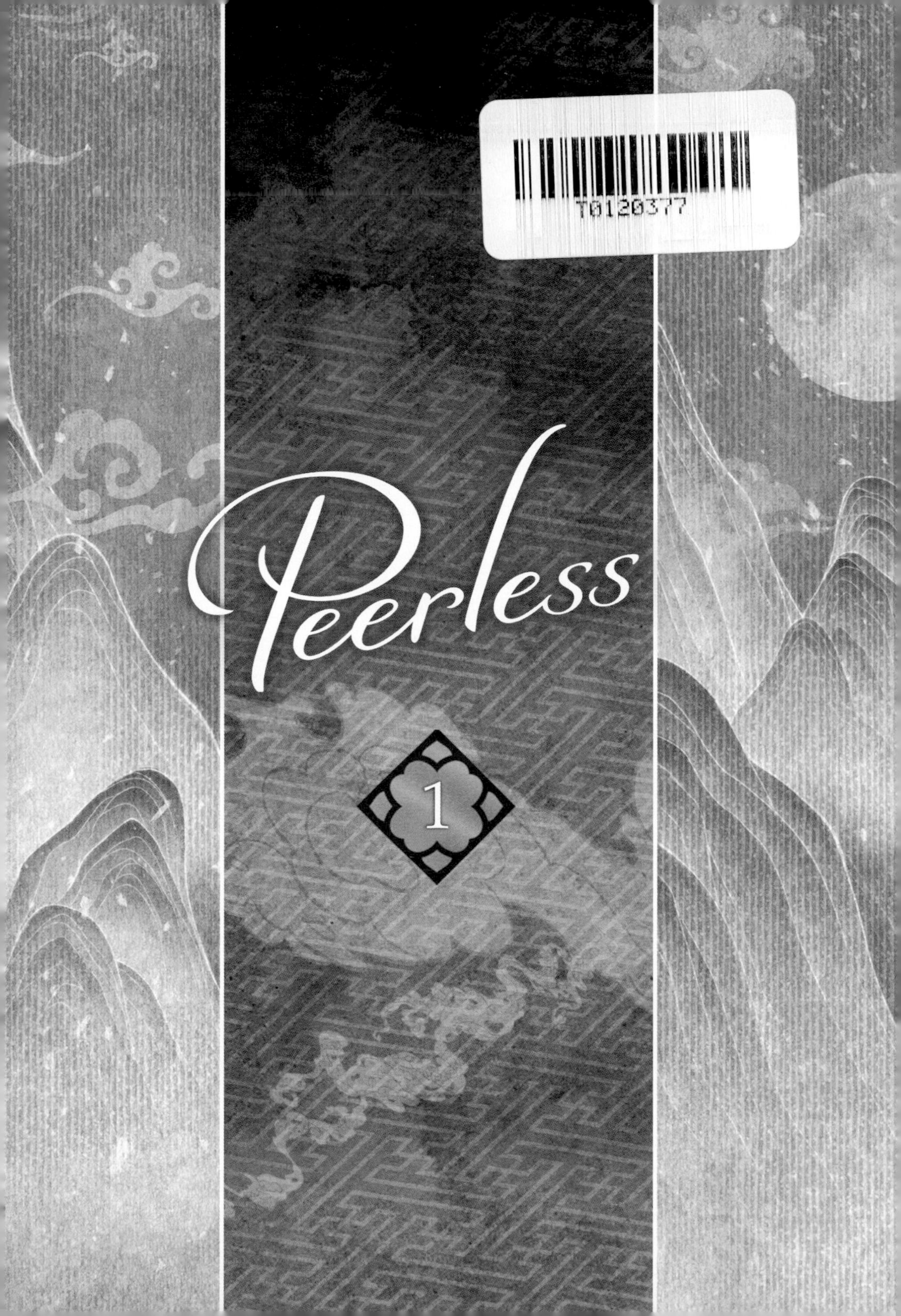
Peerless
1

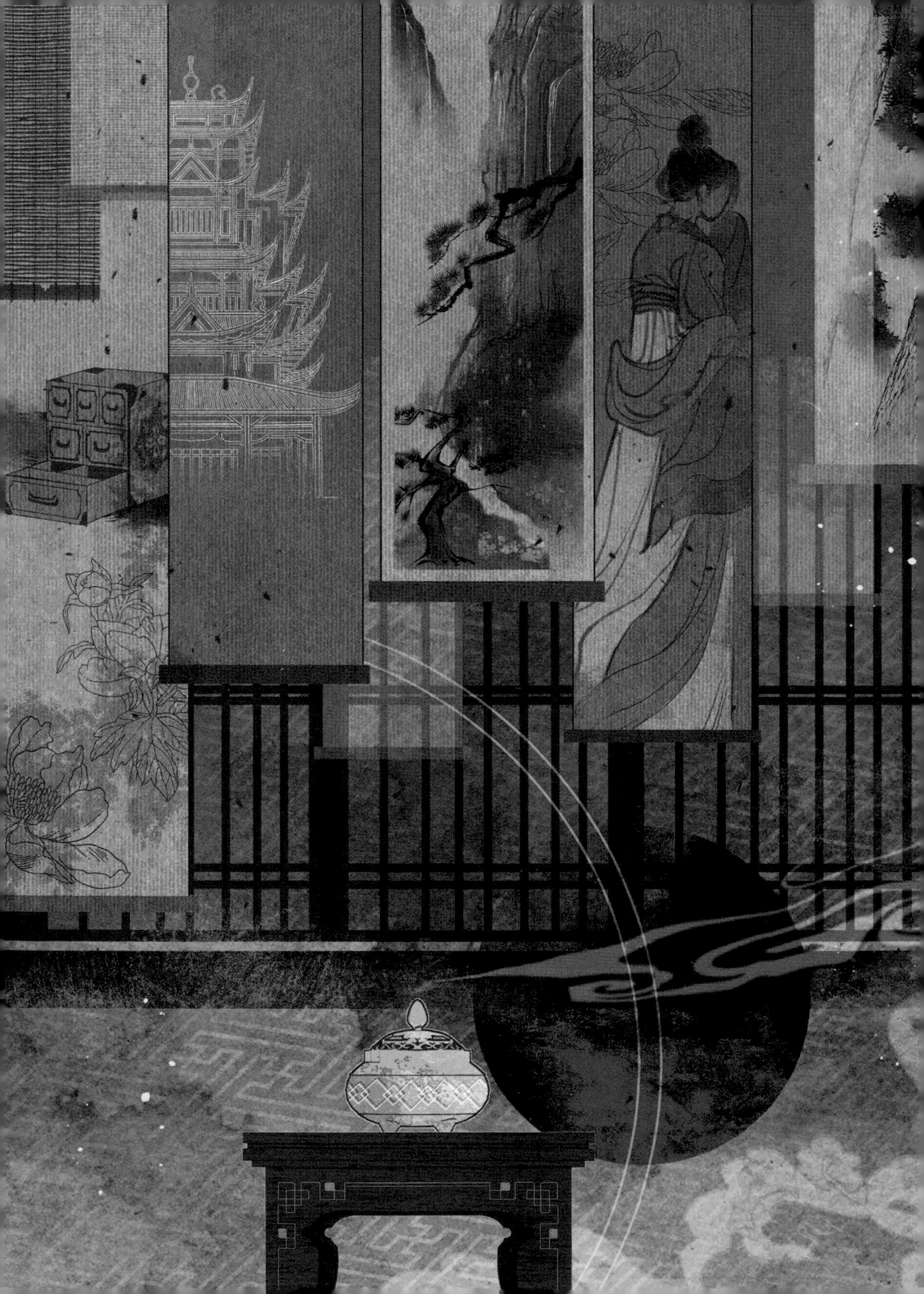

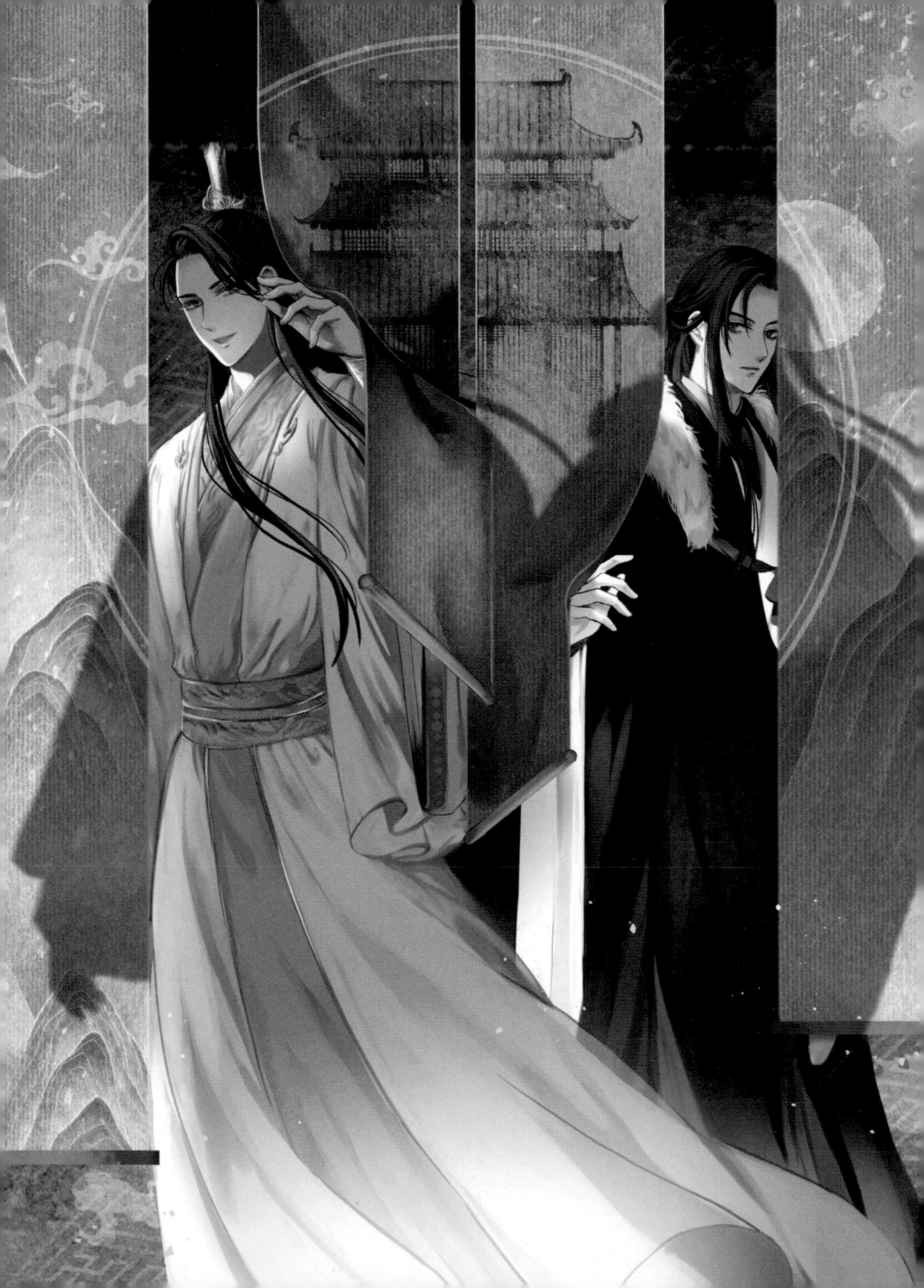

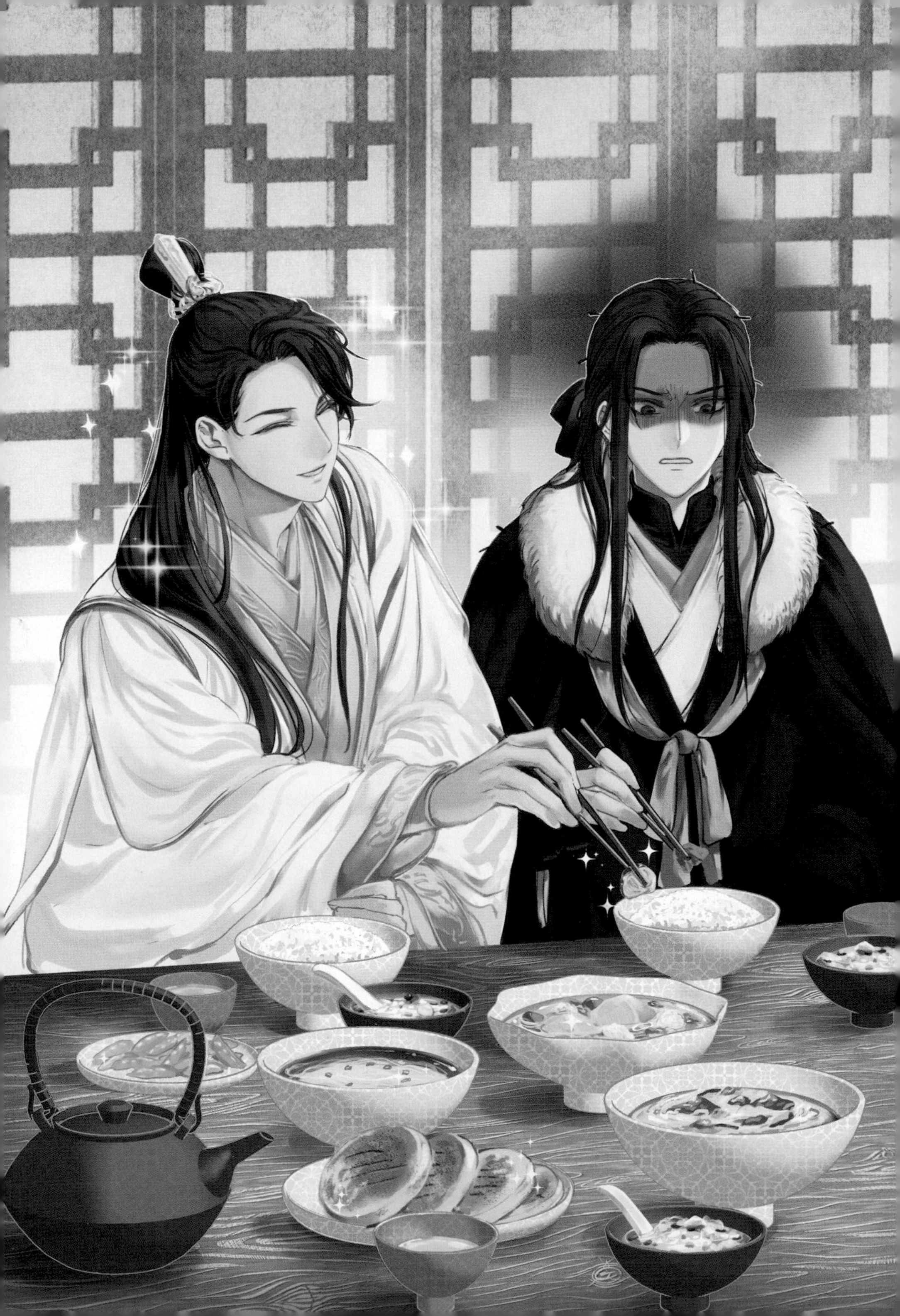

1

WRITTEN BY
Meng Xi Shi

TRANSLATED BY
Faelicy

COVER AND ILLUSTRATIONS BY
Me.Mimo

Seven Seas

Seven Seas Entertainment

Peerless: Wu Shuang (Novel) Vol. 1
Published originally under the title of 《无双》 (Peerless)
Author©梦溪石 (Meng Xi Shi)
English edition rights under license granted by 北京晋江原创网络科技有限公司
(Beijing Jinjiang Original Network Technology Co., Ltd.)
English edition copyright © 2024 Seven Seas Entertainment, LLC
Arranged through JS Agency Co., Ltd
All rights reserved

Cover and Interior Illustrations by Me.Mimo

No portion of this book may be reproduced or transmitted in any form without written
permission from the copyright holders. This is a work of fiction. Names, characters, places,
and incidents are the products of the author's imagination or are used fictitiously.
Any resemblance to actual events, locales, or persons, living or dead, is entirely coincidental.
Any information or opinions expressed by the creators of this book belong to those individual
creators and do not necessarily reflect the views of Seven Seas Entertainment or its employees.

Seven Seas press and purchase enquiries can be sent
to Marketing Manager Lauren Hill at press@gomanga.com.
Information regarding the distribution and purchase of digital editions is available
from Digital Manager CK Russell at digital@gomanga.com.

Seven Seas and the Seven Seas logo are trademarks of
Seven Seas Entertainment. All rights reserved.

Follow Seven Seas Entertainment online at
sevenseasentertainment.com.

TRANSLATION: Faelicy
ADAPTATION: Imogen Vale
COVER DESIGN: M. A. Lewife
INTERIOR DESIGN & LAYOUT: Clay Gardner
COPY EDITOR: Jehanne Bell
PROOFREADER: Kate Kishi, Hnä
EDITOR: Kelly Quinn Chiu
PREPRESS TECHNICIAN: Melanie Ujimori, Jules Valera
MANAGING EDITOR: Alyssa Scavetta
EDITOR-IN-CHIEF: Julie Davis
PUBLISHER: Lianne Sentar
VICE PRESIDENT: Adam Arnold
PRESIDENT: Jason DeAngelis

ISBN: 979-8-88843-818-3
Printed in Canada
First Printing: July 2024
10 9 8 7 6 5 4 3 2 1

1

THE NORTHERN WIND scoured the land. Here, the spring winds did not reach; the third month was approaching, but the border pass remained cold and clear as ever. One moment a hint of blue remained in thc sky, yet a blink later it'd changed without warning: a chill wind blew and clouds gathered, drowning the firmament in murky darkness like an unfading shadow lying heavy on a person's heart.

When Yuchi Jinwu noticed the convoy slowing, he couldn't help but lift the curtains and crane his neck to peer outside. Windblown sand swirled in through the window. Beside him, his favored concubine gasped in surprise and grabbed his arm.

"My lord, will we be able to cross the Great Wall before nightfall?" Her sweet, mellow voice lifted some of the worries from Yuchi Jinwu's heart. He absently patted his beloved concubine's thigh. He could feel it, supple beneath the thin fabric—it was easy to imagine the satiny skin he could caress if this troublesome material were removed. Right now, however, he was in no mood to flirt.

"I believe we should," Yuchi Jinwu said. He frowned, uncertain.

Yuchi Jinwu was a member of the Khotan royal family. Great Sui had recently established itself in the Central Plains, replacing Zhou to become the new, burgeoning dynasty of the northern regions. Now, the king of Khotan had ordered Yuchi Jinwu to travel to the Central Plains and offer tribute to this new emperor.

The emperor of Sui, Yang Jian, was a man who burned with ambition. He was diligent in governance, and the new dynasty rose like the dawning sun, its boundless rays blazing across the land. Even the Chen dynasty in the south had dispatched envoys to offer their congratulations.

Though Khotan was an insignificant kingdom beyond the Great Wall, the Göktürks had harassed them repeatedly, pestering them beyond endurance. When word came that the Sui dynasty planned to move their capital this year and had proclaimed a general amnesty, the Khotanese king seized his chance. He dispatched a party of envoys led by Yuchi Jinwu and loaded them down with lavish gifts to present to the emperor of Sui in Daxing City—first, to foster good relations between the two nations, and second, to implore the Sui dynasty to send troops to defend Khotan.

Unfortunately, their journey had been plagued with troubles.

After leaving Khotan, the procession passed through Qiemo, where their horses unexpectedly fell ill with vomiting and diarrhea. When they managed to recuperate after several days' rest and embarked once more on their travels, this awful weather had beset them. Yuchi Jinwu buzzed with anxiety—he yearned to sprout wings and fly to Daxing City in an instant.

He unconsciously cast another glance toward the corner of the carriage, where two chests were stacked. They held Yuchi Jinwu's clothes and belongings. As the carriage was spacious and the chests fairly small, Yuchi Jinwu had specially requested they be placed in his own carriage instead of stowing them in the rear of the convoy.

His concubine noticed him looking and giggled. "My lord, have you hidden a great beauty inside those chests?"

The quip eased Yuchi Jinwu's anxiety somewhat. "And what if I have? What would you do?"

She pouted playfully. "Then this concubine would have no choice but to step aside and surrender my lord to her!"

Yuchi Jinwu burst into laughter and pulled her into his arms, pressing their bodies tightly together. As they fawned and flirted, Yuchi Jinwu's dark mood dissipated.

"If I tell you what's in there, you mustn't tell another soul. At least until we arrive in Daxing City, you have to keep quiet—not a word to anyone."

The sterner and more urgent he grew, the more curious his concubine became. She clutched Yuchi Jinwu's sleeve and wheedled him sweetly as they embraced.

After a time, Yuchi Jinwu said softly, "Inside that chest is a tribute."

His concubine was puzzled. "I thought the tributes were all in the rear carriage?"

"Only ordinary objects are stowed there," said Yuchi Jinwu. "The emperor of Sui is the ruler of a mighty nation. Gold or jewels—such things are nothing to him."

His concubine's eyes widened. "Our Khotan is such a small kingdom. What wonderful treasures could we have to offer that would impress even the emperor of Sui? Could it be some kind of rare and priceless jade?"

Yuchi Jinwu pinched her lovely cheek. "How clever you are. It is indeed jade, though no ordinary kind. It's the Jade of Heaven Lake."

She exclaimed in surprise, "The legendary jade that grants eternal life—?!"

Yuchi Jinwu clapped a hand over her mouth. When she saw his stern glare, she realized what she'd done and hastily whispered, "This concubine has forgotten herself. This treasure is one of Khotan's most prized possessions, yet His Majesty is happy to give it away?"

"Even if he's unhappy, what can he do?" Yuchi Jinwu said helplessly. "His Majesty wishes to forge an alliance with the Sui dynasty. He must offer something of value if he's to demonstrate his heartfelt sincerity."

Although the Jade of Heaven Lake was named thusly, it had nothing to do with the actual lake. A Khotanese woodcutter had discovered the jade after stumbling into a cave by chance. There he found a jade stone so spectacular it was like the heart of the mountain itself. Legend had it that the jade was as clear as morning dew with a pool of icy blue-green at its center, evoking an image of the real Heaven Lake surrounded by snow-clad mountains—hence the name.

The woodcutter had presented the precious gemstone to the previous king. According to rumor, the king's mother had been ailing with a strange sickness for many years. Every treatment had failed. Yet after a shard of this jade was crushed and added to her medicine, not only did the king's mother make a full recovery, her whole body seemed to have been renewed, her appearance rejuvenated. The empress dowager lived well into her nineties, and in fact had only passed away recently.

Ever since, word of the Jade of Heaven Lake had spread like wildfire. Not only could it restore one's youth—many believed it could cure any disease, no matter how complicated or difficult, and purify the bodies of martial artists. Something so priceless was coveted by all. However, Khotan viewed the jade as a national treasure, and the king kept it well hidden. This jade was surely one of the reasons the Göktürks eyed the small nation of Khotan so hungrily.

The Khotanese king was no fool. "Holding a precious stone will cast one a sinner"—he understood this idea well. Compared with the destruction of his kingdom or the death of his family, the jade was of little import. Gifting it to the emperor of Sui in exchange for his protection would be much preferable to letting the Göktürks snatch it.

After hearing the details of the situation, the concubine was left somewhat speechless. "But my lord, is it really all right for a treasure this valuable to be escorted by so few?"

Yuchi Jinwu smiled. "Don't underestimate the men outside. Those are the best martial artists under His Majesty's command, and he sent almost all his strongest people with us. If they don't stand out, that's for the best." He thought for a moment, then repeated: "Only you and I know of this matter. You must not speak of it to anyone else."

The woman nodded again and again. "This concubine understands the gravity of the situation. If this news should leak, our lives are in danger. Of course the fewer people who know, the better."

Yuchi Jinwu stroked her hair. "You've been at my side four or five years now," he said with satisfaction. "I always knew you were the most sensible of them all. You needn't worry too much. Once we cross the Wall, the emperor of Sui will send an escort to bring us to the capital. We'll be safe and sound."

While the two of them whispered, the wind had picked up, blowing with sand and snow. Even the sturdy carriage began to sway, creaking alarmingly as if about to collapse. No longer in the mood to converse, Yuchi Jinwu bit his lip and fell silent. His concubine clutched at his robes and huddled in his arms. She dared not move an inch.

Beneath the wind's incessant howl, Yuchi Jinwu heard the sound of approaching hoofbeats.

To be traveling in such weather, the other party was unlikely to be merchants, who cherished their lives and wealth. Perhaps these were the emissaries the emperor of Sui had sent to receive them. The thought breathed new life into Yuchi Jinwu. He said to his concubine, "I'll go take a look outside…"

The carriage curtain suddenly lifted as a guard stuck his head in through the window. His words came in a rush: "The winds are too strong, my lord! We should seek shelter ahead—"

Everything happened at once.

In a split second, Yuchi Jinwu's displeasure at the guard's intrusion morphed into wide-eyed terror. He watched as blood spurted and the guard's head flew. It crashed into the carriage's ceiling before thudding heavily to the floor, where it rolled on the white wool rug, staining the pristine surface with an arc of fresh crimson blood. Finally, it rolled to a stop by Yuchi Jinwu's foot.

His concubine's shriek rang in his ear, yet just then, it sounded terribly distant—as if someone had stuffed his ears with cloth, leaving everything muffled and indiscernible. A chill wind swept over his face and a tremor wracked him. His mind roared at him to leap away, but he had lived the pampered life of a prince for too many years; his body couldn't react in time. He stared as an icy, piercing pain tore through his chest.

Yuchi Jinwu's vision was awash in the crimson of blood.

To think a person can pass from life to death in an instant.

It was his last thought before he crumpled to the floor.

※❈※

The snow fell in swirling flurries, thick enough to cloak all the world's filth beneath. But this, too, was only temporary. Once the clouds parted and the snowfall ceased, the grime would be exposed once more.

'The evil of some humans was so hideous not even the heaviest of snows could mask it.

The blood dried and blackened as it mingled with the snowdrifts, like dark rocks poking out from the piles of white. Long-stiff horses lay on the ground beside their overturned carriages. Here and there, a head lay nestled in the snow. It was clear they'd died some time ago.

Hoofbeats sounded in the distance, growing nearer.

A dozen men rode in, galloping out of the snow. Icy mist and fluttering snow churned beneath the horses' hooves, rising in hazy puffs of vapor.

The man at their fore wore a black coat, and his face was swathed tightly against the cold. The only sound from him was the rustle of his sleeves as the wind billowed through them. The ten or so men behind him were bundled more securely still—even their sleeves had been cinched tight. No one was willing to expose an inch of skin to this accursed snowstorm.

It seemed the men had expected this gruesome sight. They expressed no surprise or fear, but dismounted one after another and stepped forward, bending to examine the scene.

A corpse lay in the snow. The drifts had already swallowed it from the shoulders down, leaving visible only a head and neck the pale color of ice. A long gash stretched from throat to nape, leaving the flesh beneath splayed open, deep enough to glimpse bone. A good half of the man's neck had been sliced through—his murderer had obviously used significant force.

A hand, originally concealed beneath the black coat, reached toward the corpse.

This hand was slender and fair, delicate skin wrapped around knuckles and tendons, neither bony nor bloated. It struck the perfect balance, resembling a stalk of young bamboo as it gracefully stretched forward. Even without any flashy moves, one would find their gaze drawn to it. Such a hand could only have been nurtured within the wealthiest of noble families.

But the hand's owner didn't disdain the filth. He scooped up a handful of bloodstained snow, kneaded it for a moment, then let it fall. The snow trickled through his fingers and landed on a corner of the furs he wore, where it lingered. The man dropped his chin to look where it had fallen, and his eyebrows rose a little.

The local constable at his side had been fretting over a chance to ingratiate himself with this bigwig from the capital. When he saw the direction of the man's gaze, he swiftly fished out a clean handkerchief and came forward with a smile.

"This lowly one has a handkerchief if my lord—"

He'd yet to finish when the man shed his coat completely and tossed it behind him. Under the dumbfounded stares of the constables and petty officials, the coat was caught by a young man standing behind him.

Pei Jingzhe revealed a trace of a strained smile. "Sir..."

"Take it," the man said coolly. Without his cloak, his clothes were exposed to the wind and snow—a jade hair clasp and white robes, his sleeves dancing wildly. Just looking at him made everyone's teeth chatter. But the man's expression changed not a mote. He bent at the waist, then lowered his head to examine the corpse.

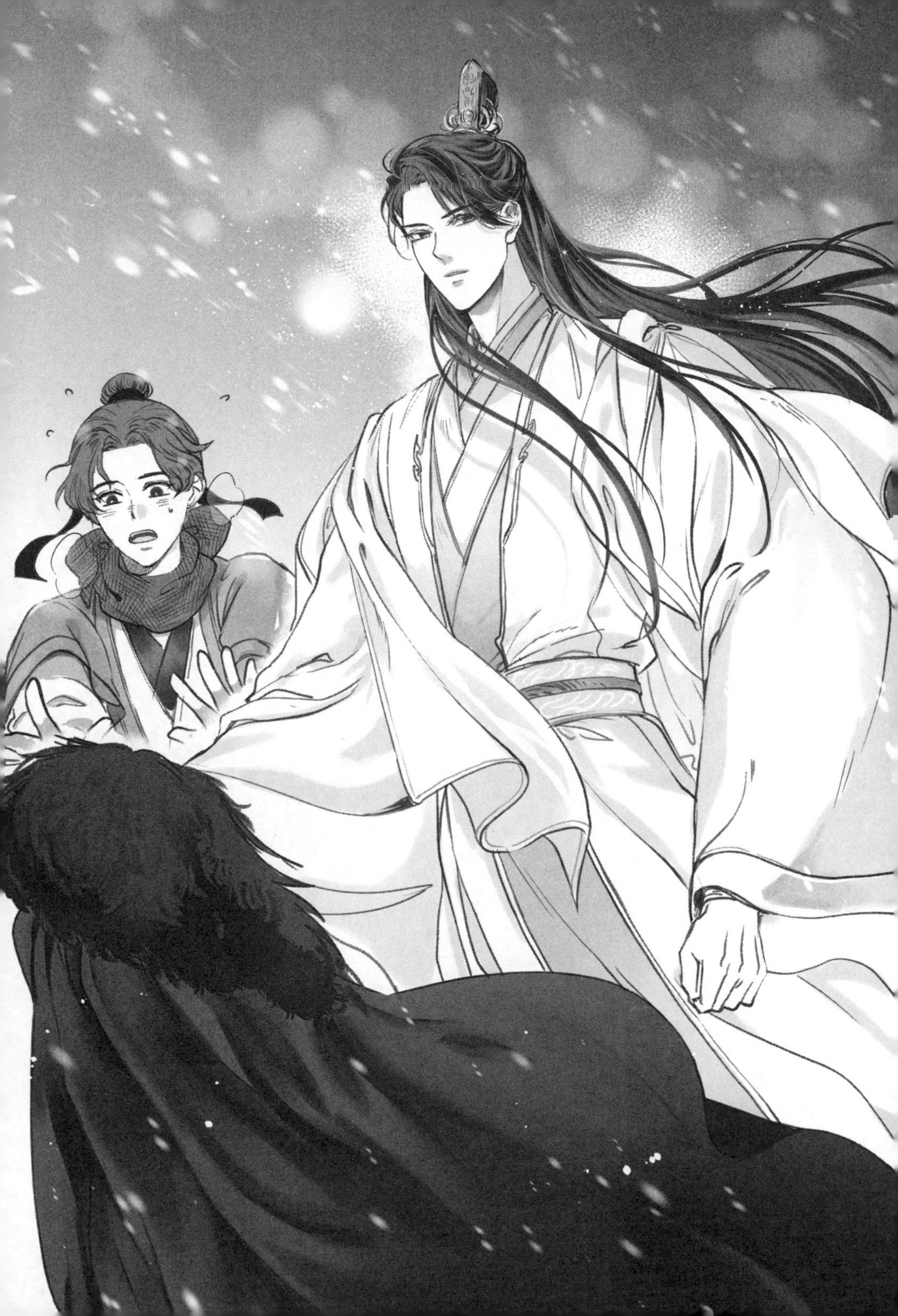

2

I NVESTIGATING A CASE that had occurred the previous
night, and in this infernal weather no less, was a horrendously
difficult task.

The ambush had occurred a stone's throw from Liugong City.
The Khotanese envoy had come to offer tribute to Great Sui yet was
assassinated along the way. News of the incident spread back to the
city, terrifying the county magistrate, who feared the blame would
land on him.

At the same time, this dignitary in white had arrived in Liugong
City under orders from the emperor to receive the Khotanese
delegation. Yet instead of greeting an envoy, he'd found himself with
a murder case on his hands.

The magistrate of Liugong County trembled with fear, deferen-
tial and subservient. He wished for nothing more than to drop this
hot potato. But what truly defied his expectations was the dignitary
from the capital. Despite the man's unfriendly demeanor, upon
receiving such shocking news, he and his companions had simply
turned and left the city to investigate without another word.

County Lieutenant Liu Lin looked up and saw the wind had
subsided and the snow abated. He heaved a long sigh. Now that
the imperial court was looking into the death of the Khotanese
envoy, Liu Lin would be hard-pressed to evade responsibility.

He wracked his brain but couldn't think of any bandits brazen enough to assassinate a foreign emissary. Come to think of it, he'd never heard of any particularly audacious bandits near Liugong City. None of those petty robbers would dare make trouble so close to the city walls...

Thoughts spiraling, he trailed behind the constables as they inspected the corpses. They had bustled about sweeping away most of the snow in the area to gradually reveal bodies strewn over the frozen ground. Most were like the first victim: throats slit with a single stroke. Only the sumptuously dressed man in the carriage had died from a blade through the chest.

Liu Lin picked up a long saber standing upright in the snow and examined it. After a moment he cried out in surprise: "A Göktürk saber!"

"Here's another!" yelled back one of the constables.

The blade was wickedly curved, its length stained with blood; it was clear at a glance that it had slain many people.

Could the Göktürks be behind this?! Liu Lin was stunned. But the more he thought about it, the likelier it seemed.

Everyone knew war would erupt between the Göktürks and Great Sui at the slightest spark. Soldiers stationed at the borders slept with their weapons, ready to leap into battle at any moment— they dared not be lax. The Göktürks had long been dissatisfied with Khotan's intent to seek protection from the Sui dynasty. Thus they'd killed a Khotanese envoy within Sui's own borders, aiming to drive a wedge between the two nations and ensure Khotan would bear a grudge against Great Sui.

Most of the others thought the same as Liu Lin.

With the discovery of the sabers, the case was as good as closed. But Liu Lin couldn't help agonizing over what came next. If the

Göktürks had been here in the night, they might already have infiltrated the city. Linlang Pavilion's annual auction would soon be held in Liugong City, and all the world's idle rich, as well as various representatives of the jianghu's many schools of thought, would gather here. For a murder related to Khotan to materialize at the exact same time...

Liu Lin saw plainly the bind he was in. Letting the Göktürks infiltrate Liugong City's borders and kill the Khotanese envoy— taking the blame for such a blunder would land him in serious trouble. At the prospect of losing his hard-won position of county lieutenant, Liu Lin's vision grew dim and his limbs weak.

The young man from earlier, Pei Jingzhe, was the mysterious dignitary's subordinate. Now Liu Lin watched as he squeezed his way out of the overturned carriage carrying a small cabinet for valuables.

The design of the cabinet was one that had become fashionable within the capital in recent years. It was exquisitely crafted, with three drawers each divided into eight compartments. The compartments were meant to hold sundries like rouge and snacks, and as the cabinet itself could easily be stowed in a carriage for long journeys, it was popular with women. The cabinets of some wealthy women were even more luxurious: not only were they decorated with tortoiseshell and agate, they might also be inlaid with gems and pearls. This transformed the cabinets from practical items into precious accouterments used to flaunt their status.

The small cabinet Pei Jingzhe currently held wasn't nearly so lavish as some in the capital, but it was still crafted from high-quality wood. A closer look revealed carvings of dancing women dressed in Khotanese garb. The design gave the cabinet an air of exotic romance.

Pei Jingzhe pulled out each of the three drawers, one by one.

The first held dried peaches, apricots, and candied fruit. The second contained hair accessories. When Pei Jingzhe opened the third, at first all Liu Lin saw was glistening yellow. Only when he looked more closely did he discover the drawer was full of forehead adornments, pieces of gold foil cut into the delicate shapes of fish, insects, moons, and stars.

There must have been women in this convoy, Liu Lin reasoned. That in itself was nothing out of the ordinary. The envoy had allegedly been a Khotanese aristocrat; that he would bring a lovely concubine and maid or two on diplomatic missions was expected. Unfortunately, the owner of this cabinet had lost her life before she'd had the chance to marvel at the prosperity of Daxing City.

At that moment, the dignitary in white spoke. "Search around; see if there's another female corpse."

When he spoke, all obeyed. The constables dismounted and one after the other began to search.

The expensive coat the dignitary had worn now lay lonely and discarded on the snowy ground. Liu Lin cast it an anguished glance, then mumbled to himself, rallying his spirits as he began searching alongside his men.

In addition to the guards on horseback, the convoy had consisted of a total of four carriages. One was for the Khotanese envoy's exclusive use, while another held the convoy's supplies. A third carried tribute meant for the emperor of Sui, and the final small carriage was most likely set aside for the envoy's maids. As the group approached that final carriage, they discovered two dead women buried beneath the snow. Like their companions, their throats had been slashed. They'd obviously been dead for some time.

The two deceased maids were lovely even in death. Liu Lin suspected they'd probably doubled as the envoy's bed warmers as well as attendants.

As he watched, the man in white leaned in nose to nose with one of the maids, almost close enough to kiss her. His handsome profile, lit by the brilliant glare off the snow, was juxtaposed with the bruised and mottled face of the corpse. The hair on the back of Liu Lin's neck stood up, yet the man seemed not to mind at all. His thin lips hovered near the cheek of the deceased maid, then moved downward. He unfastened the girl's blood-soaked collar, looking for all the world like a lecher with the worst intentions. Even the young man with him, previously so composed, couldn't hide his revulsion as he exclaimed, "Sir!"

"What are you yelling for?" the man scoffed. He strode over to the other corpse and crouched again, sniffing around her ruined throat for a long time before finally speaking again. "There's one more woman. Find her."

Was there still someone else? Liu Lin was taken aback.

"There's a fragrance lingering in the carriage," said the man impatiently. "It's different from the perfume on these women. There must be another woman. Find her!"

At this, everyone hurried to scour the area. They located a total of twenty-one corpses in the end—but aside from the two maids, they found no more women.

"Leave one team here to clean up the crime scene," the man in white ordered Liu Lin. "Take all the bodies back."

We're already done here?

The Khotanese envoy had been murdered in cold blood; the king of Khotan would certainly pursue the matter. Once the bodies were removed and the sun rose and melted the snow, any remaining evidence would disappear with it. How would they investigate the case after that? Liu Lin was baffled. But he didn't have the guts to speak up, and instead sent glance after pleading glance toward Pei Jingzhe, hoping he would take the hint.

Pei Jingzhe sighed and picked up the coat the man in white had dropped. He seemed to have accepted his fate. "We're leaving, just like that? What about the carriages and the horses, sir?"

"You tell me," the man in white countered. "What can we achieve by remaining here?"

Liu Lin stammered as he intervened. "Sh-shouldn't we at least bring the murder weapons and carriages back as evidence? That way, when Khotan questions us later, we'll at least have something to show."

"Leave the carriages," the man said. "You may bring the weapons."

Without further explanation, he strode to his horse and swung up into the saddle. Then he lifted his riding crop and galloped off, a white-robed figure on a gray steed. The remaining men looked at each other, at a loss.

The constables of a small border town couldn't compete with ones from the capital, to say nothing of a man from the infamous Jiejian Bureau. Pei Jingzhe was left to direct Liu Lin on how to clean up the crime scene. He split the party in two and sent half back to the city with the bodies and weapons. Only then did he ride back himself and head to Qiushan Manor.

Qiushan Manor was located in the southeast quarter of Liugong City, surrounded by mountains and facing the water. It was a place of tranquility amid the bustle of the city. County Magistrate Zhao's wife hailed from a prominent local family, and Qiushan Manor had been part of her dowry. Every year, the magistrate brought his family to the manor at the start of the spring holidays and stayed a few days. He'd had someone tidy the manor in anticipation of the arrival of the dignitary from the capital, and had opened the manor immediately after receiving him. If his distinguished guest enjoyed his stay, perhaps less blame would fall on Magistrate Zhao's head.

Pei Jingzhe was instantly fond of the place, especially now, when the winter snow had yet to thaw and hints of green budded anew on the branches. The place was rather more refined than his residence in the capital, and every time he entered, his mood soared. He knew that right then, however, Deputy Bureau Chief Feng's mood would be foul.

Copper chimes rang beneath the eaves. The man who sat leaning against the veranda pillar had been there for some time, having ridden back first, and had an indolent and careless demeanor. Yet his fingers were nimble as they rolled up a letter and inserted it into a bamboo tube the thickness of his thumb.

Pei Jingzhe instinctively quieted his steps, but the man's lashes quivered slightly as his eyelids flickered—he had already noticed him.

Feng Xiao passed the tube to Pei Jingzhe. "For Qiemo—send men to investigate everyone in the Khotanese convoy,"

Qiemo was situated between Khotan and Liugong City. Though the city belonged to the Sui dynasty in name, the court had its hands full dealing with the Göktürks and the Southern dynasty. For now, they gave little thought to the place. But when traveling from the Central Plains to the Western Regions, it was necessary to pass through Qiemo. Passing merchants from all over gathered there to rest, and thus, over time, it had become neutral territory. In addition to merchant goods, it was a convenient location for the collection and transmission of information. The Jiejian Bureau had long had a base of operations there.

"Yes sir," said Pei Jingzhe as he received the bamboo tube. He couldn't help but ask, "Do you already have a lead on this case?"

Feng Xiao picked up a nearby file and tossed it at him; Pei Jingzhe caught it, fumbling. When he opened it, he found a letter penned in the Khotanese king's own hand—a royal edict printed on gold foil that he'd entrusted to the envoy for the emperor of Sui, Yang Jian.

The identity of the Khotanese envoy was outlined within: the man's name was Yuchi Jinwu, nephew to the king. The Khotanese ruler expressed his admiration of the Celestial Empire, along with his hopes for an alliance to repel the Göktürks.

The Khotanese king obviously wanted Great Sui to help him deal with the Göktürks, yet he also feared the Sui dynasty would take this chance to annex Khotan. The language of the edict walked the line, striving to please the emperor of Sui while taking care not to promise too much. This edict had been meant for their sovereign's eyes—but the envoy was dead, and it had become one of their only leads in his murder case. What had been held in private keeping for the throne now passed through their hands first.

Yuchi Jinwu's convoy had been massacred on the road, yet nothing was stolen. Even this golden edict had remained in the carriage, completely intact.

Pei Jingzhe finished reading and closed the edict. "Sir, a Khotanese man was murdered within Great Sui's borders. Something like this occurring under our own noses undermines our prestige and creates friction between Khotan and Great Sui. It does seem like something the Göktürks might do."

"So the Göktürks infiltrated our borders to commit murder. In that case, why use Göktürk sabers? If they'd used weapons from the Central Plains, they'd have left neither witness nor evidence."

Pei Jingzhe scratched his chin. "The Göktürks are crude in their thoughts and savage in their actions. It's not out of the question for them to be so brazen. Both the Göktürk Khaganate and Central

Plains are sharpening their swords for war. Perhaps they were confident that even if we did realize they were behind the attack, we'd be powerless to act against them."

"Didn't you notice?" said Feng Xiao. "Something important was missing from that carriage."

Pei Jingzhe thought long and hard. Even the golden edict was there; what could be missing? The Khotanese envoy had entered Great Sui to offer tribute, and all those tributes had been left there as well...

Then it hit him. "The tribute list!" he blurted. "Earlier, I couldn't find the tribute list!"

Feng Xiao hummed acknowledgment, as if he thought Pei Jingzhe wasn't beyond hope after all.

Pei Jingzhe had long grown accustomed to the deputy bureau chief's temperament. Such a mark of approval was slightly overwhelming. Encouraged, he pressed on: "The murderer took the tribute list. Was it because they stole one of the tributes and didn't want us to know? But all we'd need to do is write a letter to the Khotanese king. Wouldn't that get us a clear answer?"

"In the time we wasted on such a back-and-forth, the murderer could do many things," said Feng Xiao. "Fetch me that cabinet from the envoy's carriage."

Pei Jingzhe went at once. He returned a short time later carrying the small cabinet and pulled the three drawers open, one at a time.

"Something's missing," said Feng Xiao.

Pei Jingzhe was confounded. He examined the drawers again. It didn't look like anything was missing to him. But saying as much out loud would almost certainly result in another scolding, so Pei Jingzhe said meekly, "My lowly self is dull-witted. I beg your instruction, sir."

Feng Xiao didn't keep him in further suspense. "Rouge."

Pei Jingzhe had worked closely under the Jiejian Bureau's deputy chief for years; he was no fool. After a moment's thought, he connected the dots. "The cabinet held forehead adornments, which means it must have held makeup and rouge as well. But the fragrance lingering within the carriage didn't match the perfume of the two maids—so there must have been another woman in the convoy, most likely a favored concubine of Yuchi Jinwu. Did the murderer kidnap her? No, that's not right... The drawers show no signs of being rifled through; the contents are neat and orderly. So she probably wasn't taken by force..." He jolted in surprise. "Could the missing woman be the murderer?!"

Feng Xiao gathered his sleeves. "Whether she is or not, she certainly has something to do with them. And though the murderer used a Göktürk saber, they might not be a Göktürk themselves. Go and investigate. Report back within three days."

Pei Jingzhe gave a slight nod. "Yes, sir."

Three days wasn't a long time, but it wasn't short either. If one spent it in idleness, the time would pass slowly and arduously—but if one had much to do, it would pass in the blink of an eye.

Pei Jingzhe knew Feng Xiao's temperament. Three days meant exactly that, and not an hour more. So after Feng Xiao gave his order, Pei Jingzhe wasted no time setting about his investigation. He sent both messenger pigeons and men on fast horses to the Jiejian Bureau's base in Qiemo. The pigeons met a sandstorm and never returned, but fortunately, his contingency plan bore fruit. On the evening of the third day, he received a letter from the men he'd dispatched.

"Speak." Feng Xiao's eyes were half-lidded; he didn't deign to look at the letter Pei Jingzhe presented to him.

Pei Jingzhe related the details: "Yuchi Jinwu came to the Central Plains several years ago and met a woman here in Liugong City. She was surnamed Qin and came from a respectable family. Yuchi Jinwu found her mesmerizing, and after pursuing her for some time, finally took her as his concubine and brought her back to Khotan. He adored this Lady Qin fiercely by all accounts. Even now, when he came to the Central Plains to offer tribute, he brought her along. The single woman missing after the massacre of the convoy must be this Lady Qin."

"Is that all?"

"I've already sent men to investigate Lady Qin's movements and daily activities in Khotan. Due to the vast distance, a timely response will be difficult to obtain. However, my subordinates did learn that she lived with her paternal aunt here in Liugong City after the death of her parents. After she left with Yuchi Jinwu, her aunt's family moved away as well. According to her old neighbors, Lady Qin was devoutly religious. Prior to her marriage, she was most commonly seen at Liugong City's Yufo Temple and at Zixia Monastery. On the first and fifteenth of practically every month, she'd go to one or the other to offer incense."

Feng Xiao finally opened his eyes and snorted. "After half a day's worth of drivel, you finally say something useful!"

"But this subordinate could only tell you the end after getting through the earlier parts!" Pei Jingzhe said indignantly. "I've already sent people to investigate Yufo Temple and Zixia Monastery. Yufo Temple has always been the most popular temple in Liugong City, but Zixia Monastery is a bit of an oddball. The temple at the monastery has been deserted for a long time; these days, few people go there. If Lady Qin wished to offer incense, why didn't she look for a busier Daoist monastery?"

When Feng Xiao didn't reply, he continued. "Even stranger, two months ago, a new abbot arrived and assumed leadership of Zixia Monastery, and its popularity rose immediately. Now everyone says Zixia Monastery is the best spot to seek medical expertise, and that the priests there are honest and kind. They say the gods receiving offerings there will answer any request, often manifesting themselves."

"What is this new abbot's name? Where did he come from?"

"His surname is Cui—Cui Buqu. They say he was a wandering Daoist; we haven't yet been able to find anything else."

Cui Buqu. *Buqu* as in "won't go"?

Where wasn't he going? And why? The world was vast. Was there any place one couldn't go? Feng Xiao rolled the name around on his tongue, and his lips tugged into a slight curve.

How interesting.

3

I N THE NORTHWEST CORNER of Liugong City, opposite Qiushan Manor, lay Zixia Monastery.

Zixia Monastery had been built during the previous dynasty. After the demise of the old abbot, the Daoists under him had scattered. Years passed, and less and less incense was burned within the monastery as the number of visitors dwindled. The younger folk in Liugong City had likely never even heard this monastery's name.

Yet this marked decline was abruptly reversed with the arrival of the new abbot.

On the third day of the third month, the birthday of the god Xuantian Shangdi,[1] Zixia Monastery thronged with visitors. Almost half of Liugong City's population had congregated there. Within the monastery people offered incense, while outside shrewd peddlers had already set up stalls selling breakfast and fresh fruit to all those who had hurried there to pray.

As little as two months ago, no one imagined the near-deserted monastery would be rejuvenated like a withered tree sprouting new leaves in spring, worshippers and believers crowded into every corner. It was the same monastery as before, with little sign of renovation. At most, the leaky roof tiles had been replaced and the

---

1   玄天上帝. *A deity worshipped in Daoism, also known as Xuanwu. His birthday is celebrated on the third day of the third lunar month with offerings and celebration rituals.*

weeds in the monastic garden uprooted. But in the eyes of the local residents, Zixia Monastery, with its thick clouds of incense and pervasive fragrance of sandalwood, looked far more sacred these days.

As the saying went: A mountain needn't be high, so long as a famous immortal lived there. The waters needn't be deep, so long as dragons swam within. Presumably, the monastery's increased appeal was all due to the new abbot.

Lady Zhang clutched an incense stick she'd just lit at the lamp platform. She waded through the crowd toward the center of the yard, trying to reach the large incense burner so she could place her joss stick there as a prayer for the peace of her family. The place was overflowing with people, yet she never thought of admitting defeat. She only wondered if she'd come too late, and if the gods might be displeased. Perhaps she ought to request a fortune slip after offering the incense. Best if she could get that young priest over there to plead with the abbot on her behalf and ask him to personally read out her fortune.

After a full hour had passed, she finally managed to place her joss stick, finish her prayers, and present her offerings. The sun was already high in the sky. Lady Zhang's rouge had grown greasy and started to peel in the baking heat; the din around her swelled as people jostled and bumped shoulders. Many of the visitors were just like Lady Zhang—they had no intention of leaving, and instead felt they'd completed some sacred and monumental task in braving the crowds.

Lady Zhang's family resided in the eastern quarter of the city. Her husband owned two tailor shops, so they lived comfortably, and their marriage was a harmonious one. Yet when it came to children, they'd met setback after setback. After much difficulty, they'd finally welcomed a son in their middle age. They treated the child like a priceless treasure, but two months later, the infant fell gravely ill and almost passed away. The couple sought out numerous doctors and visited the Yufo Temple countless times to offer incense, but nothing worked. They had nearly given up hope when they heard a new abbot with outstanding medical knowledge had arrived at Zixia Monastery. Rumor was that even the temple incense now possessed miraculous healing powers. Lady Zhang was desperate to save her son and had no time to lose. She rushed to the monastery and pleaded for help, and one way or another, her son's illness was cured. From that day on, the incense money Lady Zhang had once offered to Yufo Temple every month was transferred in full to Zixia Monastery.

Liugong City was a small place. The story of the Zhang family's infant son and his recovery spread like wildfire, and as its renown grew, people poured into the monastery in droves. Almost overnight, Zixia Monastery became famous, rivaling Yufo Temple as Liugong City's largest place of worship.

Lady Zhang fished out a handkerchief and dabbed at her fore-head. She'd finally managed to squeeze into the side hall but had been told the abbot wasn't reading fortunes today; instead, he was in the courtyard giving a lecture on Daoism. Lady Zhang was far from learned, but her blind faith in the abbot compelled her to go and listen anyway.

As she stepped into the courtyard, she was stunned to find it already packed with seated listeners. Quite a few had also gathered to stand outside the walls, creating a thronging crowd both within and without. Despite the size of the assembly, there was a hush over the courtyard, broken only by occasional mutterings and whispers.

Lady Zhang spotted the abbot over the heads of the crowd. The man was seated cross-legged on the steps beneath the eaves, his eyes slightly narrowed as he gazed into the courtyard. Lady Zhang's heart flipped as she recalled the godly statues within the main hall. Their eyes, too, had been half-lidded as they gazed benevolently down upon the joys and sorrows of the mortal world.

Abbot Cui's complexion was much paler than when she'd seen him last, though that might have been because he was illuminated by the bright noon sun. Lady Zhang came often to offer incense and had vaguely heard the novices mention it before—Abbot Cui was in poor health. As for what ailed him, no one could say. But Lady Zhang was a married woman; it would be inappropriate to inquire further.

Though she stood a fair distance from him, the crowd was so quiet that Abbot Cui's voice, when he spoke, reached almost everyone's ears. Its cadence was neither fast nor slow, but both gentle and melodious—like a cup of tea that fit perfectly in one's hands, neither too hot nor too cold, but steaming and fragrant as it seeped into one's heart. As if wherever this person went would become a place of utmost tranquility.

"Today, we shall speak on the topic of karma," Lady Zhang heard him say. In the crowd, someone gave a faint gasp of surprise, their expression revealing a trace of bewilderment.

Abbot Cui smiled. "Perhaps you believe that only Buddhism speaks of karma. But in truth, our Daoism also has much to impart on the subject. *The Treatise on the Response of the Tao* teaches that there is no road to fortune or calamity; rather, people invite both good and ill upon themselves. When it comes to blessings and disasters, neither are preordained, but tied inextricably to a person and their conduct. Is this not similar to Buddhists' teachings that good actions lead to good rewards? Despite our different origins, we arrive at the same conclusion."

Lady Zhang couldn't read, and she'd never so much as touched one of the classics. At most she'd go to the teahouse and listen to storytellers' tales of the jianghu. Nothing gave her a headache like endless preaching and sermons. But today—perhaps because so many were listening, or because Abbot Cui was expounding on these profound topics using such simple language—although Lady Zhang didn't understand completely, she wasn't frustrated. Instead, she felt an unexpected clarity suffuse her heart.

"Let us use the madam of the Zhang family as an example."

Lady Zhang started, caught completely unawares. For a moment, she thought there must be another in the crowd who shared her surname. But when she raised her head, Abbot Cui was looking right at her, and the attention of the crowd followed his gaze.

A wave of dizziness overcame her, and her ears turned bright red. For the first time in her life, she was exposed to the burning stares of a crowd. She shuffled nervously, unsure what to do with her hands and feet.

"Some time ago, Madam Zhang's son suffered a serious illness and nearly succumbed. I trust everyone here knows of this. If not for the Zhang family's frequent acts of kindness and the merits accumulated by their ancestors, how could such a calamity transform into good fortune?"

Lady Zhang had never expected Abbot Cui to praise her so. She was both moved and embarrassed, and her words came unsteadily as she hurried to say in a trembling voice, "This wife...and her husband only acted in accordance with our own hearts. These words from the abbot are really too much! Our son's recovery was all thanks to the abbot's unmatched skill. The entire Zhang family is grateful from the bottom of our hearts."

Abbot Cui's smile deepened. "It's easy to say you'll act in accordance with your heart. But how many in this world can do so successfully? If we go back further, was not my timely arrival at

Zixia Monastery also thanks to the invisible guidance of countless forefathers?"

At this, everyone nodded their agreement. When they turned back to Lady Zhang, her confusion had also transformed into admiration.

Lady Zhang's cheeks flushed crimson, her overwhelmed heart beating hard in her chest. In all her life, this was the first time anyone had so openly praised her virtue, and it had come from the abbot of the city's most famous monastery. She could hardly wait to rush home and share this account of incredible fortune with her husband. Lady Zhang decided then and there that when she visited Zixia Monastery next month, she'd increase the incense money once again.

As her thoughts went thus bounding off, something pricked at the edge of her vision, like a glint of metal in the sun. Lady Zhang blinked, but accompanying the glint was the sound of something whistling through the air, as if a bird swooped right by her ear. Her eyes grew round as she saw a gray shadow leap toward Abbot Cui where he sat on the steps. A longsword flashed, slashing with incredible speed—it was about to run Abbot Cui through.

In the blink of an eye, the point of the sword was half an inch from the abbot's forehead. No matter how swiftly the priests near him moved, it was too late for them to jump in and save him. Everything had happened so quickly—no one could react in time.

Abbot Cui jerked back on instinct, but the motion was powerless to stop the assassin's sword. In another blink, it would pierce between his brows and cut his life short.

Lady Zhang could see no way out for Abbot Cui. Terror exploded in her heart as her shriek split the air.

4

THE ASSASSIN'S PRIZE was within his grasp. As the point of the sword grazed his target's forehead, he was already imagining the sharp crack of the man's skull beneath his blade. This sword was capable of shattering stone and cleaving metal; no matter how hard a man's skull, it would be fragile as paper under the unconquerable power of a first-class sword infused with true qi.

The assassin had at first been reluctant to kill this ailing man who lacked the strength to truss a chicken. But he'd received categorical orders from his superiors: if the invalid kept his life, the assassin's would be forfeit.

In the next moment there would be a sword jutting from between this man's brows. Fresh blood would pour from the wound and a line of crimson would trickle from his nose. It was obvious from the man's sickly pallor that he'd been ill for years—but this only meant the contrast between his vivid blood and his pale corpse would be all the more pleasing to the eye.

The assassin thought all this happily as his sword sliced down. He'd witnessed such scenes far too many times, but the handsome, pale features of this man Cui managed to awaken a new and heady anticipation in him.

Yet his long-awaited prize was snatched from him by a single hand.

The assassin's eyes widened as he stared at the hand that had appeared out of nowhere. It was strong yet slender, the nails neatly trimmed, its form pleasant, its skin fair. Had this been any other day, the assassin would have loved to sever this particular hand and preserve it. If he used the right methods, he could admire it for a few days before disposing of it.

But just then he was in no mood to appreciate this hand that had become his bane. Two fingers unfurled, the movement as effortless as plucking a flower or picking up a brush. There was a deafening *clang*, and the sword trembled—the blade once capable of shattering stone and cleaving metal snapped cleanly in two.

The assassin's face showed his disbelief, but his response was immediate. He'd flirted with the boundary between life and death for years and had long ago developed a keen instinct for danger. He leapt back, evading the palm strike that followed the breaking of his sword. But there was no escape—the newcomer pursued him relentlessly, white robes billowing. Though he was bare-handed, he was more than a match for the assassin and his shattered blade. Two silhouettes interwove, their moves so quick they blurred into each other. True qi surged around them, knocking onlookers to the ground and scattering them screaming in all directions.

The previously jam-packed courtyard emptied in seconds. The few remaining novices had all taken shelter behind pillars, and Abbot Cui himself appeared scared stiff—he'd collapsed onto a reed cushion and remained there, motionless.

The assassin could tell at a glance that he was nowhere near this newcomer's match. He gritted his teeth and made a decision. Hoping to delay his opponent for at least a few breaths, he hurled the broken sword with all his might.

Those scant seconds weren't enough to make his escape; the assassin instead chose to leap toward the man sitting on the cushion. He moved with incredible speed, his dark form a smudge of shadow. In an instant he would reach his target. Abbot Cui's eyes widened slightly, and he braced his hands against the ground as if to stand. But he was too gripped with terror to dodge, and the wind from the assassin's onrushing palm already brushed his face.

"Traitor! Prepare to die a horrible death!"

Perhaps it was the pressure of the palm strike, or perhaps those hateful words had left him petrified with fear. Abbot Cui's face paled even further, and a cough spilled from his lips.

Just when it seemed the abbot would meet his end, the assassin's movements ground to a halt, and his entire body froze as his face twisted in a savage sneer. He looked down at the broken blade jutting from his chest, the steel stained with blood. It gleamed in silent mockery, cursing him to a restless death.

Feng Xiao lifted the toe of his boot, and the assassin's body was sent flying into the nearby passageway. He stared down at the bloodstain on the ground. Finally, he skirted around it and arrived before Abbot Cui, who was still frightened out of his wits.

"So you're Cui Buqu?" Feng Xiao loomed over the abbot, his back to the light and his eyes fixed on the man as if interrogating a criminal.

The novices finally returned to their senses and stumbled over. Cui Buqu coughed lightly as the young Daoists helped him to his feet. He straightened his robes and looked squarely at Feng Xiao. "Indeed, this one is Cui Buqu. Many thanks to this distinguished master for the rescue. May I ask your esteemed name?"

Feng Xiao walked up the steps. With the bright sunlight no longer casting his features in shadow, the handsome beauty of his face was revealed.

Cui Buqu had traveled far and wide across the land. The number of people he'd met surpassed the number of rice grains he'd eaten, yet Feng Xiao still left him stunned. But this man's gaze was razor-sharp, so piercing it seemed almost tangible. It felt to Cui Buqu as if those eyes were burning twin holes into his body.

"Distinguished Master, has this Cui said something to offend you? If that's the case, I must beg your forgiveness. I am deeply grateful to you for saving my life."

"Why was he trying to kill you?"

Cui Buqu shook his head. "I didn't know him."

"Right before he died, he called you a traitor."

"And yet I've never seen him before. I haven't a clue why he said that. Perhaps he mistook me for someone else."

Feng Xiao sneered. "Zixia Monastery is not the only monastery in Liugong City, nor are you the only Daoist priest. How is it that he mistook *you*, and not someone else?"

Cui Buqu's expression also cooled. "The distinguished master should ask that man. How should I know?"

"The dead cannot speak, so I must question the living. Guards!"

The moment Feng Xiao spoke, seven or eight men poured in and surrounded everyone in the courtyard. Two came forward to seize Cui Buqu, while their companions rounded up the novices. There was neither struggle nor resistance—the maneuver was carried out as painlessly as blowing away dust.

"Who do you think you are! Can you arrest someone without cause?!" Cui Buqu cried angrily. "Does Great Sui have no law and order?!"

"That's right. I can arrest anyone I find suspicious. You want to know who I am?" Feng Xiao took a step forward and grasped

Cui Buqu's chin, forcing him to meet his gaze. "I'll say this once, so remember it well: I am Feng Xiao of the Jiejian Bureau."

❖❀❖

When Emperor Wen of Sui took the throne, he appointed the Three Ducal Ministers, then established the Three Departments and Six Ministries. He enacted new laws and proclaimed a general amnesty. This emperor had seen the flames of war smoldering between the Central Plains and the Göktürks, as well as Goguryeo and its neighbors to the west. In these volatile times, he'd established the Jiejian Bureau to support him from the shadows.

Like the Six Ministries, the Jiejian Bureau answered only to the emperor. Though their duties were confidential, the power they wielded was immense. The three bureau chiefs were seen as equal to the Six Ministers in authority, and during times of crisis, it was their prerogative to act first and report later.

Within the Jiejian Bureau was an item known as the Jiejian-shi, or Sword-Relieving Stone, which had been placed there by the emperor of Sui himself. Anyone entering the bureau, regardless of position, rank, or seniority—up to and including the princes themselves— had to remove their swords before this stone. This was a mark of the Jiejian Bureau's special status.

On this occasion, a Khotanese ambassador had come to pay tribute in the Central Plains. It was an event of great significance, and the court feared foreign interference. The emperor had ordered the elites of the Jiejian Bureau to escort the envoy to the capital, and thus Feng Xiao had personally set out. He never imagined he'd be one step behind: by the time he arrived, the envoy had been murdered outside Liugong City, and a mysterious woman had vanished from the entourage along with the tribute list.

Since the culprit behind the murders had taken the tribute list, it stood to reason that they also took one of the items on the list.

Khotan possessed many beautiful jades; most of their treasures were crafted from this precious stone. Feng Xiao was a member of the Jiejian Bureau, and it was his business to be familiar with the many wonders scattered throughout the land. He'd of course heard of Khotan's natural treasure, the Jade of Heaven Lake. It was no great leap to surmise that the missing tribute was this same legendary jade.

Yet this made an already complex case more confounding. If the objective was the jade, then the murderer was motivated by riches. Perhaps they had plotted this for a long time. They were possibly a Göktürk, but they might also be someone using the Göktürks as a smokescreen. While he and Pei Jingzhe awaited a response from the men they'd dispatched to Khotan, Feng Xiao had turned his gaze to Liugong City—and to Abbot Cui, who'd risen to fame two months ago.

"Might this one inquire what kind of jianghu sect this 'Jiejian Bureau' is? I am possessed of neither power nor riches, and rarely have any dealings with wanderers from the jianghu. When, pray tell, did I offend you?"

The Jiejian Bureau guards had dragged Cui Buqu back to Qiushan Manor. Feng Xiao hadn't tortured him for answers, nor had he locked him up—he didn't need to. Cui Buqu was an ordinary man who knew nothing of martial arts.

Presently, he sat across a small table from Feng Xiao. There was even a pot of tea steaming in front of him. The atmosphere was that of two friends reminiscing about the past, a complete contrast to the earlier scene of drawn daggers pressed to throats. The about-face left Cui Buqu somewhat bewildered, as if the previous attempted assassination, rescue, interrogation, and arrest were all no more than a dream.

"You're a disciple of Liuli Palace of Fangzhang Isle. How could you not know of the Jiejian Bureau?"

From his sleeve, Feng Xiao fished out an exquisite jade token about two fingers wide and tossed it down in front of Cui Buqu. "We found this under your pillow. I trust Abbot Cui will no longer play dumb?"

Liuli Palace of Fangzhang Isle was a lone sect near the coast, remote and independent. Their disciples didn't involve themselves in the debts and favors of the jianghu, and most of their fame came from recording the annals and tales of its martial arts circles. Rumor had it that they also took in many exiles who had fled the Central Plains for one reason or another. The disciples of Liuli Palace were familiar with all major events across the land. If Cui Buqu was one of them, he would have heard of the Jiejian Bureau no matter how secret its existence.

Cui Buqu sighed. "I'll be honest. It's true I've heard of the Jiejian Bureau, but I'm only a common scholar. I've never had any run-ins with the government before. Affecting ignorance saves me some trouble. Moreover, you're mistaken. I'm not myself a disciple of Liuli Palace, though I have a senior who's a Liuli Palace consultant and studied political strategy from the Spring and Autumn period. He's given me no little guidance over the years and entrusted me with this jade token so I might visit him freely."

Feng Xiao raised an eyebrow. "So you're saying you study politics and strategy? You're a Daoist, yet you went to learn the art of debate? Don't you feel you've brought shame to your forefathers?"

Unperturbed, Cui Buqu asked, "What would you have me do? Daoists still need to eat. If I were less eloquent, how could Zixia Monastery have become what it is today?"

"Who is Qin Miaoyu to you?"

Cui Buqu was baffled. "Who?"

"A Khotanese envoy was murdered, and his favored concubine Qin Miaoyu has vanished. Before she married, Lady Qin was a resident of Liugong City, and was often seen offering incense at Yufo Temple and Zixia Monastery. Two months ago, you appeared at Zixia Monastery and single-handedly revived it. You could have gone to any sizable monastery and done well with your abilities. Why pick Zixia Monastery specifically?"

Feng Xiao's manner was aggressive, and as he spoke, he leaned in until he was mere inches from Cui Buqu, so close Cui Buqu could feel Feng Xiao's breath fanning his cheeks. Cui Buqu frowned, as if he wanted to draw back, but Feng Xiao grabbed him by the shoulder and held him in place.

"Cold plum blossom fragrance." Feng Xiao's nose was nearly pressed to Cui Buqu's neck. He inhaled, then continued in a soft voice: "This fragrance on you is the same that was within Yuchi Jinwu's carriage. What is your relationship to his concubine? Or did you disguise yourself as a woman and kill him?"

Cui Buqu was so angry he laughed. "With my looks, even if I dressed as a woman I fear no one would believe me! The distinguished master would be far more enchanting and glamorous in such a disguise. As for this plum blossom scent, there were an incredible number of worshippers at the monastery today. I have no idea how many I met and spoke to; it's no surprise if someone's fragrance lingered on me."

Feng Xiao studied him. Cui Buqu was strenuously defending his innocence, and it was true that Feng Xiao had no evidence.

But Cui Buqu's responses were far too calm—that was the most suspicious thing about him.

What had Cui Buqu done before arriving at Zixia Monastery? Where had he come from? And why was he involved with Liuli Palace of Fangzhang Isle? Too many things about this man were murky, impossible to grasp.

"It seems that no matter what, Abbot Cui refuses to tell the truth."

Feng Xiao extended a hand and gave Cui Buqu a sharp shove; caught off-guard, Cui Buqu fell backward.

As for Feng Xiao, he rose and dusted off his hands and clothes, as if afraid Cui Buqu would sully him. He asked, "Do you know why I brought you to this house?"

5

A T FIRST GLANCE, the house seemed much like any other. At most, the window paper was a little thicker, and the rafters a little lower, so that the interior was dim even in the daytime. Though the sun was still high, candles were already lit, creating a close and oppressive atmosphere. Other than that, the small house was fully furnished and looked quite new. Even the corners where the cabinets met the rugs were free of the fraying one would expect from long years of wear.

Cui Buqu gave his surroundings a quick scan before offering his assessment: "No one's ever lived here, have they?"

Feng Xiao smiled slightly. "They have, but this used to be a small house for maidservants. I had someone renovate it into a torture chamber for the Jiejian Bureau."

Faced with this naked threat, Cui Buqu said simply, "So the distinguished master means to torture me?"

Feng Xiao crouched so their eyes were level. "Look at yourself. Your reactions aren't anything like that of an ordinary, innocent citizen. How could I not suspect you?"

"Could you stop being so unreasonable?" asked Cui Buqu help-lessly. "Are you saying if I cry and plead my innocence, you'd let me go? Even if Lady Qin had some connection to Zixia Monastery, that was a Zixia Monastery before my time. I've never met the woman!

This distinguished master must have searched the monastery from floor to rafters. Tell me, did you discover anything suspicious?"

"There's a Baiyun Monastery in this city that receives far more worship than Zixia Monastery," said Feng Xiao. "Why not go there?"

"Better to lead a pack of chickens than trail after a phoenix," said Cui Buqu. "Zixia Monastery was rundown and neglected; there were a great many things to be managed. I knew if I could revive it, I'd end up calling the shots, which I much prefer to living under someone else's thumb. Surely that goes without saying?"

Feng Xiao shook his head. "That won't do. Two months ago, Linlang Pavilion announced they'd host an auction in Liugong City. You just happened to arrive at the exact same time. This in itself is suspicious. The Khotanese envoy is dead, and Lady Qin has vanished along with the treasure. It's likely the treasure is being passed from hand to hand and will eventually turn up in Liugong City. So why did you come here? For Lady Qin? Or the treasure? Where is it hidden? At Zixia Monastery, or at Linlang Pavilion's auction house?"

"I'm afraid I understand the distinguished master's words less and less."

"That's fine too," said Feng Xiao. "You can take your time pondering them here. Let me know once you understand."

"My health has always been poor," said Cui Buqu. "I fear I won't be able to endure any torture."

"Do you think physical pain is the worst suffering a person can experience?" The question was heavy with implication. Feng Xiao didn't wait for Cui Buqu's response but rose and departed.

Pei Jingzhe cast Cui Buqu a parting glance, then followed. In the blink of an eye, Cui Buqu was left alone.

The candles went out, the doors swung shut, and the window shutters came down, plunging the house into gloom. Whatever command Feng Xiao had issued, it ensured that each window was covered from the outside with layers of black netting that sealed out every last ray of light. The house drowned in darkness. Even the buzz of insects was stifled, let alone the footsteps of those outside.

The quiet of night was beloved of scholars for its ability to open the mind—but that kind of silence was a tranquil peace accompanied by the bright moonlight and the wind singing through the pines. When silence reached an extreme, as it now did, it would instead become something terrifying.

The moment the doors shut on Cui Buqu, the expression of helplessness and fury on his face was wiped clean, replaced with cool disdain. When the black netting descended over the windows, he let out a quiet snort of contempt.

He knew what Feng Xiao was trying to do.

Depriving someone of their sight and hearing would sink them into an intense silence and boredom. In such a state, one's thoughts inevitably spiraled into anxiety and confusion. Even if they shouted and screamed, they'd only hear echoes of their own voice. It was impossible to tell if it was noon or night. A day or two of this might be tolerable, but after four or five had passed—or even ten or fifteen—time would gradually lose meaning. In the end, a person subjected to such torture wouldn't know if they were dead or alive, whether they walked the mortal world or had descended into hell.

Under this kind of silent torment, even the toughest of men would find themselves weeping and begging for mercy.

Cui Buqu had seen it with his own eyes. There'd been a famed jianghu practitioner from the circles south of the Yangtze, an expert in wielding dual swords. He'd been held captive in such a house for half a month. When he at last emerged, his body was riddled with wounds—all carved by his own hand. Only through the pain of

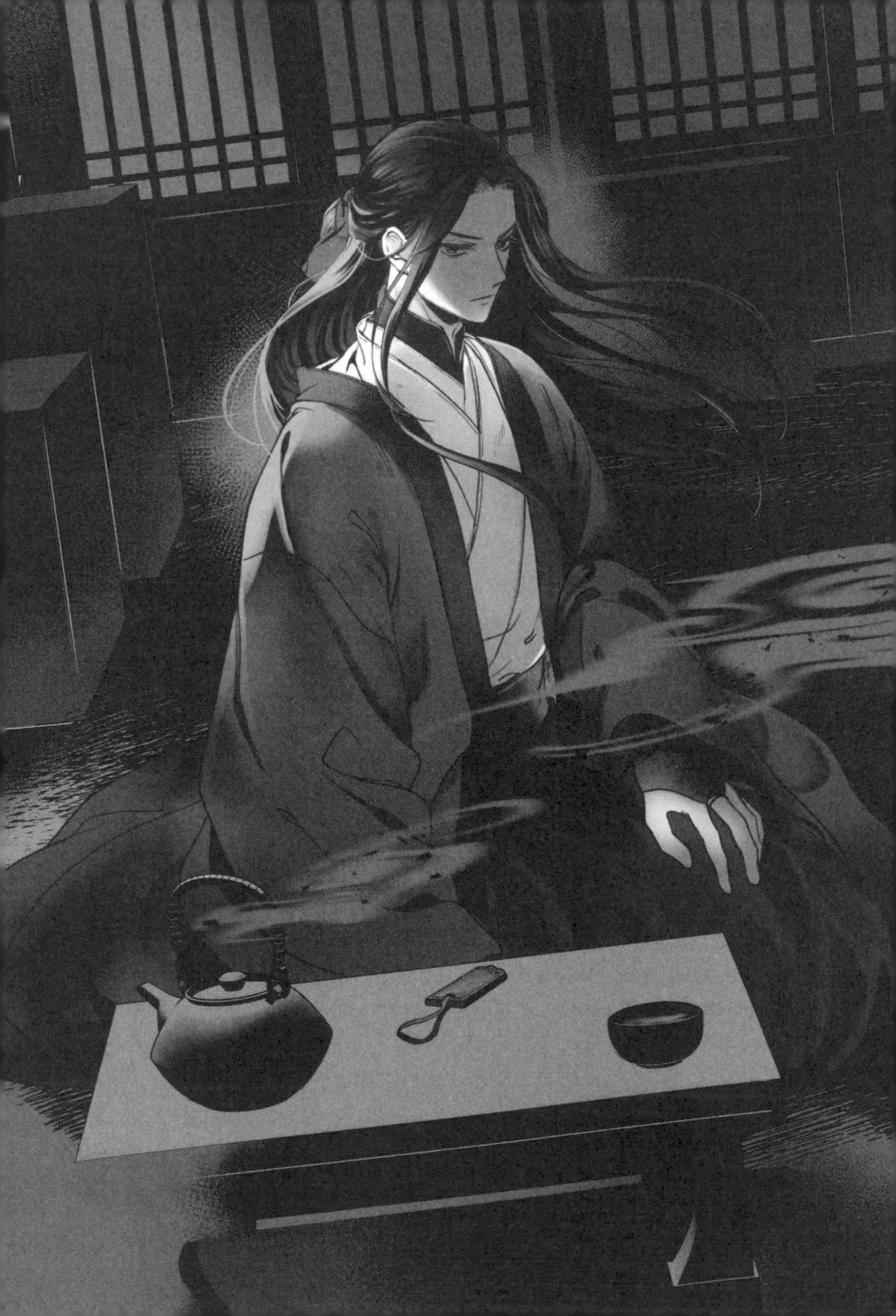

self-mutilation had he ascertained that he still lived. A method like this killed a man without drawing blood. The Jiejian Bureau had many such tricks up their sleeve. And now, one was being used on Cui Buqu.

Feng Xiao must have been confident. He was sure that however peculiar Cui Buqu might be, he couldn't withstand half a month in this house. Afterward, Cui Buqu would answer all his questions and the truth would become clear.

Cui Buqu picked up a reed cushion and searched the house. When he'd felt his way over to a pillar, he sat against it and crossed his legs. He knew nothing of martial arts, but he had learned some breathing exercises for maintaining good health. He closed his eyes and began to practice them now, looping through the techniques as he emptied his mind, isolating himself and discarding unnecessary thoughts.

Certain monks and Daoists had been known to meditate for dozens of days at a time, but those were experts who'd been thoroughly trained in the practice of nonattachment since childhood. It wasn't something the average monk could achieve, let alone common men who immersed themselves in the red dust of the secular world. Even Cui Buqu himself didn't know how long he could endure—but he did know Feng Xiao wouldn't let him off easily.

This wouldn't be the only trick the Jiejian Bureau would try.

❖❖❖

"It's been three days, sir." Pei Jingzhe set a fresh cup of tea before Feng Xiao as he spoke.

"Mm? What's been three days?" Feng Xiao asked carelessly. His head was bowed as he read through the report he'd received from Qiemo.

"Abbot Cui has been in that house for three days," Pei Jingzhe reminded him. "He's not a martial artist. If he remains there much longer, I fear he won't come out unscathed."

"Your own hands have taken no few lives. Why do you suddenly feel pity for a Daoist priest?" Feng Xiao glanced up at Pei Jingzhe.

"This subordinate is just worried it'll set us back," said Pei Jingzhe indignantly. "If he's such a suspicious character, won't we lose an important lead if he dies?"

In lieu of answering, Feng Xiao passed over the letter he held.

Pei Jingzhe read it carefully. Stunned, he said, "So it really was the Jade of Heaven Lake! The king of Khotan truly spared no effort to please His Majesty. He must be desperate for us to send troops to repel the Göktürks."

"Yuchi Jinwu is dead, so his king will send a new envoy. But his murder must be thoroughly investigated, and the jade found."

Pei Jingzhe laughed. "If you crack the case, I fear you'll no longer be able to avoid the Princess of Xiang. Won't this affect your plans to leave the capital—"

Feng Xiao's gaze flicked toward him, and Pei Jingzhe almost bit his tongue. Schooling his face to seriousness, he said, "In this subordinate's estimation, Lady Qin's disappearance is connected to the jade. Find her, and we'll find the treasure."

The jade had disappeared outside the city. If the criminal had taken it, they had only two options: enter Liugong City, or flee to Qiemo.

But Qiemo was between here and Khotan, which would presumably mean heading back the way they'd come. The culprit couldn't hide in the wilderness with the treasure forever, so the most sensible course was to lie low inside Liugong City, sell it via Linlang Pavilion's auction, then disguise it and transport it out of the city on the main roads.

"Our investigation of Lady Qin turned up three leads," said Pei Jingzhe. "As of now, we've found nothing untoward about Yufo Temple; perhaps Lady Qin only frequented it to mislead us. I've taken people to investigate Zixia Monastery several times, but we've found nothing suspicious there either. All that remains is the family of the aunt Qin Miaoyu lived with before her marriage. This aunt's entire family moved to Jincheng. However, it seems that, half a month ago, their residence in Jincheng burned down. According to the reports, this autumn was particularly dry, turning everything into potential kindling. The children were careless when playing with fire, and her aunt's entire family of six all perished in the resulting conflagration. Coincidentally, this happened at the same time Yuchi Jinwu left Khotan and set out for the Central Plains."

He paused; when Feng Xiao said nothing, he pressed ahead. "I suspect 'Qin Miaoyu' was a fake identity from the beginning. She actively plotted to catch Yuchi Jinwu's eye here in Liugong City and travel with him back to Khotan, all with the goal of getting her hands on the Jade of Heaven Lake."

"She was Yuchi Jinwu's concubine for four or five years. How could she have known five years ago that the king of Khotan would send him to the Central Plains as an envoy?"

Pei Jingzhe started, realizing he'd made a mistake in his reasoning. "Could it be that the real Qin Miaoyu was replaced by an imposter when Yuchi Jinwu was selected as envoy?"

If someone wished to frame Great Sui for an envoy's death, the ideal course of action would be to murder Yuchi Jinwu within the guest complex the Sui dynasty had prepared for him in Daxing City, then abscond with the jade. This was the most effective way to sow discord between Great Sui and Khotan.

But to get to the capital, they would have to pass through Liugong City. And, as the most favored of Yuchi Jinwu's concubines, Lady Qin would inevitably come into contact with old acquaintances there. The original Lady Qin had lived with her aunt's family; they were the ones most likely to expose her. Thus they had to die.

Perhaps some change to the plan had forced Lady Qin to make her move outside the city instead. Or perhaps the murderer wasn't in league with Lady Qin at all. The case was complex and confusing; even Feng Xiao and Pei Jingzhe were unable to clear the surrounding fog.

"This subordinate has already instructed Magistrate Zhao as you asked to enforce a daily limit on the number of people entering and exiting the city. I'll personally lead some men there to inspect everything thoroughly—I can guarantee no one will smuggle anything out on our watch. However, the situation with Linlang Pavilion is a bit trickier."

Feng Xiao's brow creased slightly. "How so?"

"Behind Linlang Pavilion stands the Li clan of Longxi County and the Cui clan of Boling County." Pei Jingzhe's smile was strained. "Princess Leping is one of their backers as well. You know His Majesty has always felt guilt in regard to Princess Leping and indulges her whenever possible. I fear the culprit will take advantage of the princess's protection to hide the jade among the auctioned items and smuggle it out of the city in plain sight."

Feng Xiao rose to his feet and sneered. "So what if Princess Leping supports them? Even she must obey the tide and bow down to her father and brothers. When does Linlang Pavilion's auction begin?"

"Tomorrow," said Pei Jingzhe. "This subordinate has already sent men to keep watch. The moment anything suspicious appears at the auction, they'll make arrests."

"Yuchi Jinwu's entire party died outside the city. It's impossible that Linlang Pavilion hasn't heard of such a significant incident; they'll be on their guard. You—"

He was still speaking when a Jiejian Bureau attendant rushed inside.

"Sir! A fight broke out near Ruyi Tavern; a man is dead! Magistrate Zhao has already sent people over; he requests your lordship come take a look."

Under normal circumstances, a death in a street brawl was far beneath the notice of the Jiejian Bureau. If Magistrate Zhao came to them, it was likely because both the suspect and victim were people he couldn't afford to offend. Instead, he'd chosen to ask Feng Xiao, that mighty buddha, to oversee it.

"Mm, I'll go."

Pei Jingzhe leapt up after him. "Sir, please wait. What if Abbot Cui still refuses to talk? What should we do then?"

"Drug him with incense of helplessness. A small amount."

Shock and hesitation filled Pei Jingzhe's face. "What if his body can't take it—"

Feng Xiao's expression was cool, almost callous. "It doesn't matter if it cripples him," he said. "So long as he still breathes."

6

THE BRANCHES OF LINLANG PAVILION spread wide throughout the north and south, and their yearly auction was a grand affair. The location of the auction changed each year: sometimes it took place in Jiangnan and sometimes Haibei, and on this occasion, in Liugong City. Regardless of the venue, people from all walks of life—from dignitaries to common folk to residents of the jianghu—came from every corner of the land to participate.

Outsiders often believed there were many priceless treasures at the auction—gold and jewels fit for a king. In truth, though the auction did feature such treasures, they were exceptionally few. Most auction lots were items like rare, precious herbs or long-lost classics, or spices and gemstones from the Western Regions. To those who didn't enjoy the idea of running around trying to obtain such things, the auction was in effect a specialized and well-stocked marketplace. That it was popular was unsurprising.

Linlang Pavilion was a vast enterprise, and their powerful backing and influence meant even those from the jianghu hesitated to provoke them. Occasionally there was a small disturbance, but never any large-scale incidents. Their yearly auctions always went smoothly.

This year, however, seemed destined to be an exception.

When Linlang Pavilion chose Liugong City for their auction, many had quietly grumbled. Liugong City was neither a wealthy

Jiangnan locale nor a famous capital like Daxing City. It was a point of connection between the east and west, but only because merchants had to pass through it when entering or leaving the Western Regions. The city itself was uncomfortably close to the Göktürk Khaganate and filled with little but wind and sand. Pampered nobles were reluctant to come, so the number of attendees was slightly lower than in previous years, and most were from the jianghu. There were plenty of traders from the north and south as well, along with merchants from the Western Regions with sharp noses and deep-set eyes, leading camels loaded with satchels full of goods.

Today's incident had occurred right at the entrance of Linlang Pavilion's Liugong City branch. A group of people had just exited when someone armed with a sword came flying from the crowd and attacked the young man at the head of the group. The two struggled, and the attacker was killed. At that point, an unknown woman had appeared. She threw herself upon the dead man and started to wail, accusing the young man of murdering her older brother.

The entire business had taken place before the eyes of the crowd, and both the killer and the killed were quickly surrounded and detained. Constables were swift to arrive; however, when they saw who the killer was, they went straight to Magistrate Zhao, who in turn asked for Feng Xiao.

When Feng Xiao stepped onto the scene, the corpse still lay where it had fallen. A young girl clutched the body, weeping loudly. When she saw a pair of black boots come to a stop in front of her, she raised her head. Her tear-filled eyes were arresting, her expression sorrowful with no sign of pretense.

But Feng Xiao's gaze only skimmed lightly over her before coming to fix on the young man nearby.

"Did you kill him?" Feng Xiao asked.

The young man froze. He obviously didn't want to answer the question, but it was equally obvious that Feng Xiao's intimidating aura was affecting him.

Magistrate Zhao hurried to intervene. "This is Feng-langjun[2] from the capital, acting under—" He glanced at Feng Xiao. He wanted to say *under authority of the Jiejian Bureau*, but he had no idea whether Feng Xiao wished his identity to be exposed. He quickly rephrased. "...acting under orders to investigate the Khotan envoy's assassination. He came specially to help."

He turned back to Feng Xiao. "This is Wen Liang, Linlang Pavilion's head broker. The deceased's surname is Ying—Ying Wuqiu from Guangzhong. This young lady is his sister."

Wen Liang seemed to see an opportunity to defend himself. He stepped forward, cupping his hands in greeting. "This one is Wen Liang. Gentlemen, please let me tell you what happened. Just now, as I came outside with the assistant brokers, this man suddenly appeared and tried to kill me. Fortunately, I studied some martial arts in my youth and barely managed to fend him off. It was sheer luck that I avoided injury. Yet for some reason, he fell down dead on the spot. I didn't kill him."

"Everyone here saw you fighting my brother in broad daylight!" the girl cried in anger. "You struck him and killed him. A murderer must pay with his life! Is that all you have to say?!"

In contrast to the girl's distress, Wen Liang appeared almost calm. "This man attacked me first. I was only defending myself, and the strikes I landed weren't fatal. A proper investigation will make things clear."

"If you hadn't killed our father, would Dage[3] have tried to kill you at the cost of his own life?"

---

2 郎君. A polite address for any man, similar to "gentleman."
3 大哥. A word meaning "eldest brother." When added as a suffix, it becomes an affectionate address for any older male.

Wen Liang scowled. "Slander and lies! When did I kill any father of yours? Miss, you've got the wrong man. This whole thing is a farce!"

The girl glared at him hatefully. "Wen Liang, I'd recognize you even if you turned to ash!"

There was obviously some story here, but Feng Xiao had no intention of carrying out an interrogation in the middle of the street. He waved a hand and ordered all related persons be brought back to the county office.

The girl refused to leave her brother's corpse and had to be hauled off by two constables. She sent a bloodshot glare at Wen Liang as she was dragged away, her face the perfect embodiment of fury. If vengeful spirits existed in truth, she'd likely have bashed her brains out against a pillar, then come roaring back from the dead to make Wen Liang pay with his life.

Yet Wen Liang didn't spare her a glance. He walked over to Feng Xiao and bowed. "May we have a word, Feng-langjun?"

"Speak."

"Linlang Pavilion has flourished in recent years; it's inevitable that petty villains will get ideas. I caught my master's eye and became head broker, which made me a bigger target. I trust Feng-langjun and Magistrate Zhao will judge this case fairly."

"This incident happened in Liugong City, so it is in the county magistrate's hands. Tell it to him, not me."

By now the corpse had been moved, leaving a bloodstain on the ground, blackening in the sun. A light breeze brushed past Feng Xiao's ear. His reflexes were excellent, and he dodged to the side at practically the same instant. Something flashed past—a glittering needle nearly grazed his nose as it hurtled toward Wen Liang only a few steps away. Wen Liang was oblivious; his skills might have been enough to deal with an open assault, but not this kind of sneak attack.

Feng Xiao's response was immediate: with a wave of his sleeve, the needle clattered to the ground.

Wen Liang saw only Feng Xiao strike out in his direction and thought he was trying to hit him. He stumbled back, shocked. "You!"

"Look down," said Feng Xiao.

Wen Liang composed himself and looked. He saw the needle, faintly blue in color—likely poisoned. Fear gripped his heart, and he looked up to see Feng Xiao scrutinizing him.

"I don't know who hates me so much that they must see me dead!" Wen Liang said with a bitter smile.

Feng Xiao turned to Magistrate Zhao. "Bring him back to the county office; detain him. I'll interrogate him myself later."

Wen Liang scowled. "I've done nothing wrong—"

"Anyone involved in the case will be considered a suspect," Feng Xiao cut in coolly. "Whether or not they are innocent will be determined *after* my interrogation."

"But I—I must oversee the auction tomorrow!"

"Do your subordinates vanish in your absence? If so, Linlang Pavilion can shut down now!"

Such imperious words, yet there was no retort he could make. Wen Liang stared back resentfully. He was about to say more when someone off to the side cut in with a sneer: "Acting high and mighty just because you're from the capital. Well, I refuse to let you arrest him. What now?"

Feng Xiao slowly turned toward the newcomer. His face was luminous under the azure sky, yet his eyes were sharp as an eagle's, able to nail a person in place and strip them of all rudeness and impudence.

"And where did you pop out from?" asked Feng Xiao, as if he'd only just noticed him.

Met with Feng Xiao's irreverent attitude, the man was hopping mad, his face twisting with rage. "I am from the house of Princess Leping! Don't tell me you haven't heard of *her*! Let's have your position in court and your name, if you have the guts. Once I return to the capital, I'll ask the princess to speak to His Majesty about this!"

From the house of Princess Leping simply meant he was her servant. Nowadays, one couldn't strike a dog without checking who their master was first. If their master was an ordinary person, there was no problem. But Princess Leping wasn't merely His Majesty's eldest daughter, Yang Lihua; she was also the empress of the previous dynasty. With the ascension of Yang Jian as Emperor Wen, the Sui dynasty had replaced the Zhou dynasty. Yang Jian had robbed his daughter's husband of his throne and relegated her from empress to princess.

Yang Lihua was a strict observer of social hierarchy. Her father's usurpation had been a great blow to her, but ultimately, she was only a daughter—there was nothing she could do about it. In an effort to make it up to her, Yang Jian and his wife doted on her fiercely and made more concessions to her than even their sons. The emperor and empress would give Princess Leping anything she wanted short of an outright revolt. Invoking the princess was sometimes more effective than invoking the Six Ministers.

Princess Leping held dividends in Linlang Pavilion, so she'd become their protective shield. On hearing her name, any outsiders who thought to make trouble for Linlang Pavilion would back off— and this was to say nothing of the figures of other noble families standing behind the Pavilion with her.

But when Feng Xiao heard the man utter the name *Princess Leping*, not only did he fail to cower in fear, he actually raised an eyebrow. His gracefully curved eyes glimmered as he flashed a radiant smile. "My name is Feng Xiao, from the Jiejian Bureau. Don't you think it's pretty?"

The moment the princess's servant heard the words *Jiejian Bureau* and *Feng Xiao*, his face drained of color. His self-satisfaction vanished completely, and he looked like he'd seen a ghost. If he could, he would have sprouted wings and flown away on the spot.

7

IN THE CAPITAL, nobles were everywhere, and officials were as common as dogs. For many dynasties, when the palace overflowed with princes and their children, even these royal scions might be regarded as worthless.

However, the current emperor and empress were exceptions.

Even back when the emperor of Sui had been an official of the previous dynasty, his wife, Lady Dugu, had accompanied him every step of the way. She wasn't the kind of woman who only knew how to hide behind her husband. Several times, when Yang Jian had suffered setbacks, it'd been Lady Dugu who'd swooped in to save the day. After Yang Jian ascended the throne, Lady Dugu had taken up her duties and became Empress Dugu. She involved herself heavily in affairs of state with her husband's wholehearted support. To their people, the emperor and empress were known as the Two Saints.

Many had noted that the relationship between this particular emperor and empress wasn't merely that of husband and wife, but an intellectual camaraderie born of mutual support. The two were inseparable. Consequently, Empress Dugu's position was more secure than that of any empress of previous dynasties, and this was without even mentioning Yang Jian's oath that he'd have "no children but hers." The princes and princesses of the current dynasty were all sons and daughters of Empress Dugu.

Thus Princess Leping's status was rather special. Not only was she the empress's daughter by birth, she was also the eldest child of the ruling couple. Due to the great upheaval she'd experienced, the emperor and empress were particularly fond of her and granted all her requests. When members of Princess Leping's household were out and about, everyone showed them commensurate respect.

But even with such a mistress, her people still found themselves bruised and bleeding after slamming into the obstacle known as the Jiejian Bureau.

Princess Leping had one child with Yuwen Yun, the emperor of the previous dynasty: a daughter named Yuwen Eying. Though she'd lost her father early in life, her mother cherished her, and her grandfather and grandmother loved her. All her relations adored her, and even the wet nurse who fed her as an infant had been uplifted in status by her. Six months prior, the nurse's son had been implicated in a case and detained by the Jiejian Bureau. The wet nurse pleaded with Yuwen Eying for help, who in turn begged her mother, Princess Leping.

Yuwen Eying was the princess's only daughter, and she was naturally unwilling to let her suffer any injustice. The princess immediately took her head guard to the Jiejian Bureau with Yuwen Eying in tow and ordered the release of the nurse's son.

The Jiejian Bureau had three bureau chiefs. The head bureau chief also held the post of Minister of Justice, so he did little of the day-to-day management. The one truly running the place was the deputy bureau chief, Feng Xiao.

Few people were present at the bureau that day. But the version of events that raced through the capital in rumors was that the princess had marched fiercely into the bureau with her people. Before the Sword-Relieving Stone, the head guard refused to remove his blade, and the princess supported him, resulting in a verbal dispute between the two sides. Feng Xiao himself had said nothing—instead, he'd snapped the head guard's sword into three pieces in front of the princess and her daughter and tossed it aside.

The head guard only felt a gust of wind. When he returned to his senses a moment later, he discovered he'd been nailed to the Sword-Relieving Stone with the three pieces of his sword driven through his clothes: one at each shoulder, and the last between his legs, pinning him firmly in place. He didn't dare move a muscle.

Everyone stared, dumbfounded. Princess Leping couldn't believe someone existed who dared humiliate her people before her very eyes. She complained to the emperor, but unexpectedly, it wasn't the Jiejian Bureau or Feng Xiao who found themselves eating crow. The emperor of Sui had laughed and said, "Feng-er[4] is just direct." He'd sent the head guard out of the capital, said a few words of comfort to the princess, and that had been that.

The incident sent a clear message: the Jiejian Bureau held an important place in the emperor's mind, and he valued Feng Xiao highly. Even Princess Leping couldn't touch Feng Xiao, let alone anyone beneath her.

Feng Xiao's infamous reputation had circulated within the capital for quite a while, and those from the princess's residence were certainly aware of it. As soon as the princess's servant heard the Jiejian Bureau's Feng Xiao was here in the flesh, he paled. He lost his previous arrogance and now itched to flee.

"Ah, perhaps there's been a mistake. If the Jiejian Bureau is handling the case, we couldn't possibly interfere. Please go ahead!" The man gave a pained laugh, all solicitude.

---

4   凤二. "Er" (二) is a character that means "second" here. "Feng-er" is an abbreviated way of saying "second in command, Feng Xiao."

But it wasn't so easy to shake off Deputy Bureau Chief Feng. He waved a hand and said to Magistrate Zhao, "These people are related to the case. Bring them in for questioning as well."

Magistrate Zhao was reluctant. "This..."

Feng Xiao didn't wait for him to finish; he called directly for the elite cavalry who'd come with the Jiejian Bureau and had them round up Wen Liang and his colleagues.

The man from the princess's residence was fuming, but he dared not sling any more insults. Helpless, he could only glare balefully at Feng Xiao and comply. If even Princess Leping herself was unable to stand against Feng Xiao in the capital, then out here in this backwater, Feng Xiao could kill him and walk away unscathed.

In the end, Feng Xiao didn't interrogate Wen Liang himself. Once everyone was safely at the county office, he handed the case over to Magistrate Zhao.

Liugong City had weathered one calamity after another in the last few weeks; Magistrate Zhao was bruised and battered. He had no clue where to begin, and wearily rushed to deal with each new event while terrified Feng Xiao would tell him off for slacking on the job. All he could do was throw himself into the work with everything he had. He didn't dare cross the line when interrogating Princess Leping's men, but he had no such scruples when it came to Wen Liang. He also extracted testimony from the sister of the dead man, and thus swiftly managed to put the pieces together.

A great many years ago, there were two households in Guangzhong: one surnamed Ying and the other surnamed Wen. Both had been merchant families for generations and got along well. Originally, the Ying and Wen families were both moderately wealthy. But the Wen family patriarch of the last generation was a talented businessman. He quickly expanded his trading network, and his family's business grew apace. In contrast, the Ying family had no such brilliant talents, and their circumstances remained unchanged. As they watched their neighbors become wealthier and wealthier, greed overcame the Ying family. They conspired with bandits, and when the Wen patriarch took his eldest son on a business trip, the Ying family had father and son murdered on the road. The Wen family, left with only women, children, and the elderly, became an easy target—the Ying family took over their business and gradually got rich off them.

The Wen family's youngest son had been brilliant from childhood but had grown up feeble and sickly. Since his grandfather was a doctor, he'd been left in his care when his father and brother set out on their trip. Upon receiving news of their deaths, suspicion took root in his heart, and he began to secretly investigate. In the end, he traced the murders back to the bandits, and the bandits back to the Ying family. Wen Liang knew his family lacked the strength to challenge the Ying household directly, so he discreetly left home. Over the course of his travels, he came to know various important people and gained work with Linlang Pavilion, all while gathering evidence of his father and brother's wrongful deaths.

Around the same time, a new magistrate had been appointed in Guangzhong. The man was desperate for merits, clearly hoping to climb the ranks quickly. This did not escape Wen Liang. Seizing his chance, he approached the magistrate with evidence of the Ying family's collusion with bandits. The magistrate was delighted to have such a juicy case fall into his lap; he immediately investigated the Ying family and confiscated their assets. The Ying patriarch was convicted and exiled, and died on the road.

The Ying siblings were spared due to their youth and were fortunate enough to keep their lives. Of course they hated Wen Liang to the bone—but they were also keenly aware that Wen Liang's current station made him difficult to touch. They'd therefore thought of a way to take him down with them. Ying Wuqiu would first drink a lethal poison, then confront Wen Liang, allowing himself to be injured in the tussle. Once the poison took effect, killing Ying Wuqiu, Wen Liang would be blamed for his murder.

The story behind the case was terribly complex, but Magistrate Zhao had seen how Feng Xiao treated the princess's men and was afraid a small pawn like himself might be discarded at any moment. He pushed his subordinates to investigate all night and through the next day, leaving no stone unturned. Finally, the coroner's autopsy found traces of a poisonous herb within Ying Wuqiu's body, proving Wen Liang's innocence.

The Ying family had moved against the Wen family first, and Wen Liang had taken an eye for an eye. His claim that he didn't know the Ying siblings was a barefaced lie, but after all, the feud between the two families was far too deep and bitter. Even Magistrate Zhao couldn't help lamenting as he reported to Feng Xiao.

Feng Xiao, however, showed little interest in this history. His focus remained on Wen Liang himself. "Aside from Wen Liang, are there no other living members of the Wen family?" he asked.

Magistrate Zhao shook his head. "Wen Liang's mother is alive, though she's been bedridden for many years. He's completely devoted to her: she's a Buddhist and strictly forbade him from slaughtering the entire Ying family. That was why he accused only the patriarch and spared the Ying siblings. I've already sent men to question the mother; it's all true enough. The Wen matriarch is frail and sickly, and medicine has no effect. I fear she hasn't long left."

He had hoped to use this opportunity to cozy up to Feng Xiao, but the man seemed indifferent, with no inclination to continue the conversation. Magistrate Zhao left disgruntled. Perhaps, he thought, he should privately ask someone closer to Feng Xiao what he liked and send him a gift. If he could get the great and mighty Deputy Bureau Chief Feng to put in a word or two with the emperor, his future prospects would be boundless.

As soon as Magistrate Zhao left, Pei Jingzhe spoke up. "Sir, this Wen Liang is very suspicious!"

Feng Xiao hummed noncommittally, the pitch carrying a musical upward lilt. It was enough to make one's heart flutter, but not with desire—this was an instinctive reaction in the face of beauty. Some beauties stood out in complexion, others in figure. Feng Xiao, however, was a rare example of peerless beauty.

Beautiful as he was, he had a sharpness about him, now on full display. His demeanor was intimidating, his every gesture filled with power. No one would harbor indecent desire for such a beauty; they were more likely to be entranced and bow down in worship.

Pei Jingzhe's thoughts drifted for a moment. He wondered whether Feng Xiao's parents had foreseen how outstanding their son would become, and if that was why they'd given him such an unusual name—*Xiao*, the high heavens. When he heard Feng Xiao click his tongue impatiently, he swiftly reeled in his fanciful musings.

"The Jade of Heaven Lake is said to possess the power to grant eternal life and raise the dead," Pei Jingzhe said. "Wen Liang's mother has been ill for a long time, and he's incredibly filial to her. A single word from his mother was all it took for him to spare the Ying siblings; if not for that, they would've had no chance to take revenge. Perhaps he plotted to steal the jade for his mother's sake. That would give him motive."

"Continue."

"If not for your lordship, Wen Liang might have died outside Linlang Pavilion today. Perhaps he was targeted because he'd been exposed somehow—perhaps his co-conspirators were terrified he'd betray them and leapt to silence him."

Pei Jingzhe went on. "Liugong City is an insignificant branch for Linlang Pavilion. They've never chosen such a remote location for their auction, yet this year they happened to select Liugong City? Couldn't Wen Liang have specifically pushed for Liugong City because it was convenient for his plans and away from prying eyes? If we examine the clues, this subordinate believes there is a high chance Wen Liang is connected to the envoy's murder, as well as the theft of the jade."

When he had finished, Feng Xiao said, "Don't you find it too convenient?"

Pei Jingzhe started. "What do you mean?"

"We scratched the surface of Linlang Pavilion and Wen Liang fell into our lap. It's like having someone put a pillow under your head right before you doze off. The coincidence is uncanny. I suspect someone is deliberately trying to confuse us."

Pei Jingzhe blinked. Privately, he thought Feng Xiao far too paranoid. "This subordinate will keep an eye on Wen Liang. I'll pry the truth out of him, whatever it takes."

Feng Xiao changed the subject. "Did you use incense of helplessness? What were the results?"

A strange expression came over Pei Jingzhe's face. "I used it, but..."

But Cui Buqu hadn't spilled a thing. Pei Jingzhe had never imagined there could exist someone so unyielding that even incense of helplessness was useless against them.

8

I THINK OF MY LORD FONDLY, *but he will never change. He is ignorant, yet I am helpless.*[5]

Incense of helplessness. The name alone elicited a thousand sorrows. It held a fragrance like the first lotus in early summer, delicate and refined, but in truth, it was a terrifyingly effective drug—a horrific poison of which people trembled at the thought.

Although its toxicity wasn't enough to kill, the incense would permeate one's body, devouring bones and marrow, until the victim gradually grew addicted. A day without the incense and they'd find themselves short of breath, their body weak and mind delirious. Three days, and they would feel as if sharp knives were scraping at their bones; their suffering would be unbearable. After five days, their only succor would be death. They'd have to cross the Bridge of Helplessness leading to the afterlife for a bowl of Mengpo's memory-erasing soup.

The moniker of "helplessness" didn't refer to the forlorn state lamented by poets, but instead to the Bridge of Helplessness that spanned the underworld's River of Oblivion.

Cui Buqu had sat in the lightless, soundless house for five full days. His tormentor had the timing down to an art: food and water

---

5   A quote from the poem "Nine Changes" in The Elegies of Chu, one of the two earliest collections of poetry from Chinese literature.

were sent only when his fatigue grew unendurable, and he was drifting in and out of consciousness. When he next regained awareness, he found sustenance an arm's length away.

It was only a tiny bit of food and water, barely enough to keep him alive. But the greatest torment was neither thirst nor starvation: it was the endless silence and the blur of time. He didn't even know what day it was. What followed the darkness was more darkness. Beyond the stillness lay eternal silence.

He tracked the hours by counting the twelve joints of his four fingers. He did his best to stretch his body and recite classics, from Daoism to Confucianism, then from Legalism to Buddhism, in an attempt to clear his mind and keep himself focused.

Gradually, his eyesight deteriorated, but his hearing became keen. At this point, even the scurrying of insects and mice, the drip of water, would have been precious treasures. But there were no such sounds. He didn't know what method Feng Xiao had used, but it was as if the house had been forsaken by the rest of the world. If not for those meager rations, Cui Buqu would have suspected they really had forgotten him.

No average person could have endured this kind of silent torment, where day and night ceased to exist. Forget ten days or half a month—even three days would drive them insane. And that was to say nothing of Cui Buqu's health, which was so poor he fell ill with every turn of the season. By the third day, frustration and anger roiled within his heart. His stomach ached from hunger, and his limbs grew weak. His mind was falling into a muddle. Chills ran through his body, yet his forehead began to burn. Sensing another major bout of illness was imminent, he simply surrendered to it. No longer did he recite classics, and he allowed his consciousness to slowly fog over.

It was then that he smelled a fragrance.

The scent was faint, almost imperceptible, like a fragrance he'd smelled at the capital's Yinhe Gardens last year: subtle yet sweet, the scent of lotus blooms carried over the breeze, mingled with the fresh aroma of lotus seeds.

Soon the capital would grow warmer, and officials and dignitaries would begin entertaining guests in their homes. Their favorite technique was to place boiled lotus seeds and silver ear mushroom broth in a jar, then lower it into a well and leave it for half a day, retrieving it once guests arrived. First they'd treat their guests to a cup of hot lotus tea to warm the stomach and quench any extra internal heat in the body, then they'd follow up with a cool bowl of lotus seed and silver ear soup. The concoction filled the mouth with fragrance, soothing one from throat to stomach and extinguishing excess heat. He himself had experienced this kind of hospitality many, many times.

Cui Buqu suddenly opened his eyes.

The darkness that greeted him snapped him instantly back to reality. He still smelled the fragrance. It wasn't a hallucination. In the darkness, he raised an eyebrow slightly and sneered to himself.

Incense of helplessness.

Though it was a terrifying poison, it was also an incredibly rare and precious one. Yet Feng Xiao was using it on him—how extravagantly wasteful.

It was impossible for Cui Buqu to leave the house, and he could hardly stop breathing. He had no choice but to inhale that bewitching, addictive fragrance, little by little. A skilled martial artist might have circulated their internal energy and thereby resisted the effects for some time, but Cui Buqu was no martial artist. The incense of helplessness would only accelerate the breakdown of his body and leave him hanging between life and death.

It seemed his tormentor didn't wish him dead and was only using the incense to force him to tell the truth. But using something like this on Cui Buqu was akin to cracking a nut with a sledgehammer.

The men of the Jiejian Bureau could have no idea that Cui Buqu had been exposed to a similar incense years ago—and for ten excruciating days. Though he'd been left half-dead, he'd maintained a basic level of awareness throughout and had never succumbed. Even his master, Fan Yun, had been astonished. He'd judged his pupil's willpower to be so strong that, if not for his weak body, he could have conquered any martial art in the world.

Yet incredible brilliance would always draw the envy of heaven. Fan Yun knew it as well: even if Cui Buqu learned no martial arts, he still stood head and shoulders above the vast majority. Some people were destined to be extraordinary from birth. To Cui Buqu, all suffering was simply the stone against which he honed himself. Only by blowing away the dust could one discover the gold beneath.

Cui Buqu slowly closed his eyes once more.

Soon, Linlang Pavilion's auction would begin. Feng Xiao couldn't wait much longer to come for him. Cui Buqu gave him ten days.

❖❖❖

"So what happened?" Feng Xiao frowned impatiently at Pei Jingzhe, who seemed to be struggling to speak.

Linlang Pavilion's auction had begun four days ago. It would last for six, so tomorrow was the final day. Up till now, it had mostly been medicinal herbs and silks at auction; the rare treasures everyone was interested in would feature at the end.

The auction had bustled with activity in the last few days. Goods and items exchanged hands, and many looked forward to returning home with bursting satchels. Still, plenty had their sights set on the final day of the auction. Even if they couldn't afford any rare treasures, if they could catch a once-in-a-lifetime glimpse, they wouldn't have traveled thousands of miles in vain.

But Feng Xiao was deeply unsatisfied.

Things were not progressing as he wished. Wen Liang and the others were still in custody, and though Linlang Pavilion didn't dare openly defy the magistrate, people still arrived daily to plead for mercy. Feng Xiao turned every one of them away and tossed Cui Buqu into the care of Pei Jingzhe, then went to personally keep an eye on the auction. But Lady Qin never appeared. It was as if she'd vanished into the sea of people, and the whereabouts of the Jade of Heaven Lake also remained unknown.

If the jade reappeared, it would be on the last day of the auction. But as Feng Xiao turned things over in his mind, he felt that he'd missed something, and it made him irritable.

Since the day he'd taken charge of the Jiejian Bureau, it'd been smooth sailing. What obstacles he'd encountered were hardly worth mentioning. It had been a long time since he'd experienced this type of elusive frustration, where everything felt hazy and indistinct. As if an invisible hand was playing chess, and Feng Xiao, originally standing beside the chessboard, had somehow been pulled into the fog and was about to become a chess piece himself...

Feng Xiao started, as if he'd suddenly grasped something—but then it was gone.

Pei Jingzhe finally got the words out: "Previously, your lordship instructed me to administer incense of helplessness to Cui Buqu for five days. The man is obviously frail; I didn't dare give him too much. Just now, I entered to take a look and found him in a daze. I splashed him with some well water to wake him and took the chance to ask him a few questions, but he maintained he had nothing to do with Lady Qin. It's my belief that this man named Cui is truly innocent!"

If he weren't innocent, he had a core and heart of steel, so strong even incense of helplessness was powerless to move him.

Was such a thing possible?

Pei Jingzhe had never seen a martial expert who could endure multiple days of exposure to incense of helplessness without begging for mercy—never mind an invalid like Cui Buqu.

"Where is he?"

"In bed in the east wing."

Feng Xiao's brows drew low in a frown. "You let him out?"

Pei Jingzhe's smile was strained. "My good lord, do you think everyone is like you, capable of spending days inhaling incense of helplessness and coming out unharmed? If they can't get his fever down, he might not survive, let alone confess."

Feng Xiao snorted. "That man still has his uses. If it looks like he won't make it, use drugs if you have to; keep him breathing."

Pei Jingzhe was gobsmacked. Feng Xiao wanted to torture Cui Buqu with drugs again already? He hurried to say, "The doctor already gave his opinion! He said his body's completely spent; he can't withstand any more torture!"

Feng Xiao made no response as he followed Pei Jingzhe to the east wing.

Sure enough, they found Cui Buqu sound asleep. His cheeks were noticeably gaunter and his complexion paler than it had been two days ago. Blue veins were faintly visible on the arm peeking out from under the covers, painting a vivid picture of a diseased and broken man at death's door.

Feng Xiao stood by the bed and watched Cui Buqu's sleeping face for a long time. The ailing man seemed to sense his burning gaze, and his forehead wrinkled a little in his sleep.

"Sir, are we going to cleanse his body of the incense?" Pei Jingzhe whispered. "Otherwise I fear he'll never recover."

Feng Xiao shook his head. He stroked his chin as he stared at Cui Buqu, watching him battle his nightmares. He seemed fascinated. After a moment he said, "Say, could he be from the Zuoyue Bureau?"

9

TOGETHER, *ZUO AND YUE* were the two components that made up the right side of the character *Sui*.[6] The name naturally brought to mind the *Sui* of the Sui dynasty.

After Yang Jian took the throne, he used a homophone of his inherited title—Duke of Sui—to name his nation, and decreed his ruling era would be called Kaihuang: "Rule of the Founding Emperor." In the second year of the Kaihuang era, six months after the Jiejian Bureau was established, another agency called the Zuoyue Bureau quietly materialized.

Much like the Jiejian Bureau, they were independent from the Three Departments and Six Ministries. But unlike the Jiejian Bureau, they did not fall under the emperor's jurisdiction. They took their orders directly from the empress.

Empress Dugu had made great contributions to the nation. She shared the emperor's rule, and he loved her above all. Thus she did something completely unprecedented: she established her own special agency.

The people referred to the emperor and empress as the Two Saints, and for good reason. Empress Dugu wielded a power that far surpassed that of any empress of bygone dynasties, even Empress Lü,

---

6   左月. "Zuoyue" is written with characters that can mean "left" and "moon." Writing the characters vertically creates the right half of "Sui" (隋), the name of the current dynasty.

the famously influential first empress of the Han dynasty. But the principal difference between her and Empress Lü was that, unlike Empress Lü's husband, Yang Jian was henpecked; he loved, feared, and respected his empress all at once.

The Zuoyue Bureau's authority had been comparable to the Jiejian Bureau's since its establishment. Their purpose was the same— to gather intelligence—and they moved freely in both the north and the south. But the emperor and empress were a loving couple; Empress Dugu was unwilling to steal the emperor's spotlight or undermine his reputation. She therefore limited the scope of the Zuoyue Bureau's duties and decreed that they would handle only disputes and cases related to the jianghu.

One chief ran the Zuoyue Bureau, supported by three deputy chiefs and a couple of cavalry riders. They were fewer in number than the Jiejian Bureau, and far more secretive in their dealings. Their members rarely appeared in public at all; even trusted, high-ranking officials and ministers knew only that the Zuoyue Bureau existed and nothing more.

Still, their similar jurisdictions meant conflicts were inevitable. Though the Jiejian Bureau and the Zuoyue Bureau had no bad blood between them and were commanded by an emperor and empress who themselves ruled harmoniously, they couldn't help competing with each other to gain the upper hand.

Pei Jingzhe had briefly interacted with members of the Zuoyue Bureau on previous cases and knew how difficult they were to handle. Consequently, he also knew more about the Zuoyue Bureau than most. Though he didn't know the chief, he knew two of its deputies. One was a woman, slender and lovely as a lady from a noble family, while the other was a man, taciturn and quiet as an ascetic monk. Though the Zuoyue Bureau thronged with eccentrics and hidden masters, these two deputy chiefs were exceptionally strange even among their number. Then there was the chief of the Zuoyue Bureau, a mysterious person who shied from the public eye. Even Pei Jingzhe had never seen them. No matter how he tried, he couldn't connect that place, more unfathomable and enigmatic than even the Jiejian Bureau, with the invalid lying before him.

Maybe the delicate woman was a martial arts master, and perhaps the taciturn man was a deadly fighter, but Abbot Cui, who couldn't even raise a shoulder or lift his hand? Could he really be a spy from the Zuoyue Bureau? Or did his sickly body and cover as a Daoist make it even easier to remain anonymous?

Pei Jingzhe thought for a moment, then said, "Do you think since Linlang Pavilion is holding their auction here, and people from the jianghu are gathering, the Zuoyue Bureau might also have planted spies here to keep an eye on things? But he knew we were from the Jiejian Bureau. If he's truly from the Zuoyue Bureau, why didn't he tell us?"

"Zixia Monastery might have been connected to Lady Qin in the past, but this man only arrived two months ago, four or five years after Lady Qin left Liugong City. I never really thought he was related to the case. However, around two months ago, the court just so happened to decide to move against the Göktürks."

Understanding dawned on Pei Jingzhe. "So right from the beginning, all you wanted was to uncover his background? But if he really is from the Zuoyue Bureau, haven't we made an enemy of them?"

Though the two agencies competed, they were still all subjects of the imperial court. Surely dealing harshly with their own and damaging the Jiejian Bureau's relationship with their sister agency would come back to bite them?

Feng Xiao seemed unconcerned. "If we become enemies, we become enemies. Whether he hates me or not makes little difference. The Khotanese envoy has been assassinated in this city; do you really believe they have no intention of meddling and claiming a piece of the glory for themselves?"

Although Liugong City was remote, Feng Xiao's people had multiple special channels that sent them constant updates from the capital. A few days ago, the emperor and his many officials had finished relocating to the new capital of Daxing City. The common folk had already moved in. The old capital that had stood for many generations was now small and cramped. On rainy days, mud and sewage backed up in the ditches, and water flooded the streets. One of the first things Yang Jian did upon taking the throne was order the construction of a new capital next to the old one. Only two years later, Daxing City was established, and the emperor of Sui proclaimed a general amnesty for the entire nation. At the request of his officials, he also began purchasing books that had been scattered by warfare in order to populate the national treasury and preserve classics for future generations.

These many examples of benevolent governance bespoke the tenor of the new dynasty and the actions of an enlightened ruler. Amid all this, Yang Jian also decided to mobilize his troops against the Khaganate and quell once and for all the disturbances in the north. No one doubted the emperor's resolve. The Three Departments and Six Ministries all got to work, while the Jiejian and Zuoyue Bureaus also took their orders and laid their plans. Anyone who played a key role in this matter would gain significant accolades. The Zuoyue Bureau had been itching to knock the Jiejian Bureau down a peg. How could they let such an opportunity slip past?

Cui Buqu, lost in fretful dreams, coughed quietly in his sleep.

Pei Jingzhe glanced at him. Before he'd suspected Cui Buqu might be from the Zuoyue Bureau, he hadn't given his condition much thought. But looking at Cui Buqu again now, he couldn't help feeling a bit of sympathy.

"Then...shall this subordinate neutralize the poison?"

Feng Xiao looked at him like he was a fool. "Why should we do that? Since he's refused to admit it, this is a perfect chance for me to do with him as I please. Even if he confesses his identity, you must insist he's lying. Don't let him lead you by the nose. In Liugong City, my word is law."

The corners of Pei Jingzhe's lips twitched. He'd long known his superior wasn't a kind or merciful person.

❖

Trapped within the agony of illness and nightmares, Cui Buqu remained completely unaware that Feng Xiao and Pei Jingzhe were freely discussing him inches away.

In his dreams, Cui Buqu walked on a very long road, one without end. Thorny briars occasionally sprouted from either side and slithered around his ankles, twining tightly about his legs. He wished to continue walking, so he ripped the briars off with his bare hands. His fingers were torn and bleeding, but the briars never thinned. Instead they multiplied, becoming thicker and more numerous. Thorns stabbed into his flesh. Every movement aggravated his wounds, sending spasms of pain through his body. But not only did Cui Buqu remain expressionless, he insisted on continuing to pull the briars away, as if he felt no pain at all.

All his life, if there was something Cui Buqu wanted to do, he wouldn't stop until he succeeded. No matter how it cost him, no matter how hard the road. None of that deterred him. And right now, he wanted to keep going, to walk to the end of the road and see what was there.

At last, unable to hinder him, the briars admitted defeat. They crumbled to ash and vanished. But Cui Buqu didn't so much as glance at his blood-slicked hands because a manor had appeared before him.

It was an old manor, hundreds of years old.

Before Great Sui's establishment, the northern dynasties had been in constant turmoil, their rulers rising and falling one after another. Yet the master of this manor remained steadfast, and his family flourished, multiplying until they became a sturdy branch no one could afford to underestimate.

Cui Buqu finally stopped walking.

The gates of the manor were tightly shut, yet on the steps stood two men. One had a head of white hair and a white beard, dignified and solemn, while the second stood somewhat closer and was far younger, his whiskers short. Within his arms was a swaddled infant, and he was speaking to the old man.

"Father, please give him a name!"

"Just call him A-Da or A-Er,"[7] the old man said coldly. "That's enough."

"He's already lost both his parents," the young man pleaded. "Can't you show him some mercy?"

"See how frail he is—he won't live more than a couple of years. What's the point in giving him a name?"

"Even so, wouldn't it be something to remember him by?"

The old man scoffed. "His parents are already dead. Who in this world would remember him?"

"I would."

---

7   阿大, 阿二. Names that essentially mean "first son" and "second son" respectively.

The two remained locked in a stalemate until the old man finally said, "Beneath my feet are stone steps. So let's name him Jie—*steps*. Stone steps are trodden on by thousands. A lowly name means he'll be easier to raise."

"Then the genealogy—"

"He's not worthy."

He's not worthy.

Those three words passed through the dense maze of fog and pierced Cui Buqu's ears.

The old man's voice creaked with age, the wear and tear of the vicissitudes of life, yet still it carried an unquestionable authority. It was like the rotting wood within this ancient manor—decayed to the point of ruin yet unwilling to retire. It still desired to claim a space for itself, to control the fates of others.

Stone steps are trodden on by thousands. A lowly name means he'll be easier to raise.

Cui Buqu suddenly loosed an icy laugh.

The sound startled the old and young man both. They turned toward him, but in an instant, they were swallowed by the mist and swept away.

All was dark once more.

Hidden behind Cui Buqu's tranquility was the ever-present abyss. But after so many years, he'd finally walked, step by step, to a place far more treacherous than that abyss—treacherous enough that he could look down into the abyss with contempt. A piercing pain tore through his chest, and a metallic taste surged up his throat. He couldn't stop himself from coughing, but it only filled his mouth with the salty-sweet tang of metal.

At last, he awoke.

His eyelids were sore and swollen, and even the slightest glimmer of light brought tears to his eyes. It was a long moment before he could see the muslin curtain before him.

A handsome face suddenly swept that curtain aside.

"You're awake." Feng Xiao looked down at him. "How do you feel?"

Cui Buqu didn't bother answering. He closed his eyes in repose.

Feng Xiao kept talking anyway. "The incense of helplessness within your body is dormant, but it's yet to be neutralized. It'll flare up again in a day or two. If you're willing to behave and follow my orders, I'll consider neutralizing the poison for you. How about it?"

Cui Buqu slowly opened his eyes. "May I refuse?" he asked hoarsely.

"No."

Then why ask? Cui Buqu rolled his eyes.

Feng Xiao seemed to not have noticed. "So?"

"I don't know martial arts," said Cui Buqu. "I won't be of any help."

Feng Xiao was all smiles. "Are you not from Fangzhang Isle's Liuli Palace? I've heard everyone there is familiar with stories from martial arts circles and knows the famous names of the jianghu. I happen to need just such a person for the Linlang Pavilion auction."

Cui Buqu was silent a moment. "I will, but I have a condition."

"Neutralizing the poison is not an option."

Cui Buqu began to cough. "I wish to eat and drink. You motherfucker, you want me to work without giving me any water?"

Some time later, Cui Buqu stared at the congee and plate of pickles in front of him, almost unable to keep a straight face.

Feng Xiao sat at Cui Buqu's bedside. Tone sickly sweet, he said, "Eat. Why aren't you eating?"

Cui Buqu spoke slowly. "I am a prisoner and completely at your mercy, yet you still want me to work for you. I'm severely ill and have yet to recover, and this is what you give me to eat?"

Perplexed, Feng Xiao asked, "What's wrong with it? You must know you shouldn't eat anything too rich when you're ill. I'm afraid you won't be able to digest it, and if you do, you'll end up bedridden again tomorrow."

"I'm not asking for any exotic delicacies. I only want a bowl of fresh vegetable soup. Surely you have *that*?"

"I apologize. We're a poor household; we really have none."

Cui Buqu was speechless. He wanted very much to upturn the bowl of congee over Feng Xiao's head, then take that plate of pickles and smear it all over his punchable face.

Feng Xiao didn't know what Cui Buqu was thinking, but he knew it was nothing good. He wasn't in a hurry, and he had no intention of leaving. He even found Cui Buqu's restrained reactions awfully amusing. He seemed almost afraid Cui Buqu *wouldn't* get angry: he paced back and forth beside him, looked at the flowers by the window, flipped through the books on the shelf, just waiting for the moment Cui Buqu would slam a hand on the table and rise, loudly proclaiming that he was from the Zuoyue Bureau.

He waited and waited, but not only did Cui Buqu not erupt, he silently picked up his bowl and brought a spoonful of the pickles and congee to his mouth.

Feng Xiao was certain he wasn't mistaken—this Abbot Cui had quite the temper. Even when he'd been pleading his innocence during their first meeting, he'd been unable to conceal the impatience bubbling under his skin. But Feng Xiao had never anticipated that within that sickly body was a core of steel, so strong even incense of helplessness couldn't break him. Someone like this could certainly

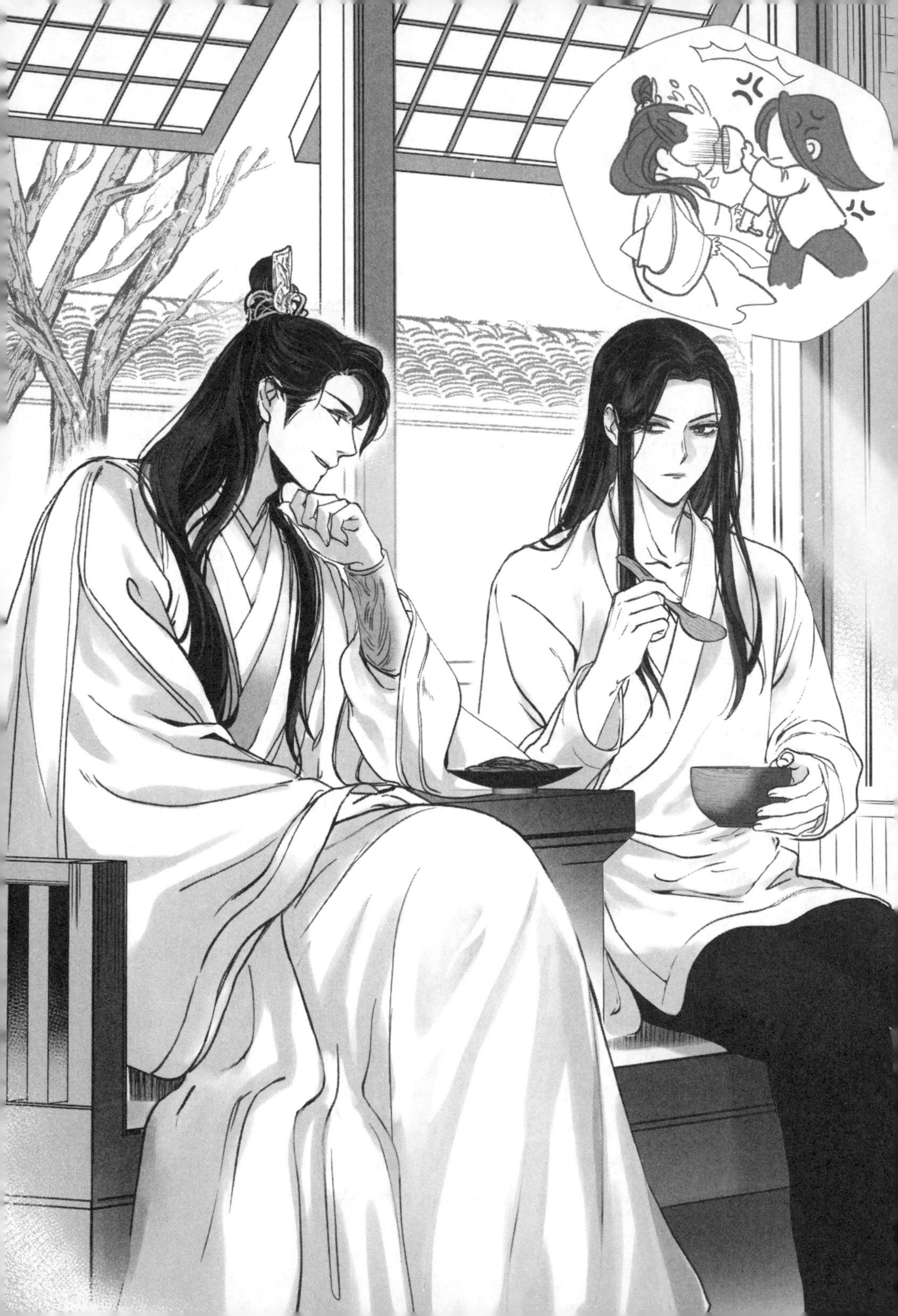

carve out a place for themselves in the Zuoyue Bureau, even if they knew no martial arts.

Feng Xiao grew even more interested.

Abbot Cui chewed and swallowed carefully. He took over an hour to finish one bowl of congee, but Feng Xiao didn't rush him. He waited at Cui Buqu's side until he finally set down his spoon.

"May I ask what service Your Excellency requires from me?"

"Why address me like we're strangers? As I recall, I've already told you my name. I'm ranked second in my household; you can call me Feng-er or Erlang."[8]

Cui Buqu ignored him. "I've been in Liugong City for two months and have heard quite a few things—such as that just before the Linlang Pavilion auction, a Khotanese envoy was murdered. If you want my help, surely you must tell me everything first?"

Feng Xiao smiled. "Naturally."

With Feng Xiao's permission, Pei Jingzhe walked through the entire sequence of events in detail: how the Khotanese envoy had died outside the city on the night of a snowstorm, and how the massacre had been discovered by passing merchants. He also described what they'd found on the bodies.

Cui Buqu listened intently. Once Pei Jingzhe finished, he said, "Did you investigate the plum blossom fragrance that was within the carriage?"

"We did." Pei Jingzhe couldn't resist a glance at Feng Xiao. He and this man had struck on exactly the same thought—in the beginning, Feng Xiao too had believed the plum blossom fragrance to be a key clue, though the idea had yet to bear fruit.

"We questioned all the perfume shops in the city and checked their formulas, but we couldn't find the fragrance we smelled in the

---

8 二郎. *"Erlang" means "second son."*

carriage. That fragrance..." Pei Jingzhe pondered as he searched for a fitting description, then blurted, "It's similar to incense of helplessness. If you smell it once, you'll never mistake it for anything else."

As soon as he said it, he felt his words had been rather inappropriate. Cui Buqu had just been tortured by this very incense. Wasn't this rubbing salt in the wound?

But Cui Buqu remained expressionless. He only nodded, coughed lightly, and asked nothing more.

10

CUI BUQU HAD ENDURED the incense of helplessness through his extraordinary willpower, but it still damaged his body. He was frail to begin with, and the effects of the incense were like piling frost atop snow. His condition, already bad, grew worse. The next day, he touched his forehead as he woke and knew his fever had returned.

He exhaled a slow, scorching breath. He'd grown accustomed to the feeling, but that didn't mean he enjoyed it. No one wanted to live under the eternal torment of illness. But as he couldn't escape, all he could do was endure.

A set of clean robes had been left at his bedside, along with a thick coat. Pei Jingzhe must have sent someone to fetch them; Feng Xiao would never bother with something so trivial. Cui Buqu put everything on without hesitation, bundling himself up tightly. Water had been prepared for him in a side room, and he used it to wash. Only then did he leisurely exit the room.

Outside, Feng Xiao had long lost patience with waiting. He sent Pei Jingzhe in to hurry Cui Buqu up. Pei Jingzhe had privately also thought Cui Buqu too slow, until he saw him: his complexion was even more pallid than the day before, and he was coughing feebly into his fist. Pei Jingzhe felt a prickle of guilt and gentled his tone. "Are the clothes suitable, Abbot Cui?"

"They're just right. Thank you."

Pei Jingzhe smiled. "We won't be eating breakfast at the manor today. My lord is taking us out to eat."

"How unexpected. Ever since I awoke, I've been hoping for a sumptuous meal. It seems I'm finally getting it."

Pei Jingzhe laughed awkwardly. "You only woke up yesterday. You shouldn't have anything too rich or oily."

Cui Buqu watched him. He could see this man's skin wasn't half as thick as Feng Xiao's. Cui Buqu's face didn't so much as twitch as he nodded, and he didn't embarrass Pei Jingzhe further.

When Feng Xiao saw them walk out, he clicked his tongue. "Must you dawdle like a maiden being wed when putting on your clothes?"

Most people's faces flushed with a fever, but Cui Buqu's paled instead. Wrapped in a white coat and standing in the snow, he practically faded into the landscape.

"My host is a cruel man," he said coolly. "He poisoned me yet wouldn't let me eat. What can I do?"

Feng Xiao seemed to be in a good mood. He smiled cheerily and said, "Then you're in luck today. A new restaurant just opened in the city, and they hired Maiden Hong as the chef. You've lived in Liugong City for two months; surely you've heard her name."

"Maiden Hong of Hong's Flatbreads?"

"The very same."

Hong's Flatbreads was a famous bakery in Liugong City that sold baked flatbreads. It was managed by the Hong family patriarch and his daughter. Remarkably, both father and daughter were skilled cooks, and though their sign only mentioned the flatbreads, all their dishes were delicious. Their name was known throughout the city, and it was said even traveling merchants from Qiemo would visit Liugong City just to taste their cooking.

Cui Buqu had eaten there once as well. The food was indeed extraordinary—broth simmered from bones, with noodles fine as strands of silver. The noodles were boiled before being added to the broth and served along with a ladleful of the Hong family's braised pork sauce and a sprinkle of green onions. Even on the coldest winter days, such fare warmed and comforted the body. Their dishes were in no way inferior to those one might find in the capital.

Unfortunately, the Hong patriarch had passed away some time ago, leaving Maiden Hong to run the business by herself. Everyone had gossiped about it, saying a woman was too delicate to handle such work, and that Hong's Flatbreads's days were numbered. Most had expected Maiden Hong to become the concubine of a wealthy family and be kept inside the house—there would be few chances, they lamented, to taste her delicious dishes ever again.

But to the astonishment of all, Maiden Hong made a fresh start. Rather than choosing a luxurious life, she accepted an invitation to become a chef at this new restaurant.

Thanks to Linlang Pavilion's auction, members of the jianghu walked up and down the streets, openly carrying their weapons. Ordinary civilians gave them a wide berth, but Feng Xiao acted like they weren't even there. With Cui Buqu and Pei Jingzhe in tow, he cut through a street toward the restaurant.

It wasn't unheard of for a martial artist to flout the law by dint of sheer power. All capable people had an arrogance about them, and those from the jianghu were no exception. Experts were rarely modest or open-minded, and indeed, most of the martial artists walking the streets were prideful young men.

Some walked in groups of three to five. Though they weren't all wearing the same uniform, the jade pendants at their waists and the scabbards across their backs were identical. These groups were usually from major sects. Others walked alone, their expressions cold and forbidding. These tended to travel solo and have short tempers. And there were still other groups where men and women walked and laughed together. The women's faces were cheerful and confident, their steps nimble. These were the young sons and daughters of influential martial arts families, out to train in the world.

Cui Buqu's gaze swept over them. A single glance was all he needed to discern everyone's backgrounds and approximate temperaments.

"Don't forget why I brought you out, Abbot Cui. Show me what you're capable of."

Cui Buqu couldn't resist rolling his eyes again. "This humble Daoist has yet to eat breakfast; he lacks the strength to speak."

Feng Xiao chuckled. "If you're good and play nicely, we'll crack the case faster and you'll be free faster as well. Is there any benefit to squabbling with me?"

"If I remember correctly," Cui Buqu said coldly, "yesterday, you told me that if I was willing to cooperate, you'd *consider* neutralizing the poison. You didn't say you'd neutralize it for sure. I was suffering under the effects of the poison yesterday, so I lacked the strength to argue. You want me to play nice with you based on such ambiguous promises?"

Feng Xiao fished out two porcelain vials from his sleeve, each the width of a finger, and held them out before Cui Buqu.

"I'll give you a chance. One of these bottles is empty, while the other is a neutralizing agent that will free you from the incense's torment for three days. Whether or not you pick the correct vial is up to you. Now don't say I'm not good to you."

There was a burning sensation in Cui Buqu's chest, as if a fire had kindled to life there. It wasn't yet a blaze, but the pain was unbearable, the agony eating down to his marrow. Thousands of invisible hands scratched at him, prickling and numbing—this was the poison wreaking havoc in his body. Though the pain of the dormant poison was less excruciating than when it flared up, it was more than enough to keep him on edge.

But he didn't touch the two vials. He didn't even glance at them; he simply pressed his lips into a tight line and kept walking.

"How can a man be so stubborn!" Feng Xiao exclaimed in surprise. "My kindness has completely gone to waste!"

Cui Buqu sneered but said nothing. A temporary antidote to this drug was as good as drinking poison to quench thirst. Feng Xiao wasn't being kind at all—it was obvious he wanted to wait for the poison to flare up again before he'd try to trick him into revealing more.

Seeing that Cui Buqu refused to take the bait, Feng Xiao simply shrugged and stashed the bottles back in his sleeve.

They walked on, and the new restaurant soon came into view. On the banner hanging by the door were written two characters: Wuwei— *Five Flavors*. People thronged at the doors; it seemed quite busy.

Pei Jingzhe had made a reservation. He skipped the line and gave his name as soon as he walked in; a waiter immediately came over to guide them to a semi-private room.

The restaurant didn't look particularly large from the outside, but the inside seemed an entirely different world. As Pei Jingzhe and the others followed the waiter down winding corridors, they realized the restaurant had purchased all the nearby shops and merged them into one. The resulting space had been divided into a main hall and smaller, semi-private rooms. The moment they entered theirs, the noise of the hall faded. Flowers and potted trees were arranged artfully around the room, creating a luxuriant atmosphere.

"The owner must have significant backing to invest so much in this place," Pei Jingzhe said in amazement. "Whose money was it, the Cui family of Boling, or the Li family of Longxi?"

Liugong City had originally been a small border town. No matter how prosperous it became, it couldn't compare to the extravagance of the capital. The itinerant merchants passing through usually stopped here for no more than a few days to trade before continuing on to their ultimate destinations. If not for Linlang Pavilion's auction, the restaurant would rarely have been this busy.

When he heard Pei Jingzhe's question, the waiter turned his head and smiled. "This esteemed guest has surmised wrongly. It wasn't the Li family or the Cui family. The owner is a local. He's worked long and hard all his life and only wishes for some good food, so he invited Maiden Hong specially to be the chef. You gentlemen are in luck today! Maiden Hong has been experimenting with some new dishes."

He led the trio to their table. There were four in the room, one already occupied by a well-dressed young man and woman. Behind them stood several maids and servants from their household. Though the room wasn't fully private, it was spacious enough that even with four tables it didn't feel cramped.

Feng Xiao put in his order, and dishes began to arrive one after another. Maiden Hong couldn't have been the only cook, but her crisp and lively style was evident on every plate.

"Snowy noodles with braised pork, pork trotter soup, hibiscus and vegetable soup, Hong-style flatbread. Eat whatever you like and stop saying I'm cruel. Surely I'm treating you well enough now?" Feng Xiao pointed out each dish with his chopsticks, then asked for three bowls of lotus seed soup.

It wasn't the season for lotus seeds, and Liugong City wasn't plentiful in lotuses to begin with. These seeds were transported from the south over thousands of miles, then wind-dried and preserved throughout the entire winter. The price of those three bowls of soup was probably more than the rest of the dishes combined.

It was the lotus seed soup that finally loosened Cui Buqu's tongue. He looked at the couple dining at the other table. "That woman's name is Lu. She's from a wealthy local family, and it's said they trace their lineage back to the Lu family of Fanyang. If so, they lost contact with the main branch long ago. Lady Lu's father is named Lu Ti, and his principal enterprise is antiques pawnshops; they say he has branches all the way in Jiangnan. He's the richest man in Liugong City and a savvy businessman."

He spoke just loudly enough for Feng Xiao and Pei Jingzhe to hear, but not so loud the other table could pick up a word.

Feng Xiao was quite pleased with Cui Buqu's tactfulness. It was rare for them to be speaking peacefully like this rather than at loggerheads.

"Is that man also from the Lu family?"

Cui Buqu shook his head. "The man is Su Xing, Lady Lu's older cousin. His parents passed away several years ago and his family's fortunes fell into decline. He sought refuge at his younger cousin's house, and Lu Ti sponsored his studies. They say Lu Ti wishes to have him as a son-in-law. If all goes well, that pair will be married within the next two years. Lu Ti has no sons, so Su Xing stands to inherit the family business."

"Then this Wuwei House is also owned by Lu Ti?"

"Of that I'm not sure," said Cui Buqu coolly. "After all, I was locked up for several days; I may have missed a lot of news."

He'd seized the chance to take a jab at Feng Xiao, but Feng Xiao acted as if he hadn't heard. He picked up a flatbread, broke off a small piece, and popped it in his mouth. "This flatbread is delicious, but it's rather chewy. Someone who's been poisoned or is recuperating from an illness generally wouldn't be able to eat it even if they wanted to. Would you like a piece, Buqu?"

Cui Buqu said nothing.

Pei Jingzhe stifled a laugh and quickly looked away. His eye caught on the young man at the neighboring table, who was picking up a piece of vegetarian goose and placing it in the girl's bowl. "Miaomiao, you love this dish, don't you?" he said warmly. "Here, have some more."

"Thank you, Cousin." The girl's voice was filled with unconcealed delight.

People of this era were quite open, especially here in the north. As long as they were chaperoned by family members and remained in public, unmarried men and women could be fairly intimate without drawing criticism. Pei Jingzhe was about to turn back around when he heard Feng Xiao speak loudly to Cui Buqu.

"Ququ, you love this dish, don't you? Here, have some more!"

Pei Jingzhe had been about to swallow his mouthful of flatbread, but on hearing this, he almost spat it back out.

Cui Buqu was even more uncomfortable. He'd just raised his chopsticks, ready to take more food, but now he stopped dead, the chopsticks hovering midair. The corners of his mouth twitched as his delicate face suddenly turned savage.

The young man, too, couldn't fail to notice Feng Xiao mimicking him. He looked furious. "Distinguished Master, we don't even know each other, so why are you trying to provoke us?"

11

"**H**OW STRANGE," said Feng Xiao. "This isn't your house, and you didn't invent those words or their pronunciation. We're in a public space, but I'm not even allowed to speak? Is there no law in this land?"

Feng Xiao kept his gaze fixed on the young man as he shoved the meat into Cui Buqu's bowl. Cui Buqu slid the bowl away, but it was like the chopsticks had eyes—they perfectly followed his movements and dipped into his bowl with unerring accuracy.

Cui Buqu glared at the meat in his bowl as if he could see traces of saliva from Feng Xiao's chopsticks on it. Never mind the food; he didn't even want to touch the bowl anymore.

But it seemed Feng Xiao wasn't done. He pushed a plate of fried beans toward Cui Buqu. "Are the meat dishes not to your taste? That's fine too. There're still beans. Here, I'll peel them for you—white and tender! Hurry up and try one. Or shall I feed you?"

Cui Buqu watched him in silence. Feng Xiao's hands were beautiful, peeling beans with the same grace as plucking flowers. In the blink of an eye, a pile of peeled beans appeared before Cui Buqu, each one neatly arranged.

Pei Jingzhe was speechless.

"Eat," said Feng Xiao.

Cui Buqu knew Feng Xiao was doing this on purpose, but still couldn't help his lips twitching. He turned his head to look out the window, pointedly ignoring Feng Xiao.

Someone else lost their temper instead.

"You!" Su Xing's face was flushed with anger. He rose from his seat to march over, but the girl next to him grabbed his sleeve.

"Let it go, Cousin!" she whispered, looking deeply embarrassed. "That man there is Abbot Cui; this person must be his friend."

"He's the one who started it. I'm gonna give that guy a piece of my mind!" Incensed, Su Xing roared at Feng Xiao. "You look like a gentleman, but you speak like a boor! Where are your manners?!"

The girl bowed to Cui Buqu. "Has Abbot Cui been well?"

Cui Buqu evidently knew her too. "May the blessings of the gods be upon you, little Lu-niangzi.⁹ Is your mother well?"

"Yes, all thanks to Abbot Cui's prescription." The girl smiled. "Her heart palpitations have been greatly alleviated."

Cui Buqu nodded. "The prescriptions of this humble Daoist can only alleviate the symptoms for a time; they cannot cure her affliction. The Lu family should look for some skilled physicians for her."

"As you say, Abbot Cui," the girl said gently.

Su Xing turned his attention to them. "So it was Daoist Master Cui who helped treat my aunt. Her health has indeed improved a lot recently. This Su thanks you deeply." He cupped his hands and bowed to Cui Buqu, then said, "Forgive me for my bluntness—the Daoist master's friend here is far too rude. Considering your reputation, it would be best if you didn't associate with such a person."

"You're mistaken," said Cui Buqu frostily. "He's not my friend; I hardly know him."

---

9   娘子. A polite term of address that can be used alone to address any woman, similar to "lady."

Su Xing eyed Feng Xiao doubtfully, his skepticism written clear on his face.

Feng Xiao smiled. "Why are you looking at me like that? Though my looks are peerless throughout the land and my charm a rare treasure few have enjoyed, all of it is quite out of your league."

Cui Buqu was speechless again.

Su Xing's complexion cycled from green to white, then from white to green, as though he'd come down with food poisoning. But with Cui Buqu and Lady Lu watching, even if he wanted to rip into Feng Xiao, he couldn't. Finally, he turned and stalked sullenly away.

Feng Xiao watched the couple leave. His frivolous smile vanished, replaced with a look of deep thought. "That Su Xing is a bit odd. Is that why you introduced him to me?"

"Since Lu Ti has no sons, he's raised Su Xing as his son-in-law ever since he took the boy in. Su Xing devotes himself to his studies, but his academic talents are average at best. However, he's shown promise as a businessman. Lu Ti was pleased to see it; he's already given Su Xing two shops to manage."

"That's still odd," said Feng Xiao. "If his skill is in managing businesses, you'd expect him to know how to handle prickly customers. Why did he lose his temper just because I mimicked him?"

Cui Buqu sniped, "Perhaps Feng-langjun's face simply enrages whoever looks at it. No matter where you go, everyone finds you disagreeable."

Feng Xiao smiled. "How can that be? Just now, Lady Lu was gazing at me with such awe and admiration."

Cui Buqu had met narcissists before, but this was the first time he'd encountered such an extreme example. He stared at Feng Xiao in disbelief. "Does Feng-langjun often look in the mirror to admire his own reflection?"

Not often, always, Pei Jingzhe observed silently.

Feng Xiao raised an eyebrow. "Did I not speak the truth?"

Cui Buqu snorted coldly. He couldn't be bothered to keep arguing. "The natural conclusion is that he acts differently before Lady Lu than his customers."

"Lady Lu likes his fiery temper, so he flares up in front of her. Lu Ti likes clever people, so he plays the bright and studious youth for him. Most interesting!" said Feng Xiao. "Ququ, you've figured out practically everyone during your two-month stay in Liugong City. Even the women of the Lu family haven't escaped your eyes! Those who know you know you're a Daoist, but those who don't might think you're planning something shady!"

Cui Buqu chuckled, his smile bright and fake. "But haven't I still fallen into the demonic clutches of the Jiejian Bureau's Feng-erlang?"

"Now you're incorrect," said Feng Xiao. "The Jiejian Bureau was established by decree of the emperor, with equal authority to the Ministry of Justice. All this about 'demonic clutches'—aren't you criticizing His Majesty? Rest assured, I won't forget this."

Worry not. I've got a longer memory than you, Cui Buqu thought. He coughed feebly twice, trying to conserve his strength.

When the three had finished their meal, they walked together to Linlang Pavilion's Liugong City branch.

Unbeknownst to Feng Xiao and Pei Jingzhe, soon after they left, a man and woman entered the private second-floor room.

The woman spoke first: "The lord chief's complexion looked very poor just now. Has he fallen ill again?"

She had a voice as cold as snow and ice, yet her face was extraordinarily beautiful. The contradiction existed in perfect harmony—like a soaring swan, or an orchid in bloom. Even without an observer to appreciate it, her beauty illuminated heaven and earth.

The man beside her didn't answer. He walked over to the table where Cui Buqu and the others had been eating. After leaning down to look for a while, he suddenly swept aside the beans on the table.

The woman came around the table to join him. "What did the lord chief leave us?"

"Cold plum blossom fragrance," the man said quietly.

The woman frowned.

"The lord chief wants us to find a perfume with the fragrance of cold plum blossom?"

The man said shortly, "Khotan. Homicide case." He treasured words like gold and spoke as little as possible.

Luckily, the woman had worked alongside him for many years; she could extract a complete thought from these few syllables. "The cold plum blossom fragrance has something to do with the Khotanese homicide case," she said. "But if the connection was obvious, the Jiejian Bureau would have found it already, and the lord chief wouldn't have left a clue for us. Either way, we should head to a perfume shop and ask some questions."

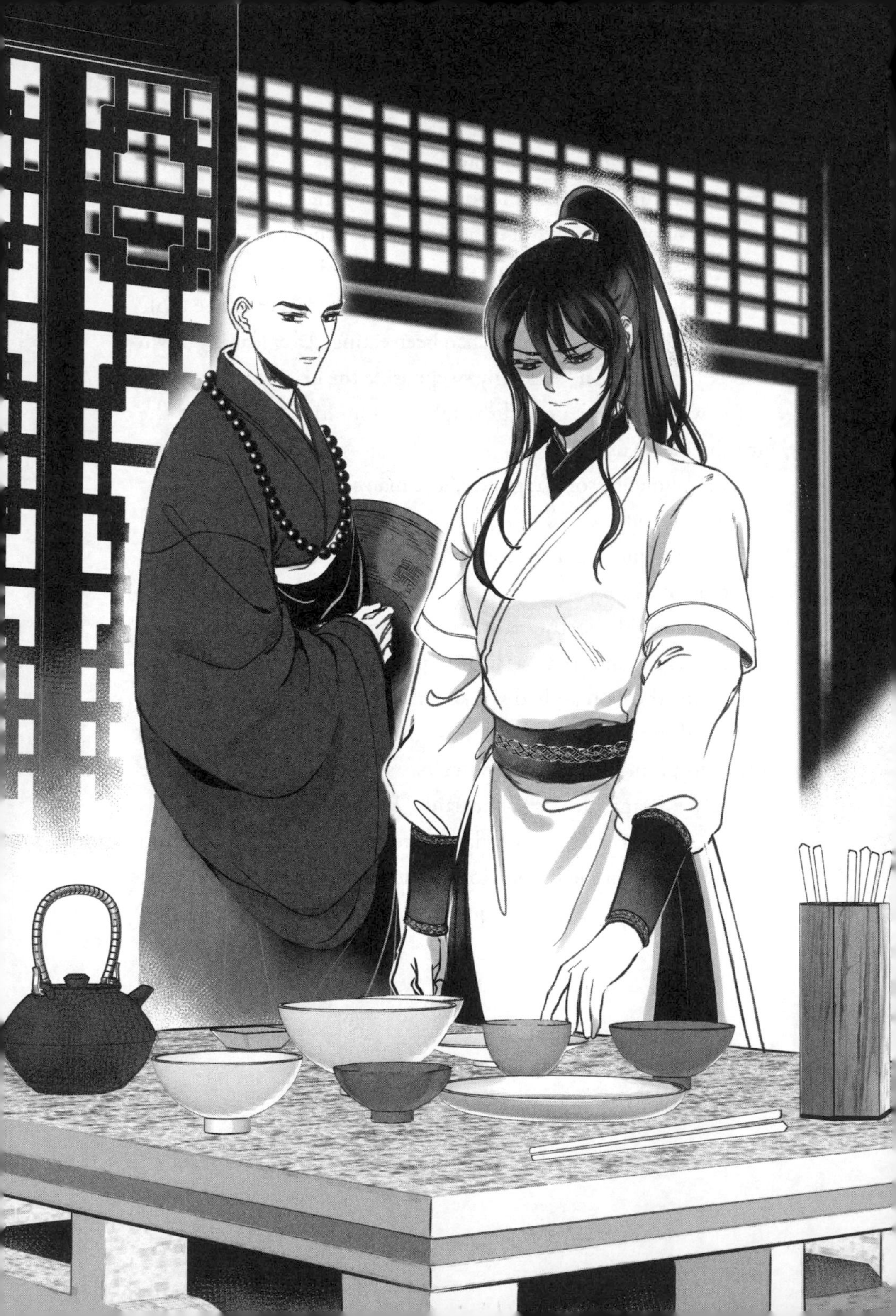

12

O N THE EDGE OF THE TABLE, where Cui Buqu had sat earlier, four faint words had been carved into the wood with a fingernail: *Cold plum blossom fragrance.*

The woman stared at those four words, worry lining her brow. "The amount of strength the lord chief put into writing this...it looks like he's grown even weaker. I fear he's injured again."

The man had never been talkative, but he couldn't help giving her a reminder. "Qiao Xian, the lord chief has always done things his own way."

Qiao Xian was unhappy. "You've been with the lord chief this long and you still don't understand him? He knows his limits when it comes to cases, but never when it comes to his own body!"

Zhangsun Bodhi didn't answer. He only looked at her with a gaze that said, *But what can you do?*

Qiao Xian was disheartened, but indeed, there was nothing she could do. Cui Buqu had always been a man who never stopped until he achieved his goal. At present, their options were to run straight to Feng Xiao, expose Cui Buqu's identity, and drag him back to their own headquarters, or follow his orders and proceed with the investigation of the murder. If Qiao Xian ruined their lord chief's plans for the sake of his health, she could kiss her post at the Zuoyue Bureau goodbye.

Of course she'd considered all this. Qiao Xian sighed silently.

"It's late. The perfume shop," Zhangsun Bodhi reminded her.

"Let's go." Qiao Xian swept a slender hand over the table, and the marks scratched into the surface vanished. The wood was now as smooth as if those words had never been.

⁕⟡⁕

Liugong City had more than a few perfume shops. Lying as it did at the nexus of east and west, the city's perfume shops were known for using spices unique to the Western Regions; the number and diversity of their fragrances surpassed even the shops of the capital. Qiao Xian and Zhangsun Bodhi had imagined that this cold plum blossom fragrance would therefore be easy to find. But after asking around all morning and visiting well-nigh every perfume shop in the city, they ultimately managed to purchase only three plum blossom perfumes.

"Come to think of it, it's quite a coincidence. Just before you two, another gentleman was in here asking about cold plum blossom fragrance. Tall and thin, and fairly young and handsome." The owner of the perfume shop raised his palm to mark the man's height.

Qiao Xian and Zhangsun Bodhi exchanged a glance. There was no question of whom the man was talking about: this was Feng Xiao's subordinate, Pei Jingzhe.

But that meant someone from the Jiejian Bureau had already followed this lead. Surely they would have found anything worth examining—so why had the lord chief gone out of his way to set his own people on the trail? Cui Buqu would never do anything pointless. There must be some detail they'd yet to discover.

"I can't speak for other shops, but my selection of perfumes is the most complete in Liugong City. If you're looking for plum blossom fragrances, we have three here. One of these recipes was gifted to me by an itinerant merchant from the Western Regions a few years back, after I saved his life."

As he spoke, the shop assistant brought out three round cakes of compressed perfume.

Most martial arts practitioners possessed a keen sense of smell. Wearing perfume would give away their whereabouts if they needed to flee or hide from an enemy. In Qiao Xian's position, she used perfumes even less. People like her, who rarely came into contact with such fragrances, were more sensitive to them—she could discern the scents presented almost instantaneously.

"These are...plum and apricot blossoms?" Qian Xian sniffed the perfume cake in her hand, then handed it to Zhangsun Bodhi.

The shopkeeper nodded. "Correct. This perfume is called Spring Snow; it's the most popular fragrance in the capital currently. Young ladies adore it, especially ones from wealthy families. When spring comes they put on fresh new clothes, then daub themselves with the perfume. A touch of this fragrance, and a celestial maiden like yourself would have suitors practically breaking down your door!"

The man had a silver tongue. Even when confronted with customers who'd only come to make inquiries, he was doing his utmost to persuade them into a purchase.

"Now this perfume is called Still Waters Run Deep." The shopkeeper picked up a second cake. "It contains the scents of both sandalwood and plum; nothing's better for calming one's nerves and driving away evil."

Zhangsun Bodhi sniffed it and shook his head. Qiao Xian agreed. "It's not the cold plum blossom fragrance we're looking for."

The shopkeeper handed them the third cake. "If it's a *pure* plum blossom fragrance you're after, this is the only one."

Zhangsun Bodhi took it in hand. The thick scent of plum blossoms burned like fire as it wafted toward his nose. Yet the biting crispness intrinsic to the flower seemed to be missing—instead, this fragrance smelled closer to the rich, sweet scent of peonies.

When Qiao Xian saw Zhangsun shake his head, she took the round of compressed perfume and sniffed it herself. Sure enough, this wasn't the fragrance they sought. "Master, you're quite knowledgeable. Is cold plum blossom fragrance really so difficult to create?"

The shopkeeper considered a moment. "For normal perfumes, the stronger the scent, the better. But cold perfumes are called *cold* for a reason; they're different from the rest. If it's a true cold plum blossom fragrance, a first sniff will merely yield the faint, clean scent of snow and ice—only after an hour or so will the aroma of plum blossoms gradually emerge. Even then, it will be sharp but not strong. The scent lingers and can last for several days."

Qiao Xian recalled that Feng Xiao and his men hadn't arrived on scene until the morning after the murders, yet they'd still detected the fragrance. She nodded in agreement. "So I'd imagine only extraordinary people can wear such a fragrance?"

"There are different types of cold fragrances," the shopkeeper said. "Cold lotus fragrances and cold bamboo fragrances, for example. But the term 'cold' is especially fitting for plum blossom fragrance; plum blossoms bloom in late winter and carry the scent of snow and ice. Such fragrances are terribly rare. Several years ago, I got my hands on a cold lotus perfume and couldn't bring myself to sell it. I intend to leave it to my daughter as part of her dowry. Cold plum blossom perfumes are even more exceptional. Anyone who could create such a fragrance would certainly treasure it and hide it away. They wouldn't share the formulation lightly, or everyone on the street would be wearing it. Then it would no longer be precious."

CHAPTER 12 🕸 111

"Can you think of anyone who knows how to create this cold plum blossom fragrance?"

The shop owner's smile was strained. "If I did, I would have hired them long ago for a vast quantity of gold, and I certainly wouldn't be telling you all this. Rare fragrances can't be sought out, only encountered through serendipity. I've been in the perfume business half my life. If you find a person with such a skill, please don't hesitate to inform me."

He paused, then smacked his head. "That's right. Last month, little Yunyun-niangzi from Chunxiang House won a dance championship, stunning most of Liugong City. I heard that lately she changes the fragrance she wears every day, but she's never sent anyone to purchase from me. She must be consulting some expert. Why not ask her?"

Both Qiao Xian and Zhangsun Bodhi's eyes lit up.

"When the previous gentleman came to ask, did you tell him about this?" asked Qiao Xian.

The shop owner shook his head. "I didn't recall it then, so of course not."

"Chunxiang House is a dance house?"

The shop owner gave a suggestive smile then—one all men understood. Qiao Xian understood too. She realized her question was rather foolish.

Fragrant flowers, herbs, and spices had always been medicinal ingredients; in this way, perfumery and medicine were not unalike. Cui Buqu had a superior understanding of medicine, so it was unsurprising that he also had some understanding of perfumes. He'd inferred the rarity of the perfume merely from the words "cold plum blossom fragrance" and pieced the clues together from there.

Qiao Xian and Zhangsun Bodhi were well acquainted with their lord chief's incredible aptitude. Most people were superficial;

they saw Cui Buqu's weak and ailing body and underestimated him. But if a man in his circumstances could manage to stake out a place for himself within the vast and changeable world, they must certainly be possessed of extraordinary abilities. Even if Cui Buqu lay bedridden eight out of ten days, not a single person in the Zuoyue Bureau dared underestimate him.

Qiao Xian's mood had lightened considerably with this discovery. "If the Jiejian Bureau knew Wuwei House was the Zuoyue Bureau's base, wouldn't they vomit blood in rage?" Though her face remained icy, her tone was now relaxed.

Zhangsun Bodhi responded with a different question: "Chunxiang House. Shall you go, or shall I?"

"I'll go, of course," said Qiao Xian. "With that face of yours, if you go, you'll be taken for a debt collector. No one would think you're there for entertainment."

Zhangsun Bodhi couldn't refute it. He turned the prayer beads in his hand and said no more.

⊷≋⊱

Linlang Pavilion.

Today was the final day of the auction, and the hall was more crowded than ever. The threshold for entering had likewise risen: not only did attendees require invitations, they also had to pay a deposit at the door. If they bid on something, the deposit would be put toward their item; if nothing caught their fancy, Linlang Pavilion would return them their fee when they left.

This approach effectively weeded out those who came to make trouble, those who couldn't afford anything, or those who only wished to spectate.

Feng Xiao had just led Cui Buqu and Pei Jingzhe inside when a voice behind them exclaimed, "If it isn't Feng-er!"

The newcomer caught up to them with quick strides and regarded Feng Xiao with surprise and joy. "Feng-er, long time no see! I didn't expect to find you here."

The man was in his mid-twenties, wearing a tall crown and red clothes. He had the graceful and confident bearing of an aristocratic young master. But Cui Buqu's eyes were sharper than most—he immediately observed that this man's attitude toward Feng Xiao was rather unusual.

Even when old friends reunited, this level of enthusiasm, an eagerness bordering on solicitude, was odd. Yet it didn't seem like this man was trying to ingratiate himself with Feng Xiao either.

As Cui Buqu considered this puzzle, Feng Xiao's eyebrows shot up in surprise and he smiled. "Young Estate Master Lin! It's been a while."

When Cui Buqu heard this name, in combination with the man's age and conduct, the young master's background instantly fell into place.

Yandang Mountain Estate housed a middle-class family prominent in the jianghu. They were primarily merchants, and wealthy ones at that. The thirteen forms of the Yandang sword technique had been passed down through the generations, but Estate Master Lin Ling had only managed to sire a son in his later years. Not unexpectedly, this meant he heeded his child's every whim and gave him whatever he wanted, even turning a blind eye to his more ridiculous habits. Yandang Mountain Estate's renown within the jianghu came not from the Lin family's wealth nor the Yandang sword techniques they wielded, but from Lin Yong.

Just as Lin Yong, beaming, was about to step forward and grab Feng Xiao's hand, Feng Xiao seamlessly took a small step back and slid his arm around Cui Buqu's shoulders. Before Cui Buqu could react, he'd been dragged to Feng Xiao's side. Their shoulders knocked against each other.

"Allow me to introduce you two. Young Estate Master, this is a dear friend of mine, Cui Buqu. Ququ, this is the young master of Yandang Mountain Estate, Lin Yong."

He put deliberate emphasis on the words *dear friend*, his lips curving in an ambiguous smile. Any listener would find it dubious, and their imagination would run wild.

Cui Buqu was utterly flummoxed.

13

THE MOMENT THE WORDS *dear friend* were spoken, the
eyes Lin Yong had turned upon Cui Buqu narrowed with
hostility.

Now that Cui Buqu had placed Lin Yong, he also remembered
the rumors about him. He made to brush Feng Xiao's hand away
without a second thought, but that hand clung to him as if it was
glued. He couldn't push it off no matter how he tried.

Lin Yong's eyes flashed as he smiled. "Cui-langjun must be very
special indeed if he is Feng-er's dear friend. The Cui in Cui-langjun's
name—would that be the Cui family of Boling or the Cui family of
Qinghe?"

"It's just Cui." Cui Buqu's face was carefully blank. "I'm from
neither Boling nor Qinghe; I'm only a commoner. My humble name
is not worth mentioning."

The more he insisted on his ordinariness, the more unconvincing
Lin Yong found him.

Cui Buqu's steps were weak and unsteady, his face drawn and
pale. His brow and eyes were lined with fatigue. It was obvious he
didn't know any martial arts and was plagued by illness. Why would
such a man receive Feng-er's favor? It was truly bizarre.

Several years ago, Feng-er had encountered Lin Yong as the latter
was embroiled in some minor trouble. With his help, Lin Yong had
managed to extricate himself from the situation.

Back then, Feng-er had seemed to descend from the heavens, awing Lin Yong at first sight. No one had been able to catch his eye since. Feng-er, however, wasn't remotely interested in him that way. What was more, Feng Xiao was a powerful martial artist; even if he wanted to, Lin Yong couldn't force himself on him. He might end up losing his life if he tried. Thus he restrained his lustful impulses and acted as warm and attentive as possible toward Feng Xiao, hoping the man would come around eventually. But Feng-er's whereabouts were erratic, and Lin Yong to date hadn't pinned down his background or identity. He never knew where Feng-er would resurface, so reuniting with him at this moment was truly a pleasant surprise.

Lin Yong thought himself quite handsome, so the idea that Feng Xiao preferred this invalid elicited a wave of resentment. He was about to say more when Feng Xiao smiled and led Cui Buqu inside, throwing a "We'll be going ahead" over his shoulder.

Cui Buqu found himself alternately dragged and prodded into the room. Feng Xiao's gestures looked soft and intimate, but they left no room for resistance.

Linlang Pavilion had two floors arranged around a central atrium. The lower level held the auction floor surrounded by guest seating. From the second level, one had a full view of the central area over the railing.

Feng Xiao and Cui Buqu took their seat on the second floor's south side. Tea and snacks had already been placed on the low table, and the waiters didn't shout the way those in wine pavilions or restaurants usually did—even their footsteps were soundless. The hush was contagious; most guests kept their voices down as well, while the melody of the pipa drifted in from afar and lent the whole a hint of sophisticated charm. It felt more like they were inside a dance house than in Linlang Pavilion's branch doing business.

Cui Buqu gave the hall a quick scan. The first floor was mostly composed of ordinary wealthy merchants and residents of the jianghu, while the second held young people from noble families. In contrast to the tranquility of the second floor, the first was far rowdier. Linlang Pavilion had obviously separated the two on purpose, perhaps to avoid any unnecessary trouble.

They ascended the stairs and turned a corner, slipping behind the screen and finally shaking off Lin Yong's unswerving gaze. At almost the same time, Feng Xiao released Cui Buqu and shoved him aside, as if terrified he'd catch something nasty if he touched him a moment longer.

Cui Buqu silently made another black mark in his mental ledger, then found a place to sit with no change in expression.

Feng Xiao seemed oblivious, his face wreathed in smiles. "Judging by your expression, you know of Lin Yong's predilections."

"Is that why you used me to mess with him?" Cui Buqu was annoyed. "This wasn't included in the conditions of our agreement."

Feng Xiao looked back at him innocently. "I still took you out to see the world today, did I not? What's wrong with asking for a little something in return? Anyway, he can't hurt you with me around."

"Lin Yong might have some indecent hobbies, but he's no fool," said Cui Buqu coolly. "It'd be far more believable if you used Pei Jingzhe rather than me."

Pei Jingzhe, who'd been drinking his tea in silence, choked and coughed.

Feng Xiao smiled. "It wouldn't work. You're better looking."

He'd hardly finished speaking when Lin Yong's silhouette appeared behind the screen. "It's really too noisy downstairs; I can't get a moment of peace. Would Feng-erlang mind if I intruded?"

Seconds before, there'd been more than a foot of space between Feng Xiao and Cui Buqu. But the instant Lin Yong's voice rang out, Feng Xiao grabbed Cui Buqu's wrist and leaned in close, lips curving in a doting smile. "Ququ, there's dust on your nose. Let me brush it off for you."

The stare Lin Yong directed at Cui Buqu became increasingly intense. Cui Buqu saw a flash of killing intent in his eyes—but only a flash. Lin Yong quickly regained his graceful and confident demeanor, as if what Cui Buqu saw had been an illusion.

Though Yandang Mountain Estate was only a mid-tier martial arts family in context of the entire jianghu, people still showed Lin Yong respect on account of his father's generosity and hospitality. Feng Xiao, however, cared not a whit for such things.

"My apologies, I'm afraid there's no more room." Feng Xiao's smile was pleasant, but his words were a blunt rejection.

Lin Yong hadn't given up yet. But before he could say more, Pei Jingzhe stepped in front of him. "This way, Young Estate Master Lin."

"Then...let's talk another day," Lin Yong said reluctantly.

Feng Xiao gave a slight nod.

He'd showed Lin Yong no respect at all, but Lin Yong didn't express any displeasure. To Lin Yong, Feng Xiao was like the shadow of a soaring bird—a man who revealed no hints as to his true name and background. He seemed to appear out of thin air in the jianghu, coming and going without a trace. That mysterious allure of his had snared Lin Yong completely; otherwise, why would he still be yearning for him?

Lin Yong couldn't help but shoot one last glance at Cui Buqu as he went. Cui Buqu's lashes were lowered, leaving his expression unclear as Feng Xiao lightly grasped his wrist and swung it back and forth. Lin Yong sneered in his heart—so Cui Buqu was only a plaything. He shook out his sleeves and left.

By the time Feng Xiao released his wrist, Cui Buqu had lost his look of displeasure. Instead, he looked thoughtful.

As deputy chief of the Jiejian Bureau, there was no need for Feng Xiao to treat Lin Yong's feelings with any delicacy, let alone hold up Cui Buqu as a shield. Yet despite Lin Yong's repeated advances, Feng Xiao hadn't fallen out with him; in fact, he'd even left the door open. There had to be a reason behind it.

"What are you thinking? Need me to clarify something?" Feng Xiao's voice was right beside his ear.

Cui Buqu suddenly had a thought. "Is the Jiejian Bureau investigating Lin Yong?"

Feng Xiao's eyes flashed. "What makes you think so?"

Cui Buqu didn't answer immediately. *Could Lin Yong be connected to the assassination of the envoy?* he thought. No, that couldn't be it. Yandang Mountain Estate was thousands of miles from Liugong City. In the normal course of things, they had no dealings with Khotan or even with Linlang Pavilion. Lin Yong had likely only turned up to watch the show.

There was, however, a small point of connection. One of the products the Lin family traded in was a silk called sky-cleansed gauze, which was produced in the south. Its luster was bright as the sky, its texture smooth as ice on a frozen lake. Officials and nobles alike adored it, and it'd been listed as one of the tributes in the convoy— the Lin family sent some to the Sui palace every year. Trading this silk had been key to the Lin family's early success, and rumor had it that, lately, they'd been trying to use it to approach the Sui crown prince.

Feng Xiao allowed him to ponder. "Ququ, with your abilities, remaining an unnamed and lowly spy within the Zuoyue Bureau is really too unfair to you. Right now, the Jiejian Bureau has three chiefs. If you wish to join us, I'll tell my superiors to have you established as the fourth bureau chief."

Off to the side, Pei Jingzhe's eyes widened. He held his tongue with some effort.

The Jiejian Bureau stood on equal footing with the Six Ministries. The bureau chief was also the Minister of Justice, and Feng Xiao, his deputy, had the authority to act independently when necessary. The power he held was enormous. Cui Buqu might be from the Zuoyue Bureau, but his rank and identity were unknown. Yet now Feng Xiao wanted to appoint him as the fourth bureau chief? It was a grand offer—almost too grand. Pei Jingzhe couldn't tell whether Feng Xiao truly wished to recruit more talent or if he was only trying to test Cui Buqu.

Cui Buqu's expression was placid as he slowly raised his head. "What is this *Zuoyue Bureau*? I don't understand a word you're saying."

Feng Xiao took Cui Buqu's hand in his. "You're in poor health, yet here you are toiling in this border city, plotting and scheming with no one to appreciate your efforts. I just think it's a pity. The Jiejian Bureau lacks a strategist like you. If you're willing, I'll tell the Zuoyue Bureau myself; I promise I won't offend your superiors. What do you think?" He tucked away his smile and stared intently at Cui Buqu, his face shining with sincerity. The sight was enough to make an iron tree bloom and a stone shed tears.

For the first time, Cui Buqu realized there existed someone who could drive others out of their mind with looks alone. Perhaps he himself had escaped being bewitched, but that didn't stop him from marveling at Feng Xiao's beauty, as brilliant as spring blooms.

"Feng-langjun, though your words are very touching, I don't know any Zuoyue Bureau. I just want to live in peace as a Daoist priest. I hope you'll keep your promise and let me go."

Seeing his attempts at seduction had failed, Feng Xiao's lip curled, and he released Cui Buqu's hand. He leaned back and revealed his true colors. "When did I promise to let you go? I said I'd *consider* letting you go. As for whether I can be persuaded, that all depends on your performance."

Even acting the part of a scoundrel, Feng Xiao managed to be captivating. Cui Buqu couldn't help but silently curse him. *Shameless man.*

As the two of them traded barbs, the crisp sound of a bell rang out, and a middle-aged man walked to the center of the floor downstairs. Everyone's attention was immediately drawn to him.

The main event had begun.

14

LINLANG PAVILION'S AUCTION was famous. As their name spread, many pawnshops and jewelry stores imitated them and put on their own auctions using various gimmicks. Unfortunately, none could compare to the wealth and scale of Linlang Pavilion. An invitation to Linlang Pavilion's auction was rarer and more precious than gold. Many regarded them as a status symbol, and receiving one was considered a great honor.

If Feng Xiao wanted an invitation, he had no problem obtaining one even without flaunting his identity—but others treasured what might be a once-in-a-lifetime chance. On this occasion, there were more than a few first-time attendees. They immediately quieted down when they saw the auctioneer appear.

"Esteemed guests, today is the final day of the auction. Thank you for taking time out of your busy schedules to join us; Linlang Pavilion has been honored by your presence. Now, we know everyone is waiting eagerly. Without further ado, we present our first item."

The auctioneer didn't strain to be heard; his voice effortlessly resonated across the entire space. Though the special design of the atrium was a factor, he was likely also a master of internal cultivation. Linlang Pavilion was a grand enterprise and would naturally attract outside envy. It was no surprise that they'd hired martial artists from all over to oversee the auction.

As the man's last words rang out, a beautiful maid came forward and presented a tray draped in golden silk. Two young waiters, one on either side, whisked the cloth away to reveal a bronze wine vessel.

"This wine vessel was used by Duke Huan of Qi during the Spring and Autumn Period. Three characters are inscribed on the base of the vessel, which prove the owner's identity. This item has been appraised and judged genuine by Dong Yang-xiansheng[10] of Linlang Pavilion. The starting price is ten thousand coppers, and we'll do the final call thrice. Let us begin!"

The maid pulled on a rope and the bell rang again. Someone called, "Eleven thousand coppers!"

"Twelve thousand!"

"Thirteen thousand!"

Once the bidding started, noise in the hall swelled. Soon, someone called out a costly bid of thirty thousand.

It wasn't that any of them were particularly interested in the bronze wine vessel in itself. Most treasures from Linlang Pavilion would at least double in value once purchased. Even if the buyer didn't sell the item and instead gave it out as a gift, all they needed to say was, "verified by Dong Yang-xiansheng from Linlang Pavilion," and the recipient would be suitably impressed.

"Who was the one who bid thirty thousand?" Feng Xiao asked Cui Buqu with great curiosity. He didn't participate in the bidding—he was far more interested in the bidders. And he was sure Cui Buqu would know the answer.

As expected, Cui Buqu said, "The bidder's name is Leng Du, the adopted son of the chief helmsman of the Nine Guilds of Water

---

10 先生. A polite address for men, originally only for those of great learning or those who had made significant contributions to society.

Transport. Recently, Chief Helmsman Ning Shewo gifted a rare beauty to the emperor of Southern Chen, Chen Shubao. She won Chen Shubao's favor, and he dotes on her. It seems she pleased Chen Shubao so much he handed a portion of the south's canal transport market to Ning Shewo. Leng Du likely intends this wine vessel as a gift. Chen Shubao is the mighty emperor himself, so he'd see such a trinket as beneath him—the gift might instead be for one of Chen Shubao's attendants. I suspect he was determined to obtain this item, perhaps because he knew bidding wouldn't be as fierce for the first one."

The Nine Guilds of Water Transport weren't a single entity, but, as the name suggested, a conglomeration of nine. Within the southern martial arts circles, they were a force none could afford to underestimate. Among the nine guilds, the Jinhuan Guild held the greatest power, and this Ning Shewo, as their leader, was elected chief helmsman.

Ning Shewo was an ambitious man. Under his management, the Nine Guilds of Water Transport had risen quickly, transforming with unstoppable momentum from a medium-sized business alliance into the leader of Jiangnan's martial arts circles.

Though it was trivial for the Jiejian Bureau to investigate whomever they wished, it was ultimately more convenient to bring Cui Buqu along. He had every story and figure of the jianghu committed to memory and could rattle off anyone's background and motives with a moment's thought. Even Pei Jingzhe was in awe of his abilities; he privately thought the Zuoyue Bureau was indeed full of talent.

By the time Cui Buqu finished speaking, the final call for the bronze wine vessel had gone out and Leng Du had claimed the item. All had gone as Cui Buqu predicted.

Cui Buqu had always been a pale and sickly person, and the collar of his thick coat was pulled up so high it obscured almost half his face. The mere sight of him slumped in his seat elicited a sympathetic wave of fatigue, yet when he spoke, it was with the clear confidence of a seasoned strategist. Listeners couldn't help but believe him.

Feng Xiao clapped his hands in praise. "A-Cui really is amazing. Out of the masses here, only you possess any flicker of brilliance— I'll give you three out of ten."

Cui Buqu pressed his lips together, refusing to respond.

But Feng Xiao wouldn't be denied. He said, "Why don't you ask me where the remaining seven points are?"

"Even without asking, I already know," Cui Buqu said icily.

Feng Xiao smiled. "It seems that you think the same—as they say, heroes are of one mind. Seven-tenths of the world's brilliance already belongs to me. Thus the remaining three-tenths goes to you!"

Cui Buqu rolled his eyes in answer.

Pei Jingzhe asked curiously, "Does Ning Shewo have no children by birth?"

Shaking his head, Cui Buqu answered, "Ning Shewo and his wife have been married nineteen years, but they were never blessed with a child. They adopted Leng Du and treat him as their son by birth. Ning Shewo has already made it known that he'll retire next year. Barring any last-minute surprises, the position of Jinhuan Guild's leader should go to Leng Du. But Leng Du is young yet; even the pressure of managing the Jinhuan Guild is too much for him. How the situation will develop remains to be seen."

Pei Jingzhe listened to these remarks as he might to marketplace rumors, smiling but paying them little mind. To him, the feuds of the jianghu lay too far to the south and were merely the internal trivialities of this or that guild—they had little to do with the north, or Great Sui.

Cui Buqu seemed to sense his thoughts. He said evenly, "If the emperor wishes to invade Chen, he must cross the river southward; transportation by water will become vitally important. Should that time come, surely dividing these guilds from within and allowing chaos to break out is superior to seeing the Nine Guilds of Water Transport assist the Southern dynasty against Great Sui?"

Feng Xiao smiled but said nothing; he'd already thought that far ahead.

But Pei Jingzhe had no such insight. He was stunned and cupped his hands toward Cui Buqu. "Ah, I see now!"

Pei Jingzhe's first impression of Cui Buqu had been that the man couldn't go more than a handful of words without coughing. Though he'd never said so aloud, he'd inevitably found himself looking down on him. After all, the Jiejian and Zuoyue Bureaus were fundamentally unlike the Three Departments and Six Ministries. These sister agencies moved seamlessly between light and shadow— they had to summit the heights of the court while also walking the vastness of the jianghu. Martial arts weren't a strict necessity, but with no skills at all, it was terrifically difficult to make one's way in martial arts circles where strength was king.

Cui Buqu was an exception. This man was from Liuli Palace and knew the jianghu and its people like the back of his hand, yet he had no martial skill of his own. Even now, though Feng Xiao was currently holding him hostage, he showed no sign of being at a disadvantage in word or action—no hint of flattery, nor pleas for mercy.

Pei Jingzhe felt that, for a person like Cui Buqu, ignorance of martial arts posed no problem. If they could convince this man to work under their deputy chief, the Jiejian Bureau would be like a tiger that'd grown wings.

Next up for auction were two antiques: the zither Luqi, and a sword known as Baihong.

This zither was a famous one, and the sword was also a quality blade. Countless people jumped in with bids. Feng Xiao seemed mildly interested in Luqi and participated in several rounds of bidding. Finally, someone offered three thousand taels of silver to secure the zither. Feng Xiao immediately dropped out—it seemed his interest didn't extend that far.

Cui Buqu watched him give up on the zither halfway though he clearly wanted it, and he couldn't help but shoot him a questioning glance or two.

Feng Xiao caught his look, and his lips quirked up in a smile. "I can let Luqi go; I have a much bigger and better treasure already. Would you like to see it?"

Cui Buqu said nothing. He wasn't usually a person who hesitated to speak. If he wished, his words had the power to strip someone of their dignity and leave them ashen and disgraced. But when it came to dealing with scoundrels like Feng Xiao, he rarely needed to say anything—there had always been someone around to handle such people for him. Now he was like a dragon in shallow waters, temporarily trapped; he had to take action himself to confront Feng Xiao in this war of words. Besides, Cui Buqu was no blushing maiden. Why should he give Feng Xiao the satisfaction of a flustered reaction?

Thus he fell quiet for only a moment before calmly saying, "I'm waiting. Please pull it out."

Feng Xiao clicked his tongue twice and said, "A-Qu, you're too frivolous. Valuable things deserve respect; how could you tell me to *pull it out* so crudely? You should tell me to *present it* instead."

"I'm afraid if you do, your treasure will shrink to the size of a finger, and I'll be greatly disappointed."

"I'm talking about a zither," Feng Xiao exclaimed in surprise. "What are *you* talking about?"

Cui Buqu snorted. "I'm also talking about a zither. Why do you think I'm not?"

Pei Jingzhe couldn't bear to listen to their conversation any longer. He raised his teacup to hide his twitching lips.

Feng Xiao looked at Cui Buqu with an expression that said, *Keep it up, I dare you.* "And what kind of zither, pray tell, can both grow and shrink?"

"Li Xuanji from Tiangong Workshop has recently invented a folding zither. When fully folded, it's only the size of a palm, but when unfolded, it's the size of a pipa. Feng-langjun is from the Jiejian Bureau. He should know all there is to know in the world, yet he doesn't know this?"

"Although Li Xuanji is a genius craftsman, my zither is certainly finer than his." Feng Xiao smiled. "It's also finer than Luqi. Still, Luqi is a famous zither; even seeing it is a rare joy. If I could borrow this instrument and play it for a few days, I'd be even happier."

"The man who made the winning bid is named Cui Hao. He's the legitimate grandson of the patriarch of the Cui family of Boling, born to his second wife. The eighth day of the next month is his grandfather Cui Yong's birthday. Cui Yong loves the zither more than his life, and he's always loved Cui Hao in the same measure."

The obvious conclusion was that Cui Hao had purchased the zither as a gift for his grandfather.

Several more treasures were presented and quickly auctioned off one by one. Anyone who secured an invitation to Linlang Pavilion didn't lack for money. In fact, publicly purchasing an item was sometimes a method of flaunting one's name and status and stoking one's vanity. These people rushed to bid on the auctioned items no matter how expensive.

Most of the buyers were strangers to Feng Xiao and Pei Jingzhe, but Cui Buqu recited all their details with ease. With the aid of his introductions, Feng Xiao could make a rough determination as to whether or not each person was connected to the case of the missing jade.

Near noon, as the auction reached its halfway point, Linlang Pavilion's staff brought plates of hot dishes and snacks to each table. Refreshed and with full stomachs, the crowd's anticipation once again grew over the upcoming treasures.

Pei Jingzhe could hardly sit still. He was starting to suspect that the Jade of Heaven Lake wouldn't appear here at all. But seeing that Feng Xiao and Cui Buqu remained perfectly composed, he quashed his anxiety and sat back once more.

At last he heard the auctioneer's voice ring out. "The next item is a jade with no origin or name. It was delivered to Linlang Pavilion just yesterday, and Dong Yang-xiansheng has yet to appraise it. Guests purchase this item at their own risk; whether it is genuine or not, we at Linlang Pavilion take no responsibility. We hope our esteemed guests understand."

The man had mentioned this rule before, but now emphasized it again. Many of the more cautious bidders were already shrinking back.

The item was removed from its carved lacquer box. When the sunlight streaming through the window rippled over its surface, the crowd gasped in surprise.

Now Pei Jingzhe really couldn't remain still. He sat straight up and stared at the object in the maid's hand.

The Jade of Heaven Lake!

15

As FENG XIAO AND CUI BUQU were waiting for the Jade of Heaven Lake to appear at Linlang Pavilion, a strange guest arrived at Chunxiang House in Liugong City.

The man had a shaved head and held prayer beads in his hand. One couldn't call him a monk, because he was wearing common clothing—yet one couldn't say he wasn't, because his expression was serene and devoid of all earthly desire. He didn't look like he'd come for entertainment, but more like he'd come to preach.

The house's owner, Madam Xue, had received many odd guests over the years, but this was the first time she'd met one *this* odd. When she heard a man had ignored their closed doors and proceeded to enter, she pulled her hair haphazardly into a bun, yawned, and walked out under the protection of her armed escort.

At the sight of the guest, Madam Xue was momentarily stunned. She buried her anger and donned a smile. "Good sir, Chunxiang House doesn't entertain guests during the day. If you're interested, please return around six this evening."

Zhangsun Bodhi said, "I heard little Yunyun-niangzi moved half the city with her dancing recently. I came specially to see her."

Madam Xue covered her mouth coyly and smiled. "Little Yunyun-niangzi? I'm afraid she's still dawdling at this hour, struggling to get out of bed and put on her makeup!"

If the regular customers of Chunxiang House had seen the fiery and impatient Madam Xue being this courteous with a man who didn't understand the rules, their jaws would have hit the floor. But though Madam Xue had seen countless people come and go in her time, Zhangsun Bodhi's handsome face cooled her early morning temper enough that she could greet him with a smile.

Zhangsun Bodhi frowned slightly. "I'm only passing through Liugong City and will be gone by tonight. Can't I meet her just this once?" He took out a brocade pouch and handed it to Madam Xue.

When she opened it, she found herself stunned again. The pouch was filled with golden pearls from the South China Sea, round and heavy and glistening in the morning sunlight.

Combined with Zhangsun Bodhi's handsome face, the bag of golden pearls shattered her resistance. Forget Yunyun; if he'd requested Madam Xue herself, she'd have had no objection.

"Please step this way, sir. I'll call Yunyun right now!"

Zhangsun Bodhi gave a slight nod, his gaze sweeping furtively around the front room. A lithe silhouette flashed past, then vanished from sight.

If they'd wished to move in secret, it would of course have been best to come at night. Then there would be people coming and going from Chunxiang House, decked in finery and fragrances, and it'd be easier for Zhangsun Bodhi and Qiao Xian to conceal their activities.

But this advantage cut both ways—night made it easier for their adversary to hide as well. Zhangsun and Qiao Xian had discussed it, and both believed a daytime visit gave them a better chance of catching their target off guard. Perhaps they could even lure the snake from its hole.

Chunxiang House was actually a sprawling complex of pavilions connected by winding walkways and corridors. A faint fragrance hung in the air, giving visitors the impression of beauties tucked away in their boudoirs. But as Zhangsun walked behind Madam Xue, he only thought that this place had too many concealed corners and hidden nooks. Even if a martial expert sought someone here, as long as their target held their breath and stayed still, the sounds of the birds, fish, and insects would provide cover, and they might avoid discovery.

"This is Yunyun's residence. You may go up, though she might not be awake yet," Madam Xue said with a smile.

Yunyun was both a performer and a prostitute, and she wasn't a woman just anyone could have. But Zhangsun had been too extravagant in offering this pouch of golden pearls right off the bat. There was only one Yunyun, yet it could've purchased ten of her.

Madam Xue took her leave. Zhangsun knocked twice, and the door opened promptly. A young girl stood in the doorway.

"I'm here to see Yunyun."

The girl was immediately angry. "Sir, you don't know the rules. The mistress doesn't entertain customers before dark. Please leave, or I'll call someone over."

"Madam Xue brought me here."

The girl was stunned. Her anger turned to sadness, but in a flash that, too, was gone. Her face smoothed to placidity as she said, "My apologies—please come in, sir. May I trouble you to wait in the front room for a moment? Little Yunyun-niangzi has not yet risen, so I will go and wake her up."

Zhangsun nodded. "Thank you."

The women in such houses took a great deal of care when dressing and adorning themselves; he settled in to wait. Zhangsun looked around and saw a potted wintersweet plum before the window. It was curious to see it blooming in spring. He stepped over for a look and realized they were silk flowers, but finely crafted. The evenness of their color and the variety of shades made them indistinguishable from the real thing.

"Do you think they're pretty?" came a gentle and melodious female voice from behind him.

"I do." Zhangsun Bodhi turned to look at her. "Did you make them yourself?"

Yunyun smiled without speaking. Her dark hair had been casually pulled into a knot and an outer garment draped loosely over her thin robe, creating an aura of languid intimacy.

"As long as they're pretty, does it matter where they came from? Why has this gentleman arrived before evening? Did Madam Xue not stop you?"

Zhangsun Bodhi's answer was typically concise: "A bag of golden pearls."

Yunyun understood at once. A giggle slipped from her. "No wonder Madam Xue was willing to make an exception." She moved to hold Zhangsun's hand, pressing herself against him.

No matter how enthralling Yunyun's dancing might be, what most of the men willing to spend thousands on her wanted was her body. The pleasure of a woman could be more cheaply obtained elsewhere—the real reason men flocked to her was to satisfy their ego by possessing her. Yunyun understood this well, so she didn't play hard to get like other girls of the dance house.

But Zhangsun Bodhi pushed her hand away. "I wish to see you dance."

Yunyun sputtered out a laugh. "Is the gentleman shy? Does he wish to see a dance first? That's also fine. However, there's no accompanying music here; I'll have to ask my maid to play the pipa."

"I'm not shy," said Zhangsun Bodhi. "And I'm not putting on a virtuous act. I simply wish to see you dance." His expression was placid and unsmiling, yet this somehow gave more weight to his words. "Do you remember this?" He took a golden hairpin from his sleeve and handed it to her.

A look of confusion passed over Yunyun's face. Then her expression slowly cleared, as if recalling something. "You couldn't be the one in the alley on the east side..."

Zhangsun nodded. "Eight years ago, there was a young man living on the streets, starving and cold, close to death. You gave him a golden hairpin from your own hair and told him to pawn it to weather those difficult times. Later, when his circumstances improved, he re-purchased the hairpin and kept it with him always. Today that young man has come to return it to you and finish what he started."

Yunyun stared at the golden hairpin for a long time. Tears brimmed in her eyes, rolling down her cheeks to fall onto Zhangsun Bodhi's palm.

"It's been eight years. You've become a strong and stalwart man, while I've grown old."

"If you wish, I can redeem you," said Zhangsun.

Yunyun wiped at her tears and smiled as she shook her head. "I love the life I have, where everyone's eyes are on me, and I can indulge in what luxuries I wish. You needn't worry about me. Keep this golden hairpin to remember me by. What dance do you want to see? I'll perform it for you."

After this reminiscence, Yunyun's attitude toward Zhangsun Bodhi had become genuinely intimate. No longer was she so distantly polite as she'd been at the beginning.

Zhangsun gazed at her intently for a moment, then tucked the golden hairpin back in his sleeve. "In that case, I'd like a dance to the song 'The Drunken East Wind.'"[11]

❖❃❁❃❖

Linlang Pavilion was a flurry of chatter; the quiet scene had boiled over. People craned their necks to get a look at the lustrous, crystalline jade in the maid's hand. Any further introduction from the auctioneer was unnecessary—even those who knew nothing about jade could see this was a priceless treasure.

"So that's what the Jade of Heaven Lake looks like?" Pei Jingzhe asked.

It was true they'd speculated that the Jade of Heaven Lake would appear at the auction, but none of them had imagined it'd be so openly. If the Jiejian Bureau simply shut down the auction and took the jade away, wouldn't their adversary's careful planning have been all in vain?

He immediately considered the possibility it was a fake.

But since Linlang Pavilion had brought the item out, there was no going back. Whether it was real or fake, they would have to obtain the jade to verify it.

"Due to the unknown provenance of this item, Linlang Pavilion isn't confident in our appraisal. The starting price is therefore lower than the other treasures we've seen here today, tentatively set at five thousand. If any honored guest is interested in increasing the price, please make your bid."

As the auctioneer finished, someone called out a bid of six thousand coppers and the price began to climb. Soon it had increased

---

11 醉東風. In ancient China, poems were often composed to certain established tunes, of which "The Drunken East Wind" was one.

to fifty thousand—but the hall roiled, and the bids kept coming. Clearly the bidding wouldn't conclude any time soon. Even Lin Yong, who'd stayed out of the spotlight, joined in and called out a bid of one hundred thousand. Someone immediately bid up the price again.

Even if it wasn't the Jade of Heaven Lake, a jade as precious as this one still had countless people vying for it. Additionally, news of the theft of the Jade of Heaven Lake had spread underground, and quite a few well-informed people had caught wind of it. Despite the caveats of the auctioneer, the jade quickly became more coveted than any of the previous items.

Pei Jingzhe began, "Sir, should we—"

"Wait a little longer," said Feng Xiao.

The bidding had reached three thousand taels of silver. Feng Xiao saw the bidders were restless and eager to continue. On his orders, Pei Jingzhe called out a bid of five thousand taels, throwing in ten golden pearls from the South China Sea for good measure.

The hall fell instantly silent as the crowd turned to look toward the source of this outrageous bid.

Cui Buqu tugged his coat further up around his chin and turned aside, avoiding the many unwanted stares.

Feng Xiao leaned over deliberately. "You're not some young maiden. Why act so shy? What, are they not even allowed to look at you?"

"You're so flashy," Cui Buqu said coldly. "I fear if I'm seen with you I'll end up dead in my bed one night with no one the wiser."

Feng Xiao chuckled and looped an arm around his waist. "Then you can share a bed with me," he said silkily. "I can guarantee you a peaceful night's sleep."

Suddenly Cui Buqu stood and slapped Feng Xiao soundly across the face. The move was so blisteringly fast not even Feng Xiao, the martial arts master, could react in time. He'd taken half the force of the blow before he managed to flinch backward.

"Shameless cad! Sleeping with my little sister wasn't enough for you, so now you're coming after me? This humble Daoist fled all the way to Liugong City, yet I still can't escape you. Is there no law or order in this world?"

Cui Buqu was in full view of the crowd, his tone severe and his expression fearsome. His face was white with anger, bringing to mind a slender stalk of bamboo amid snow—brittle, yet refusing to break.

Feng Xiao was struck speechless.

He hadn't anticipated that Cui Buqu's silent forbearance had simply been him biding his time for this moment. All eyes were on Feng Xiao, and his image in them had completely transformed.

Now this is truly awful luck, Feng Xiao thought to himself. *Playing with fire and burning myself—that's a first.*

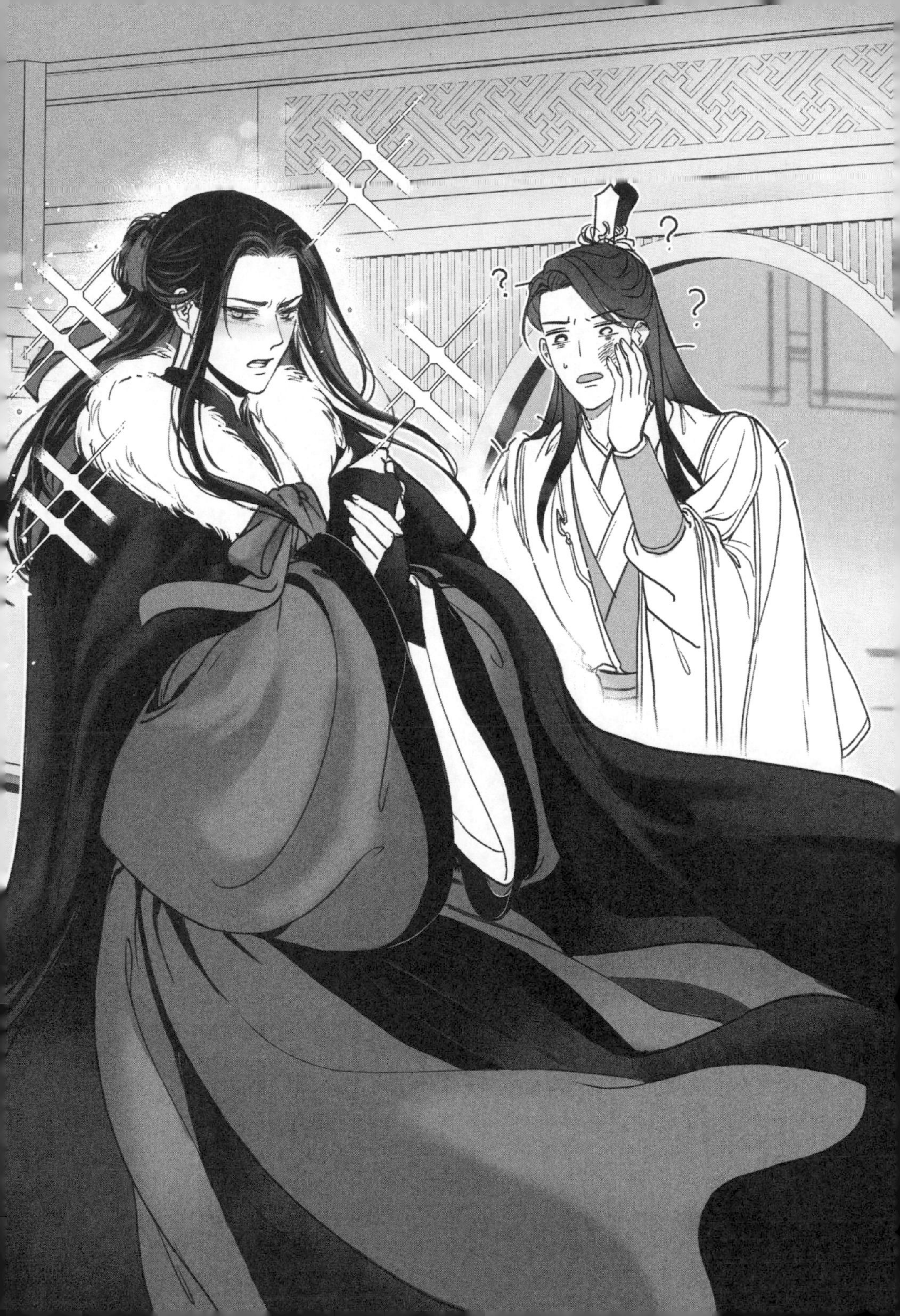

16

CUI BUQU'S ACCUSATIONS trailed off as he covered his mouth to cough. One cough followed another, each more punishing than the last. He was forced to double over, coughing until his body trembled, like frost-rimed bamboo struggling in the wind.

In the past two months, Zixia Monastery's reputation in Liugong City had soared. Though not all of those present were locals, there were plenty who recognized Cui Buqu. They called out, "Abbot Cui, what's wrong? Do you need help?"

"To think someone would commit such filthy and despicable acts in broad daylight! Abbot Cui, come downstairs quick! We'll report it to the county magistrate this instant!" someone else chimed in.

Cui Buqu coughed a few times, then smiled bitterly. "This is Feng-langjun from the Jiejian Bureau. He has been ordered to investigate the Khotanese envoy's murder case. He insists I'm related to the case and has detained me against my will; going to the county magistrate would be pointless. Thank you, everyone, for your kindness. I just...really can't bear it!"

His eyes were watering with how violently he'd been coughing, but no one cared about the reason. All they saw was Cui Buqu's wan complexion and his piteous appearance, tears clinging to his eyelashes. Even Lin Yong, who thought highly of Feng Xiao, couldn't help wondering if Feng Xiao only looked like he had high standards and in fact had some peculiar fetishes. Not only did he pay no mind to gender, he had specifically gone for a barely breathing invalid.

If that was the way of it, Feng Xiao's rejection of him made sense too.

Lin Yong had begun to seriously contemplate whether he should start acting like an ailing beauty when Cui Buqu revealed Feng Xiao's background and gave him yet another shock. The Lin family had connections in the palace; Lin Yong was far better informed than the average member of the jianghu. He was therefore aware of the significance of the name *Jiejian Bureau*. To think—he'd known nothing of Feng Xiao's identity yet had held such improper intentions toward him. On reflection, he couldn't help finding his own bloated self-confidence rather laughable.

The Linlang Pavilion auction had been brought to a halt. Even the auctioneer, a capable man prepared for all sorts of contingencies, found himself stunned and unsure what to do.

That is, until Feng Xiao laughed.

"Who says you can't have your cake and eat it too. Your little sister is a fair and lovely thing, and you're a brilliant man. What's wrong with having both of you? The Jiejian Bureau's status under the emperor is high enough that I can do as I please! Why call on the law for something so trivial. A-Cui, I've already trained your sister. Now it's your turn. If you come with me willingly, I guarantee that from now on you'll live a life of luxury and never suffer the slightest indignity!"

He smiled evilly at Cui Buqu, as if Cui Buqu really did have a sister Feng Xiao had abducted and kept as his personal property. *You have your schemes, but I have my countermeasures. Aren't we both tearing each other down? Who's afraid of you?*

Cui Buqu sneered. "But is this the proper way to court someone? My sister told me that when she was with you, you had strange, secret hobbies. Not only did you enjoy stripping down and letting her whip you, you wanted the whipping to be as painful as possible. If it wasn't painful enough, you'd torment her to within an inch of her life in bed. Aren't you afraid outsiders will find out about *that*?"

The hall erupted.

Pei Jingzhe was completely numb, watching without expression as these two engaged in public mutilation of each other's reputations.

Lin Yong's mouth was agape; he looked utterly dumbfounded. Never had he expected Feng Xiao, with his dignified air and lofty demeanor, to have such private hobbies. Lin Yong considered his own situation. While being a cut-sleeve wasn't something he could openly tell others, at least he was more normal in other areas...

Feng Xiao's mouth twitched. He'd thought his reflexes fast, his willingness to debase himself strong. Yet now he realized there was always a higher mountain, always a greater man. This Cui Buqu had appeared like a bolt from the blue, and he was somehow even readier to debase himself than Feng Xiao.

The two stared at each other, locked in a stalemate. Finally, Feng Xiao decided to call a temporary truce—they must first deal with the business at hand. He flicked his sleeves and said to the auctioneer, "These are my private affairs; no one else need concern themselves. If anyone has doubts they'd like to air, they may come to the Jiejian Bureau. Today's auction is not over yet. Surely it can't end here, in such disarray?"

The auctioneer came to his senses and hastily said, "Of course! We still have no idea to which family this beautiful jade will go! Please take your seats, honored guests!"

Cui Buqu sat down once more, his expression serene. Falling into Feng Xiao's hands had been unexpected, but the plan he'd laid was still in play. He, too, was a pawn in this game; he couldn't extricate himself too early. Still, getting under Feng Xiao's skin in the process wasn't a bad deal at all.

At the auctioneer's reminder, the crowd finally settled. No one made a higher bid for the jade, so Feng Xiao won it without further disruption. Several more treasures were unveiled, and the crowd began vying for them, but Feng Xiao no longer participated—he waited for the auction to end, then swept out of Linlang Pavilion's auction hall and returned to Qiushan Manor with Pei Jingzhe and Cui Buqu trailing behind him.

"Abbot Cui's tongue is too sharp! You ruined my lord's reputation with that little speech!" Pei Jingzhe recalled the scene at the table and felt a wave of frustration. His tongue wasn't so quick as Feng Xiao's, and at the time, he hadn't managed to think of anything impactful to say. And if he'd struck Cui Buqu, it would only have reinforced his claims.

"My body is still full of the incense of helplessness you drugged me with. Am I not permitted to vent my anger? I could have vomited blood back there to substantiate my words—that I didn't was already showing you more respect than you deserve."

Cui Buqu's expression was mild, without the rancor he'd previously affected. He sat there, all his previous intensity extinguished, as tranquil as the distant, misty mountains.

Pei Jingzhe was deeply unhappy. "Then go ahead and vomit some blood; let's see it!"

As soon as he said it, Cui Buqu opened his mouth and coughed. Red seeped between his lips and splattered over his clothes.

Pei Jingzhe practically leapt three feet into the air, ready to run up to Cui Buqu and check his vitals.

Feng Xiao's voice drifted over. "Fool, it's just mulberry juice."

Getting ahold of himself, Pei Jingzhe examined it: the color was indeed not the dark crimson of blood, but instead a purplish red.

Pei Jingzhe was silent.

Cui Buqu raised his sleeve and calmly wiped the juice from his lips. He didn't seem the slightest bit embarrassed at being exposed. "Pardon, I choked."

Pei Jingzhe's eye twitched uncontrollably as he remembered that, back at Linlang Pavilion, the maid had brought out several fruit drinks. Cui Buqu had asked for mulberry juice. But to keep the juice in his mouth for that long, only to spit it out now... Who would do such a thing?

Feng Xiao only smiled. "Oh, Ququ. I find you more and more pleasing to the eye. You really won't consider joining the Jiejian Bureau? The position of fourth chief is waiting for you. The words of an upright gentleman are like swift horses—once released, they can't be taken back."

"Upright gentleman? Are you one?"

"All right," said Feng Xiao. "Even if I'm not an upright gentleman, the words of a scoundrel are surely worth a horse or two, no? Or is your standing within the Zuoyue Bureau higher than I'd imagined?"

"I've already said I've never heard of any Zuoyue Bureau."

"Then let's talk about the jade."

Feng Xiao gestured for Pei Jingzhe to place the jade he'd bought on the table. It shimmered in the sunlight, scattering rays in all directions. They could almost see their own reflections in the jade's lustrous surface.

"Earlier, six people joined the bidding, including me. Do you know who they were?"

Cui Buqu hummed in affirmation. "Lin Yong from Yandang Mountain Estate. Zhou Pei, a wealthy merchant from Khotan. Cui Hao from the Cui family of Boling. Go Nyeong, a Goguryeon. Zhang Yingshui from the Zhang family of Anlu."

He'd clearly expected the question and reported each person's name and background without a moment's hesitation.

"Whom among them do you find most suspicious?"

Pei Jingzhe had thought Cui Buqu would retort with something like, *How should I know?* But for once, he cooperated.

"Zhou Pei. His father is a Göktürk, and they say he's the younger cousin of Fo'er, the foremost martial artist under Ishbara Khagan. He's the most suspicious, along with the martial artist from Goguryeo, Go Nyeong."

17

ZHANGSUN BODHI wasn't a man who indulged in pleasure. In the eyes of others, he was an ascetic. At the Zuoyue Bureau, he spent his spare time brewing tea and reciting scripture, his days more monotonous than a monk's. He didn't consider this lifestyle punishment; in fact, he was quite content.

Yet at that moment, he was sitting within a boudoir men flocked to, watching a dance that had bewitched half the city. Snow-white ankles twirled and golden bells jingled. Despite the sensual atmosphere, Zhangsun wasn't relaxed. He sat straight as a poker, hands clasped together and prayer beads tucked against his palms, watching with rapt attention. He looked less like he was enjoying a dance and more like he was watching a demonstration of unparalleled martial arts.

The maiden Yunyun had danced for all sorts at Chunxiang House. Even under his scorching gaze, she finished her dance with grace.

"Was it beautiful?" she asked with a smile, taking the handkerchief from her maid and dabbing at the slight sheen of sweat on her forehead.

"It was." Zhangsun said only two words, but to Yunyun's ears, they were far more sincere than the lengthy and extravagant praise she received from others.

"Then tonight, you'll…" She stopped.

It wasn't the first time she'd tried to keep a guest, but for some reason, she found herself unable to go on. Perhaps it was because Zhangsun's expression was so solemn—how could he possibly be there to sleep with a prostitute?

Though the city had praised maiden Yunyun's dancing to the skies, extolling her as a treasure money couldn't buy, Yunyun herself understood that she was no more than a drifting piece of duckweed. She had no control over her fate, no choice but to struggle futilely in the fisherman's net.

Zhangsun suddenly leaned in.

Yunyun's composure shattered. Heat rushed from her neck to her cheeks, and her body stopped obeying her orders. She found herself unable to retreat, frozen as his proximity overwhelmed her.

"The fragrance you're wearing," said Zhangsun. "It's very unique."

Yunyun's face was scarlet, and her ears were hot. "Yes—it's the scent of mandarins, with a note of grass and trees."

"It's a lovely scent."

Now the two of them were practically pressed up against each other. A strong arm looped around Yunyun's slender waist, fixing her to the spot. Yet her heart beat faster and faster. This man was more handsome, more full of strength and vigor than anyone she'd ever met. They were even linked by fate.

"Did you create this perfume yourself?" Zhangsun Bodhi asked.

Confused and infatuated, Yunyun dropped her guard entirely. "No, someone created it for me."

"Ask her to make one for me as well."

"All right..." Yunyun murmured. Puzzled, she realized he'd released her.

"It's not yet dark," said Zhangsun.

Yunyun flushed. It was true that it was inappropriate to indulge in such activities during the day. Even if propriety was of little concern within Chunxiang House, she wanted to leave the best possible impression on Zhangsun.

"Then what does the gentleman wish to do? Shall I perform another dance for you?" She tucked her hair back, her crimson lips lightly parted.

"I wish to paint you," said Zhangsun Bodhi.

Yunyun was taken aback.

"I've seen the dancers and musicians of the palace," he said, "and you are just as skilled as them. I wish to paint you so you can see what I see."

If a promiscuous young master had uttered those words, she'd have brushed them aside with a smile. But Zhangsun Bodhi's gaze was steady, his expression earnest. She believed him completely. No one had ever said they wished to paint her before.

Yunyun lowered her head in thought. When she looked up again, it was with a radiant smile. "All right."

Outside, the maid Hong Zhu had approached with food and wine only to find the doors tightly shut; no sound could be heard from within. She stopped, feeling a hint of nervous excitement, then quietly nudged the door open a crack with her shoulder and peered through the gauzy curtains. Yet she didn't see the amorous scene she'd imagined; instead, Yunyun was posing with her back to the door.

Hong Zhu snuck a peek at the uninvited customer who'd barged in offering a huge sum of money. He wasn't embracing or kissing the beauty—instead he was standing before the desk, brush sweeping back and forth as he painted.

Hong Zhu watched the hazy outline of Zhangsun Bodhi for a while, her eyes filled with unconcealed envy. But the pair inside the room continued, oblivious to their audience. Finally she grew bored. Pursing her lips, she turned and left soundlessly, taking the food and drink back to her own room to enjoy. She was completely unaware that another white figure had been watching behind her.

Initially Qiao Xian had wanted to restrain and question the maid, but on seeing her actions, she reconsidered. Everyone had their weaknesses. Having weaknesses wasn't frightening—but being unable to find them was.

And Hong Zhu's weakness was obvious.

Questioning her using a different method might be more effective.

Back at Qiushan Manor, Cui Buqu looked at the suspected Jade of Heaven Lake and said slowly, "Goguryeo is currently ruled by Go Tang, as King Pyeongwon of Goguryeo, the twenty-fifth-generation ruler. *Go* is a Goguryeon surname; though few people in the Central Plains know Go Nyeong, he's quite famous in Goguryeo. It's said he achieved transcendence in his swordsmanship and defeated twelve preeminent experts in the three kingdoms of Goguryeo, Baekje, and Silla in the space of ten days. Pyeongwon was delighted and bestowed the title of Goguryeo's number-one sword expert on him. He's even permitted to carry his sword and ride horses within the palace grounds. In Goguryeo, this is the highest of honors."

Pei Jingzhe, who had just been the victim of Cui Buqu's little prank, was still unhappy. He said irritably, "Goguryeo is a nation in a small corner of the northeast. I fear their naming someone a 'preeminent expert' is no more than a boast. He can't compare to the martial artists of the Central Plains."

Cui Buqu gave a rare nod of agreement. "Correct. However, it is highly likely Go Nyeong is after the jade's medicinal properties. Like all martial artists, he wishes to climb to higher heights. It's not uncommon for martial artists to plateau and make no more progress their entire lives; with the jade's assistance, perhaps he can find a shortcut to the heavens."

"But that's only hearsay," said Pei Jingzhe. "No one knows whether the jade really has such a power."

"Hearsay is enough. As long as there's some hope, there will be people willing to take risks." Feng Xiao rapped on the table. "Back to the matter at hand. What do you think? If you wanted to steal something, would you expose it to the public eye and draw everyone's attention?"

Pei Jingzhe considered it. "I'd get someone inside Linlang Pavilion to have the jade listed as one of the auction items, then quietly snatch it out from under their noses. A connection with Linlang Pavilion would also make it easier to avoid detection when leaving the city. The head broker, Wen Liang, would have been able to do it, but he's still in prison. Could it be that Wen Liang's arrest ruined their plans, and that's why the jade appeared at the auction?"

Feng Xiao shook his head. Things couldn't be that simple; he was certain he'd missed a link somewhere.

This case looked straightforward at a glance: a murder and robbery. But as he disentangled each element bit by bit, he realized how intricate it was, thread wound tightly around thread. Whenever they managed to hit on a promising lead, it was upended the next moment.

Feng Xiao felt the presence of several invisible hands, all trying to scramble the chessboard. Some attempted to conceal their own motives, while others attempted to obscure the facts of the case.

At that thought, he couldn't help looking at Cui Buqu. Cui Buqu noticed his gaze and met it, frank and impassive. Each suppressed a cold smile.

Damn fox, Feng Xiao thought, sneering to himself.

Swaggering oleander spirit. Cui Buqu curved his lips in secret amusement. The oleander flower—beautiful but toxic. It was perfect for Feng Xiao.

Pei Jingzhe paid no heed to the undercurrents surging between the two. After a long bout of careful consideration, he asked hesitantly, "Could there be two Jades of Heaven Lake? A fake we have here, and a real one elsewhere?"

18

A SINGLE BRILLIANT TREASURE like this was hard enough to come by. Where would one find another?

Cui Buqu reached out and laid his hand over the jade. The chill of it seeped into his palm. None of them had seen the real Jade of Heaven Lake before, so it was impossible to know whether this was the genuine article.

"What did Linlang Pavilion say?" asked Feng Xiao.

"When I asked, they said all the treasures at this auction were handled by the head broker Wen Liang. So I went to interrogate Wen Liang again, and he said this item was delivered to them yesterday by an old servant in gray. It was brought to them in an ordinary wooden chest, and the man claimed it was a family heirloom. He said his master's household was in decline, and he'd therefore been ordered to sell the jade to a pawnbroker, relinquishing their claim to it for good. Linlang Pavilion would normally never accept goods from unknown sources—if it became known they'd sold stolen items, that would damage their reputation. However, because the item had arrived on their doorstep on the eve of the annual auction, Wen Liang considered carefully. He concluded that even if the item was stolen, the owner might be present at the auction and recognize it. If so, it would make returning the jade easy. He therefore decided to include it in the auction."

"What if he'd decided not to put it up for bidding?" asked Cui Buqu. "What would Linlang Pavilion have done with it?"

"According to Linlang Pavilion's rules, they'd hold it for one year," said Pei Jingzhe. "If no owner came to claim it, it would then be auctioned off. So they only moved the date forward by a year."

"Is Khotan still sending another envoy?" asked Cui Buqu.

Pei Jingzhe looked at Feng Xiao and saw him nod. "Yes, the new envoy dispatched by the king of Khotan is already on his way. We sent someone to receive him in Qiemo, but it'll take three or more days for them to reach Liugong City."

Until he arrived, no one could prove the jade in front of them was the true Jade of Heaven Lake.

Cui Buqu stroked the jade and said slowly, "After you won the auction today, at least ten people had their eyes on you. Three looked dissatisfied, but two held murderous intent."

He noticed all that? Pei Jingzhe was shocked. He couldn't stop himself from asking, "Who?"

Cui Buqu didn't hold back. "The three people who frowned in dissatisfaction were the young leader of Jinhuan Guild, Leng Du; the wealthy businessman from Khotan, Zhou Pei; and Zhang Yingshui from the Zhang family of Anlu. Of the two with murderous intent, one was a Göktürk man dressed in black, while the other was a man in his mid-twenties, dressed in gray and wearing a bamboo hat. I've never seen either of them before. Their faces didn't stand out and they didn't do anything to give away their training, so I can't guess at their identities."

"A Göktürk man?" Pei Jingzhe looked suddenly wary.

But Feng Xiao was amused. "Whether or not this Jade of Heaven Lake is the real one, now that it's in my hands, we can expect plenty of people to come knocking."

"Correct," said Cui Buqu.

Pei Jingzhe was alarmed. "They dare make enemies of the Jiejian Bureau?!"

Cui Buqu laughed mockingly. "The Jiejian Bureau's authority comes from the emperor. The various ministries might be willing to tiptoe around you because of it, but what meaning does that hold in the jianghu? If the jade really has the power to purify the body or bring the dead back to life, of course they won't hesitate to steal it."

Pei Jingzhe opened his mouth to refute it but couldn't think of anything to say.

At that moment, Feng Xiao chuckled. "The weather is cold, the dew heavy. You've been outside listening to us for so long; why not come in for a cup of hot tea?"

There was someone outside?

Pei Jingzhe's ears pricked up. He had no small skill himself, but throughout the entire conversation, he hadn't noticed any sounds from without.

A blithe female voice rang out, clear as spring water: "I'm afraid the house is too crowded. There's nowhere to sit."

There really was someone there! Pei Jingzhe leapt up.

Feng Xiao snatched the wooden chest off the table and flung it at the door. Obviously he wasn't trying to smash a hole through the door and hit the person outside. The box hit the door just so, and it flew open. This skillful display of strength was something only a martial arts expert could achieve.

The wind swept into the house through the opening, and they beheld, on the eaves of the building opposite, a woman in yellow. She sat looking at them, leisurely swinging her legs back and forth. Her face was ordinary, her features unexceptional. Comparing her to Feng Xiao was like comparing a clod of mud to a cloud, but her voice was unmistakable.

"My apologies for disturbing you this late at night. Perhaps Feng-langjun would allow me a glimpse of the jade? Then I'll leave without delay."

Pei Jingzhe followed Feng Xiao as he stepped through the door. He noticed instantly that the woman in yellow wasn't the only one outside: three more people waited in the dark. One stood on the left rooftop, one on the right, and a third was beneath a tree.

The first wore a hat with a white veil. They were clad in white from head to toe, and it was impossible to tell if they were a man or a woman. The second was a tall man with wheat-colored hair. It was clear at a glance that he was foreign—a Göktürk. The last was another man dressed in gray, his face frosty and his thin lips drawn into a line. A deep scar ran between his brows, and he wore a longsword at his side.

So many martial experts were just outside, and yet Pei Jingzhe had failed to notice. He couldn't even sense them—if a fight broke out, he would be of no assistance to Feng Xiao. All the hair on Pei Jingzhe's body stood on end.

The woman in yellow seemed to take note of his nervousness. She chuckled. "Fear not, young man. I came alone; I'm not with them."

Cui Buqu gave two quiet coughs and slowly stepped outside.

Everyone was dressed in thin clothing, as if it was the height of summer. In contrast, Cui Buqu was tightly swaddled in a thick coat, his face the color of snow. It was clear at a glance that he was chronically ill; he looked like a man with only a few days to live. Then there were his footsteps, utterly insubstantial and lacking even a trace of the power and surety one would expect of a martial artist. Everyone's gazes alighted on him then flitted away, paying him no further heed.

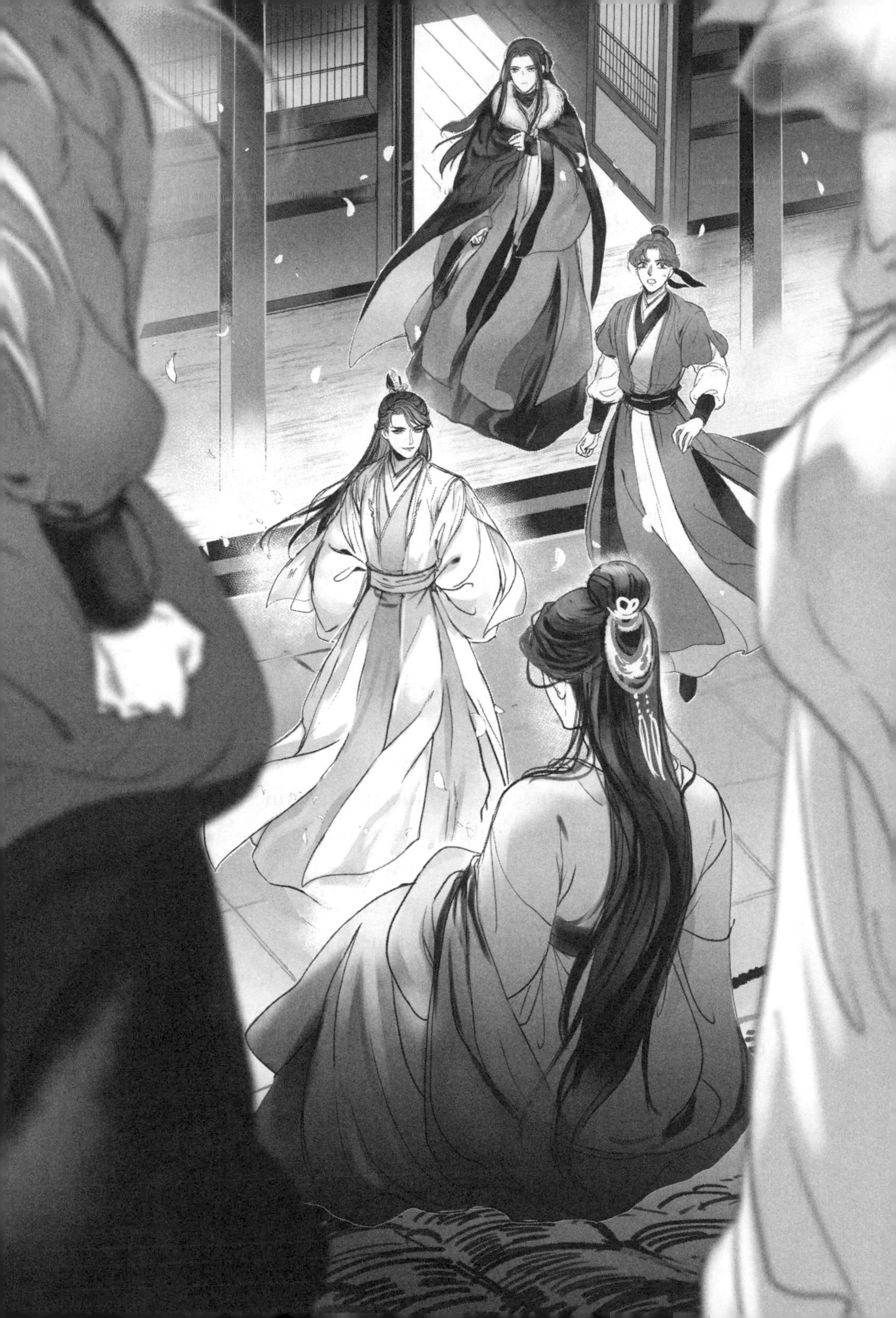

Feng Xiao strolled forward, hands clasped behind his back. He showed no hint of nervousness—rather, it was as if he'd been looking forward to this night for a long time. His eyes were sparkling with amusement.

"There are still two more. Why don't you all just come out at once?"

No one spoke as they waited for the two he'd addressed to appear. The silence stretched for a long moment before a shape emerged from a dark corner. The figure might have been that of a tall and slender woman. Half their body remained cloaked in darkness beyond the reach of the moonlight, as if they belonged in the shadows.

"Who else is there?" Pei Jingzhe demanded. "Can you only hide like a rat?!"

"The last person has already left," said the woman in yellow. "If I'm not mistaken, they were an assassin from the Thirteen Floors of Yunhai."

At the sound of that name, both Feng Xiao and Cui Buqu's expressions shifted.

The Thirteen Floors of Yunhai was a new and rising sect in the jianghu. They worked in secret, and their main business was providing killers for hire. There would always be people whose existence was an obstacle to others, but it wasn't always convenient to remove the obstacle oneself. Perhaps some even lacked the ability to do so. Hence the Thirteen Floors of Yunhai came to be.

Rumor had it that business was booming for the Thirteen Floors of Yunhai. They had grown increasingly audacious and even dared to target court officials. Last month, an official from the Ministry of Justice had passed away suddenly. A discreet investigation from the Jiejian Bureau had found the cause of death irregular—they suspected murder. Thanks to that, the Thirteen Floors of Yunhai had carved their mark in the case files of the Jiejian Bureau's deputy chief.

Assassinations were a shady business. This opponent had realized Feng Xiao was no easy target, not to mention the other experts on the scene tonight. It made sense that they'd seen the confrontation wouldn't go smoothly and chosen to leave first.

But that was one. Five still remained.

Cui Buqu looked around furtively, then coughed softly twice, suppressing a smile tinged with malicious glee. *Now, how will the oleander spirit deal with this gathering of heroes?*

19

QIAO XIAN SAT IN THE TEAHOUSE, staring dazedly down into her cup. The amber liquid rippled, reflecting the evening sunset. Gradually, the sun sank below the horizon. The stallkeeper lit the candles, then asked Qiao Xian if she'd like a hot bowl of noodles.

She declined. Qiao Xian wasn't accustomed to the taste of this tea, bitter with a hint of salt. At the Zuoyue Bureau, everyone knew the lord chief's subordinate Qiao Xian loved sour plum soup. But this was a remote area, at a time of year when the chill had yet to subside. There was not a drop of sour plum soup to be found.

Raising her bowl for the fifth time, Qiao Xian took a tiny sip of the tea, then frowned and put it down. At that moment, the person she was waiting for finally appeared. She watched Zhangsun Bodhi step out of Chunxiang House from afar, then stride unhurriedly toward the teahouse where they'd agreed to meet.

"You're an hour late," she said as soon as Zhangsun sat down.

"You're early."

"What did you learn?"

Zhangsun hesitated—a rare sight. "The fragrance she wears was created by a woman called Miao-niangzi. Miao-niangzi is familiar with many types of perfumes and capable of creating unique scents.

Yunyun was able to distinguish herself among Chunxiang House's top courtesans recently partly thanks to her perfumes."

Had Cui Buqu or Feng Xiao been there, the name "Miao-niangzi" would have instantly called to mind Lady Qin Miaoyu, the Khotanese envoy's concubine who'd disappeared. But they were far on the other side of the city, and Zhangsun and Qiao Xian had no way of knowing that name's significance.

Even so, they could more or less guess Cui Buqu's intentions in sending them to investigate the cold plum blossom fragrance.

"This Miao-niangzi must be related to the person the lord chief is looking for," said Qiao Xian. "But you wasted half the day with Yunyun-niangzi, and this is all you have to show for it?"

Zhangsun Bodhi shot her a look that seemed to say, *And what did you find yourself?*

"I planned to follow her maid," said Qiao Xian. "But when I saw her standing outside little Yunyun-niangzi's room, all envy and dissatisfaction, I changed my plans. I pretended to be an injured man from the jianghu who'd mistakenly entered Chunxiang House and begged her to treat me. I was so pitiful she dropped her guard, and I coaxed some information out of her."

As a woman, Qiao Xian was a cold, untouchable beauty; when she disguised herself as a man, that quality became an aura of cold austerity that drove women crazy. In fact, the longer one looked at Qiao Xian, the more androgynous she seemed.

For the first time, Zhangsun Bodhi's gaze lingered on her face. Confusion surfaced on his features. "You...which are you, a man or a woman?"

"You've been practicing Buddhism for how long?" said Qiao Xian coolly. "Don't you know all things are ephemeral, and all appearances but empty vanity?"

Zhangsun silently turned the prayer beads in his hand and murmured a few *Amitabhas* "You're right, I have strayed. My training is not yet complete."

Qiao Xian was surprised. "Did nothing happen between you and that little Yunyun-niangzi?"

"After questioning her, I tapped her sleep acupoint and left," Zhangsun said placidly.

Once Yunyun awakened, she might remember Zhangsun Bodhi, but she wouldn't remember how she fell asleep. She'd only remember it as a spring night filled with romance, a dream that left no trace. They'd never see each other again.

Zhangsun Bodhi sank into reverie but was quickly pulled back by the roughness of the prayer beads in his hand. "What did you find?" he asked belatedly, though he rarely took the initiative to inquire.

"I asked about the whereabouts of this Miao-niangzi. She said Yunyun had secretly purchased a private manor—originally, she'd planned to live there after redeeming herself and earning her freedom. But she'd established herself at Chunxiang House with Miao-niangzi's help, so she returned the favor and recently invited Miao-niangzi to take up temporary residence at the manor. I, too, would like to see just who this Miao-niangzi is."

Zhangsun Bodhi's expression asked: *It's already dark, so why aren't we going?*

Qiao Xian didn't answer. Instead she called the owner over and asked for two bowls of noodle soup. "It's still early. We can leave after we eat."

Zhangsun Bodhi nodded.

In truth, obtaining intelligence like this, through conversation, was not his strong suit. Given the choice, he'd much rather take up a weapon and fight the enemy head-on. Yunyun had been stunningly cooperative, but when he'd walked out of Chunxiang House, his tightly pursed lips had betrayed his nervousness. Only now did he finally relax.

Qiao Xian regarded him for a moment and said, "The Zuoyue Bureau still has fewer people than the Jiejian Bureau. If the lord chief could find more subordinates with both wits and courage, perhaps he wouldn't need to personally carry out his strategies as he has this time."

"Compared to seeing him confined to bed for weeks at a time, I'd rather see him run around. At least that would mean he wasn't sick as often." It was rare to hear Zhangsun say such a long sentence.

Qiao Xian frowned. "But he can't be having a good time with Feng Xiao."

As they spoke, the noodles arrived. They set the conversation aside and silently applied themselves to their meal.

The noodles were ordinary, plain noodles. The quality of the flour couldn't compare to the flour of the capital, and the soup base was boiled well water. Some green onions and vegetables had been scattered over top, but there was not a sliver of meat to be seen. It was a meal to sate the common people. These noodles were much worse than anything Zhangsun and Qiao Xian were used to eating. But in the face of hunger and cold, a bowl of hot soup warmed the stomach, wiping away fatigue and enveloping them in coziness.

Qiao Xian and Zhangsun Bodhi both had the same thought: *If only the lord chief were here.*

Where he was, would anyone offer him a bowl of hot noodle soup?

❧❀❧

Of course there was no bowl of hot noodle soup for Cui Buqu.

He currently stood outside the manor, getting battered by cold winds and suppressing the urge to cough.

But he was still in an unusually good mood. Because right before his eyes, Feng Xiao had been cornered five to one.

"Bring the jade out," he heard Feng Xiao say to Pei Jingzhe.

Pei Jingzhe stood momentarily frozen, unsure what Feng Xiao intended. Then he turned and entered the manor, swiftly returning with the jade.

The moonlight was bright and clear, and the jade shone radiantly in Pei Jingzhe's hand. A hint of rippling green was visible in the center of the crystal-clear stone. Whether or not it was the real Jade of Heaven Lake, it was certainly a jade of unmatched quality.

Multiple shining eyes fixed upon the jade.

Feng Xiao drew himself up and said with perfect composure, "I assume you're all here for this?"

He was met with silence. Except for the woman in yellow, who had already claimed she only wanted to borrow the jade for a look, the identities and aims of these uninvited guests remained unknown. It seemed no one was willing to speak first, as if they were competing to see who could be most patient.

Feng Xiao wasn't bothered, and Cui Buqu even less so. Only Pei Jingzhe was growing anxious. He was aware he had his own lack of discipline to blame, but he didn't want his failings to reflect poorly on Feng Xiao. He silently drew a deep breath, doing what he could to control his restlessness.

As before, the woman in yellow broke the silence. "This one came first and doesn't wish to make an enemy of the Jiejian Bureau. I'm but a weak woman, and I've been shivering in these cold winds for most of the night. Take pity on me, Feng-langjun. Let me see it, so I can return with my report."

She gave a small smile. Though her face was unremarkable, her mellifluous voice drew involuntary glances from the assembly.

Cui Buqu quietly looked around and found only two people who didn't look at her. One was the androgynous person clad in white with the veiled hat, and the other was the Göktürk man. Right from the beginning, the Göktürk man's attention had been focused on no one but Feng Xiao.

Only a martial arts master with a heart clean of desires would maintain such unwavering focus on their target.

As for the figure in black, still half-shrouded in shadow... That person was a distance away and turned to the side. Their left hand gripped their right wrist, stroking it occasionally.

Cui Buqu's eyes narrowed slightly.

Feng Xiao didn't look at the others. His gaze was locked on the woman in yellow, as if she was the only guest in the courtyard. Seeing her smile, he followed suit and said, "How polite you are; I'd certainly lend you the jade first, but I know neither your name nor your origins. If you take it and run, how will I find you?"

"This one is Bing Xian," said the woman in yellow.

Feng Xiao raised an eyebrow. "Your surname is Bing? That's unusual."

"Names are merely what others call us. For example, even if you didn't call yourself anything so lofty as Feng-langjun, you'd still be magnificent and without peer in this world. Isn't that right?"

Feng Xiao chuckled. "Unlike these other mannerless guests, your words have won my heart. Say, why not come to my Jiejian Bureau? I guarantee I'd help and protect you; never would I let you sit on a roof in the middle of the night, shivering in the wind."

Smiling, Bing Xian was about to reply when Feng Xiao snatched the jade from Pei Jingzhe's hand and threw it at her. "Since I like you the most, I'm lending you the jade first!"

Bing Xian was taken aback; she'd never expected Feng Xiao would really follow through. She had no time to think—her delicate toes pushed off the ground and she leapt into the air, featherlight, toward the jade.

She was fast, but others were faster. The veiled person in white and the scarred man in gray also grabbed for the jade.

Yet the Göktürk man didn't even look at it. As others dove for the treasure, his saber sprang from its sheath, its churning, tumultuous qi bearing down on Feng Xiao like a tidal wave.

The saber qi was so powerful that even Cui Buqu, who stood behind Feng Xiao, felt it as a gale roaring toward him. He stumbled back, about to slam into the wall, when someone dragged him viciously forward by his collar. With a start, he realized he was trapped within Feng Xiao's arms.

But the Göktürk man had already reached them. Saber qi cut down from above, and Cui Buqu felt his topknot loosen and hair flutter down. An expert at Feng Xiao's level knew the Göktürk man's surprise attack would at minimum knock his clasp loose. In order to preserve his hairstyle, he'd pulled Cui Buqu forward and used him as a shield.

Cui Buqu didn't need a mirror to know he looked like a disheveled madman. Rage surged in his heart, and he spat, "Feng Xiao, you motherfucking son of a bastard!"

He soon realized the Göktürk man was aiding his revenge—the man immediately engaged Feng Xiao in a fierce battle, leaving Feng Xiao no chance to respond.

Meanwhile, the man in gray, one step ahead of the others, had just wrapped his fingers around the jade. Yet before he could rejoice, it splintered in his hands and crumbled to powder, dissipating on the wind.

The three fighting over the jade froze, completely dumbfounded.

20

THE MAN IN GRAY could have sworn he'd done nothing to the jade, let alone smashed it. But the stone had truly crumbled to dust, and he had no good explanation.

The other two left off tussling and moved together to block his retreat, one from the front and the other from the back.

Bing Xian smiled. "This distinguished master has a terrible temper. He's destroyed something he can't have just so no one else can have it either."

The person in white made no reply, but it was clear from the way they closed in that they wouldn't let the man in gray off easily.

"I didn't do anything. It shattered by itself," the man in gray said coldly.

"Both of us saw it plainly. We witnessed it with our own eyes—are you claiming we saw wrong?" Bing Xian raised an eyebrow.

Cui Buqu leaned against the door and coughed quietly. The instant the man in gray moved, he'd ascertained his identity. But now wasn't a good time to step into the limelight. No one paid him any heed because he was sickly and had no fighting ability. He wasn't about to take the initiative to put himself in danger. Besides, there were surely others here capable of recognizing the man in gray.

Sure enough, the person in white finally spoke: "You wield a sword like a katana user, and your style is reminiscent of the famous

Soga clan of Japan. But there are some differences. I heard Goguryeo has a rising star known for his innovation whose master was Japanese. Go Nyeong—that must be you, right?"

These words were spoken gently, with a cadence as refreshing as a spring breeze. It was rather out of place in such a bloodthirsty moment.

Bing Xian couldn't help but examine the person in white anew. They'd been able to identify the man in gray with ease, so they couldn't be an ordinary person. But though she wracked her brain, she couldn't match this description to any of the top figures of the jianghu.

Unless—they weren't from the jianghu?

Bing Xian's brow furrowed. She'd come for the jade with full awareness that the Jiejian Bureau was no pushover. She'd known getting her hands on it would be no easy task—and this was before she'd seen how many other experts had appeared with the same goal. The Göktürk man alone was headache enough.

At that thought, Bing Xian smiled slightly and tucked back a lock of her hair that had whipped loose in the wind.

"Feng-langjun has too many honored guests right now. I can see you don't have time to entertain me, so I'll take my leave first. I'll trouble you another day." Without waiting for Feng Xiao to respond, she leapt into the air, light as a feather. She touched down on the eaves and disappeared into the darkness.

Across the way, Fo'er, the Göktürk man Bing Xian had identified as the greatest threat, was getting a shock. The reason was simple: Feng Xiao's appearance belied his skills. Those who underestimated him due to his excessive beauty would find themselves blindsided by his incredible martial arts.

The Göktürk man had never set foot in the Central Plains, but he had considerable confidence in his own skill. He'd been convinced that if he stepped into the jianghu he'd have few equals, that he was strong enough to stand among the best of grandmasters. Since entering the Central Plains, the man had challenged several sect and guild leaders, all top martial experts. Just as he'd expected, even within the expansive jianghu, there were few who could match him.

Until he met Feng Xiao.

Feng Xiao's martial arts were not bold and powerful like his, but fluid and agile, as if he were shaking dew from his sleeves or snow from his robes. They conjured the image of plucking flowers with a smile or taking a graceful stroll—every motion was beautiful. But Fo'er saw bloodlust concealed in that beauty. Feng Xiao's moves seemed effortless, yet each and every one threatened ambush from all directions. Fo'er discarded his initial carelessness and regarded his opponent with a renewed caution. Even the jade shattering didn't distract him.

A battle between two peerless martial artists was a rare sight. The person in white and the Goguryeon in gray, Go Nyeong, called a temporary truce in order to watch.

Cui Buqu coughed twice lightly, then whispered, "That man didn't come for the jade. He wants to kill Feng Xiao."

The words were meant for Pei Jingzhe, who was standing beside him. Pei Jingzhe was stunned. "How do you know?"

Cui Buqu scoffed. "Haven't you realized? From the moment he appeared, he's only had eyes for Feng Xiao. He didn't even glance at the jade, and he didn't participate in the scuffle for it either."

"Do you know who he is?"

"I've never seen him before, but if I'm not mistaken, his name is Fo'er and he's the top martial artist under Ishbara Khagan. He was taught by great masters, and his martial skill combines the strengths of various schools. That man has yet to lose a fight since entering the Central Plains. He's what they call a grandmaster."

Pei Jingzhe gasped in surprise. He'd never expected an ordinary night like this could attract such a powerful martial artist.

"Who's stronger? Him or my lord?"

"I don't know any martial arts," said Cui Buqu. "Why are you asking me?"

Pei Jingzhe didn't bother replying. He watched for some time as the fighters' sleeves swirled and their silhouettes flickered. But they were simply too fast; even Pei Jingzhe couldn't tell who had the upper hand. He was so anxious he turned and ran back into the house, reappearing with an object cradled in his arms. Peng Jingzhe called to Feng Xiao, "Sir, your zither!"

"Toss it over." Feng Xiao's voice was clear and calm with no sign of surrender. Pei Jingzhe's eyes lit up, and he threw the zither into the air.

They heard but a single *twang*, yet the sound called to mind a vast army, the charge of a thousand valiant soldiers. The very air went stagnant, and everyone's hair stood on end as they watched with bated breath.

There were many weapons in the jianghu—knives, swords, and spears. But this was the first time Fo'er had ever seen someone use a zither as a weapon. The zither was carved from lacquered black wood, and despite being solid and heavy, it looked weightless in Feng Xiao's hands, an obedient plaything. He attacked and defended, the thrum of the strings disturbing the minds of all who heard their sound.

"What a zither!" the person in white exclaimed.

Go Nyeong, however, turned away from the fight between Feng Xiao and Fo'er. His brow furrowed as he looked at Pei Jingzhe and Cui Buqu, who were still observing the battle. In a flash, he dove toward them. His katana transformed into a tide of qi as it swept toward the pair. Pei Jingzhe yanked Cui Buqu out of the way, but at the last second, Go Nyeong changed tactics and grabbed at them with his free hand.

Pei Jingzhe thought he was trying to take Cui Buqu as a hostage; he shoved Cui Buqu back and drew his sword to parry his opponent's strike. However, Go Nyeong's goal wasn't Cui Buqu, but Pei Jingzhe. His blade immediately reversed its trajectory to meet Pei Jingzhe's sword. His internal energy was deep and strong, the wind from his katana ferocious. Pei Jingzhe felt a numbness in his wrist, then a sharp agony between thumb and forefinger. His sword almost tumbled from his hand, and a moment later Go Nyeong's sword was against his neck.

"Hand over the jade if you value your life!" Go Nyeong rasped.

"You destroyed the jade!" Pei Jingzhe spat back.

Go Nyeong scowled. "Don't mess with me. That was obviously a fake!" He yelled to Feng Xiao, "If that jade were real, you would never have handed it over so readily! Give me the real jade or I'll kill him!"

Even inches away from death, Pei Jingzhe couldn't help asking, "Why me?!"

Didn't common sense dictate that Cui Buqu was a more suitable hostage, since he was essentially defenseless?

"Don't take me for a fool," said Go Nyeong coldly. "That man is Feng Xiao's lover, capable of traveling the jianghu with him; he must know at least a technique or two. You, on the other hand, are both weak and expendable. Why would I grab anyone else?"

Pei Jingzhe was utterly flummoxed.

As if Go Nyeong's words hadn't dealt his self-esteem a severe enough blow, Feng Xiao's quiet chuckle drifted down from above. "If you know he's expendable, why grab him? Grabbing my lover would be better! Maybe then I'd cooperate."

The moment these words were uttered, the person in white smiled. "Is that so? Then I'll give it a try."

A flash of white robes and he was at Cui Buqu's side.

Cui Buqu felt pain slam through his shoulder, rendering him completely immobile.

21

IN THE BLINK OF AN EYE, Cui Buqu had fallen into the hands of the person in white. What looked like a palm lightly placed on his shoulder seemed somehow to weigh thousands of pounds. Cui Buqu felt as if his shoulder had been removed entirely: in an instant, one side of his body went completely numb.

His throat grew itchy, like it was being tickled by a feather, and he broke into another fit of coughing. The motion aggravated his injured shoulder, and pain raced through his body.

The person in white saw his paling face and the cold sweat that soaked him, and reached out to support him with their other hand.

"Are you all right?" Their tone was gentle and concerned, as if speaking to an old friend of many years, yet each word was probing. "Your footsteps are unsteady, and your face is wan. But that didn't just happen now. It looks like you've been poisoned." They clicked their tongue. "You're dragging this sickly body around, yet still helping the Jiejian Bureau look for the jade? Is it worth it? Why not come with me instead? I'll neutralize this poison and set you free; you'll be spared the pain of being trapped at the mercy of others."

Cui Buqu looked up sharply, his gaze piercing both the darkness and the veil, locking onto his captor's eyes. The veiled figure didn't shy away from his stare. They gazed back; perhaps there was even a kind and gentle smile on their lips.

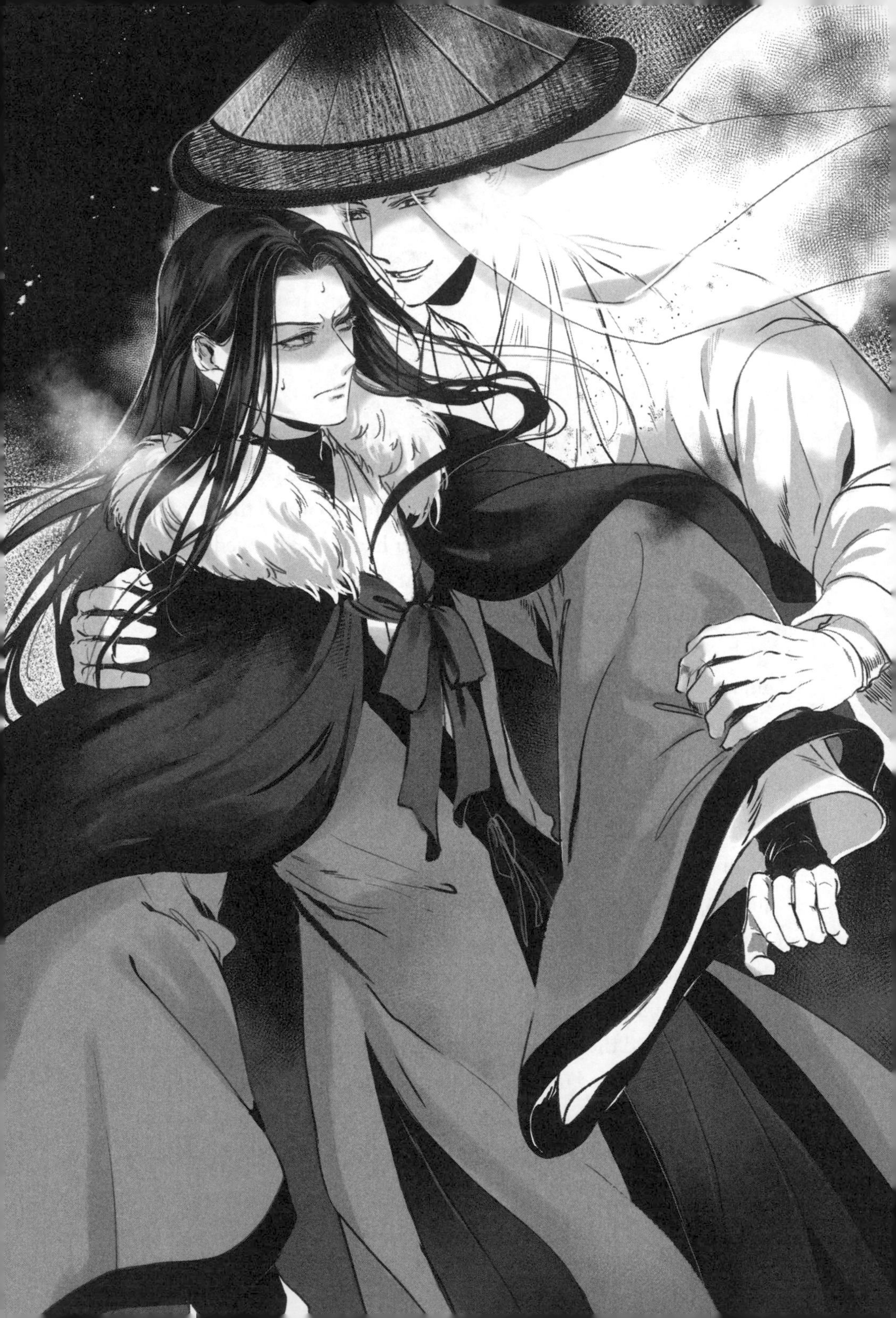

"Oh my," said Feng Xiao. "My lover and my subordinate have both been captured. Whom shall I save first? Now you're making things difficult for me on purpose!"

Fo'er didn't slow his attack to let Feng Xiao speak; he pressed forward with strike after strike. The sea of qi surged and roiled, enveloping Feng Xiao and leaving him no avenue of escape. Fo'er leapt from the ground, sending a palm toward Feng Xiao in midair.

The gesture was like a wave breaking against the shore or a storm at sea—relentless, and leaving its target with nowhere to run or hide. It was as if Feng Xiao was surrounded on all sides by enemies, with an abyss before him and a cliff behind him, precarious and on the verge of plummeting into the void.

This palm technique was part of the first set Fo'er had created after completing his apprenticeship, and it was also the one he took the most pride in. He'd named it Qiluo—*Invincible*. Fo'er had used it to defeat many experts in the Central Plains, and now his mind was made up: he vowed to himself that he'd slay Feng Xiao with this strike.

"It seems Feng-langjun is occupied." The person in white smiled, then grabbed Cui Buqu's arm and dragged him upward. Cui Buqu felt a sharp pain in his shoulder as he rose into the air.

Go Nyeong snorted coldly at the sight. Then he grabbed Pei Jingzhe and he, too, left.

But just as Fo'er's palm was about to slam down on his opponent's head, Feng Xiao's long sleeves swished, and the ancient zither in his arms soared into the air to block Fo'er. The strings twanged and the zither shuddered, but it didn't splinter or break—instead, the sound of the zither slowed Fo'er just enough that Feng Xiao's attack connected first. When the ancient zither fell, he caught it smoothly in his arms and stopped before Fo'er, taking the chance to slam the zither outward again.

Startled, Fo'er withdrew, but the sound of the zither was like a towering wave. Its powerful energy transformed notes into weapons, piercing every orifice of Fo'er's face. The sound waves slammed into his organs and scoured his body. A sweet taste rose in the back of his throat; blood trickled from the corner of his mouth.

He swiped at the bloody foam and glared icily at his opponent.

Feng Xiao was unruffled. He didn't even glance toward where Cui Buqu and Pei Jingzhe had disappeared. He simply stood, his hands behind his back as he leisurely raised his eyes to meet Fo'er's.

"You're quite strong," Feng Xiao said. "You've already caught your first glimpse of the grandmaster's path, but unfortunately you encountered me tonight." He continued, smiling brightly. "If everyone has a destined nemesis, the heavens must have sent me to polish you. You're talented to be sure, but now that you've met a true genius like me you'll have to admit defeat. Go back to your grasslands and practice for another five years or so. Then maybe you'll be my match, hm?"

Fo'er was panting lightly. Pain twinged in his chest; Feng Xiao's counterattack had left him with internal injuries. He knew his opponent must have suffered some injuries himself, but they were at most lacerations caused by the flaring of Fo'er's true qi. Between the two of them, Fo'er was worse off.

It would be impossible for him to kill Feng Xiao tonight.

Earlier, when it'd been five to one, he'd easily have achieved his goal if someone else had made a dramatic move. But those who had come for the Jade of Heaven Lake chose either to stand aside, run when things didn't go their way, or capture someone close to Feng Xiao—anything but attack Feng Xiao directly. Certain victory had turned to failure.

All of these were factors in his current predicament. But ultimately, Fo'er lost because he was the weaker of the two.

"A warrior must be wholly focused in order to reach greater heights, but tonight you are clearly distracted. I disdain such opponents," Fo'er said coldly, then turned and left. Though his martial skills were strong and domineering, his qinggong was light and agile. In a blink, he'd leapt several yards away and disappeared into the night.

His words were nothing but a salve to his dignity. The Göktürk Khagan's best martial artist was most certainly someone who cared deeply for his own reputation.

Feng Xiao didn't give chase. He watched as Fo'er's figure vanished from sight, then discarded his careless demeanor and turned to enter the house.

Unsurprisingly, various buildings within Qiushan Manor were now in shambles. The servants had hidden themselves where they could, too afraid to make a peep. When they saw Feng Xiao, they crawled out, trembling, from under the tables and wailed at him. "Sir, just now while you were outside, two people burst in and started tearing up the place. They left emptyhanded—whatever they were looking for, it seems they didn't find it!"

Feng Xiao hummed in affirmation. Their guests tonight had been certain the destroyed jade was a fake, so they were trying to locate the real one.

And as for the real Jade of Heaven Lake...

Feng Xiao's mouth slanted in a mocking smile.

Any expression looked different on the face of a beauty. The servants were terrified and crying, but when they raised their heads and saw this smile, they were caught off guard and froze in awe.

The person in white had whisked Cui Buqu away, but now that they had him, they took their time. Cui Buqu was forced to blindly follow. If not for the sharp pain in his shoulder and his old illness flaring up, he'd have almost believed his kidnapper was simply looking for someone with whom to take a stroll.

From afar came the clang of the night gong, and in the distance several lights flickered. The night was deep, and the heavy dew added to the chill. Cui Buqu was wearing several layers, yet he still felt the cold and shuddered.

"You're not from the jianghu," he said, then followed it with two hoarse coughs. He thought absently that he must have gotten a fever from the chill: his entire body was sore, and he longed to find a bed and lie down as soon as possible. But life was unpredictable; instead, he had to follow this stranger and play a game of riddles.

The person in white smiled and said, "I'm not. Are you?"

Cui Buqu acted like he hadn't heard him. "You came here tonight and joined the excitement, so you must want the jade. But if you're not from the jianghu, the legends about it strengthening one's martial arts wouldn't interest you. People like you seem easygoing on the surface, but deep down they're arrogant. You're not the type to readily submit to another, yet you came here personally. That means the one whose orders you follow must be of high status indeed. You wish to obtain the jade and present it to them."

"Has anyone ever told you that clever people die quicker deaths?"

"You needn't waste so many words," Cui Buqu said coolly. "Four are enough to sum me up: *heaven envies the talented.*"

The person in white chuckled. "Daoist Cui, you're really too fascinating. If we hadn't met at such an inopportune time, I'd have liked to take you tea-tasting and enjoyed some scenery together."

"If it was with you, I wouldn't be able to drink any tea, nor enjoy any scenery."

The person in white ignored this quip. "Are you hungry?" they asked. "Is there anything to eat in the city at this time of night? Take me around for a look. Hot soup would be best."

"My shoulder hurts, and I'm not hungry."

The person in white smiled behind their veil. "If you don't take me, your shoulder will hurt rather more, I'm afraid." He spoke with complete politeness and without a hint of anger, but his threats were extraordinarily vicious.

"Even if I don't take you, someone else will," Cui Buqu said.

The person in white laughed. "Who?"

"Me." A tall and slender figure strode forward out of the night. He stopped several paces away, his back to the lights of the city.

"Feng-langjun is so fast. You dismissed the Göktürks' number one martial arts master, just like that?" the man in white exclaimed in surprise.

Feng Xiao said, "Not so. You caught my lover, so why shouldn't I be a bit faster?"

22

THE PERSON IN WHITE was rather bemused. Fo'er's skill and battle lust were such that even if he failed to kill Feng Xiao, he should still have held him up. Who would have expected the foremost martial artist of the Göktürks would fail to live up to his reputation? Less than two hours had passed, yet Feng Xiao had already extricated himself and caught up with them.

"Feng-langjun's martial arts have exceeded my expectations."

"You never intended to go far in the first place," said Feng Xiao. "Of all the people who appeared tonight, your background alone remains a mystery. Doesn't this distinguished master wish to introduce themselves? Or do you wish to come and go without even leaving your name?"

"A name is just a word," the person in white said. "Hundreds of years from now, ash will return to ash, and dust to dust. Why does Feng-langjun persist in asking?"

Feng Xiao sneered. "The more someone says something like this, the more they must care about their own reputation. You're dressed in white, your clothes free of dust, so you're the kind who's deeply critical on the inside, to both yourself and others. Certainly nothing like the untrammeled image you're presenting now."

The person in white smiled. "I'm not interested in Feng-langjun's evaluation of me. What interests me is that you detained Daoist Cui and poisoned him, subjecting him to a fate worse than death. Why does he still hope for you to rescue him? Are there really people in this world who enjoy being tortured?"

"I don't enjoy torture, but compared to falling into your hands, I'd rather land in his," Cui Buqu said coldly.

The person in white said with mild surprise, "Other than the small bit of force I used to bring you away, have I not treated you with courtesy?"

"He at least has his own goals and limits regarding how far he's willing to go. You don't value anyone's life at all," Cui Buqu said.

"Oh, Ququ. It's so rare to hear you praise me in front of others. I'm overwhelmed by this show of favor." As he spoke, Feng Xiao flitted toward them.

The person in white reacted swiftly, retreating while keeping hold of Cui Buqu. They shoved Cui Buqu forward slightly, ready to use him as a shield. Unexpectedly, Feng Xiao didn't target anything vital, but instead extended his hand to remove their veiled hat.

The person in white flinched, but it was too late. Their head was bared, and a cold wind blew over them, leaving its lingering chill.

Cui Buqu coughed twice, not hiding his surprise.

Feng Xiao smiled. "So even monks are dishonest nowadays. Rather than staying in their temples and chanting scriptures, they come to steal precious jades. Which abbot are you under? I'd like a word."

The moonlight glinted off the smooth and shiny head of the man in white, and Feng Xiao couldn't help but think of a boiled egg, freshly peeled. Still in the man's clutches, Cui Buqu began coughing again. Feng Xiao glanced over; he could swear Cui Buqu was using his cough to conceal his laughter. Feng Xiao suddenly felt that he and this invalid were quite in sync.

In the instant the man in white's hat was removed, fury flashed over his face. But he quickly composed himself and said, "This humble monk has no fixed residence; he lives like the drifting clouds, free and untethered. My dharma name is a humble one, not worth mentioning."

"Oho," said Feng Xiao. "So you're a monk living in the wilds? Then you can't call yourself a monk. Who knows, maybe you're running from forced labor in the guise of one. It seems I need to take you in for some careful questioning!"

He reached to grab the man in white, but his opponent was vigilant—he'd swept back as Feng Xiao spoke, retreating a dozen paces in a single step. Feng Xiao pursued him closely, leaping after him. He seemed determined to capture the man.

The man's brow furrowed. He didn't fear a fight with Feng Xiao, but he was reluctant to waste time or use his martial arts, which would reveal his training. When Feng Xiao attacked, the man in white shoved Cui Buqu toward him, then turned and leapt away, intent on fleeing.

He'd gone only a few feet when a dark shadow fell from the sky and a longsword sang as it slashed through the air. The clouds were thin, the stars few and scattered. The moon shone brightly. By its light, the man in white saw the newcomer's face.

It was Pei Jingzhe, who'd been kidnapped by Go Nyeong. So he'd managed to escape!

Feng Xiao alone was difficult to handle, and now there was Pei Jingzhe to deal with as well. Even if the subordinate wasn't as strong as his superior, having a fly buzzing around one's head was still an annoyance. The man in white saw victory had slipped from his grasp and had no desire to linger. He spun to avoid the sword glare, and in the same motion leapt off a tree branch and touched down on a nearby rooftop. By the time Pei Jingzhe made to give chase, the man was already a distance away.

"Don't pursue him," said Feng Xiao.

Pei Jingzhe jumped down from the tree and said shamefacedly, "This subordinate was lacking. I didn't manage to capture Go Nyeong."

"He's a far stronger martial artist than you," said Feng Xiao. "Your escape from him saved me the time I'd have spent on a rescue. I should be thanking you."

Pei Jingzhe couldn't tell if these were words of praise or derision. After thinking a while, he ventured cautiously, "Thank you very much for the praise, sir. This subordinate is unworthy."

Cui Buqu piped up: "He was mocking you. You thought it was praise?"

"My apologies," Feng Xiao said. "This child is a bit silly. He's made a fool of himself."

"I'm used to it."

Pei Jingzhe, watching them, barely managed to suppress the twitch of his lips. "Sir, shall I investigate that monk's identity?"

Feng Xiao looked at Cui Buqu. "Daoist Master Cui must already know."

"I do have a guess, but I don't know if it's correct," said Cui Buqu.

"Tell us."

"The monk Yuxiu."

Who? Pei Jingzhe was bewildered. He searched his memory but couldn't remember anyone by that name appearing in the jianghu.

"He's apprenticed to the Buddhist master and sage of Tiantai Sect," Cui Buqu continued. "He rarely wanders the jianghu and is not considered one of their number. Most recently, he works for a certain eminent personage and advises them from behind the scenes."

Upon hearing the words *eminent personage*, a guess rose to Pei Jingzhe's lips, but he couldn't bring himself to voice it.

"The Prince of Jin," said Feng Xiao. It wasn't a question.

"That's right," said Cui Buqu.

The Prince of Jin, Yang Guang, was the emperor's second son. Like the crown prince Yang Yong, his mother was Empress Dugu. This second son of hers, however, was much livelier and more sociable than his elder brother. The crying child receives the most candy; since their eldest son didn't act cute or play pranks, the younger Yang Guang naturally drew more of his parents' affection. This was no secret in the court.

Pei Jingzhe had heard it whispered that the emperor was selecting a marshal to carry out his plan of conquering Chen and unifying the north and south. According to rumor, the empress intended to appoint the Prince of Jin as deputy marshal and send him on the expedition. If the Prince of Jin contributed to such a significant military achievement, no one would dare label him merely an unruly child the emperor and empress had spoiled since infancy. At that point, the Prince of Jin's contributions would likely surpass even those of His Highness the Crown Prince.

As the counselor to a prince with such prospects, there was no doubt that the monk Yuxiu had a promising future. An appointment as state preceptor was far superior to wandering the jianghu. Pei Jingzhe drew in a cold breath. It wasn't Yuxiu he feared, but this eminent personage behind him.

"He's a subordinate of the Prince of Jin. Doesn't he know about the Jiejian Bureau? Why would he wade into this mess?" Pei Jingzhe looked toward Feng Xiao.

"Why else? He wants the jade."

"For the Prince of...for his master?"

"Mm," said Feng Xiao. "Consider the situation. The Jiejian Bureau failed in their mission to see the envoy safely to the capital, and the jade was stolen. The first person to find it will be a meritorious subject in the eyes of the emperor and empress. It's no surprise the Prince of Jin wishes to intervene. Even the Zuoyue Bureau behind Daoist Master Cui couldn't help sticking their noses in, no?"

"The what bureau?" said Cui Buqu.

"Your attempts at playing dumb are getting quite lazy."

"Then I'll try harder." Cui Buqu adopted a look of faint surprise. "What's this now? The Zuoyue Bureau? I don't understand you at all."

Feng Xiao nodded. "Your tone needs work, but your expression gets a pass."

Pei Jingzhe was speechless.

A low rumble sounded, breaking the awkward silence. Cui Buqu said calmly, "I'm hungry."

23

LIUGONG CITY DIDN'T ENFORCE a curfew; the city merely shut its gates at night, preventing people from coming and going as they pleased. But small border counties weren't like the unsleeping capital, where lamps were lit at all hours. This late, on nights this cold, only watchmen roamed the streets. Few respectable citizens skulked about in the small hours, and even fewer came looking for a meal.

The trio wandered for some time before finally fumbling their way into the rear kitchen of a restaurant. They slipped in from the back, and Pei Jingzhe went forward to tap the acupoints of the kitchen maid and servant on night watch, knocking them out. He found some firewood for the stove and rummaged through the shelves until he discovered some eggs and noodles, then boiled three portions.

This wasn't because Feng Xiao's treatment of Cui Buqu had suddenly improved, but because Feng Xiao himself was hungry.

Cui Buqu didn't stand on courtesy either—the word *courtesy* didn't exist in his personal dictionary, and that went doubly toward a man who'd poisoned him. When Pei Jingzhe brought the noodles, he grabbed the largest bowl and ducked his head to eat.

Feng Xiao clicked his tongue. "A-Cui, have you never heard the story of how Kong Rong gave up the pears to his brothers?"[12]

Cui Buqu didn't raise his head. "Are you my brother?"

But he quickly discovered he had no reason to gloat. He chewed the mouthful of noodles for several long moments before finally choking them down. His brow was pinched. "Why is this so tasteless? Didn't you add salt? Why are the noodles so tough? Did you only boil them for a second?"

Pei Jingzhe was indignant. "I've never cooked anything before." What he meant was, they were lucky the noodles were remotely edible.

Feng Xiao snickered. "Why else did you think I chose the bowl with the most soup and least noodles? It's impressive he managed to serve anything! Just take it and eat."

The monk Yuxiu's pace had seemed leisurely when he fled with Cui Buqu, but they'd still ended up in the far northwest corner of the city. Qiushan Manor was nearly opposite, in the southeast. Cui Buqu would have keeled over from hunger if they tried to return to the manor first, so the three had wandered half the night searching for a meal.

Pei Jingzhe was so full of questions he couldn't focus on his noodles. He blurted, "Sir, did the jade truly shatter?"

"It did. Didn't you see with your own eyes?"

"But what if that was the real jade?"

Feng Xiao set down his bowl. "There are at least two parties involved in the theft of the jade," he drawled.

Pei Jingzhe was stunned. "How do you figure?"

---

12 A well-known anecdote featuring Kong Rong, a second-century scholar. The story goes that as a child, he was given the largest pear by his father, but chose to give it up to his older and younger brothers and took the smallest for himself.

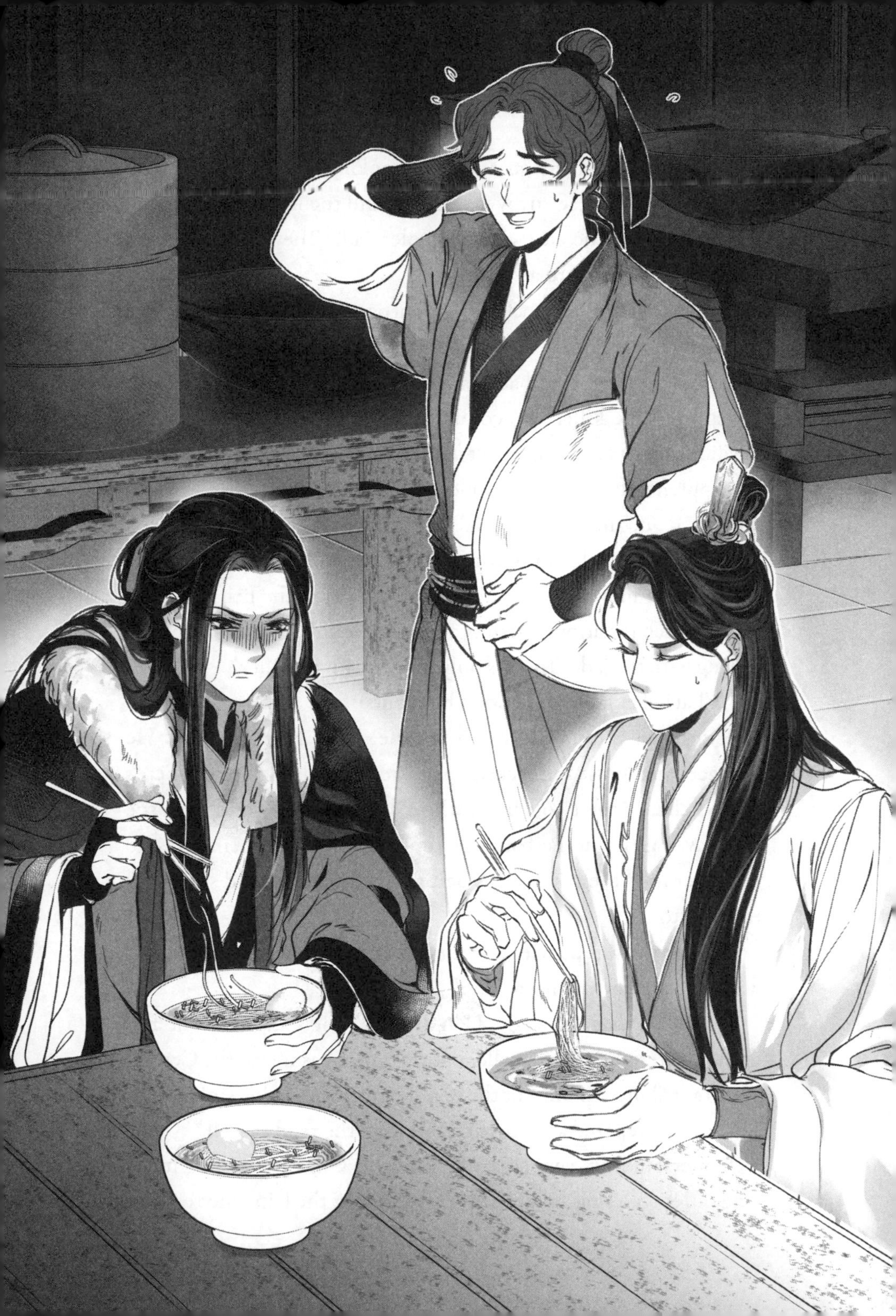

"Your brain is as inadequate as your cooking skills," Cui Buqu said icily. "The Khotanese envoy was killed, and the murderer has been lying low inside the city with the stolen jade. They must have had help from an insider to achieve this."

Cui Buqu was now mocking him outright—yet not only did Feng Xiao fail to defend him, he agreed. "If they have help from someone in the city, it will be even harder for us to find the real jade. Previously, I suspected the killer was colluding with Wen Liang of Linlang Pavilion and trying to misdirect us and lead us astray. But Wen Liang was apprehended, and the supposed Jade of Heaven Lake was still auctioned off. Then it looked like they might offer a fake to draw our attention and use that opportunity to transport the real stone out of the city. But after today's auction, the eagle riders the Jiejian Bureau left on watch in various quarters of the city found no trace of anyone leaving with the jade. There is only one other possibility."

"What?" Pei Jingzhe couldn't help but ask.

Cui Buqu couldn't stomach another bite of the noodles. He grimaced in disgust and picked up where Feng Xiao left off: "There's a good chance the two parties who killed the envoy and stole the jade have fallen out. Perhaps one took the stone for themselves, so the other used the fake jade as bait to lure them out and steal back the real stone."

Pei Jingzhe was puzzled. "If they already had the real stone, why would they come out for a fake?"

"I've heard that during the Han dynasty," said Cui Buqu, "no few of the Western Regions' smaller nations sent treasures to the Central Plains as tribute. To prevent the real treasure from being stolen, they sometimes prepared a decoy and sent it on the road as well."

Understanding dawned on Pei Jingzhe. Cui Buqu thought the king of Khotan might have sent two jades on the trip, one real and one fake. Though a counterfeit was a counterfeit, it must still be a priceless jade, or no one would mistake it for the real one. Perhaps only Yuchi Jinwu had known which jade was which. After killing him, the murderers had taken both jades, one for each party. But both would naturally come to suspect the one they held was fake, and that the real jade was in the hands of the other.

This hypothesis was convoluted, but after Pei Jingzhe thought it carefully through, he felt there was no way to refute it. In a few days, when the new envoy dispatched by the king of Khotan arrived, they'd confirm whether Feng Xiao and Cui Buqu were correct.

But first, they had to find the jade.

"So Daoist Master Cui is saying that since the suspected Jade of Heaven Lake appeared in Linlang Pavilion's auction, the other party would definitely send someone to check the outcome."

Cui Buqu nodded. Maybe Pei Jingzhe wasn't quite so stupid after all.

"Of those present tonight, at least one must be connected to the murderer. They might even be the murderer themselves." Pei Jingzhe thought back. "Six people came for the jade tonight. The assassin from the Thirteen Floors of Yunhai left at the start, so we can ignore him. Other than the monk, there was also the Göktürk expert Fo'er, and the Goguryeon Go Nyeong. Then the woman in yellow, and one more..."

Cui Buqu had only had a vague impression of the last person. All he recalled was that they'd been dressed in black. Half their body had been shrouded in shadow, so even their gender was unclear. By the time Fo'er attacked, that person had already vanished.

Feng Xiao took the six chopsticks they'd used and heaped them in a pile. Then he began to move them out of the group, one at a time. "Fo'er wanted to kill me. He didn't come for the jade. Though we don't yet know *why* he wanted to kill me, we can set him aside for now. Go Nyeong and Yuxiu both came for the jade, but they made no attempt to test it. So it's probably not them either. As for the woman, Bing Xian..."

Feng Xiao gazed at Cui Buqu.

Sure enough, Cui Buqu knew her background. "There's a sect in the jianghu called the Hehuan Sect, known for utilizing pair and parasitic cultivation[13] to improve their martial arts. Bing Xian is a disciple of the current sect leader, who's said to value her greatly. The leader's mantle may one day pass to her."

A subtle change came over Feng Xiao's expression on hearing the words *Hehuan Sect*. Slight as it was, it didn't escape Cui Buqu's notice. "Is there some connection between Deputy Chief Feng and the Hehuan Sect?"

"I'll tell you the truth. My younger cousin's daughter-in-law's aunt's uncle's aunt is also a disciple of the Hehuan Sect. So when I hear the name, my heart warms a little," Feng Xiao said with a smile.

Cui Buqu's face was blank. "So your younger cousin's daughter-in-law's aunt's uncle's aunt enjoys draining men to strengthen her martial arts?"

"Perhaps. They say women are wolves at thirty and tigers at forty. She may have taken to the Hehuan Sect like a fish to water."

Pei Jingzhe's mouth twitched, and he steered them back on topic. "So, Bing Xian and the other mysterious person are the likeliest suspects?"

"It's true the jade is useful to those from the jianghu. Bing Xian has sufficient motive. But if she really were one of the murderers,

---

13   双修, 采补. Pair cultivation, also translated as dual cultivation, a practice that uses sex to improve cultivation. Parasitic cultivation is the practice of draining yin or yang energy from a host to strengthen oneself.

she wouldn't need to reveal her presence and give her name just to check its authenticity. She could have simply hidden in the dark, then slipped away unnoticed."

After considering this, Pei Jingzhe thought it made sense. When he saw Feng Xiao pluck away the penultimate chopstick and leave only one, he knew Feng Xiao, too, agreed with Cui Buqu's analysis.

The likeliest suspect was the person in black, whose gender they'd been unable to discern.

Feng Xiao stood and said, "Before that person left, I secretly ordered a rider to tail them. When we get back to the manor, we can expect an update."

This card Feng Xiao had hidden up his sleeve was news to Pei Jingzhe as well. But he suddenly remembered a more important point. "Sir, the jade was shattered. If it was real, wouldn't that... wouldn't that mean the whole thing has been a wild goose chase and we don't have anything to present the emperor?"

Feng Xiao glanced at him but didn't speak.

Cui Buqu did. "Next time, I suggest you bring someone a little smarter, so you waste less of your breath."

Smiling, Feng Xiao said, "With someone as brilliant as me around, no matter how smart my subordinate, they'd be as a firefly's glow to the moon."

"If that's the case, what use does Feng-langjun have for me? You should let me go."

"No can do," said Feng Xiao. "Perhaps you're not as dazzling as the sun or the moon like I am, but when you stand beside me and bask in my light you're still a radiant star. A-Cui, if you're willing to join the Jiejian Bureau, the title of fourth chief is nothing. Even if you fell for me and asked me to warm your bed, my venerable self would not decline." He spoke tenderly, taking Cui Buqu's hand.

Cui Buqu was so repulsed the hairs on the back of his hand stood on end. He shook Feng Xiao's hand off as if it was something filthy and answered Pei Jingzhe: "Whether the broken jade was real or fake, the jade you recover must be the real one!"

Realization hit Pei Jingzhe. He couldn't help muttering to himself that a sly old fox would always be a sly old fox. Anyone who caught Feng Xiao's eye must of course have an aptitude far beyond that of the common man.

The three of them at last made their way back to Qiushan Manor. As expected, the eagle rider who'd tailed the person in black was waiting for them as they approached.

"My apologies, sir," he said. "Halfway through, the other party noticed me, and I was forced to give up the chase. But I saw where they were heading when they disappeared—it was the backyard of Lu Manor."

The surname Lu was a popular one in the city, but there was only one clan famous enough to own something that could be called a manor. It was of course the wealthy Lu household, the same rumored to be distantly related to the Lu family of Fanyang.

A stunning coincidence. That morning, Feng Xiao and Cui Buqu had met the daughter of this very Lu family and her cousin at the restaurant. Feng Xiao and Cui Buqu glanced at each other.

"A-Cui, her cousin," said Feng Xiao. "What was his name again?"

"Su Xing."

"Judging by their figure, the person in black looked more like Lady Lu. Let's go take a look."

It was still the middle of the night and freezing out, yet Feng Xiao moved to stand. He was really about to go search Lu Manor this instant.

"Feng-langjun," Cui Buqu said icily, "I just ate the half-cooked egg noodles your subordinate made. Now I have such a stomachache I'm about to vomit blood again. Could you please show me a bit of sympathy?"

His plea for mercy was spoken as if brandishing a thousand swords and halberds. Pei Jingzhe could practically see a whizzing arrow shooting straight at him. He took an involuntary step back, not wanting to be drawn onto the battlefield.

But Feng Xiao didn't take Cui Buqu seriously in the least. "As if you're that delicate. You withstood incense of helplessness. What are a few egg noodles? Jingzhe, go take a look in the kitchen. Fetch some snacks; Daoist Master Cui can pad his stomach with those. Then we'll head to the Lu residence."

Still cold, Cui Buqu said, "I'm quite serious."

But Feng Xiao didn't believe a word. "Go ahead and vomit then; let's see."

To his great surprise, Cui Buqu really did open his mouth and retch.

They were standing close together; Feng Xiao couldn't avoid it. But as the reek assaulted him, he realized Cui Buqu hadn't vomited blood—he'd brought up the bowl of egg noodles he'd eaten earlier.

To the fastidious Deputy Chief Feng, this was far more intolerable than any blood. His face immediately drained of color.

24

THE MANOR WAS NONDESCRIPT and of no interest to anyone, one among many like it in the city. Its gates were shut year-round, and only a single elderly woman, hard of hearing, occasionally came and went for food and necessities.

When the neighbors asked, they learned the owner of the manor was gravely ill and had been unable to go out for many years. Of course they were all sympathetic, but they couldn't help worrying the disease was contagious. Thus people gradually stopped making inquiries, and the owner of the manor obtained peace and tranquility free from disturbance.

Now the night was late, and silence was all around. Every household had blown out their candles and gone quietly to bed, and the manor in their midst was quietest of all. Not a whisper could be heard. Around the corner, Qiao Xian and Zhangsun Bodhi exchanged glances.

Zhangsun's expression said, *Are you sure this is the place?*

Qiao Xian had no patience for his questions. She leapt onto the tiled roof in a single bound.

Zhangsun shook his head and followed a step behind.

They both landed soundlessly on the roof. Qiao Xian bent to remove a tile, but Zhangsun Bodhi stayed her hand. He pointed to the luminous moon in the sky, and Qiao Xian drew back.

Tonight the moon was bright, the stars sparse. With no candles lit in the manor, the interior would be black as pitch. If a trickle of moonlight seeped down from overhead, an ordinary person mightn't notice, but a martial artist certainly would.

Qiao Xian couldn't sense anyone inside the room—but it was better to be cautious.

Zhangsun Bodhi looked around, then jumped off the roof and circled the building. After a few seconds, he leapt back up. Qiao Xian was confounded as she watched him crouch and spring outward. He hooked his feet around the eaves and hung upside down, facing the house, his movements silent.

Qiao Xian too hopped down to look. She found a broken window and a pillar beside it that blocked Zhangsun from sight while allowing him a clear view of the interior. She hid beneath the tree and threw him a hand signal. *Is someone there?*

After a moment's observation, Zhangsun gave her an unexpected answer: *Yes.*

Qiao Xian was stunned. There was merely a wall between them, yet they hadn't detected this person's presence at all. Whoever it was must be a master of internal martial arts and breath control. This wouldn't be easy. Had the other party already noticed their presence and made their preparations?

Just then, a noise came from behind the house. It was faint, but not so faint as to escape Qiao Xian and Zhangsun's ears.

Nor had it escaped the ears of the person inside.

"You're already here. Why keep sneaking around?" The woman in the room—presumably Miao-niangzi—snorted. Though she didn't conceal her anger, her voice had a charming lilt that drove one to imagine an equally charming face.

Qiao Xian and Zhangsun looked at each other, then simultaneously hid themselves in the darkness. Better to let the exposed third person take the blame.

"Come out!" The woman's tone was frigid as an arrow of ice, and she let out another delicate *hmph*.

A quiet noise came from behind the house, and a black shadow leapt out to smash through the broken window and attack the woman inside.

Qiao Xian's ears pricked up. They were at a distance, but she could vaguely tell that the woman in the room wielded something like a whip. The intruder swung a sword, the blade ringing in the air, overflowing with murderous intent. Each move was made to kill. The woman blocked each blow, one by one, but struggled to gain the upper hand. Such a stalemate couldn't last. Once the woman's patience was worn thin and her strength exhausted, the intruder would slay her with a single strike.

Miao-niangzi was an important lead in the case; Qiao Xian and Zhangsun couldn't let her die. They hesitated no longer and charged into the house.

The woman was embroiled in a life-and-death struggle with a masked figure in black. Qiao Xian saw at once that the weapon she'd heard from outside wasn't a whip, but the woman's own belt. The white belt was made of some unknown material, flexible yet unyielding—even sword qi was unable to cut it. The figure in black seemed to specialize in killing blows; each move left them wide open as they focused only on taking her life. If not for her advantage in weaponry, she'd never have held on this long.

When Qiao Xian and Zhangsun rushed in, the woman's expression changed. She thought two more enemies had appeared, and her focus slipped. Immediately, the black-clad person's sword stabbed toward her forehead—Qiao Xian and Zhangsun sprang into action. Zhangsun grabbed a prayer bead and flicked it toward the person in black, while Qiao Xian drew her sword and hacked down toward their wrist.

To their shock, the intruder disregarded the danger completely and pressed forward, determined to slaughter Miao-niangzi.

At the last moment, Miao-niangzi leaned back and raised herself onto her toes, contorting into an almost impossible position as she spun away. She avoided a fatal strike by half an inch, and the black-clad person's sword skimmed past her temple. Where the sword qi brushed her, dark hairs drifted down. Miao-niangzi felt a pain in her scalp and reached up to touch it. Fear filled her face.

The slash had sliced a lock of hair from her temple, and her scalp was now cut and bleeding. If she'd taken the two newcomers for helpers and not fought with all she had, her body would be cooling.

The black-clad person's attack had failed, and now there were two more obstacles in their way. Their eyes shone with anger behind their mask, and every strike grew fiercer. Zhangsun shot bead after bead, each aimed perfectly through the gaps in the opponent's sword qi so that they were unable to advance or retreat—much less approach Miao-niangzi.

Qiao Xian, fearing Miao-niangzi might seize the chance to escape, left Zhangsun to deal with the person in black. She grabbed for Miao-niangzi, intending to capture her.

Miao-niangzi barked something in a harsh tone, but Qiao Xian couldn't understand her and didn't stop. Surprise came over Miao-niangzi's face, and she immediately switched to Chinese. "Who are you?!"

"Someone who can protect you," said Qiao Xian. "If you want to live, come with us!"

Miao-niangzi scoffed. "There are many people who wish me dead, but they haven't succeeded yet!"

Across the room, Zhangsun had no desire to waste time with this enemy. He reached into his clothes and produced a short wooden rod. With a flick of his wrist, the inch-long rod extended into a two-foot baton, which he thrust toward the black-clad person's chest. They instinctively raised their sword to parry, but Zhangsun's thrust had profound internal energy behind it; its momentum was unstoppable. Not only did the sword fail to block his strike, it snapped in two. The rod slammed heavily into flesh.

Zhangsun Bodhi had thought to capture this person alive to find out who was so intent on taking Miao-niangzi's life. But when the masked intruder saw they'd failed in their mission, they bit down on the poison capsule in their mouth before Zhangsun could stop them and died on the spot.

"You saw that person's skills," said Qiao Xian to Miao-niangzi. "The Thirteen Floors of Yunhai have many such experts. Even if this one is dead, a second will follow. We can guarantee you your life."

Miao-niangzi's lovely eyes flashed. "Who are you? And why should I believe you?"

"Because of this." Qiao Xian fished a token from her sleeve. Miao-niangzi looked closely and saw two words carved upon it: *Kaihuang Zuoyue*. Though the token was wood, it gleamed like gold. It was clear at a glance that it was a valuable object. "We are members of the Zuoyue Bureau working under the emperor of Great Sui. We hold the same authority as the Six Ministries. However great the danger you're in, the Zuoyue Bureau can ensure your safety."

Miao-niangzi eyed the token with suspicion. "I heard the emperor ordered the Jiejian Bureau to investigate this case. I've never heard of any Zuoyue Bureau."

"The Jiejian Bureau was established by the emperor, and the Zuoyue Bureau by the empress. The court has its Two Saints who rule side by side. Surely you've heard this?"

Watching Qiao Xian patiently try to convince her, Miao-niangzi could see she wasn't out for blood. She relaxed and wound her hair around her finger, then said with a smile, "I'm afraid the one I've offended is a person even you can't afford to provoke."

"The chief of the Zuoyue Bureau wields the same authority as the Minister of Justice, and he's in Liugong City as we speak. If you cooperate and help us locate the Jade of Heaven Lake, even if you killed the Khotanese envoy, we can still ensure you live a life free from threat and escape to whatever distant place you wish. Surely it's better to choose to trust us than to remain hunted and on the run with no guarantee you'll live to see the next day."

Miao-niangzi blinked. The injury on her scalp had stopped bleeding, though the wound was ugly. Even so, her incredible beauty made it easy to overlook such a flaw.

"In that case, you already know my relationship to Yuchi?"

Yuchi? Yuchi Jinwu—the dead Khotanese envoy? Qiao Xian and Zhangsun Bodhi exchanged a glance. Their minds went quickly to work, though their expressions remained unchanged. "That's right," Qiao Xian said, "we've already looked into your relationship."

"All right, then I'll tell you this: the one who murdered the envoy and the one who took the jade are the same person. He's still in the city."

"What's his name, and where is he now?" Qiao Xian pressed.

"His name is—"

25

As Miao-niangzi parted her lips to speak, Qiao Xian and Zhangsun unconsciously moved closer. Miao-niangzi suddenly raised her sleeves and shot two darts, their tips glinting a blackish blue: poisoned.

Shocked, both dodged. Zhangsun flicked a prayer bead with extraordinary swiftness, intent on stopping Miao-niangzi. But she was faster still—her figure flickered and vanished, reappearing several feet away in a blink.

"Stop her!" Qiao Xian cried.

Zhangsun Bodhi gathered his qi and rushed after Miao-niangzi. His palm flew out with almost his full strength behind it. Miao-niangzi's back was to him as she fled, leaving her wide open. Yet when the wind from Zhangsun's palm strike hit her, she didn't crumple; she merely faltered slightly and sped on. Even if he gathered more qi and gave chase, it was too late; he'd lost his chance. Within seconds, Miao-niangzi had vanished.

Qiao Xian rushed over. "What was that?!"

Everything had happened in an instant. Neither had expected their cooked duck to get up and fly away.

"She hid her true strength earlier," Zhangsun rasped. He'd realized it the instant Miao-niangzi withstood his attack with only a stumble.

"Impossible!" Qiao Xian refuted it on reflex. "If that was the case, why couldn't she defeat the assassin?"

"Two reasons: First, she knew we were here and wished to see which side we were on. When she saw we came to save her, she grew more secure. Second, the fact that we tried to negotiate with her proved we weren't the type to kill indiscriminately, which meant she had more room to catch us off guard."

It was rare for Zhangsun to talk so much. Qiao Xian would have preferred him to remain silent—or at least not just stand there and watch an important lead run off. Now that Miao-niangzi had slipped their grasp, finding her again would be terribly difficult.

"Now all we can do is ask the lord chief for instructions," said Qiao Xian.

Zhangsun said nothing, because he had no better ideas. After a moment, he mused, "She took my palm strike. Even if she managed to escape, she must be seriously injured."

"If she wishes to disguise herself to sneak out of the city, she won't find it easy," Qiao Xian said thoughtfully. "But mobilizing the city guard and constables to search for her would reveal our identities and alert the Jiejian Bureau, and that would affect the lord chief's plans."

"It wouldn't," said Zhangsun Bodhi.

Qiao Xian frowned. "Why not?"

"I heard the strongest martial expert under Ishbara Khagan, Fo'er, is in the city as well. He must be after the lord chief."

They couldn't know that earlier that night, this very man had fought Feng Xiao.

Qiao Xian started. "Then we must protect the lord chief!"

"No need. The lord chief is under the protection of the Jiejian Bureau. But if Fo'er has arrived, Apa Khagan's men must be here as well. Our official duties come first. We no longer have time to make trouble for the Jiejian Bureau."

Qiao Xian pondered this. "So you're saying..."

The Jiejian Bureau and the Zuoyue Bureau had always performed their respective duties independently, and their presence in Liugong City was no exception. Of course Cui Buqu hadn't brought the members of Zuoyue Bureau here for the sole purpose of hindering the Jiejian Bureau—they had their own important matters to attend to. However, after hearing of the murder of the Khotanese envoy and the theft of the jade, Cui Buqu had elected to obstruct Feng Xiao's investigation while they waited. If the Zuoyue Bureau were to find the jade first, they'd earn another merit in the eyes of the emperor.

But with the appearance of Fo'er, the situation had changed; the case of the jade must be set aside. Miao-niangzi had fled, but her flight was a lead in itself. Rather than let the Jiejian Bureau run around like headless chickens, Cui Buqu would certainly choose to negotiate and offer Feng Xiao some limited cooperation.

What Zhangsun Bodhi was saying was that, thanks to Cui Buqu's incredible shrewdness, the Zuoyue Bureau would have something to show for their presence here either way.

Qiao Xian nodded. "Then I'll have someone send word to the lord chief."

Zhangsun Bodhi raised his head in time to see a dark wisp of cloud drift over and swallow the luminous moon. The sky above them darkened.

Each understood the other. They said no more but parted ways and headed in separate directions.

Few people in the world were capable of harming Feng Xiao. Cui Buqu was an ordinary man who knew no martial arts and lacked the strength to truss a chicken, yet he'd achieved this tremendous feat. Pei Jingzhe's eyes had been greatly opened.

Feng Xiao could ignore Cui Buqu's hunger, but he couldn't run an investigation covered in filth. In the end, Pei Jingzhe headed to Lu Manor first to investigate, while Feng Xiao took Cui Buqu back to Qiushan Manor for a change of clothes.

Using every skill at his disposal, Feng Xiao rushed back to the manor like the wind. He'd probably expended less effort fighting Fo'er earlier. All the night patrolman saw was a black shadow hurtling toward him. Before he could get a clear look, a blistering gale had blown past his cheek and swept into the distance, scaring the living daylights out of him. He wondered if all his night walks had finally led to a ghostly encounter.

Cui Buqu wasn't much better off. He'd just been taken hostage by the monk Yuxiu, which had left one shoulder numb, and now he was being dragged along by his other arm at a sprint. Both his shoulders had lost almost all feeling. Despite his discomfort, Cui Buqu felt Feng Xiao's reaction had been worth it.

Feng Xiao's voice drifted over, a tight smile audible in his voice. "Daoist Master Cui looks quite pleased with himself."

Cui Buqu suppressed the slight curve of his lips and said, "I'm just happy for Deputy Chief Feng. You've obtained new clues in the case, so perhaps the veil will soon fall away and reveal the truth."

Feng Xiao snorted faintly. He didn't deign to reply, but Cui Buqu sensed multiple meanings contained within that snort.

First: *Once I change, I'll get you for this.*

Second: *You've got a lot of nerve, still jumping about while you're at my mercy. Don't you have anything better to do?*

Third: *I'm going to make you beg for death and cry for your mother. I'll make you regret you were ever born.*

Cui Buqu raised his eyebrows, entirely unafraid. *So what?*

When they arrived at Qiushan Manor, Feng Xiao tossed him aside without a word and rushed to bathe and change.

Cui Buqu was no martial artist. He was hauling around an ailing body and couldn't run even if he wanted to. Besides, those Jiejian Bureau cavalry, the eagle riders, were still about, so Feng Xiao wasn't worried he might overestimate himself and make a break for it. In any case, Cui Buqu would never run—he returned to his room, washed up, and asked the maid for some snacks.

This late at night, the stoves were no longer lit; it would be some time before they could cook anything. But there were pre-prepared snacks, and the maid worked fast. Soon enough, she brought a tray, along with some information.

"About the lead you gave them—Qiao-niangzi's group pursued the target but lost her. She wants to know what they should do next."

The maid was called Tang Li. The steward had given this name to her when Qiushan Manor employed her. Previously, she'd been known as Tao-niang, meaning *peach*. It was an unremarkable name that suited her dull appearance—there was nothing memorable about her.

All the way back when Feng Xiao had received orders to escort the Khotanese envoy to the capital, Cui Buqu had guessed Magistrate Zhao would open his private manor to host Feng Xiao. And with that, Tang Li smoothly became a woman whose poor family had sold her into the manor.

She hadn't been assigned to Cui Buqu at first. But the maid attending him had come down with a sudden stomach bug yesterday and was now bedridden with vomiting and diarrhea. The work couldn't wait, so the steward had reassigned the ever-dutiful and obedient Tang Li.

Whether she was truly dutiful and obedient or only allowing the steward to believe so no longer mattered.

Feng Xiao and Pei Jingzhe were absorbed in their investigation and paid little attention to trivial details like the reassignment of a household maid. Thus Tang Li brought Cui Buqu all the information Qiao Xian and Zhangsun Bodhi had obtained in the past two days with no one the wiser.

Cui Buqu looked contemplative. The cold moonlight illuminated his profile and lent it a hint of translucency.

Tang Li snatched the briefest look before dropping her head. The esteemed guest in residence at the manor possessed a peerless beauty and elegance. Yet compared to Feng Xiao's bright and dazzling looks, Tang Li found Lord Chief Cui Buqu more pleasing to the eye.

It was just that his complexion was rather awful.

"Was your lordship injured? Should this subordinate bring some medicine?" Tang Li asked.

"Do you know anything of massage?" asked Cui Buqu. "Both my shoulders are sore."

"This subordinate will try," she said, and stepped behind Cui Buqu. When she attempted to press his acupoints, she heard him hiss softly. "Your lordship probably pulled some muscles, but your bones are unharmed. The massage will hurt a little."

"Do what you need to do. I've always been good at enduring pain," Cui Buqu's words were self-mocking, but his tone was relaxed.

Tang Li stopped hesitating and kneaded Cui Buqu's shoulders as she continued her report. When she mentioned that Miao-niangzi had said something strange to Qiao Xian, then repeated herself in Chinese when Qiao Xian and Zhangsun couldn't understand her, Cui Buqu stopped her. "What exactly did the target say? Did she tell you?"

"She did." Tang Li nodded. Anyone who was admitted to the Zuoyue Bureau was no ordinary person, and those assigned here even less so. Tang Li obediently parroted Miao-niangzi's words. Though they'd been passed to her via Qiao Xian, she repeated them with near-perfect accuracy.

Cui Buqu sat up, completely ignoring the pain from Tang Li accidentally using too much strength in her surprise.

"Lord Chief?"

"It's Goguryeon. Qin Miaoyu is from Goguryeo, and the Jade of Heaven Lake is certainly on her person."

How are you so sure? Tang Li was befuddled, but she didn't press for answers. Cui Buqu's theories were always grounded in reason, and besides, it wasn't her place to ask.

Sure enough, Cui Buqu said no more.

In the meantime, Feng Xiao had finished bathing and dressing, and now sent someone to hurry Cui Buqu along. Cui Buqu was satisfied—he'd eaten the snacks and his shoulders had loosened up nicely. He rose and went to Feng Xiao without further delay.

The change of clothes had not improved Feng Xiao's mood.

When Cui Buqu arrived, he found Feng Xiao holding a letter and a token. The letter was a scant few lines saying Pei Jingzhe had been kidnapped and inviting Feng Xiao to visit Huyang Forest to ransom him. The token was the one Pei Jingzhe always carried with him, belonging to the Jiejian Bureau. Separated from its owner, it proved the letter was no empty threat.

As the saying went, "Xiang Zhuang's sword dance is for the Duke of Pei."[14] The true target of this maneuver was obvious—they weren't after Pei Jingzhe at all, but Feng Xiao. And presumably, the Jade of Heaven Lake.

"Oh for the love of—he never accomplishes anything, yet he can always make things worse!" Feng Xiao cursed.

"Fo'er?" Cui Buqu speculated.

"Perhaps." Feng Xiao rubbed his fingers together, and the letter crumbled to powder.

"You're going?"

"What else can I do?"

Cui Buqu was surprised. "Deputy Chief Feng doesn't seem like a man who values sentiment and righteousness. Yet he cares so deeply for the life of a subordinate!"

"His father saved me once."

Cui Buqu shook his head. "That still doesn't seem like you."

"Then in your opinion, what should I do?"

"Send them a reply: *kill him if you wish*."

---

14   A saying that originates in the Hongmen Banquet incident of 206 BC, in which future Han emperor Liu Bang, the Duke of Pei, escaped an attempted murder by his rival, Xiang Yu, during a sword dance at a feast held in Liu Bang's honor.

26

NEEDLESS TO SAY, Feng Xiao would send no such response. Pei Jingzhe was incompetent, but he was still a member of the Jiejian Bureau—it wasn't for outsiders to execute him. Feng Xiao sent his cavalry to surround Lu Manor with orders to monitor the situation and allow no one out. Then he took Cui Buqu to the outskirts of Huyang Forest.

Cui Buqu was baffled. "Why are you taking *me* to save Pei Jingzhe?"

"They have a hostage. They'll be secure, while I'll be panicking with no idea what to do." Feng Xiao's tone was leisurely. "But if the resourceful Daoist Master Cui is with me, perhaps he can come up with a few ideas."

Cui Buqu took in his serene countenance. There was nothing there that could be described as panic. As expected, Feng Xiao's next sentence was, "If we meet with any danger, I'll feel so much more at ease with you there."

"So." Cui Buqu coolly exposed him: "You wish to use me as a meat shield."

"How clever you are," said Feng Xiao.

His steps were swift as the wind—such was his skill in qinggong that he flowed like drifting clouds or running water. So that Cui Buqu didn't slow him down, Feng Xiao had looped an arm securely around his waist as he sped forward, carrying him along. Cui Buqu's feet didn't even touch the ground; with no effort from him, they arrived at their destination.

The moon emerged from behind the dark clouds, bathing the world in light once more. Huyang Forest was cloaked in moonlight, its swaying branches limned in a hazy silver glow that gave it a tranquility not present during the day.

But any sense of peace was an illusion. Perhaps Cui Buqu hadn't noticed, but Feng Xiao immediately sensed something unusual about the place. He slowed his steps. "It was you who invited me here. Why hide?"

The grass on the ground was sparse, tussocks scattered across the sandy soil. Cui Buqu heard no movement—but when he looked, a figure had appeared beneath a nearby tree.

The Goguryeon expert, Go Nyeong.

Though Go Nyeong carried the Goguryeon royal surname and ranked as a first-class martial artist even in the Central Plains, his clothes were simple to the point of shabbiness. He'd traveled thousands of miles in the same gray robe, growing ever dustier and more travel-worn, yet he cared little for such things. From the moment he appeared, his eyes were fixed unswervingly on Feng Xiao. He didn't so much as glance at Cui Buqu beside him.

Obviously this wasn't because Feng Xiao's beauty had captivated him. He now regarded Feng Xiao as a sworn and lifelong enemy, and was determined to defeat him.

"Where is my subordinate?" asked Feng Xiao.

Go Nyeong's reply was succinct. "Not here."

His Chinese was halting and his tone was brusque, harsher than the cold night wind.

Feng Xiao chuckled. "I knew Pei Jingzhe wouldn't be so foolish. Even if you managed to take his token, he wouldn't allow himself to be captured. So tell me, who are your accomplices? Does the number one martial artist of Goguryeo make a habit of slinking around like a rat? It seems Goguryeons only know how to scurry about in the dark!"

Anger shone on Go Nyeong's face. His hand went to his sword, but before he could draw it a voice drifted over.

"He's trying to provoke you. Pay him no mind."

Another man stepped out from behind a stone. Until that moment, he'd kept his breathing so low and remained so still even Feng Xiao had failed to notice him. Someone that skilled, who also happened to be in Liugong City and wanted Feng Xiao dead? It could be no one else.

"If it's not the number one Göktürk martial artist! Did you lose something here? Shall I help you search?" Feng Xiao's eyes widened in mock surprise.

"You were distracted during our fight tonight. I seek a rematch," said Fo'er.

"This is the first time I've heard someone describe an ambush in such a novel and refined way," said Cui Buqu. "You're not from the Central Plains, so perhaps you don't know these more apt words: brash, brazen, underhanded, unscrupulous, debased, shameless, treacherous, and conniving. Does that about cover it?"

His tone was cool, yet he listed them all in a single breath, growing increasingly sarcastic. Judging from the way Fo'er and Go Nyeong's faces flashed alternately green and white, they certainly understood at least some of it.

"Never have I found you as adorable and amiable as I do now, Ququ," chirped Feng Xiao happily.

"I beg Feng-langjun not to read anything into it. Just stick to calling me Daoist Master Cui, or I'll break out in hives."

"These Central Plainsmen!" Go Nyeong snarled, interrupting them. "A quick tongue and nothing more!" He drew his sword, sweeping toward Feng Xiao.

The sword glare came cold and swift like a spear of light piercing the moon, faster than when he'd moved to take Pei Jingzhe hostage earlier. At the same time, Fo'er attacked from the other side, and the two closed in on Feng Xiao from the left and right. They were clearly determined to kill him tonight.

Yet Feng Xiao showed no sign of fear. He remained motionless until both men were within striking distance. Then, with a tap of his toes, he leapt from the ground to avoid their joint attack.

He gathered up his zither and tossed it forward; in the same moment, he reversed direction, diving toward the ground, his palm strike accompanied by the zither's notes as they bombarded his adversaries. Fo'er and Go Nyeong had him surrounded, yet he handled them with ease and lost not an inch of ground.

Though Cui Buqu was hardly on good terms with Feng Xiao, they were in the same boat. If Feng Xiao lost here, no good fate awaited Cui Buqu.

Fo'er and Go Nyeong were a formidable combination, but Feng Xiao was a force to be reckoned with as well. For a time, the three seemed evenly matched. If Feng Xiao seized the momentum, he might even win. After observing this, Cui Buqu relaxed and edged toward a nearby boulder, ready to sit and watch the fight.

Suddenly the hair on the back of his neck stood on end as if someone had blown lightly on his nape.

There was no one there—it was an instinctive reaction to danger. Cui Buqu knew no martial arts, but over his many years of illness, his body had absorbed all sorts of drugs. As a result, his five senses were greatly sharpened. The instant he felt that coolness, he flung himself to the ground. At the same moment, he heard the faint sound of something whistling over his head. Several long needles appeared just in front of him, sticking neatly out from the dirt.

No doubt poisoned.

Cui Buqu realized he'd flung himself a bit too vigorously. His knees were sore, and he lacked the strength to get up and run. But his attackers were right behind him, so he was forced to roll to the side. His pose was wretched, but it might save his life.

As he tumbled in the dirt, he saw two black-clad men sweep toward him, one behind the other, cold swords glinting. He'd survived their first attempt, but avoiding the second would be impossible.

Truly, disaster followed that flamboyant oleander spirit!

For all his plots and calculations, Cui Buqu never imagined he'd die not at the hands of his foes, nor even from illness, but instead thanks to Feng Xiao dragging him into this business. Death was close at hand; he had no time to curse, but in his racing mind, he'd already paid his respects to dozens of generations of Feng Xiao's ancestors, right through the dynasties of Xia, Shang, Zhou, and the Three Sovereigns and Five Emperors.[15]

On the outside, he simply closed his eyes and accepted his fate.

Perhaps Cui Buqu's frenzied cursing had some effect—those two swords never landed, and no unexpected agony tore through his body. He instead heard the sounds of fighting. He opened his eyes to find Feng Xiao had leapt over in time to block the killing blows of the assassins.

---

15   三皇五帝. *Prehistoric mythological deities and sages said to have ruled China between the creation of the world and the Xia dynasty. Credited with many critical cultural developments, such as writing, farming, medicine, fire, architecture, and silk.*

With this, the number of his enemies increased from two to four.

Feng Xiao didn't even spare a second to mock Cui Buqu. It was clear the fight was beginning to tax him.

The moment he was out of danger, Cui Buqu cried, "Those two are assassins from the Thirteen Floors of Yunhai. They carry poisoned needles!"

A representative of the Thirteen Floors of Yunhai had appeared earlier that night. Bing Xian, the woman in yellow, had exposed their identity; this, combined with a lack of opportunity, meant they'd simply turned and left. Neither Cui Buqu nor Feng Xiao had expected them to join forces with Fo'er and Go Nyeong.

"No one told me the Thirteen Floors of Yunhai now carries out robberies as well as assassinations!"

The two in black didn't answer. They attacked Feng Xiao without reserve, and without even looking at Cui Buqu, who'd barely managed to escape with his life. It was plain their target had been Feng Xiao from the start.

Here in the uplands late at night, the wind rose and sandstorms spun up out of nothing. The fight drifted from east to west, until the combatants found themselves at the edge of the plateau. It was no vast abyss below, but the cliff was steep and treacherous—any ordinary person who fell here would lose their life.

Sandy wind blew grit into Cui Buqu's mouth and nose. He yearned to cough but swallowed it down. There was no room for mistakes when masters exchanged blows. If Feng Xiao should lose due to a tiny distraction, Cui Buqu would also meet a dreadful fate.

He moved slowly, retreating into a blind spot behind the towering boulders where he might go unnoticed. Between the howling sandstorm and the combined assault on Feng Xiao, no one realized he'd disappeared.

From the moment the two members of the Thirteen Floors of Yunhai had joined the fight, the balance had begun to tip. In the face of four martial experts attacking at once, even if Feng Xiao were first in the world, he would find it difficult to escape unharmed. On top of that, two of the attackers were from outside the Central Plains, while two others were assassins. None were beholden to martial codes of morality and chivalry, and they had no scruples about fighting many-on-one or using underhanded tactics. They'd already launched several volleys of hidden weapons: Feng Xiao had been hit twice, once in the shoulder and once in the abdomen. His attacks began to slow.

Fo'er saw his opportunity and took it—he flung out a palm and knocked Feng Xiao off the cliff, while Go Nyeong kicked his zither in the opposite direction.

Feng Xiao fell from the edge and disappeared from sight. The assassins from the Thirteen Floors of Yunhai were determined to finish the job; they dove down after him. The sand swirled wildly, mixing with the rain and snow. Even the best of fighters would find it hard to withstand. Go Nyeong and Fo'er weren't acquainted; they'd only allied to take down Feng Xiao. Now their foe had fallen, and they were on guard once more. Unlike the assassins, they weren't desperate enough to press on in such terrible weather. They turned and left, one to the east and one to the west, their figures quickly vanishing into the wind and snow.

Cui Buqu waited a long interval, until he deemed both were sufficiently far away. Then he slowly inched toward the edge of the plateau and peered down.

No matter how keen his eyesight, there was a limit to what he could see in the dark of the night. Even if Feng Xiao had survived the fall, a single stab from those assassins would put him in his grave.

Cui Buqu clicked his tongue. He did feel it was rather a shame for such an unparalleled beauty to be reduced to bone. At the same time, he rejoiced: Feng Xiao's death meant the Jiejian Bureau's glory was certain to wane, and that would make room for the Zuoyue Bureau to shine brighter.

As he considered this, a faint voice reached his ears.

"Pull me up."

Cui Buqu looked around for the source of the sound, then reached over the edge and groped at the side of the cliff. After fumbling a moment, he touched a hand.

The hand clutched his fiercely, and Cui Buqu was almost dragged over the edge. He barely managed to stop his downward slide.

"Pull—me—up!"

Feng Xiao's voice was weak. Its softness sounded like more than fear of being overheard; he must have suffered serious injury.

"How lucky you are!" Cui Buqu couldn't help but sigh.

Feng Xiao snorted. "Someone like me, unmatched in both beauty and charm, is naturally afforded the protection of heaven. How could those thugs do me serious harm?"

"But now you need me to save you."

"Once we're back, I'll give you your freedom," said Feng Xiao. "You may come and go as you please."

Cui Buqu thought, *If I wanted to go, there's already nothing you can do to stop me.* "That's worthless. Promise me something and I'll pull you up."

"Anything," Feng Xiao said impatiently. "Just pull me up first!" He kept his voice low, lest the assassins from the Thirteen Floors of Yunhai overhear.

"Call me 'Daddy' three times and I'll do it," said Cui Buqu.

Feng Xiao was speechless.

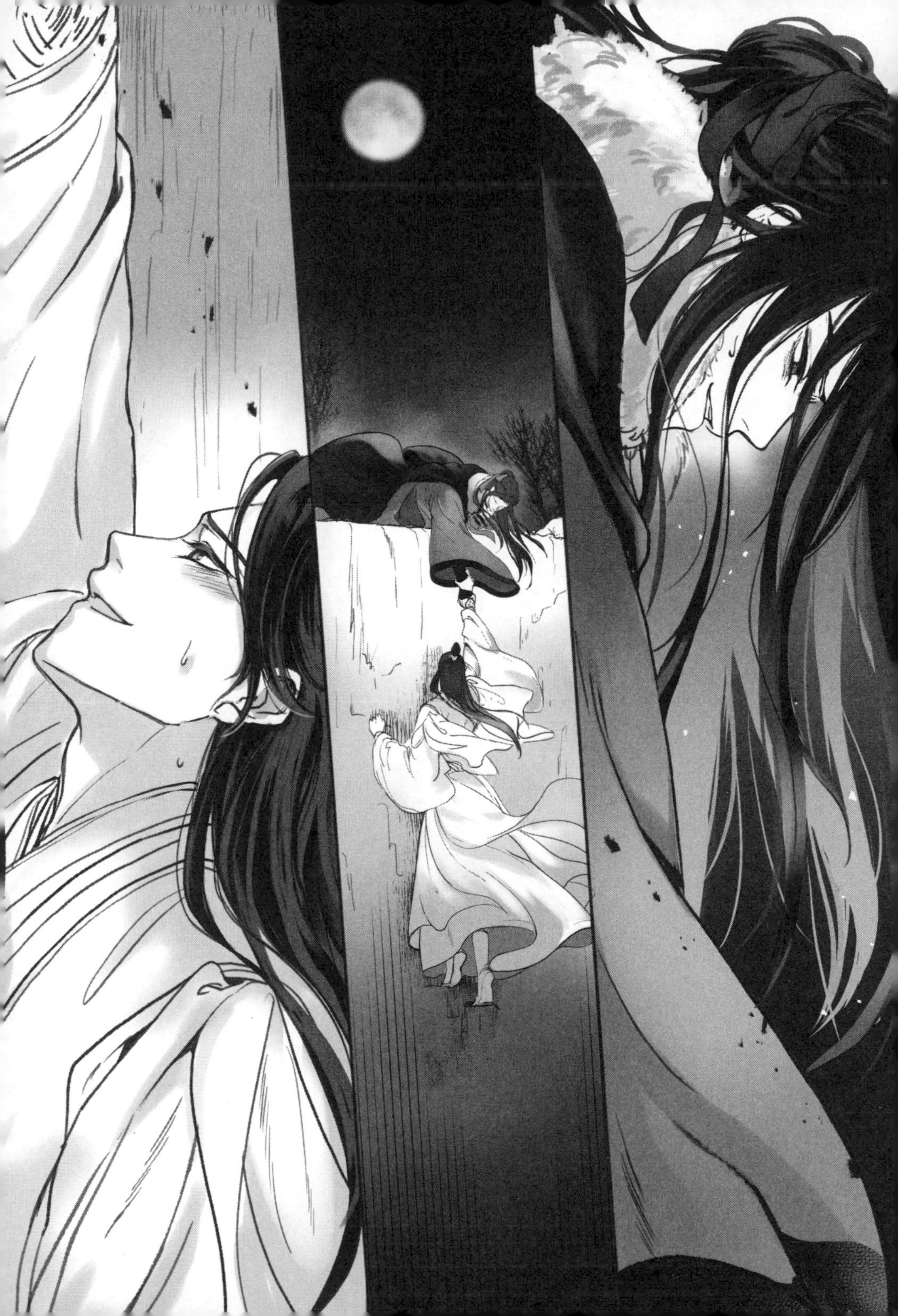

27

ONE'S DIGNITY or one's life—which was more important? Perhaps some would cling to their dignity even in the face of hellish torture, but that was certainly not Feng Xiao's style. He chose the second option without hesitation.

"Daddy..." he said. His voice was feeble, carried away by the wind and snow. It sounded more like a moan.

"I can't hear you."

"Pull me up. I don't have the strength."

Cui Buqu sneered. "You can say all that when you have no strength, yet you can't manage a single 'Daddy?'"

Thanks to Tang Li's earlier shoulder massage, Cui Buqu had regained some function in both arms. Feng Xiao must also have found some foothold among the rocks; otherwise, after Cui Buqu had almost lost his arm earlier that night, there was no way he'd have been able to support Feng Xiao's weight.

"Daddy! Daddy..."

The first *daddy* was inflected upward, the second down. These lilting syllables weren't from the strain of yelling over the wail of the blizzard, but the product of Feng Xiao's boundless chagrin. If a delicate woman had cried out like that, it might have been pitiful. But Feng Xiao calling out in falsetto only made Cui Buqu break out in gooseflesh, and he almost lost his grip and dropped him.

At that moment, Feng Xiao suddenly plummeted downward, dragging Cui Buqu with him. The gale tore past, and sand blinded his eyes. He'd fallen without even time to grab at the stones on the cliff's edge.

There were many situations in this world that no amount of wisdom could anticipate, and this was one of them. Cui Buqu had never expected Feng Xiao would really fall. Feng Xiao had his martial arts, so the fall wouldn't necessarily kill him. But at this height it would undoubtedly be fatal for an ordinary man like Cui Buqu. The instant he was yanked down, Cui Buqu resigned himself to death.

He quickly realized, however, that Feng Xiao wasn't actually plummeting. After a quick drop, he'd found his footing and pulled Cui Buqu into a recess in the rocks—a narrow cave.

They stared blankly at each other across the darkness, panting harshly. Outside, the blizzard screamed, and the moon hid behind the clouds; no trace of light filtered into their hideout.

Over the sound of the wind, Cui Buqu gasped, "You—"

A hand was clapped over his mouth, and Feng Xiao pressed against him, pinning him to the cave wall so he could no longer move. The cave was halfway down the steep side of the plateau, likely carved out by years of wind erosion. There was little space, and it grew only more cramped with two people squeezed together inside.

Cui Buqu was fairly confident Feng Xiao wasn't doing this just to mess with him; he remained motionless and didn't struggle. Sure enough, there was a lull in the wind and snow, and a black shadow swept past outside. Cui Buqu's eyes were sharp. He recognized the shadow as one of the assassins who'd jumped down to find Feng Xiao.

In Feng Xiao's current condition, there was no question of him fighting one against two. If he and Cui Buqu had remained on the cliff's edge, they'd have doubtless been discovered.

The figure suddenly stopped and hooked their feet around the stones jutting out over the crevice, hanging upside down to peer inside. The interior was narrow and black as pitch; it was impossible to make out anything within. Feng Xiao didn't need to speak. Cui Buqu was already holding his breath, perfectly focused. The only thing he didn't do was slow his heartbeat.

The assassin hesitated a moment, as if considering whether to search inside. Cui Buqu, pressed against him, felt Feng Xiao shift and heard a brief rustling. Then something seemed to explode overhead, bursting outward with the sound of wings flapping.

The unsuspecting assassin reeled back as the flock of bats burst from the crevice. They struck out with a palm but only drew a denser mass of bats. Caught entirely off guard, the assassin's face was scratched bloody. They lost their balance and tumbled down the cliff.

Cui Buqu never imagined there could be so many slumbering bats hidden in this small crevice. The feeling of the massive flock sweeping down past his head wasn't much better than the feeling of staring death in the face. It was worse still for the fastidious Feng Xiao. All the washing and changing he'd done before they left was completely in vain. If they made it back, the man would probably have to scrub off a layer or two of skin. The thought gave Cui Buqu a fierce pleasure, and his current treacherous circumstances no longer felt so unbearable.

Feng Xiao finally moved his hand away from Cui Buqu's mouth. But before Cui Buqu could breathe a sigh of relief, he heard him say, "There's still one more."

Almost as he spoke, a shadow flew in from outside, swift and violent, a sword glinting coldly in their hand as they thrust straight toward Feng Xiao.

Feng Xiao had long lost his zither. Sleeve flying, he met his opponent's blade with a palm. Just as the point of the sword was about to pierce his shoulder through, he angled his body and let the blade slice through his clothes and flesh as his palm slammed into his assailant's neck.

Cui Buqu heard the crack of bones breaking, and the person was sent flying out of the cave.

"Shall we go?" said Cui Buqu.

This was their moment to escape. Go Nyeong and Fo'er were long gone, unlikely to return. As for the two assassins from the Thirteen Floors of Yunhai, Feng Xiao had killed one, and the other had plummeted down the slope and was probably more dead than alive. Even if they survived, they'd be unconscious for a while yet.

"I can't walk," said Feng Xiao feebly.

"This cave isn't far from the top. I'll climb up and go get help."

"Oh," said Feng Xiao. "Then go."

Cui Buqu's mouth twitched. "Let go of me."

Feng Xiao was clutching his wrist in an iron grip. "I really do want to let go," said Feng Xiao innocently. "But my hand won't obey me; there's nothing I can do."

He was sure that if Cui Buqu left, he would never return. Even if Pei Jingzhe could find him here, he likely wouldn't make it until daybreak. The night was young; much could happen.

"We can work together," said Cui Buqu.

"Explain," said Feng Xiao.

"You're investigating a case right now. I happen to have a lead that will help you crack it. I can tell you what I know."

"Why didn't you say so earlier?"

"I was only recently informed."

"So you've been passing secret messages behind my back."

Cui Buqu was unmoved. "Do you want to know or not?"

Realizing he would be stuck here for a while, Feng Xiao decided to put the danger of his current predicament out of his mind. He relaxed, leaning back against the rocks to rest. However, he still refused to release Cui Buqu's wrist. "Why should I believe you?"

"Didn't you guess my identity long ago?"

"Oho?" Feng Xiao's tone pitched upward. "So Daoist Master Cui is finally willing to confess?"

"That's right," said Cui Buqu. "The Zuoyue Bureau has no connection to the Jiejian Bureau, but we are both subjects of the throne. And right now, we are both in Liugong City, so we're all in the same boat. Even if you resent me, we must deal with our common enemy before our private grievance."

"What was your objective in coming here?" asked Feng Xiao. "The Jade of Heaven Lake?"

Cui Buqu paused. "No. I arrived in Liugong City two months ago. How could I have known the jade would be stolen? The Zuoyue Bureau is executing another important mission."

Feng Xiao sighed. "We've come so far, but Ququ, you still won't be honest with me. How am I supposed to believe you?"

Cui Buqu rolled his eyes. "Ishbara is restless, ready to invade the Central Plains. However, the Göktürks have many tribes, and though Ishbara Khagan's authority is far-reaching, he doesn't hold supreme power. I came here to spearhead the court's move against the Khaganate. This is a matter of utmost secrecy; no unrelated persons are permitted to know of it. That's as much as I can tell you. With your smarts you can easily guess the truth, so surely I needn't say more."

Feng Xiao pondered this. Cui Buqu couldn't make out his features in the darkness, but he guessed he was mulling over the trustworthiness of this information. Feng Xiao abruptly asked, "In that case, was Wen Liang a fake lead you left on purpose?"

Cui Buqu said nothing—but his silence was tacit confirmation.

Feng Xiao swiftly linked together a winding string of cause and effect and realized something. Although Cui Buqu had been at his side all this time, drugged with incense of helplessness, sickly and feeble, he'd somehow managed to lead Feng Xiao by the nose throughout the entire case. Feng Xiao's fingers itched, and he longed to yank Cui Buqu's head off and kick it around like a ball.

Feng Xiao should have had victory within his grasp, looking down on Cui Buqu from on high. Yet for the first time in his life, this man had completely jerked him around.

After he finally, and with much difficulty, managed to curb his more violent impulses, Feng Xiao flashed Cui Buqu a fake smile. "Could I trouble Daoist Master Cui to explain more clearly? When we went to capture Wen Liang, people plotting against him suddenly emerged. You incited them to action in order to mislead me, right?"

28

SINCE THE TIME of the Wei and Zhou dynasties hundreds of years before, the shadow of the Göktürk Khaganate had loomed over the north. In the interest of maintaining a fragile peace, generations of emperors had practiced appeasement and reconciliation, narrowly avoiding direct conflict with the Göktürks. But a wolf was a wolf: it didn't forget its hunter's instincts just because it was fed for a while. The moment a meal was late, its ferocity would surge to the surface, and it would bare its fangs to bite.

During the Northern Zhou dynasty, Princess Qianjin had married Ishbara Khagan to seal the alliance between the Central Plains and the Khaganate. Peace reigned between the two sides for some time, but after Yang Jian ascended and Sui replaced Zhou, Princess Qianjin resented the new emperor for usurping the throne and killing her family and parents. She encouraged her husband Ishbara to invade the Central Plains. Ishbara himself wasn't a timid man; he was driven, and saw the Sui dynasty surrounded by foes on all sides. Glimpsing an opportunity for the Khaganate to crush their enemies and expand, he steered his boat into the current and agreed to his wife's request, dispatching troops to invade the Sui dynasty.

The war had begun the year before last, and fighting had continued intermittently since. Ishbara Khagan, along with the surrounding tribe leaders such as Apa Khagan, had deployed hundreds of thousands of troops. They crossed the Great Wall, then pushed southward from Mayi, Keluo Mountain, and elsewhere. Though the Sui army rose up in its own defense and achieved both victories and defeats, overall, they were at a disadvantage. Yang Jian had to preserve sufficient strength to guard against attack from Southern Chen and Goguryeo; he couldn't throw everything he had against the Göktürks. Thus he had no choice but to take a multipronged approach: he made overtures to Princess Qianjin, aimed to stabilize his relationship with the Chen dynasty, and leveraged existing conflicts between the various Göktürk tribes to divide them and diminish their strength.

It was under these circumstances that Cui Buqu had arrived in this remote western city.

Cavalry Commander Zhangsun Sheng and Crown Servant Yuan Hui had received secret orders from the emperor and set out, one to Huanglong and one to Yiwu, to treat with Bagha and Tardu Khagan, who had conflicting interests and a poor relationship with Ishbara Khagan. Meanwhile, Cui Buqu was ordered to liaise with the envoys of Apa Khagan and persuade him out of an alliance with Ishbara. Thus did they plan to divide the Khaganate from within.

But Ishbara Khagan held enormous power. Even if Apa Khagan wished to make contact with the Sui dynasty, he didn't dare do so openly. He had dispatched envoys in secret to Liugong City.

Over a month ago, shortly after Cui Buqu arrived in Liugong City, Apa Khagan had sent his envoy to meet them. But the envoy contracted food poisoning while stopping overnight in Qiemo and ultimately died puking his guts out. Qiao Xian and Zhangsun Bodhi had quietly arrived in Liugong City on Cui Buqu's orders around the same time. Cui Buqu sent them to investigate, but though the envoy's death was suspicious, their search turned up nothing. This only put them more on their guard.

The news traveled back and forth, eating up several weeks. It wasn't until recently that Apa Khagan secretly dispatched a second envoy. This trip had been arranged with even greater secrecy, and it had been agreed that the Zuoyue Bureau's scouts would only send word to their chief when the envoy arrived in Qiemo. Now that word had come, the envoy was sure to arrive within the next handful of days.

That was Cui Buqu's mission, and it should've had nothing to do with the duties of the Jiejian Bureau. But then the Khotanese envoy had been murdered and the jade stolen. He was already in Liugong City. He wouldn't have been Cui Buqu if he'd sat by and done nothing.

Feng Xiao himself had shared the leads in the case with him, and it was from this that he hit upon the key evidence of the cold plum blossom fragrance. He'd passed the message to Qiao Xian and Zhangsun Bodhi, sending them to investigate this clue in an attempt to find the jade first and steal the credit for the Zuoyue Bureau. Feng Xiao had hardly let Cui Buqu out of his sight, yet he'd never imagined the newly opened Wuwei House they'd patronized had been established by the Zuoyue Bureau for the purposes of espionage.

Cui Buqu had also intentionally misled Feng Xiao. It was he who passed word to Zhangsun to hide in the crowd and attack Wen Liang with the needle. Feng Xiao had noticed and stopped it, leading him and his team to mistakenly believe Wen Liang was a key figure in the investigation.

Now that he'd agreed to cooperate with Feng Xiao, Cui Buqu briefly outlined the details. He didn't reveal everything, but only what he thought was necessary.

After listening, Feng Xiao sighed. "Daoist Master Cui was by my side the entire time, never leaving for a moment. Yet he was capable of hamstringing my entire investigation. Truly amazing!"

Even sitting in a cramped, dark, and smelly crevice, Cui Buqu couldn't help his buoyant mood. The corners of his lips curled slightly. "Hadn't you already guessed Wen Liang was a red herring?"

Feng Xiao sighed again. "If I'm not mistaken, Fo'er's target isn't me, but you."

Apa Khagan had approached the Sui court; even if he didn't pledge his loyalty, he wanted to ally with them. The various Göktürk tribes were wary of their fellows, but they also provided mutual assistance. Word of this would inevitably make its way back to Ishbara Khagan. And at the very same time, Fo'er, Ishbara Khagan's number one martial expert, had arrived in Liugong City. What—or who—was his goal? It was an intriguing question.

Fo'er had no interest in the jade, but he was determined to kill Feng Xiao. There was only one explanation: he mistakenly thought Feng Xiao was here to represent the court with Apa Khagan's envoy. If he wished to stop their secret negotiations, the surest way was to kill Feng Xiao. He could intimidate the Sui dynasty and the other Göktürk tribes in one fell swoop, thereby demonstrating the power of Ishbara Khagan. They'd be too fearful to act recklessly then.

The deputy bureau chief was flamboyant and well known, and thus he'd become Fo'er's target. Fo'er had never guessed that the one preparing to meet Apa Khagan's envoy in secret negotiations wasn't Feng Xiao at all, but Cui Buqu.

"We both serve the throne; what's the difference between targeting you or targeting me? If we want to get into specifics, Deputy Bureau Chief Feng also used incense of helplessness on me, subjecting me to rather horrific torture. How should we settle this score?"

Feng Xiao shrugged, the picture of innocence. "If you'd confessed your identity sooner, it would never have happened."

"If I'd confessed it sooner, you'd have been wary around me, hampering all my movements. Then how would I have found this crucial lead for you?"

They stared at each other, unblinking.

Finally, Feng Xiao said, "What kind of cooperation are you proposing?"

"Within the next few days, the envoy sent by Apa will arrive in Liugong City. Continue to keep Fo'er and anyone else with ulterior motives occupied. Don't let them upset the negotiations."

"Very well. Then what's this lead you mentioned?"

Cui Buqu gave a rough overview of how Qiao Xian's team had followed the trail of the cold plum blossom fragrance to discover Lady Qin. When he was done, he said, "Qin Miaoyu is likely a Goguryeon, and the jade is on her."

"How do you know?"

"Had she always been such a skilled martial artist, she could have fled right after murdering him. There was no need for her to lurk in the city. My two subordinates fought her together, yet she managed to escape. We must presume her martial arts have improved greatly in a short period of time. Otherwise how could she survive an impossible battle with only blind courage?"

"The Jade of Heaven Lake."

Cui Buqu nodded. "The jade possesses the legendary ability to enhance one's martial arts within ten days. She's injured now, so she won't be able to sneak out of the city at night. When you head back in the morning, gather some people and search the city. It shouldn't be difficult to find her."

Feng Xiao mulled this over. "Then, considering what her strength would have been a few days ago, she couldn't possibly have killed Yuchi Jinwu and his entire party by herself."

"Yet she escaped alone with the jade," Cui Buqu continued. "Whoever her companions are, they may also be searching for her. The jade stone Linlang Pavilion auctioned off was likely placed there by her accomplices. It wasn't done to deceive us, but to lure out Qin Miaoyu."

"But Qin Miaoyu discovered the secret of using the jade to improve her martial abilities," added Feng Xiao. "She knows she's holding the real thing; she would never take the bait."

The two of them finished each other's thoughts, one after the other. In this manner, they pieced together most of the original story. Finding Qin Miaoyu wasn't enough. They had to catch her accomplices too if they were to eliminate any future difficulties.

"What about Go Nyeong? How does he figure into this?"

"He may have nothing to do with the case. Or perhaps someone was worried about Qin Miaoyu and her accomplices, and sent him here as insurance. If you're interested, send people to look into him."

"Mm." Feng Xiao changed the subject: "Ququ was sent here to meet privately with Apa's envoy. Your position in the Zuoyue Bureau must be quite high, no? You already know my identity; shouldn't you be honest with me as well? After all, we're so familiar with each other now."

Who's familiar with you? Cui couldn't help but mutter to himself. Feng-er's shamelessness knew no bounds. But outwardly he remained composed and pretended to ponder a moment. "At this point, I may as well come clean. In truth, my surname isn't Cui, and my given name isn't Buqu."

"Oh?" Feng Xiao said, his tone rising.

"My surname is Zhangsun, and my given name is Bodhi. Deputy chief of the Zuoyue Bureau."

Somewhere in the city, Zhangsun Bodhi sneezed.

29

As Feng Xiao listened, the corners of his eyes curved—almost a smile, yet not. "Unfortunately, I happen to have seen both of the Zuoyue Bureau's deputy chiefs, a man and a woman. Don't tell me you're one of them."

Woven into his tone was, *Go on, keep bluffing. Let's see what you come up with.*

"How do you know the Zhangsun Bodhi you saw was the real Zhangsun Bodhi?" asked Cui Buqu.

"Oh?"

Cui Buqu's expression didn't shift a mote as he lied through his teeth: "As the saying goes, 'the crafty hare keeps three burrows.' This is especially true for the Zuoyue Bureau. We work for the court and our whereabouts and identities are need-to-know. It's normal to use a double or two. After all, I rely on my brain to make a living. I'm not like Deputy Chief Feng, a skilled martial artist who can go about as he pleases."

Feng Xiao suspected Cui Buqu was calling him a musclebound simpleton, but his tone was neutral; it was hard to take exception.

"Then who is the chief of the Zuoyue Bureau? What's their name?"

"You know, I've never seen them before either. They never show their face—they give their orders from behind a screen in a dark house. They sound old from their voice; they must be quite advanced in age." Cui Buqu continued his improvisation, his lies so convincing they sounded like truth.

Feng Xiao furrowed his brow in thought. He mused to himself, *Could it be the empress's trusted eunuch, Chamberlain Zhang?*

"Does the voice sound masculine or feminine?"

"Apart from sounding old, it has no distinctive features."

Feng Xiao sighed. "Daoist Master Cui is a gifted man of peerless intellect and cunning. How unfortunate that there's yet another person on top pressing him down. A capable man cannot lose his authority for even a day, lest he find himself impeded by all around him. In the end, being one's own master is the best way to live!"

Even now, they never missed a chance to tear into each other.

"Is that so?" said Cui Buqu. "Feng-langjun is in the same position, since the Minister of Justice is your superior."

Feng Xiao smiled. "The Minister of Justice is a figurehead. My Jiejian Bureau is unlike the Zuoyue Bureau. Though the empress and the emperor are called the Two Saints, when all's said and done, the world can belong to only one. Being under His Majesty's jurisdiction or his wife's jurisdiction—there's a distinction. In my opinion, giving up your seat as deputy chief is a no-brainer. Why not join the Jiejian Bureau instead? I'll grant you the position of fourth deputy chief, as well as the authority to take or spare a life, to punish or reward. Whatever the Zuoyue Bureau can give you, the Jiejian Bureau can give. Whatever the Zuoyue Bureau cannot give you, the Jiejian Bureau can still provide."

Cui Buqu asked curiously, "I'm already a deputy chief of the Zuoyue Bureau, and if I joined your organization, I'd still be your subordinate. What's the difference between what you're offering and what I have now?"

"Of course it's different," said Feng Xiao. "How can an awful old man who gets in your way compare to me, an elegant, exceptional, and heaven-sent genius? Not to mention I'm far more pleasing to the eye."

Cui Buqu didn't know what to say.

"Look upon me every day, and your mood will improve. If your mind is at peace, your body will heal without the use of medicine. Is this not a great boon?"

After a moment of silence, Cui Buqu said, "Deputy Chief Feng. You really are the best-looking person I've ever met."

Feng Xiao arched a brow and said, "Naturally. Did you only just realize?"

"But you're also the most thick-skinned and shameless person I've ever met." Cui Buqu spoke sincerely.

Feng Xiao laughed. "Does there exist a man capable of achieving great things who also has skin as thin as paper? These things called reputation and dignity are merely traps people set for themselves— they constrain you and prevent you from moving forward. Look at Fo'er. He obviously can't defeat me, but to safeguard his own dignity, he claims it's because I wasn't focused. He cherishes his reputation above all. Whether he pursues the martial path or runs after wealth and power, reaching the summit will be nigh impossible for him. If Ishbara Khagan's subordinates are all the same, I fear it'll be difficult for him to accomplish great works."

"As far as I know, though they call Fo'er the number one Göktürk expert, many powerful Göktürk martial artists have appeared in recent years," said Cui Buqu. "There are enough of them that we can set aside the late Hulugu for now. Bagha Khagan from the Eastern Khaganate is an extraordinary martial artist in his own right, and there's also a man under Apa Khagan called Yeluohe. He looks as delicate as a woman, but his moves are ferocious and brutal, his skills incredible. They are strong enemies all who mustn't be under—"

Feng Xiao was listening attentively, but before Cui Buqu could finish the word *underestimated*, he began to cough. He covered his mouth, but the harsh sounds of his coughing seeped between his fingers, growing more and more intense. If not for Feng Xiao taking care of the assassins from the Thirteen Floors of Yunhai earlier, they would surely have been discovered now.

As he coughed, a bone-searing pain flared to life in his chest. It spread rapidly through his body in wave after wave from his fingertips to his heart and lungs, even bringing a searing ache to his temples. The incense of helplessness was stirring inside him. His body was frail to begin with, and as the poison took hold, he endured an agony several magnitudes greater than the average person would have experienced.

Even so, he made no sound other than to cough—no groans or cries of pain escaped his lips.

It wasn't as if the Jiejian Bureau had never used incense of helplessness before. Feng Xiao had witnessed at least one powerful martial artist break down weeping under the influence of the incense, answering any and all questions as his resistance collapsed. Even after the poison had been neutralized, his eroded willpower dragged his body down with it. He hadn't lost his health completely, but he'd never be what he was.

Yet Cui Buqu, who knew no martial arts at all, had somehow managed to accompany Feng Xiao, running around all over Liugong City with the poison working inside him, enduring it in silence until it finally flared up. When it came down to it, Cui Buqu was from the Zuoyue Bureau; he wasn't a mortal enemy. Hadn't using incense of helplessness on him been a bit much?

For the first time in his life, Feng Xiao, Deputy Bureau Chief Feng, spent the span of several breaths reflecting on his actions.

But he quickly cast aside such a useless emotion—surely he merely felt sympathetic because he too was poisoned and injured. "I still have some incense of helplessness with me," he said to Cui Buqu.

"...No need." Cui Buqu curled up against the cold, drawing all his meager warmth into himself.

Incense of helplessness had no antidote—the only way to be free of it was to endure the endless, torturous agony, waiting for the poison to fade as the body expelled it. Some martial arts practitioners could temporarily suppress the poison using internal energy; aside from that, one could alleviate the pain by treating poison with poison—suppressing the effects of the incense with another dose. Yet afterward, the next flare-up would be more agonizing than the last.

Still, those who were subjected to this poison would often take more incense to bring themselves relief. They chose a temporary, short-term comfort and ignored the long-term harm it wrought.

"The cave is cold and damp," Feng Xiao's tone was disapproving. "You're exhausted, so flare-ups will affect you more severely. A wise man accepts his circumstances. The next time it flares, you can recuperate somewhere warm and comfortable. You'll still feel better then than you do now."

Cui Buqu's forehead burned hotter and hotter as his consciousness grew hazy. There seemed to be something between him and the sound of Feng Xiao's voice—it came to him soft and muffled. He said, "If I take a first step, I will take a second step. If I wish to defeat the poison completely, I must not take the first step at all." His eyes were tightly shut, his brow furrowed as he struggled in the grip of unrelenting agony. Somehow, he still managed a self-deprecating laugh. "I've suffered pain far greater than this. This...is nothing."

Feng Xiao raised a brow and was about to ask more when he heard a wail from outside. The wind that had died down suddenly picked up again, blowing snow and rain into the cave. A wave of bone-chilling cold swirled inside, the icy gust sweeping right into his open mouth and aggravating the poisoned wound in his shoulder. Feng Xiao bent his head in a coughing fit of his own.

Once it began, it seemed it'd never stop. The night was long, and they were crammed together in this small space. Their coughs rose and fell in tandem like echoes.

A tiger ripped from its mountain may be bullied even by dogs. All that was missing were the howls of wolves outside.

The instant he thought it, Feng Xiao heard the faint howl of wolves on the cliffs amid the wind and snow. The corners of his lips quirked up. He looked at Cui Buqu just a short distance away. "Hey."

Cui Buqu was using all that remained of his consciousness to fight the poison; he had no attention to spare for Feng Xiao.

Feng Xiao coughed twice. "I'm injured too. Why not come closer? We can huddle for warmth."

Opening his eyes a crack, Cui Buqu frowned as his sluggish thoughts processed Feng Xiao's words. "Get the fuck over here then," he said.

Feng Xiao was stupefied. He eyed the unmoving Cui Buqu and concluded he probably hadn't the strength. Feng Xiao was left with no choice but to debase himself and scoot over, pulling the other man into his arms. Deep inside, he thought in both anger and sorrow, *How did my venerable fucking self fall this far?*

No matter how he looked at it, it was all one person's fault.

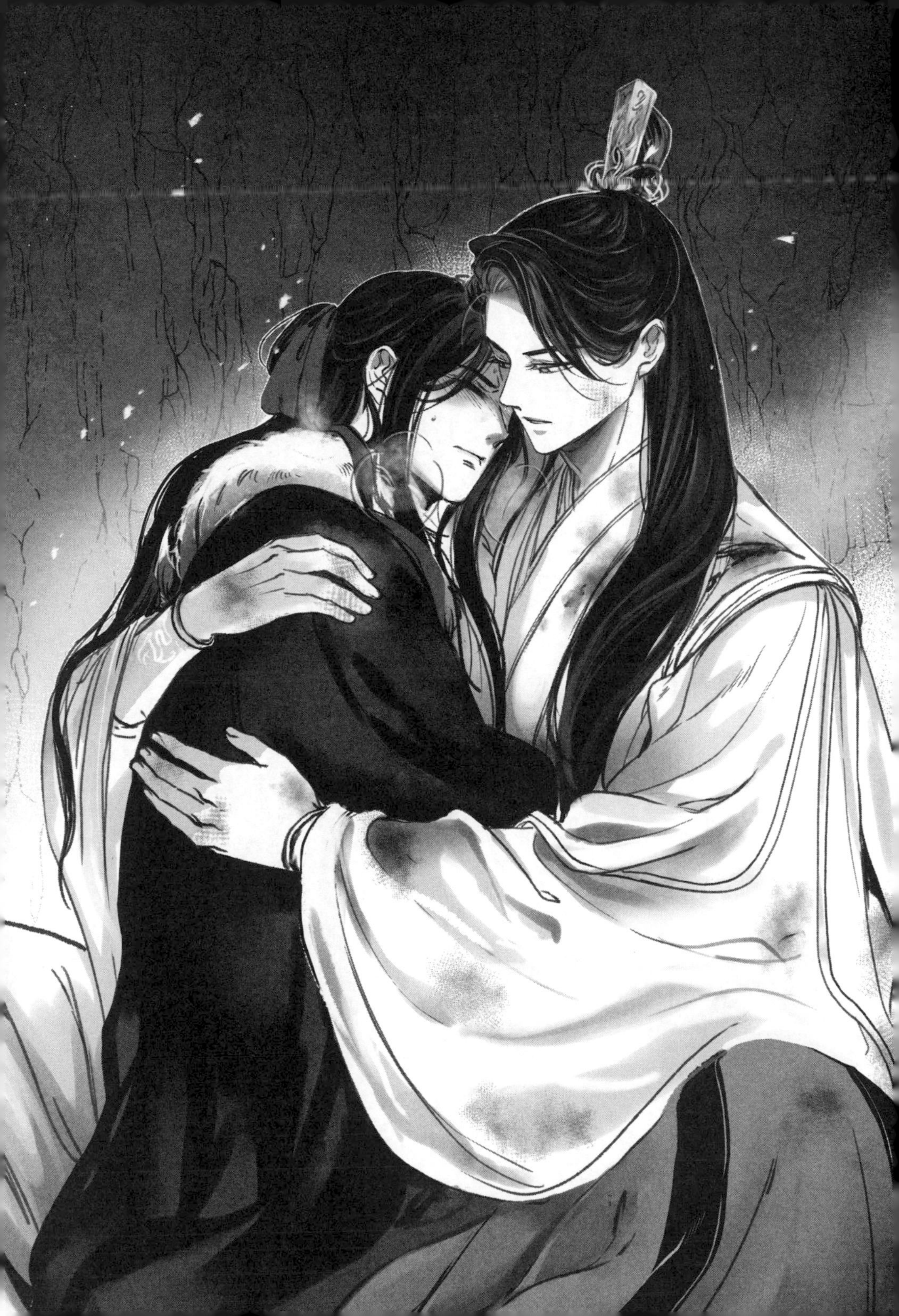

Pei Jingzhe, standing at the gates of Lu Manor, sneezed thrice in rapid succession. Whether due to the chill of the wind or someone discussing him out of earshot, he had no time to wonder. He, too, had encountered the unexpected.

30

PEI JINGZHE HAD ARRIVED at Lu Manor and found himself in trouble.

It was impossible for him to monitor all of Lu Manor alone. Even if he infiltrated to get an inside look, the other party was more familiar with the layout and terrain. Unless he explained his identity to the owner and had the Jiejian Bureau's eagle riders surround the entire complex, his quarry could easily slip away without him noticing.

But if he did all that, it'd spook his target. They'd flee for sure, and he would lose the lead completely.

Thus Pei Jingzhe was in a dilemma.

He'd always felt he lacked wisdom and maturity, that he couldn't solve problems the way the deputy chief could, while smiling and chatting. And if he'd possessed fantastic martial abilities like the third chief, he wouldn't have been standing here at a loss either. At the very least, he might have captured the person in black as they left Qiushan Manor.

Pei Jingzhe had just about made up his mind to sneak inside when a scream from within Lu Manor shattered the night and sent a chill through his heart.

Lanterns all over the manor flickered to life, and the murmur of its occupants swelled to a clamor Pei Jingzhe could hear through the doors. Infiltration was impossible now. Pei Jingzhe frowned.

The clatter of hoofbeats sounded from behind. Pei Jingzhe looked back: six of the Jiejian Bureau's eagle riders had followed him.

"Weren't you supposed to stay at Qiushan Manor?" said Pei Jingzhe.

The leader of the unit cupped his fist in a salute. "We come by order of the deputy chief to assist Pei-langjun!"

Pei Jingzhe understood at once. Feng Xiao had anticipated his hesitation and had sent the cavalry to prod him into making a decision. So decide he did: "Split up and surround Lu Manor. No one leaves without direct orders from me!"

The eagle riders saluted and left to take up their posts. Lu Manor was sprawling, but the eagle riders were trained by the Jiejian Bureau. Six was enough.

Pei Jingzhe was about to knock on the door when he felt a gust of wind at his back. His heart thumped, and he instinctively dodged to the side as a white light flashed past the corner of his eye and punched through the wooden door in front of him. The brutality of the attack put Pei Jingzhe instantly on alert. He drew his sword and spun to meet his opponent.

As they came face to face, he saw his attacker was an elegant figure in white robes, radiating the cold and otherworldly aura of a celestial being from the Moon Palace.

"Who is this distinguished master?" asked Pei Jingzhe.

Qiao Xian sneered. "You detained one of ours, yet you ask such a question? Hand over Cui Buqu!"

Pei Jingzhe was startled. "You?!"

He saw another person approach. It was a man dressed in black, an eye-catching figure with a bamboo hat on his head and prayer beads wound around his hand.

"Deputy Chief Zhangsun?"

Qiao Xian answered no questions. Her attacks grew fiercer as she demanded, "Where is he?!"

Pei Jingzhe composed himself and said, "I don't know what you're talking about!"

Although Lu Manor was in chaos, the family was not deaf. The noise they were making at the entrance was considerable; of course they could hear it inside. Someone rushed to open the door and was greeted with the sight of Pei Jingzhe and Qiao Xian clashing on their doorstep. They exclaimed in shock and fury, "Stop right there! Who are you—you dare fight on the doorstep of the Lu family?! Quick, get help!"

On hearing the clamor, the Jiejian Bureau's eagle riders rushed over and surrounded Zhangsun and Qiao Xian. The situation was quickly spinning out of control.

Pei Jingzhe's mind was a mess. "Everyone, stop!" he shouted, and immediately withdrew half a step to prove his intent. When he saw Qiao Xian and Zhangsun had also ceased their attack, he let out a breath of relief.

The Lu family looked out over this bizarre scene, unsure how to react. It was Pei Jingzhe who broke the stalemate. "What is Deputy Chief Zhangsun doing in Liugong City?"

It was impossible for the Jiejian Bureau and the Zuoyue Bureau to have never crossed paths. Pei Jingzhe had met the Zuoyue Bureau's two deputy chiefs, at least. Though this wasn't exactly the time to reminisce, he couldn't pretend not to recognize Zhangsun.

"Looking for someone," said Zhangsun Bodhi.

Pei Jingzhe smiled. "I have an urgent task to attend to at the moment. Once I complete it, I'll organize a banquet to welcome you both, then help you find whoever it is you're looking for. How about it?"

"Hand him over," said Qiao Xian coldly.

Pei Jingzhe guessed whom she meant, but still affected surprise. "Hand *whom* over?"

"Cui Buqu!"

Coughing lightly, Pei Jingzhe squashed down his guilt. "My apologies, I've never heard of any such person."

Anger darkened Qiao Xian's face. She stepped forward, ready to attack again, but Zhangsun Bodhi stopped her. "Hand him over or don't even think about leaving here tonight," he said.

Pei Jingzhe laughed. "Bold words, Deputy Chief Zhangsun! You may be powerful, but you can't beat all seven of us!"

"Try me," said Zhangsun Bodhi. His shadow flickered as he swept toward Pei Jingzhe, swifter than lightning. By the time the cavalry riders surrounding them realized what had happened, Zhangsun had reached Pei Jingzhe and was grabbing for his shoulder. Pei Jingzhe dodged narrowly, but his longsword was still halfway out of its sheath when it was forced back in by a strike from Zhangsun's palm.

Thrice he tried to draw his sword, and thrice he was prevented. Pei Jingzhe's face flushed crimson. He knew he was nowhere near a match for the deputy chief of the Zuoyue Bureau in martial arts; still, he'd never expected to be humiliated such that he couldn't even unsheathe his sword. For a martial artist, this was shameful beyond belief.

The truth was, Zhangsun Bodhi was going easy on him. Otherwise, even with the eagle riders present, he could have killed Pei Jingzhe as easily as breathing.

"Where is he?!" Zhangsun Bodhi brought his palm down, aiming for the top of Pei Jingzhe's skull.

Pei Jingzhe couldn't avoid it. He reflexively squeezed his eyes shut and cried, "Qiushan Manor!"

From all around came the shocked gasps of the eagle riders. Two rushed over, but they were too late. The wind from Zhangsun's palm strike howled—then disappeared. Pei Jingzhe opened his eyes and saw Zhangsun had abandoned his attack and was now standing in place.

Having just raced to the gates of hell and back, Pei Jingzhe stared in shock. Zhangsun Bodhi gathered his sleeves and threw his arms wide, forcing the eagle riders of the Jiejian Bureau to stumble backward.

The eagle riders who'd hurried over were elite members of the Jiejian Bureau. At minimum they qualified as first-rate martial artists in the jianghu. Yet Zhangsun shoved them away effortlessly, leaving no room for a counterattack.

That one move alone was enough to show Pei Jingzhe that while Zhangsun Bodhi might be Feng Xiao's inferior in martial arts, the gap was a narrow one. In attempting to fight him, Pei Jingzhe had grossly overestimated his own abilities.

Qiao Xian fixed Pei Jingzhe with a chilly glare. "Didn't you just say you've never heard of any such person?"

Pei Jingzhe's smile was strained. "How could I know your intentions? A little wariness is reasonable, is it not?"

"You knew Cui Buqu was a member of the Zuoyue Bureau, yet you detained him, tormented him, and harassed him. The Zuoyue Bureau will remember this debt. Once we've retrieved him, we'll take our time collecting."

Pei Jingzhe's head throbbed. "It's true Daoist Master Cui is with us, but we haven't harassed him. My lord brings him wherever he goes..."

He felt a stab of guilt, but he couldn't very well say, *We drugged him with incense of helplessness and it flares up every three to five days.*

He's yet to recover, but our boss dragged him out this morning to identify suspects!

Qiao Xian saw his hesitation. She stepped forward and fisted a hand in his collar. "What did you do to him?!"

Pei Jingzhe hadn't expected this celestial beauty to spring over and strangle him to the point he could barely breathe. "He's fine, honestly! If you don't believe me, I'll take you there and you can see for yourself. But you'll have to wait until I've finished here—"

An angry voice interrupted them. "Excuse me, but who are you?! How dare you show such discourtesy at the doors of Lu Manor?! Hurry up and leave!"

The Lu family patriarch, Lu Ti, stood aggressively at the door, flanked by his courtyard guards. His eyes were bloodshot, his whiskers frazzled. Yet he seemed less like he was irritated at being disturbed by a late-night altercation at his entranceway, and more like he'd suffered some terrible calamity.

Recalling the scream he'd heard, Pei Jingzhe set aside his conflict with Zhangsun's group and gave the eagle riders their orders. "Surround Lu Manor. Don't let anyone leave!"

He turned to the Lu patriarch. "I am a member of the Jiejian Bureau with orders to investigate the murder of the Khotanese envoy. We've received a report that a suspect is hiding in your mansion. Patriarch Lu, please cooperate and let us search inside!"

Lu Ti reeled back as if he'd suffered a great blow. Pei Jingzhe's words seemed to strike some chord within his brain, and he finally snapped completely. "This is Lu Manor! It's not a place you can enter at will! My Lu family is diligent and frugal, and we've never conducted ourselves against our conscience in business nor in anything else. So what if you're with the Jiejian Bureau? You think you can come here and throw your weight around?! I heard you even waltzed up and arrested someone from Linlang Pavilion—but as long as I, Lu Ti, am here, you'll not take a single step inside!"

He had the look of a wounded lion roaring fiercely in defense of his territory. Pei Jingzhe and his men could force their way in, but if they did, Lu Manor would descend into chaos. This would only aid the person he was seeking in their escape.

"Please, sirs," another voice rose from the crowd. "Our master has experienced a tragic accident tonight. The young lady of the household has drowned, and the doctor is still trying to save her. Our master is deeply anxious, so I ask your lordships to show some mercy tonight. Please come back in a few days!"

The speaker was a man standing beside Lu Ti with a mournful expression on his face. His dress and manner placed him as the manor's steward.

Pei Jingzhe's heart thudded. They'd followed the trail here, and now the Lu family had experienced misfortune. It was far too great a coincidence.

He hadn't gone in, but Lu Manor had still descended into chaos. Yet he couldn't leave things like this either. He struggled for a moment but was too afraid of Zhangsun Bodhi to shake Qiao Xian off. Qiao Xian gave him a cold look, then released his collar.

Pei Jingzhe breathed a sigh of relief and turned to Lu Ti. "Patriarch Lu, I'm deeply sorry to hear about your daughter. However, your daughter's accident occurred just after we discovered a key lead in a murder case. The two may not be unrelated. It will benefit us both to uncover the truth!"

"No need! We merely wish for peace and quiet!" snapped Lu Ti.

Pei Jingzhe ignored him. He turned and instructed the eagle riders to go at once to Magistrate Zhao and have him mobilize enough constables to surround Lu Manor and stop a single soul from leaving.

Lu Ti was furious. He roared, "Looks like you're determined to cause trouble for me tonight!"

"Patriarch Lu is the one causing trouble for me," Pei Jingzhe said. "The Jiejian Bureau has an important mission, and unrelated persons may not interfere. Arrest him!"

A wave of his hand brought the eagle riders trotting up from either side. The residents of Lu Manor watched as their master was detained. The servants of the Lu family surged forward to wrest their master back from the eagle riders, and the scene devolved into confusion. In desperation, Pei Jingzhe shouted, "If anyone dares act recklessly, I will execute Lu Ti on the spot!"

This declaration stopped the Lu family in their tracks. They all looked at each other, too afraid to move.

Lu Ti had gone blue in the face. He held nothing back as he thundered, "You lot are completely lawless! Don't you know we're related to the Lu family of Fanyang? I'll bring you before the magistrate for contempt toward our noble family!"

Qiao Xian scoffed. "How many generations have passed since the Lu family of Liugong City split from the Lu family of Fanyang? Even if you were a legitimate branch of the Fanyang Lu, contempt for a noble is not a valid charge under the Kaihuang Code.[16] All land belongs only to the emperor. Don't think too highly of yourself, then complain when your death comes that you don't understand why!"

Pei Jingzhe had never imagined Qiao Xian would speak up for him. He glanced at her in surprise.

Lu Ti was so incensed his eyes were rolling back in his head; he was unable to utter another word.

---

16 开皇律. *A series of laws instituted by Emperor Wen of Sui that simplified and reformed older laws. These statutes provided a pattern for the legal codes of the Tang and other Chinese dynasties that followed.*

But this was a night full of twists and turns. Just as Pei Jingzhe was preparing to have Lu Manor searched, he heard someone else pelting down the road.

"Young Pei-langjun! What is your lordship doing here? This is terrible news!"

A man ran up, heaving for breath. Pei Jingzhe recognized him as a servant from Qiushan Manor.

When Magistrate Zhao had ordered Qiushan Manor offered to Feng Xiao, he'd sent a group of servants to attend his honored guests. These servants were efficient and capable. They never asked what shouldn't be asked, and never said what shouldn't be said. Even the fussy Feng Xiao hadn't found fault with them.

Now one of those servants was running pell-mell toward Pei Jingzhe. He cried out, "Feng-langjun received a letter saying you were kidnapped; the kidnapper told him to come to Huyang Forest outside the city. He asked this humble servant to tell the eagle riders to find County Magistrate Zhao, then surround Lu Manor and ensure no one leaves. He said he'd deal with them on his return! But...why is your lordship here? Was Feng-langjun deceived?!"

Pei Jingzhe's face paled in horror. "Did he go alone?"

The servant was still panting as he shook his head. "He took... took Daoist Master Cui with him!"

At that, Qiao Xian and Zhangsun Bodhi blanched as well.

"When did he leave?!" Peri Jingzhe demanded.

"The same time this humble servant left the manor, around an hour ago!"

Qiao Xian raged, "If he wanted to die, he could have done it on his own! Instead he's dragged our people into it!" With no thought for anything else, she rushed off with Zhangsun Bodhi toward the city outskirts, not forgetting to threaten Pei Jingzhe as they left: "If anything happens to Cui Buqu, I'll never forgive you!"

Pei Jingzhe was worn out and frazzled; now he understood how Lu Ti felt. Fortunately, County Magistrate Zhao didn't dawdle. He ran over at once, his haste evident—he hadn't even fixed his hair clasp. But Pei Jingzhe wasn't in the mood to praise him. After giving him a quick summary of the night's events, he left him to handle Lu Manor while he took two eagle riders and sped to Huyang Forest as fast as their horses would carry them.

❄☙❈❧❄

The wind and snow had somewhat abated, but the interior of the cave was still frigid.

Feng Xiao had used his internal energy to expel most of the poison from his body, but residual toxins remained. His limbs were numb, and his body shook with chills.

Cui Buqu was the opposite—his body was blazingly, worryingly hot. He felt like a soldering iron as he lay in Feng Xiao's arms. It did keep Feng Xiao warm, but he suspected that if Cui Buqu's fever stayed this high, he'd give up the ghost before any rescuers could find them.

Confidants were hard to find, opponents difficult to meet—but the latter were far rarer than the former. So of course Feng Xiao didn't want Cui Buqu to die like this. He guessed that even if Cui Buqu did go, judging by his penchant for tormenting others, he wouldn't go in peace. He'd definitely have left behind a huge pile of traps for Feng Xiao to fall into.

Feng Xiao felt he absolutely couldn't let Cui Buqu die.

"Hey, say something." He patted Cui Buqu's cheek. His touch wasn't gentle, but Cui Buqu didn't open his eyes.

"You can't sleep. If you fall asleep, you won't wake up again." Feng Xiao said. He pinched Cui Buqu's wrist and channeled a wisp of internal energy into his feverish body. Perhaps this wisp had some effect; after a moment, Cui Buqu twitched, though his brow furrowed more deeply.

Still, any response was a good one. "Ququ, what do you think of my looks and charm?"

Cui Buqu's lips moved, but no sound came out.

"I know, I know. They're unmatched throughout the land. You don't have to keep praising me; I've long grown bored of such flattery. It seems you're no different from the vulgar masses. But today, I'll tell you a story from my youth."

Cui Buqu's eyes remained closed as he sighed softly, almost like a reply.

"When I was young, I traveled to the southwest and heard a story there. It was about a man from a local noble family and a beautiful woman. The woman's family was impoverished, but the man fell in love with her at first sight. He overcame every obstacle, insisting he'd make her his wife. At first, the young lady refused to believe him. She wished to marry a man of her own station and live a simple life. But the man slowly convinced her, and her heart was moved as she saw the many things he did for her. He persuaded the elders of his family, eliminated everything that stood in their way, and gradually, she fell in love with him as well." As Feng Xiao spoke, he warmed to his story. "I happened to meet that young lady. She saw my looks and charm, peerless in all the land, and begged me to do something for her. Can you guess what it was?"

Cui Buqu's face was lined with fatigue. His brows were tightly pinched as he finally opened his eyes a crack. Feng Xiao felt him shift in his arms, trying to escape. He smiled. "You must be curious.

Why don't you guess what she asked of me? If you're right, I'll let you stay by my side a few extra days, granting you the precious opportunity to further admire me."

Even a dead man would have twitched at hearing that sentence, let alone Cui Buqu, who wasn't dead quite yet.

"Could you..."

"Hm?"

Cui Buqu's breathing was weak. Close as they were, Feng Xiao had to lower his head and lean in so he could hear the rest. Feebly, Cui Buqu finished, "...shut your fucking mouth?"

His thoughts were muddled; he wanted only to sleep soundly, dead to the world. But someone kept prattling in his ear, like a fly buzzing around his head. He couldn't swat it or drive it off. Cui Buqu wanted to rip that "fly's" head off and toss it far beyond the clouds—then force that irritating creature to reincarnate as a mute fly for eighteen lifetimes straight.

Feng Xiao raised a brow and said, "That's not right. How can you refer to my mouth in such a vulgar way? You should call it a 'fortunate mouth.' Everything I say is as precious as jade or gold. My words are something all yearn for, but few are fortunate to receive— yet you get to be held in my arms. This is a fortune that only comes once in three lives! You should appreciate it."

Cui Buqu didn't bother replying. He could admit Feng Xiao's face was gorgeous enough to fell any living creature, to bewitch men and women alike—but there was a condition attached: Feng Xiao must not be allowed to speak.

It seemed there was no stopping him till he finished the story. Cui Buqu sighed and reluctantly opened his eyes. All around him was unrelieved darkness. He felt another bout of drowsiness surge over him and did his best to resist his fatigue and stay awake.

"...She wanted you to test her lover. She wanted to see if he could remain indifferent in the face of your stunning looks."

Feng Xiao smiled. "Just as I'd expect of the man I have my eye on! Then you must have guessed the conclusion as well."

Cui Buqu's tone was indifferent. "With your looks, if you disguised yourself as a woman, no one would be the wiser. Nations would topple before your beauty; only a scant few wouldn't be swayed. That noble son was a man like any other. How could his heart not falter in the face of such provocation? That woman wished to test the human heart and ended up dropping a stone on her own foot."

"What about you? Have you been swayed?" Feng Xiao lowered his head, his breath fanning over Cui Buqu's cheek.

At any other time, Cui Buqu would have shoved Feng Xiao's face away or moved out of his reach. But he was completely drained. He couldn't even turn his face aside, let alone lift an arm to push him off. "Just because someone's heart is swayed doesn't mean they've fallen in love," he whispered, "Feng-er, your face could sway anyone, but not every heart will become your plaything."

"Someone entreated me to test the faithfulness of their lover," Feng Xiao said innocently. "He was unable to withstand the temptation I presented; how is that my fault? The human heart will always crumble when tested. If it doesn't, it just means the temptation wasn't strong enough. Lover or spouse, parent or child—they're all the same. That woman didn't understand this truth, so she couldn't accept the outcome. She deluded herself into thinking she was the exception. Isn't that absurd?"

"What happened to her afterward?"

"Guess."

"The man had a sudden change of heart and fell for another.

The woman was unable to bear it. She either fled or ended her own life. In this world, women have no third option."

"How clever you are," said Feng Xiao. "That young lady threw herself into a well. The man was heartbroken for a time, but two years later he married someone else. They lived happily ever after, a loving and harmonious union. So what do you think? Wasn't that a fun story?"

Cui Buqu didn't reply.

Feng Xiao was mildly surprised. "I didn't expect someone as cold and calculating as Daoist Master Cui to believe in true love."

"Whether true love exists or not has nothing to do with me," said Cui Buqu coolly. "I just want to know when you're going to shut up so I can sleep."

"You probably won't be able to sleep at all tonight, because I have another tale to tell you."

Cui Buqu was at a loss for words.

Feng Xiao talked most of the night. By dawn, it didn't matter how loudly he spoke—Cui Buqu no longer stirred. He was barely conscious as he weathered the incense of helplessness flare-up, but at least his temperature had fallen slightly. Finally, he was no longer radiating that blazing, terrifying heat.

However able Feng Xiao might be, by now, his throat and tongue were dry and painful. He no longer had any desire to move.

The snowstorm had calmed, and the sky overhead was a brilliant white. From within the cave, he could just make out the gilt edges of the clouds. It looked to be a cold, sunny day. Feng Xiao sighed and muttered to himself, "A whole night has passed. I'm cutting Pei Jingzhe's next three months' salary by half."

He slowly got up, then half-dragged, half-carried Cui Buqu outside. He pinched underneath Cui Buqu's nose, trying to wake him.

"I'm going to carry you up. Wake up a bit. At least enough that you won't fall off my back."

Cui Buqu grunted faintly and followed Feng Xiao's instructions. He wrapped both arms around Feng Xiao and lay against his back, obedient and docile. His usual acumen was nowhere in sight.

Feng Xiao sighed again. He far preferred an awake, alert Cui Buqu. Even if every thought in Cui Buqu's brain touched off countless malicious designs, that version of him was far more entertaining than the man before him now. And more pressingly, Feng Xiao now had to carry his dead weight while climbing back up the steep slope of the plateau.

Feng Xiao muttered to himself again. "I'll cut Pei Jingzhe's salary down to nothing for the next three years. That will save the Jiejian Bureau some expense."

31

ALL HIS LIFE, Feng Xiao had seldom found himself pushed to his very limit. This was one of those times.

He'd been a prodigy since childhood, achieving twice the results with half the effort in both academics and martial arts. The things ordinary men spent their lives seeking without success were child's play to Feng Xiao. When it came to the Jiejian Bureau, his authority had been personally bestowed by the emperor. Wheresoever he went, none dared challenge his brilliance, and whatever difficulties arose, his wits and intelligence were sufficient to handle them with ease.

This was the first time he'd been too cocksure, too careless, and had fallen into the trap someone else had laid for him. Though he hadn't lost his life, it had caused him some serious grief. Fortunately for him, he still didn't have it as bad as Cui Buqu. No matter how dark one's mood, nothing lifted the spirits quite like seeing someone worse off than oneself.

So it was that, as Feng Xiao watched the completely insensate Cui Buqu, he began humming a jaunty tune. "If you still refuse to wake up," he said between bars, "I'll leave you here and go back to the city by myself."

He climbed onward. "Actually, now that I've taken a closer look at your face, while it's not even a thousandth so lovely as mine, it's rather outstanding compared to the great unwashed."

And a little later: "Cui Buqu, Cui Buqu, no matter how I urge you, you won't go... That probably isn't your real name."

Feng Xiao leaned back against a rocky ledge and squinted at the dawn sun as it rose from the east, staining the clouds and turning the pale sky a brilliant red-gold. In the distance the mountains rose and fell, silently recounting the passage of glorious eons through this land, and the smoke of wars past.

He nudged Cui Buqu with his toe, giving the fallen man a light kick. "Don't you think it's a pity to miss such a beautiful scene?"

Naturally, Cui Buqu didn't answer.

Had he been conscious, he might have picked up a rock and stuffed it into Feng Xiao's mouth to stop his chatter. But right then he only lay quietly next to Feng Xiao. If not for the dawn light pouring over his face and provoking a frown of discomfort, he would have looked like he was immersed in a sweet dream, unable to wake.

Feng Xiao had mentally docked the totality of Pei Jingzhe's salary for the next five years, yet the latter still hadn't appeared. Feng Xiao sighed softly and began to consider transferring Pei Jingzhe to the Jiejian Bureau's remote base in Qiemo.

"Your complexion is poor. Let me help you," he said to Cui Buqu. An idea seemed to occur to him, and his face lit up with joy. "In the old days, people used to enjoy drawing on their eyebrows. Now we can share the joy of painting on faces. A great reimagining of an old tradition, if I do say so myself."

Cui Buqu's lashes trembled slightly, as if he was trying to open his eyes yet couldn't find the strength. But he wasn't a man who gave up easily. Heaven had come for him many times, and every time it had left him his frail, flickering life, clawing his way back to the light.

Though he was left wandering on the banks of the underworld, even the reaper's soul-restraining chains couldn't drag him through the gates of hell.

He'd never lost before. And he wasn't going to start now.

He opened his eyes.

Above him was a vast world of azure skies and an extraordinarily beautiful face. "You're awake," Feng Xiao said, sounding pleased. "How do you feel?"

Cui Buqu tried to move his fingers and found he was still without strength. It was practically all he could do to lie there like a corpse. Perhaps it was the touch of the sun's first rays, but he no longer felt cold. The early morning breeze skimmed over his face, filling him with a profound sense of peace.

If only that aggravating man were a little farther away, it would've been perfect.

"Are you thirsty?" Feng Xiao asked.

Obviously he was. He'd gone a day and a night without water; at this point his throat was practically on fire. But he knew Feng Xiao wouldn't help him for nothing.

Sure enough, Feng Xiao smiled. "Call me 'Daddy' three times, and I'll use my internal energy to melt some snow for you to drink."

Of course he'd take his revenge. He'd only been waiting for the opportune moment. Cui Buqu decided to get it over with. He opened his mouth without hesitation: "Daddy, Daddy, Daddy."

His voice was rough and grating, but he got the words out.

Feng Xiao took a handful of snow and got to work. The snowmelt seeped through his fingers, dripping into Cui Buqu's open mouth.

Cui Buqu wasn't as fastidious as Feng Xiao, who would rather die of thirst than accept melted snow mixed with sand. After swallowing a few mouthfuls, Cui Buqu's throat felt much better.

"My dad's dead," he said.

Feng Xiao eyed him. Seeing as Cui Buqu was at death's door, he decided to be magnanimous and let it slide. After all, if Cui Buqu really did die, Feng Xiao would have a hard time finding someone anywhere near as interesting.

"Give me a couple more mouthfuls," Cui Buqu said. As long as someone hadn't had anything to drink, they could endure their thirst. But the moment they drank, their body would demand more.

"It's so dirty, yet you can stand to drink it." Feng Xiao pursed his lips but picked up another handful of snow and melted it for him.

"I've drunk water dirtier than this before," Cui Buqu said coolly. "After heavy rain, there are puddles on the roadside. Have you seen them? People come and go, stepping in the puddles, and the mud from their shoes mingles with the water. I've drunk even that kind of water."

Compared to that, snowmelt was indeed much cleaner. When someone was in truly dire straits, they could eat rotten food and drink stagnant water—rainwater from a puddle was nothing. But Cui Buqu had never felt those experiences worth bragging about, so his tone remained neutral, as if he were talking about his meals for the day.

"Chief Cui," Feng Xiao said suddenly.

Cui Buqu blinked. His expression remained unchanged—but that blink was enough to confirm Feng Xiao's guess.

"The great and mighty chief of the Zuoyue Bureau has been lurking beside me all this time. In order to hinder my investigation, he even sacrificed his body to poison. Your resolve is unmatched— I'm quite blown away!"

"Would the chief of the Zuoyue Bureau risk his life for this endeavor, let you drag him out of the city, and almost perish as a consequence?" Cui Buqu asked.

Feng Xiao was all smiles. "Others might not, but you definitely would. Someone like you never bows to adversity, nor submits willingly to others. As long as you're in the Zuoyue Bureau, no one else can stand above you. Daoist Master Cui, you've deceived me for so long! You're truly so capable!"

There was no way to deny it, so Cui Buqu no longer bothered to make excuses. "The head of the Jiejian Bureau himself traveled to this remote border city; what's so special about me coming with my ailing body and precarious health?"

Feng Xiao smiled again. "If I killed you here, not a single soul would know. I could throw your body down the cliffside and let the wind and sand bury it. Even if your men found this place, they wouldn't find any evidence. From then on, the Zuoyue Bureau would no longer pose a threat to the Jiejian Bureau. What do you think?"

"Not a bad idea. However, I'm not the only capable person in the world. In time, a new leader of the Zuoyue Bureau would emerge. Killing me is pointless."

"But there aren't many as intelligent as you. Even dragging around your half-dead body, you set stumbling blocks for me at every turn. If you were gone, I'd have a lot less to worry about."

He reached for Cui Buqu's neck.

Cui Buqu looked back at him indifferently. His gaze was calmer than the sky, blissfully unconcerned.

⋇⊰℥⊱⋇

Qiao Xian and Zhangsun dashed all the way to Huyang Forest without pause, Pei Jingzhe and his eagle riders at their heels. But when the group arrived, they found the area deserted. Careful searching revealed traces of a battle.

Now everyone was in the same boat; there was no time for further disagreements. They split in three directions and began to search.

The blizzard was howling, and their shouts were snatched by the wind. Qiao Xian and others had their martial arts, but they weren't any kind of winged deities. The longer they spent running about in the snowy night, the more anxious they became. Qiao Xian fretted that Feng Xiao had already used Cui Buqu as a meat shield, or that he'd met with some other dire misfortune.

The vast wilderness, the mighty Gobi Desert, the endless horizon. It seemed like they'd never find their way back. They searched until the black of night paled into the white of day, until the wind and snow subsided. At long last, Qiao Xian found Feng Xiao and Cui Buqu huddled behind a snow-covered boulder.

Feng Xiao was fine, sitting leaned against the boulder. He was tired but still alert. He cast Qiao Xian and Zhangsun a lazy glance when they appeared, completely unsurprised. "Finally. Another few minutes and your Daoist Master Cui might have been an icy corpse."

Before looking at Cui Buqu, Qiao Xian retained some composure. But the instant she looked, rage exploded over her face.

Cui Buqu's face, his forehead and cheeks and even his neck, were covered in words. The handwriting was strong and lively, each brushstroke carrying the elegance of a master calligrapher—but that was beside the point.

The point was the content.

"I, Cui Buqu, owe Feng Xiao a life debt. When I see him in the future, I must call him 'Daddy.' Let this be my evidence. Should I refuse, may I be struck by lightning and perish of thirst; should I flee from my fate, may I break my legs first."

Before Qiao Xian could erase the words, Pei Jingzhe, who'd scurried after her, had already read them aloud.

The corners of Zhangsun Bodhi's eyes and mouth twitched. He bent down to try and wipe the words on Cui Buqu's forehead away with his sleeve but found the task tremendously difficult.

From the side, Feng Xiao said coolly, "Don't bother. That kind of mud is everywhere here. Once dissolved in water, it's nigh impossible to get off. I tried it several times before I wrote on him. If the life debt he owes me could be so easily erased, how would this demonstrate its sanctity?"

Cui Buqu rolled his eyes.

Qiao Xian didn't say another word; she drew her sword and lunged at Feng Xiao. Pei Jingzhe sprang forward to stop her, and the two eagle riders with him also stepped forward to protect their lord. Another fierce battle was about to erupt.

"Bring me back," Cui Buqu cut in. "Zhangsun, your hat."

Zhangsun Bodhi removed the bamboo hat that never left his head. He silently put it on Cui Buqu, then heaved him onto his back.

Feng Xiao didn't stop them. He waved cheerfully. "Daoist Master Cui, take care; I'll visit you in a few days. Don't forget the life debt you owe me."

Cui Buqu's smile didn't reach his eyes. "Oh, I'll remember it for eight lifetimes."

The tangled knot that had formed between them over the past few days was nowhere near unraveling.

❁❁❁

Qiao Xian could tell Cui Buqu had relaxed after seeing her and Zhangsun. It wasn't something outsiders would notice—but she'd been his subordinate too long not to recognize his likes and dislikes. Someone as wary and guarded as Cui Buqu only relaxed for a very special reason, and Qiao Xian and Zhangsun were fortunate enough to have become one.

They had no interest in exchanging pleasantries with the Jiejian Bureau; the moment they recovered Cui Buqu, they left. Feng Xiao didn't intervene—he needed some time to recuperate himself.

The murderer of the Khotanese envoy had yet to be brought to justice, and the jade had yet to be retrieved. Thanks to Cui Buqu's plotting, the Göktürk warrior targeting him had been misled into attacking Feng Xiao. But then Feng Xiao had brought him outside the city, and Cui Buqu found himself in a three-way ambush that almost ended in his total defeat. In the game between the Zuoyue Bureau and the Jiejian Bureau, neither had achieved victory. Both sides beat a temporary retreat, making tallies in their own mental ledgers and waiting for the day they could settle the score.

On the return trip, Cui Buqu fell asleep on Zhangsun's back.

Zhangsun Bodhi's shoulders were steady as he walked, and Cui Buqu felt not a single bump or jolt.

"The lord chief appears to have been poisoned," whispered Qiao Xian.

"Mm," said Zhangsun. He'd already detected the strange aroma. "It's incense of helplessness."

Qiao Xian was taken aback; anger instantly darkened her face. "The Jiejian Bureau did it. How dare they?!"

Zhangsun was silent. Feng Xiao's reputation as a disagreeable man with questionable morals was well-known. Zhangsun wasn't remotely surprised he'd used such a method on their lord chief.

"Don't make any move. Wait and see what the lord chief has to say. He must have a plan for this as well."

Cui Buqu slept for a full two days. When he woke, his entire body felt heavy and limp. There was no part of him that wasn't exhausted. Only his mind was unusually clear, perhaps because he was finally well-rested. The moment he opened his eyes, he was alert. He called over Qiao Xian and Zhangsun.

"What have I missed in the past few days? Have Apa's men arrived?"

When the maid brought in chicken soup, Cui Buqu refused to let anyone feed him. He took the bowl himself and sipped slowly. Qiao Xian and Zhangsun had already made their inquiries and were only waiting for him to wake so they could report.

"Apa Khagan's envoy arrived in secret yesterday. We have him settled in already; now you're awake, you can meet him," said Qiao Xian.

Cui Buqu nodded. "And what's happening at the Jiejian Bureau?"

"Feng Xiao had Magistrate Zhao lock down the entire city to search for the Goguryeo woman Qin Miaoyu, the one who fought us that night. There was also the accident in the Lu family. The night you and Feng Xiao left the city, Lu Ti's daughter drowned. Her body is still at the county office. Feng Xiao is busy searching for Qin Miaoyu, so he ordered men to surround Lu Manor; no one is allowed out. Lu Ti is furious. He wrote a letter to his distant relatives, the Lu family of Fanyang, asking them to intercede with the Jiejian Bureau."

At this point, Qiao Xian paused. "There's one more thing. Yesterday, I caught a glimpse of the number one Göktürk martial artist, Fo'er, in the city. He seemed to have noticed me as well, because I was unable to tail him."

Though the city was currently under lockdown, that wouldn't stop an expert like Fo'er or Go Nyeong from sneaking back in if they wished.

"He must have received word that Apa Khagan's envoy arrived and realized he'd been misled. Go fetch Apa's envoy here. Then stay close to me in case Fo'er attempts something."

"Yes," said Qiao Xian.

She'd expected Cui Buqu would meet immediately with the envoy of Apa Khagan, but to her surprise, he seemed more interested in the affairs of the Lu family.

"What happened to Lady Lu? Tell me."

"It's a long story," said Qiao Xian.

Lu Ti's daughter was his only child, and he'd adored her beyond measure. She'd been the apple of his eye, the pearl in his palm, and he'd yearned to give her all that was wonderful in the world. He couldn't stand the idea of his daughter marrying into another family, so the moment she came of age, he sought a husband to whom he could pass the Lu family's business and inheritance.

The young maiden Lu had a cousin: Su Xing, whom Feng Xiao and Cui Buqu had encountered at Wuwei House. His parents had passed early, and he lived and studied at Lu Manor. He was of an age with Lady Lu, and they made a perfect couple. It was only natural that they developed feelings for each other. Privately, Lu Ti felt Su Xing's fate was too full of hardship—he had lost both his parents already—but his daughter loved him. The fact that Su Xing had no family to whom he owed loyalty also meant he was uniquely suited to join the Lu family. Lu Ti had arranged for them to marry two years from now.

But recently, Lu Ti had reconnected with the branch of the Lu family in Fanyang for business reasons, and the two sides had exchanged letters and visits. Upon meeting the young Lady Lu, one of the elders of the Fanyang Lu family became enamored of her and offered to play matchmaker between Lady Lu and the young son of the Wang family of Taiyuan.

The son of the Wang family was two years older than Lady Lu, a talented young man with great academic achievements. Several of his uncles served as officials in the imperial court. Everyone expected the young man would follow in the footsteps of his elders and become a minister. His future was bright, his prospects boundless.

The lad's noble background and excellent character made him hundreds of times more desirable as a son-in-law than Su Xing. Lu Ti had changed his mind, but Lady Lu was unwilling. The ever-gentle and obedient Lady Lu quarreled fiercely with her father and threw a tantrum. She had drowned that very night.

It was the same night the Jiejian Bureau's eagle rider had pursued a suspicious figure to Lu Manor. The incident with Lady Lu must have occurred at almost the same time.

32

AFTER LISTENING TO THE whole story from beginning to end, Cui Buqu pondered in silence.

Qiao Xian could tell from his expression that he was interested. "Your lordship wishes to involve yourself in this matter of the Lu family?"

"It's a good opportunity to force the Jiejian Bureau to share credit with us," he said.

Qiao Xian thought he'd already washed his hands of this case of the Khotanese envoy's murder. For a moment, she was speechless.

"Feng Xiao is not the easiest to work with," she finally managed.

"There's no need for us to take the initiative to work with him. Compared to the Lu family, Qin Miaoyu, who has the jade in her possession, is much more important. He's got his hands full searching the city for her; he has no time for the Lu family. Feng Xiao also knows Pei Jingzhe can't resolve this matter on his own. He'll definitely send him to our door."

After this explanation, his appetite seemed to return, and he ate voraciously. Not only did he finish the chicken soup, he followed it with a bowl of noodles. The instant he set down his spoon, the word came: Pei Jingzhe had indeed come to call.

Qiao Xian heaved a sigh. "The lord chief truly accounts for everything!"

"Feng Xiao is a formidable man, but he's flexible in his think-ing. The Zuoyue Bureau hindered him, but cracking the case and recovering the jade are far more important than a petty grudge." Cui Buqu stopped for a moment, puzzled. "Why did those noodles I just ate taste like the ones at the Zuoyue Bureau?"

Qiao Xian beamed at him. "Were they good?"

Outsiders only saw her cold, frosty demeanor, an unapproach-able beauty. Few had glimpsed this hidden gentleness.

"Of course they were good. The noodles and soup the Zuoyue Bureau makes are the only kind I like."

"Qiao Xian made them," said Zhangsun.

Cui Buqu revealed a rare expression of surprise. "When did you learn to cook?"

"Before we left, I asked the madam chef to teach me. I was worried you wouldn't be able to stomach the food out here. But I never thought..." When she remembered all the suffering Cui Buqu had been through in the past few days, she wanted to wring Feng Xiao's neck.

"I was the one who let myself be caught. I expected I'd have to suffer a little to stay near him," Cui Buqu said evenly. He seldom detailed his reasoning to others. But in the same way Qiao Xian was completely loyal to him, he was always willing to explain patiently to her.

They were still talking when the servants showed Pei Jingzhe in. He didn't miss the fierce glare Qiao Xian sent in his direction. Pei Jingzhe privately thought this was totally uncalled for.

"Good day, Cui-langjun." He politely cupped his hands. Feng Xiao had already told him Cui Buqu's identity. When he reflected on what this man had suffered at their hands, he felt a sharp pang of guilt.

"Where's my gift?" Cui Buqu held out a hand expectantly.

"What?" Pei Jingzhe was taken aback.

"You've come to me for a favor," Cui Buqu said lazily, "yet you're empty-handed? Are these the manners of the Jiejian Bureau?"

How did you know I'm here for a favor? The words crowded at the tip of Pei Jingzhe's tongue, but he swallowed them down. He smiled. "My lord knows your health is poor. Considering the suffering you've endured, he was sure you needed bed rest. I only came to see how you fared today. I've left the gift with your servants."

When Qiao Xian and Zhangsun had arrived in Liugong City, they had purchased a small house with a courtyard and a handful of deaf and mute servants. Unlike Zixia Monastery and Wuwei House, this house was more suitable for convalescence—secluded, quiet, and secret.

However, Feng Xiao had guessed Cui Buqu's position in the Zuoyue Bureau correctly. It was easy for him to guess that this manor, along with the incredibly popular restaurant Wuwei House, were all bases of the Zuoyue Bureau.

"I'm tired. Show our guest out." Cui Buqu had no interest in listening to Pei Jingzhe prevaricate. He lay down and turned his back to him.

Pei Jingzhe started to step forward again, but Zhangsun Bodhi strode over to block his path. He had no choice but to steel himself and tell the truth. "This subordinate indeed has a favor to request."

Qiao Xian said coldly, "Is the request from you, or Feng Xiao?"

"Is there a difference?"

"There's a big difference."

The message was clear: Pei Jingzhe was a nobody. If Feng Xiao didn't send him, they'd kick him out.

Pei Jingzhe silently cursed his lot. He was like a sheep entering the wolves' den, utterly defenseless. No wonder Feng Xiao had warned him to be direct and not bother hiding anything. He knew Pei Jingzhe was no match for these members of the Zuoyue Bureau.

The thought brought Pei Jingzhe no satisfaction. All he could say was, "I'll be honest. It was my lord who asked me to come."

Cui Buqu didn't turn to look at him. He lay motionless on his side with his back to Pei Jingzhe.

Pei Jingzhe pressed on: "My lord requests Cui-langjun intervene in the matter of the Lu family in order to find Qin Miaoyu's accomplice."

"And what about the gift?"

Understanding dawned on Pei Jingzhe as he finally realized what Cui Buqu meant by *gift*. If you wanted something from someone, you had to give something in return.

"My lord is willing to split the credit with you. Once it's all settled, he'll submit a memorial to the emperor declaring that he relied heavily on the support of the Zuoyue Bureau in this case and asking the emperor to reward you for your contributions."

Feng Xiao's choice of words hadn't been so polite—in fact, Deputy Chief Feng had crossed his legs and said carelessly, *Do I look like someone who'll let myself be cheated? I'll split the credit with him now, but next time will be different. Just go. If his price is too high, I'll make him repay it a few times over.*

There was no way around it: his boss sounded more like he was picking a fight than asking a favor. Pei Jingzhe was forced to polish his words a bit.

Cui Buqu snorted. "He'd never say something like that. I bet he told you, 'Find out what Cui Buqu wants for it. If he's too greedy, I'll make him repay it a few times over.'"

Pei Jingzhe's mouth twitched, and he thought to himself, *You really know each other too well.*

"I can help you," Cui Buqu said, "but on one condition. I want Fo'er's head."

"That's..."

"You can agree now, or this discussion is over. Feel free to see yourself out."

"Don't be so hasty, Cui-langjun," said Pei Jingzhe in a rush. "Whatever you want, I'll promise on behalf of my lord!"

The Lu family's case was pressing, and Lu Ti had already written letters asking for support. Keeping all of Lu Manor under house arrest wasn't a long-term solution. The longer this dragged on, the more trouble it would cause; it was best to resolve the matter as soon as possible.

Only now did Cui Buqu turn back over and sit up to slowly slip into his shoes. "You should have agreed earlier. Instead you made me lie down in bed right after I ate. My stomach hurts."

Pei Jingzhe's mouth twitched. "The fault is all mine, sir!"

With this settled, he led Cui Buqu and the others to Lu Manor. Pei Jingzhe furtively observed Qiao Xian along the way. He thought he'd been subtle until she shot him a cold glance—he was forced to look away and trade his secret observation for open inquiry. "Cui-langjun, how should this lady be addressed?"

Cui Buqu's lips quirked in something that wasn't quite a smile. "Is it you who's interested? Or Feng Xiao?"

Pei Jingzhe mumbled, "Is there a difference here as well?"

"If you're interested, go ask her yourself. If Feng Xiao wants to know..." Pei Jingzhe waited for Cui Buqu's next words, but he seemed to reconsider what he was about to say. "...then I definitely won't tell you."

Pei Jingzhe pressed his lips together in silence. He finally realized that, from top to bottom, there was no one at the Zuoyue Bureau with whom he was on friendly terms.

But who'd asked the deputy chief to be so ruthless that he'd even drug Cui Buqu with incense of helplessness? Pei Jingzhe had thought the Zuoyue Bureau and the Jiejian Bureau were sister agencies with the same goals, and thus their cooperation would make things twice as efficient and fruitful. But a grudge once formed was not so easily dissolved.

Lu Manor was shrouded under the thick fog of grief.

Lu Ti's cherished daughter had died; he was heartbroken. On top of this tragedy, his manor was surrounded, and now his sorrow was tempered with rage.

Feng Xiao only had so many eagle riders, so he'd borrowed some men from Magistrate Zhao. Yet Magistrate Zhao was also plagued by troubles he dared not mention—he didn't want to offend Lu Ti, but he also couldn't disobey Feng Xiao's orders. Caught between the two, he held his nose and told Lieutenant Liu Lin to do as the Jiejian Bureau instructed, while also asking him to show the Lu family leniency.

Regardless of all else, Lady Lu had to have a funeral, and the family lacked the necessary supplies. Liu Lin had been ordered to keep Lu Manor surrounded, but Magistrate Zhao had privately instructed him to turn a blind eye if he saw them sneak out the back. Unfortunately, Pei Jingzhe and Cui Buqu happened to come upon this very scene as they arrived.

"Stop! Who gave you permission to leave!" Pei Jingzhe cried in anger. He moved forward at once to stop them.

Leading the group was the Lu family steward. He choked down his grief and anger to cup his hands and plead, "The young lady of our house has passed away. We must hold a funeral—surely we can't leave her without a place to rest? Please, have some mercy!"

"What do you want?" Pei Jingzhe asked. "I'll have Liu Lin send someone to buy it—but no one from the Lu household is allowed to leave!"

The steward finally snapped. "Who do you people think you are! The dead come first! Our lady suffered a terrible misfortune before she could marry. The mistress wants to make things livelier for her, lest she feel lonely on the road. Everything must be of the highest quality! If we let outsiders buy supplies, how would that demonstrate our devotion toward our young lady?! Are you so cruel, so unreasonable, that you show no respect even for the dead?"

"The one disrespecting the dead isn't us, but you," Cui Buqu said coldly. He pointed out a maid who was standing behind the steward with her head lowered. "That's a man. Seize him."

Pei Jingzhe was stunned, but Qiao Xian and Zhangsun Bodhi didn't hesitate. The last word had barely left Cui Buqu's lips when they swept forward to restrain the tall and slender maid.

The maid was forced to raise her head. At first glance, Pei Jingzhe merely felt she looked familiar—but then he recognized her. It was none other than Lady Lu's cousin, the one who should have married into the family: Su Xing.

Su Xing was fair and delicate even as a man. He'd followed the steward, hiding himself among a couple of tall servants. At a glance, he passed for any other servant of the manor. If Pei Jingzhe's group hadn't happened to run into them, and if Cui Buqu hadn't exposed him, his disguise would have succeeded.

"Su Xing?" asked Pei Jingzhe.

The young man showed no alarm at being discovered. His voice was calm as he said, "I've been close with my cousin for a long time. Her likes, her dislikes—even my aunt and uncle might not know as well as I. I left the house with the steward so I could buy the things she loves most; at least then she won't feel so lonely down there. What's wrong with that?"

His eyes were bloodshot, his cheeks markedly gaunter, and a dusting of stubble shadowed his chin. On his face was the calm left behind by old sorrow. No one who saw him could say he was cold-blooded and ruthless; they would be more likely to sigh about star-crossed fates and the separation of death.

"Then why did you disguise yourself as a woman?" Pei Jingzhe asked.

"My cousin and I were engaged for some time, but we weren't married. If I bought something for her in the name of the Lu family and rumor of it spread, it would tarnish her reputation. My cousin was pure and unsullied. She came into this world that way, and she should leave that way too."

Cui Buqu regarded him for a moment, then turned to the steward. "Perhaps we can bring this matter to a close today. When all are satisfied, I will return you your freedom myself. I too share some small destiny with the Lu family. Please allow me to enter and offer a stick of incense to your young lady."

The steward recognized Cui Buqu. When he'd first arrived and Zixia Monastery had begun to flourish, talk of the medical skills of its abbot had spread through the city. The Lu family matriarch had also benefitted from his kindness.

The steward sighed and beckoned them back toward the manor. "This way."

This manor housed three generations of the Lu family. Lu Ti had an old mother who still lived. Last year, he'd had a coffin made and placed in the cellar in preparation for her passing, in accordance with local custom. Yet fate had other plans—the coffin never held the old mother. Instead, it was the young Lady Lu who lay inside.

Though a coffin was on hand, the memorial tablet, candles, and funeral flags were missing. Thus the steward had bribed Liu Lin so he might go out and purchase them.

When Liu Lin saw Pei Jingzhe and the others come in with the steward, he looked horribly embarrassed and braced himself for a scolding. But Pei Jingzhe ignored him. He asked the steward to take them to the hall and sent someone to invite Lu Ti.

The coffin was already closed, and the hall once used to entertain guests had been temporarily transformed into a place of mourning. The pots for burning paper money had been prepared, but there was nothing inside. Lu Ti's wife, Madam Li, was dressed in plain clothes and sitting in the hall, staring at the coffin with blank eyes. The maids at her side murmured words of comfort, but she turned a deaf ear to them all. Lu Manor, which had once thronged with guests, was now cold and somber.

Cui Buqu crossed the threshold, took an incense stick from a maid, and bowed to the coffin. He personally went up to offer the incense before crossing the hall to stand before Madam Li.

"Be at peace."

Madam Li was thoroughly heartbroken, her complexion a waxy yellow—she had always taken great pains with her appearance, yet in her grief she paid it no heed. She barely reacted to Cui Buqu's words, so the old female servant beside her greeted him in her stead. "Thank you very much, Daoist Master Cui."

"I wish to examine the body in the coffin."

These words shocked the entire hall. The servants of the Lu family burst into furious chatter, and even Madam Li jolted out of her daze and raised her head to look at him.

The Lu family steward was furious. "Didn't you come to offer incense?!"

"I'm here to offer my condolences, as well as investigate this case. I suspect foul play in the death of your young lady."

"Daoist Master Cui, I respect the kindness you've shown to our mistress, but you can't just say whatever you please! And to think you've become a lackey of the Jiejian Bureau as well!"

Pei Jingzhe's lip curled. He thought to himself, *No sir, our Jiejian Bureau is incapable of recruiting this great buddha.*

Cui Buqu hadn't fully recuperated even after his long sleep. The walk here had fatigued him; he didn't wait for the host's invitation and found an empty place to sit. He looked up at them. "Enough. If I say open it, then open it. Or do I have to do it myself?" At this, he shot an impatient glance at Pei Jingzhe.

"Who dares open the coffin?! You'll do it over my dead body!" Lu Ti had rushed over just in time to hear the end of Cui Buqu's speech. He strode forward in a rage, longing for nothing more than to roll up his sleeves and beat Cui Buqu half to death on the spot.

Qiao Xian saw him barreling toward Cui Buqu and stepped forward. She resembled a celestial being in her fluttering white robes, yet a single airy push from her hand sent Lu Ti stumbling back five or six paces. He grabbed at the wall for balance.

Cui Buqu wasted no more breath on them. He said three words only: *"Open the coffin!"*

Pei Jingzhe had received strict instructions before he left Feng Xiao. As long as Cui Buqu agreed to help, he was to follow Cui Buqu's orders to the letter, no matter what they were.

And at that moment, Cui Buqu had given him an order, albeit a rather unconventional one. Still, the Jiejian Bureau and the Lu family had been at loggerheads for so long that piling one more offense on top of the rest didn't mean much. He steeled himself and stepped forward, heading toward the coffin. Reaching out a hand, he circulated his internal energy, then pushed the lid hard and bared the interior of the coffin to the daylight.

The husband and wife of the Lu family wailed at the sight before them.

33

I**T WAS STILL EARLY SPRING**, and the weather had yet to warm. Lady Lu had been lying in the coffin for two days, but no unpleasant odor wafted from her body. Nevertheless, the dead were not to be disturbed—now that her corpse was revealed once more, the servants of the Lu family took two involuntary steps back. Only Su Xing didn't retreat. He approached the coffin and stared dazedly at the girl within.

As she watched, Madam Li's eyes grew even redder.

Lu Ti was wracked with guilt. If he hadn't gotten so mixed up, his beloved daughter and potential son-in-law would never have met such an end. His heart was fit to burst with pain and regret, but he couldn't turn all his suffering and remorse on himself. He glared at Pei Jingzhe and Cui Buqu's backs as Qiao Xian effortlessly held him in place.

Cui Buqu walked up to the coffin and gazed at the girl within. Her eyes were closed, her expression serene. They'd wiped her face clean and reapplied rouge, then changed her into a fresh set of robes. It was impossible to tell she'd been waterlogged and disheveled when they pulled her from the water.

Under the eyes of the hall, Cui Buqu reached out and touched Lady Lu's face. He opened her collar, then flipped her body over to touch and examine it.

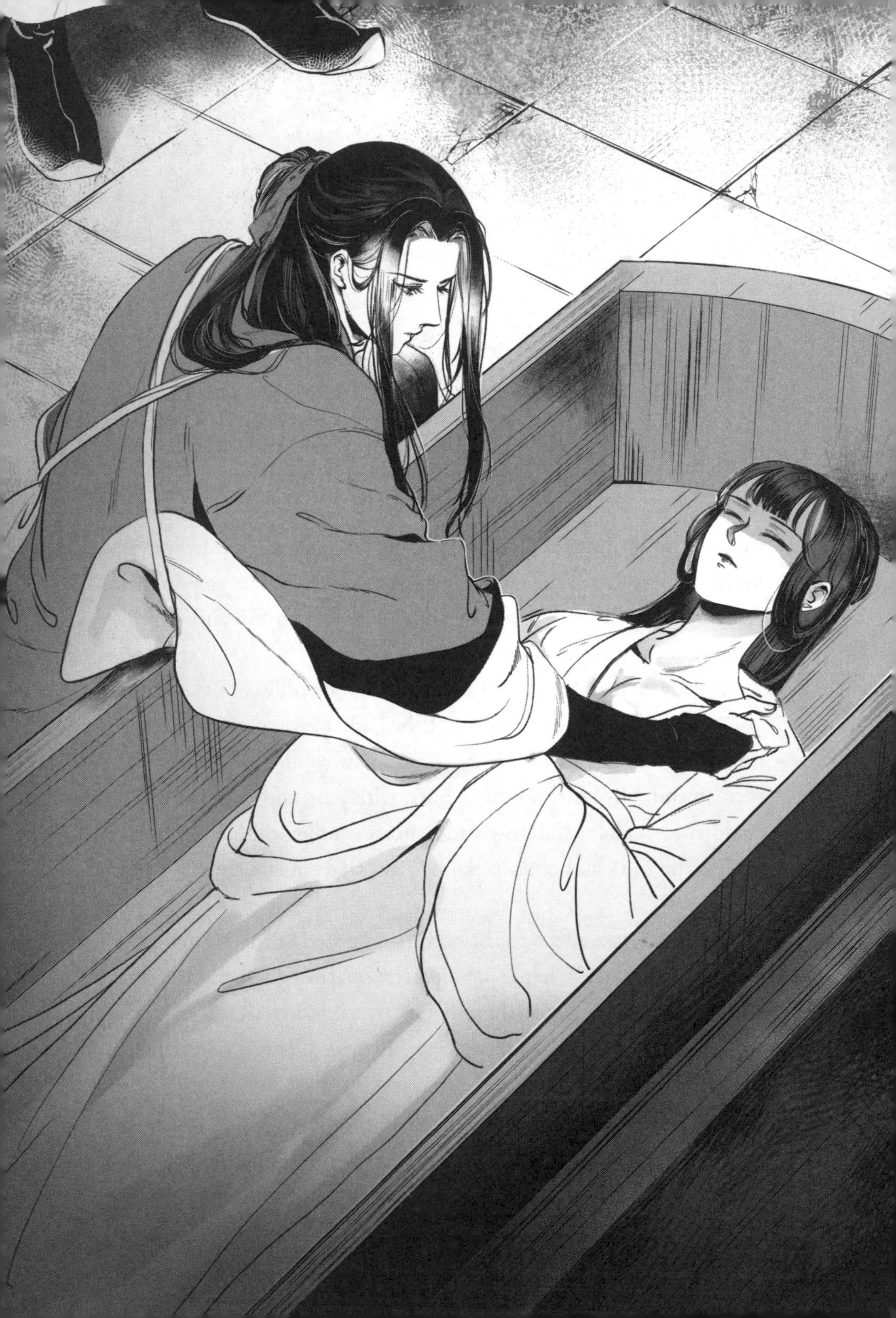

Lu Ti saw red. If he hadn't been restrained, he would have long since dashed over to punch Cui Buqu's sickly face. What he couldn't manage physically he made up in words: he and the rest of the Lu family shouted and cursed Cui Buqu without cease.

Cui Buqu didn't look up from his work. "Silence everyone aside from Lu Ti and Su Xing," he said impatiently.

"You think I'll thank you for this?!" Lu Ti raged. "My little girl is dead. Do you wish to steal her peace, even in death?! I'll never forgive the Jiejian Bureau as long as I live!"

Pei Jingzhe coughed twice. "This Cui-langjun is from the Zuoyue Bureau, not the Jiejian Bureau."

With his back to him, Cui Buqu said carelessly, "I'm unhappy to hear that. If Feng Xiao hadn't sent you to me for help, I wouldn't be here now. Lao-Lu, you're right to place the blame on the Jiejian Bureau."

"I don't care if it's the Jiejian Bureau or the Zuoyue Bureau! Either way, today's humiliation is engraved upon my heart!"

"There's no point snarling like that. Even if you did summon someone from the Fanyang Lu family, my Jiejian Bureau wouldn't fear you."

Qiao Xian and Zhangsun Bodhi were both speechless.

The corner of Pei Jingzhe's lips twitched. He was admittedly disturbed by the obscene acts Cui Buqu was performing in the name of investigation—he had the niggling feeling the man was merely taking this opportunity to smear the Jiejian Bureau's good name. But just as he was about to put a stop to it, his eyes widened. Cui Buqu had bent and pried Lady Lu's mouth open, then shoved his fingers deep into her throat.

"You—"

Cui Buqu withdrew his hand and turned nonchalantly back to Pei Jingzhe. "Do you have a handkerchief?"

Pei Jingzhe produced one from his sleeve and handed it over. He'd seen it for sale earlier on the street and liked the look of it, so he'd bought it with the intention of giving it as a gift.

Cui Buqu took the handkerchief and wiped his hand.

Pei Jingzhe felt a wave of nausea as he watched Cui Buqu rub the filth from his hand onto the handkerchief. But Cui Buqu acted like it was nothing out of the ordinary. He said to Lu Ti, "Your daughter didn't drown. She was murdered."

Lu Ti's enraged expression froze in a terrifying rictus. "Don't speak nonsense!" he yelled.

Cui Buqu extended his hand to show some kind of sticky, yellow residue smeared on the handkerchief. "What did Lady Lu eat before her death?"

Lu Ti didn't know; he looked to his wife Madam Li, but she didn't know either. In large, wealthy families like theirs, parents didn't stick close to their children. They were usually only together during the morning and evening greetings.

Madam Li immediately summoned her daughter's nurse and maid for questioning.

The nurse was over forty years old, with a frank and honest face. The maid was fifteen or sixteen and dressed in pink. Though she wore neither makeup nor accessories, a palm-sized lotus flower was embroidered near the hem of her skirt, which lent her a splash of brightness.

Cui Buqu prompted them to explain what they'd been doing the night of Lady Lu's death.

The nurse had been watching a pot as she prepared a portion of spun-sugar swallow's nest for the young lady. The swallow's nest had to be simmered for two hours, and she'd planned to serve it to Lady Lu right before bed. The nurse therefore hadn't seen her all evening and didn't know what the lady might have eaten.

The maid spoke next: "That night, Daniang ate some green bean pastries. This lowly one brought them to her."

These days, it was common for servants to refer to their masters by their place in the family. As Lady Lu was an only daughter, the maid addressed her as *Daniang*—eldest lady.

"Was there anything unusual about her that night?" asked Cui Buqu.

The maid glanced at Lu Ti and hesitated before saying, "Earlier in the day, the master summoned Daniang. When Daniang returned, she was deeply unhappy. I asked why, but she refused to tell me. Su-gongzi[17] sent someone to invite Daniang to go flower viewing, but she didn't want to go. She insisted on staying alone inside the house."

The nurse added, "He-niang is right. Early that morning, Daniang went to pay respects to the master, and she stayed for about two hours longer than usual. I thought it strange at the time and sent someone to hurry them up, but one of the master's servants said Daniang had already left."

Previously, Lu Ti had been overwhelmed by his rage. Now, listening to the servants recall the events of the day, he got himself under control and did his best to remember as well. "That's right. That day, I mentioned to Daniang the prospect of marrying into the Wang family of Taiyuan, but she refused. She said she and Su Xing were in love. I... Hah, if only I had known! How could I have made such a terrible mistake?"

"How long did the two of you talk?" asked Cui Buqu.

"Around half an hour," said Lu Ti. "Her mother came in to persuade her, and then I asked her to go home and think about it. Who knew she would..."

"How long does it take to walk from where you spoke to the house she lived in?"

---

17   公子. *A respectful address for young men, originally only for those from affluent households.*

Lady Lu's nurse was the one to answer. "We servants move quickly, so we can get there in about five minutes. Daniang walks slower, so she'd take around ten."

"So you chatted for half an hour. Even adding on the ten-minute walk, there's still more than an hour left to account for. Where did she go?"

Everyone looked at the maid who daily accompanied Lady Lu and never left her side. The girl stuttered, "D-Daniang said she wanted to enjoy some fresh air, so she walked more slowly than usual."

"Is that the truth?" Cui Buqu countered. "Or did she go somewhere after, and you're too afraid to say?"

"How could my lowly self lie?!" exclaimed He-niang.

"Call every servant in the manor; ask if anyone saw Lady Lu that day. Then we'll know for certain," said Cui Buqu coldly.

Pei Jingzhe didn't know why Cui Buqu had suddenly jumped from examining the corpse to interrogating Lady Lu's maid, but when he saw how flustered she looked and heard how hesitant her speech was, he too became sure she was hiding something. He watched quietly from the side, waiting to see where this led.

He-niang panicked; she fell to her knees. "Daniang went to find Su-gongzi!"

Furrows appeared on Lu Ti's brow. Without waiting for Cui Buqu to ask more, he cut in: "Why did she go to Su Xing? And why would you lie about it?!"

"Uncle, Cousin rushed in while I was painting," said Su Xing. "She was upset and told me you wished her to marry another man. I gave her some advice and calmed her down, then told her to go back home. I thought I could talk to her again when she regained her composure and then everything would be fine. I didn't expect her to succumb to despair and..." The words faded into a deep sigh. His haggard expression tore at the heart.

The rims of Lu Ti's eyes grew red as he held back his tears. "I failed you both..."

"Please wait," Cui Buqu interrupted. "He-niang, Su Xing resides with the Lu family, and he and Lady Lu went out often together. That she would run to Su Xing after hearing bad news is to be expected. So why were you afraid to tell the truth?"

He-niang hesitated, so Su Xing answered instead. "I asked her to keep it secret. I was the cause of the disagreement between my uncle and my cousin. If Uncle learned she came straight to me, he might have thought I was trying to influence her. I only sought to avoid any accusations."

Pei Jingzhe was appalled. "She stood up to her father for you, yet all you worried about was staying out of it and keeping your nose clean?"

Su Xing's smile was bitter. "You are unaware of the difficulties that come with living under someone else's roof. My cousin and I were in love, but I have neither family, home, nor career. A place with the Wang family of Taiyuan was far more suitable for her. If I were Uncle, I too would wish my daughter to marry into a good family!"

Lu Ti opened his mouth to say something, then stopped. His face was written with guilt.

Madam Li sobbed and lowered her head to wipe at her tears.

Yet Cui Buqu remained unmoved. "You say you were painting. What did you paint?"

"*Summer Sun on Lotuses,*" replied Su Xing.

"Show me."

Su Xing frowned. "Daoist Master Cui, what does this have to do with my cousin's death?"

Pei Jingzhe also felt that Cui Buqu's questions were starting to stray off course. But Cui Buqu insisted. "Bring all the paintings from your room here, including *Summer Sun on Lotuses*."

Even Madam Li couldn't help but speak up. "Daoist Master Cui, this..."

"This is related to your daughter's death," said Cui Buqu.

Lu Ti was confused, his mind in turmoil. He gestured for his steward to follow Cui Buqu's instructions, and the paintings were swiftly brought over from Su Xing's room.

Su Xing's paintings filled an entire basket, but Cui Buqu had Qiao Xian unroll each scroll in turn. Most of the paintings were of various kinds of lotuses: some with new buds yet to bloom, and some with blossoms withering in death.

Pei Jingzhe didn't know much about painting, but those who haven't eaten pork have still seen pigs run. Su Xing's paintings were average at best; he had some ability but not much talent. If he'd had talent, he wouldn't have spent so many years living with his relatives—he could've left to blaze his own trail long ago.

Lady Lu lay quietly in the coffin as it was surrounded by dozens of scrolls blossoming with lotus flowers. It was a scene to make anyone sigh.

"He-niang," Cui Buqu said suddenly, "Was your daniang good to you?"

The maid was taken aback. "Of course. Daniang was wonderful to me!"

"Then why did you betray her and help Su Xing conceal her murder?" asked Cui Buqu.

Everyone was dumbfounded.

"Daoist Master Cui, what are you saying?!" Lu Ti blurted.

"Your daniang is dead. Even if your house currently lacks for mourning clothes, there's no reason you should be wearing pink. That dress is embroidered with lotuses, and you are called He-niang, which means *lotus*. What a coincidence that Su Xing here also likes to paint lotuses. Can it really be chance? You tell me."

"Watch what you say, Daoist Master Cui!" said Su Xing coldly. "He-niang likes lotuses because her name is He-niang. What does that have to do with me?"

"Is that so?" Cui Buqu sneered, then turned to the steward and Madam Li. "Was her name He-niang when she entered the manor?"

Madam Li shook her head. She paid a great deal of attention to the maids who served her daughter. "She used to be called Shi-niang because she was the tenth child in her family. They were poor, and her parents couldn't afford to raise her. We purchased her at the age of six, and two years ago, Daniang personally changed her name to He-niang."

Cui Buqu looked at Su Xing. "Two years ago, you would already have been living at this manor."

"So what if I was?" said Su Xing.

"Do you know why I put my fingers into Lady Lu's mouth just now? She'd eaten some green bean pastries that night, and the residue remains in her mouth. If she'd drowned, water would have poured into her mouth and nose and these traces would have been washed away. Yet there was no sediment from the water in her mouth, and the leftover bean paste remained. This proves she was placed in the water after her death, when she was no longer breathing. That's why the water couldn't enter."

Lu Ti was stunned. He began struggling fiercely, and at Cui Buqu's signal, Zhangsun let him go. Lu Ti wobbled and stumbled forward to look down into the coffin.

Cui Buqu looked at Su Xing and said, "The night Feng Xiao won the jade at the auction, many experts visited Qiushan Manor. The one in black was you, was it not?"

"I see Daoist Master Cui wishes to frame me," said Su Xing coldly. "You're trying to pin everything on me!"

"You were the one who sent that jade to Linlang Pavilion," said Cui Buqu. "You did it to test everyone's reactions and lure out your accomplice. That's why you acted differently than the others. You didn't come to steal the jade; you were there to hide and observe. Once you confirmed your accomplice wasn't present, you left. Do you know how I recognized you? Because that night, the person in black stood with his right wrist in his left hand, just as you do now. You can disguise and conceal your face, but your body tells the truth!"

Su Xing remained unmoved. "That's because I spend too much time painting and writing," he said evenly. "I overtax my wrist, so sometimes it's sore. Many scholars experience this issue. If you don't believe me, find another scholar and examine them. Then you'll see."

At that moment, Zhangsun attacked him from behind with a powerful strike. He put eight-tenths of his full strength into the blow, enough to kill Su Xing where he stood. Su Xing turned his head slightly aside but remained still as Zhangsun's blow came closer and closer. At the last second, Zhangsun withdrew his palm and stepped back.

Su Xing knew he'd made the right call—they'd only wanted to test him.

But Cui Buqu wasn't going to let him off so easily. "Why pretend? The exact reaction you just tried to avoid has demonstrated you're a martial artist, and a powerful one at that."

Su Xing scoffed. "If all you want is to add to my charges, why should I stand here and listen to your slander? I'm leaving!"

He flicked his sleeves and turned to go. In a flash, Qiao Xian's sword glare swept toward his back, brimming with the murderous force of a thousand troops crushing their enemies. This killing intent was naked, unlike Zhangsun Bodhi's probing blow. At last, Su Xing could no longer feign ignorance; he stepped aside to evade.

That one sidestep removed all doubt—this man was a martial artist.

Exposed, he no longer hesitated. He reached for his waist, and a rippling, glinting blade appeared in his hand. He turned and sped toward Qiao Xian—but halfway across, he made a sharp turn and grabbed Lu Ti instead. In an instant, Lu Ti became a hostage, Su Xing's whip sword coiling around his neck.

"Stay back, or I'll kill him!"

Cui Buqu shook his head. "What's the use in taking him hostage? When the Jiejian Bureau wishes to settle something, we won't stop for anyone!"

Pei Jingzhe was at a loss for words.

Deputy Bureau Chief, this man is throwing your authority around and directing all blame to the Jiejian Bureau, yet still you want his help? Doesn't the Jiejian Bureau have enough enemies already?!

34

L U TI HAD BEEN TAKEN HOSTAGE, and his life now hung by a thread. Yet he showed no fear. Rather, upon his face was written disbelief, shock, and rage.

"Sanlang, let go of your uncle!" Madam Li sobbed.

"You bastard! When have your aunt or I ever wronged you? How could you kill Daniang?!" Lu Ti was trembling all over, paying no heed to the whip sword slowly tightening around his neck. Blood dripped down the blade and over his skin. Madam Li's terror overwhelmed her: her vision went dark, and she crumpled limply to the floor.

"I'm sorry. You did treat me well, but I haven't forgotten my hometown and family. I can't become the real Su Xing!"

Everyone was shocked, including the group with Cui Buqu.

"If you're not Su Xing, then who are you?!" asked Pei Jingzhe.

Su Xing was silent.

Lu Ti was filled with anguish and sorrow. "Even if you aren't Su Xing, you've been part of the Lu family for many years. I have no sons and have always treated you as my own child. Daniang was devoted to you; she never wavered. The proposed marriage with the Wang family of Taiyuan was my own fixation. It had nothing to do with Daniang. If you were dissatisfied, why not kill me instead?! Why kill Daniang?! Have...have you no conscience?"

Su Xing sighed. "You misunderstand. I didn't kill Daniang because of the marriage. If you wish to blame someone for Daniang's death, blame her for being in the wrong place at the wrong time. That's why she had to die!"

"Did she discover you were a Goguryeon?" Cui Buqu cut in. "Or did she discover you killed the Khotanese envoy and stole the Jade of Heaven Lake?"

Su Xing narrowed his eyes and looked at Cui Buqu. "The Jiejian Bureau deserves its reputation. I thought this was well concealed and I could escape without issue. I never imagined simply killing Lu Youniang would cause so much trouble!"

Cui Buqu smirked. "You think the Jiejian Bureau has anyone as talented and resourceful as me? I'm from the Zuoyue Bureau, remember that! The characters *Zuo*, *Er*, *Yue* together make *Sui*. Don't mistake one enemy for another, lest you find yourself dead without knowing who killed you!"

Pei Jingzhe stared.

Now he finally understood. Cui Buqu used the Jiejian Bureau's name when he was offending his enemies, and the Zuoyue Bureau's name when he was intimidating them and burnishing his reputation.

Must you debase our Jiejian Bureau? What right do you have to make the Zuoyue Bureau sound superior? A crowd of complaints stampeded through Pei Jingzhe's heart, but now wasn't the time to speak them aloud. All he could do was wait till this was all over so he could run and tattle to Feng Xiao. Of everyone present, only Pei Jingzhe had attention to spare for these complex, agitated thoughts swirling in his heart. The rest of the hall's focus was drawn to the conversation between Su Xing and Cui Buqu.

Lu Ti was aghast. He shook like a leaf. "You... You're Goguryeon? Then what happened to the real Su Xing?!"

"He died long ago," Su Xing said coolly. "Six years ago, there was a plague in Su Xing's hometown; all five members of his family died. I happened to be passing through and took on his identity. I pretended I'd had a narrow escape and came to the Lu family for shelter."

Lu Ti was panting. "Why...why choose the Lu family?! The Lu clan has no connection to Goguryeo!"

"Whether it's the son-in-law of the Lu family or Su Xing, to me it's just a shell. Wherever they need me, that's where I go. Whoever they need me to be, that's who I become."

"Who's 'they'?" asked Pei Jingzhe.

Su Xing ignored him and continued. "After I settled down with the Lu family, they made no attempt to contact me. I originally planned to marry Youniang and become Su Xing in truth. That would have been rather nice. Unfortunately, when news came that Khotan wished to meet with the emperor of Sui, they claimed me again. So you see, I was unable to stay out of the matter."

"But what does that have to do with your murder of Lu Youniang?" Pei Jingzhe asked. "She was a girl who lived in ladies' chambers; she had nothing to do with your schemes and plotting!"

"I also wish to know!" Lu Ti wailed. "Su Xing, whether or not that's really your name, you've never suffered any injustice at the hands of the Lu family. Your aunt was afraid the servants in the family would look down on you, so she specifically instructed them to treat you as they would treat Youniang. And the way Youniang regarded you was even more... Why, why?!"

"Does this need to be asked?" Cui Buqu said coldly. "Lu Youniang has nothing to do with the Khotanese envoy, but she must have seen something she shouldn't. Su Xing was forced to silence the witness!"

"That's right," said Su Xing. "That day, when Youniang left her father's, she rushed right over to find me, but I happened to be out. Normally she's very well-mannered; this was the first time she entered my study without permission."

"People like you are meticulous and careful, otherwise you wouldn't be able to conceal yourself for so many years. Even if Lu Youniang did enter the study, what could she possibly have seen that she shouldn't have?"

"I have a book filled with codes. I use those codes to decipher messages sent by my accomplices. The book itself is unremarkable; normally, no one would bother flipping through it. Unfortunately, of all the books on the bookshelf, that was the one she took out to read."

Su Xing closed his eyes. He didn't have to tell them all this; he could simply remain silent. Perhaps Cui Buqu's group would never have found out what Lu Youniang discovered that ended her life. And yet he'd spilled the entire story. It was clear the lovely, ill-fated Lu Youniang wasn't nothing to him.

The dead could never return. Only in this way could he soothe the tiny sliver of guilt pricking his heart.

"When I returned, I noted my cousin's flustered expression and the way she stumbled over her words. I went to find the book and saw signs it'd been read. My cousin was sharp—I knew she'd connected the dots. But I hadn't obtained the jade; I couldn't afford to be exposed. Youniang had to die." He heaved a weary sigh.

Lu Ti's face streamed with tears—but they were tears of rage, the tears of a father powerless before the villain who'd killed his beloved daughter. "Youniang loved you with all her heart. She refused a marriage into the Wang family of Taiyuan. Even if she discovered something, she would never betray you. Why couldn't you let her live?!"

"I couldn't take the risk. If my identity was exposed and the mission failed, death awaits my family in Goguryeo. I can only repay Youniang's love for me in the next life." Su Xing looked at Cui Buqu. "You must also know by now that the real Jade of Heaven Lake isn't on me. I can offer you Lu Ti's life and some valuable information—would you be willing to let me go in exchange?"

Pei Jingzhe sniffed contemptuously. "You mean to give up your accomplice? She's been seriously injured, and we're combing the city for her as we speak. She'll be caught any minute."

Su Xing shook his head. "Only I know where she'll be hiding. You won't find her even if you search for three days and three nights. And don't forget, the jade is in her hands. She's capable; she likely already discovered the jade's secret—that it can be used to enhance martial arts. Even healing internal injuries might be possible with the help of the jade. Once she recuperates and sneaks out of the city, good luck catching her."

As he spoke, his gaze never left Cui Buqu. He clearly knew who was in charge here.

"Very well," said Cui Buqu. "If your information is accurate, I will drop the charges against you for the murder of Lu Youniang. You needn't release Lu Ti now if you don't trust me. You can release him once we've caught your accomplice."

Lu Ti hissed and spit. "Absolutely not! Even if he drops the charges, I won't let you go. I'll kill you!"

Su Xing paid him no heed. He tapped the acupoint that would render Lu Ti mute, and Lu Ti fell silent.

"I need a guarantee. Something strong enough to reassure me," Su Xing said to Cui Buqu.

Cui Buqu addressed Zhangsun Bodhi. "Head to Feng Xiao's place to help out. No need to come back for now. I'll find you if I need you."

Zhangsun nodded. He asked no questions but turned and left.

Su Xing watched Zhangsun disappear and secretly breathed a sigh of relief. The one person on the scene he feared was Zhangsun Bodhi. Su Xing was an elite martial artist himself; with Zhangsun gone, he considered no one else here his match. He was no longer afraid.

Cui Buqu thrust a hand out toward Pei Jingzhe. "Give it here."

Pei Jingzhe looked back at him, flummoxed.

Impatiently, Cui Buqu said, "Your deputy chief asked me to help, so he must have given you some kind of certificate or seal. I need it now, so give it here."

Pei Jingzhe couldn't help saying, "But your lordship is from the Zuo—" His voice died out as Cui Buqu nailed him with a sinister glare. With great reluctance, he reached into his lapels and produced a small seal, then tossed it to Cui Buqu.

Cui Buqu looked down at the seal, then threw it in turn to Su Xing. "This is the seal of the Jiejian Bureau's deputy chief. Any gate within Great Sui's borders will open to you with this seal. Though leaving this place means leaving the country, with this certification in hand you'll feel some measure of reassurance, no?"

Su Xing's true background was a tightly kept secret, but his six-year stay with the Lu family had influenced him. He'd seen no few treasures, and the moment he weighed the seal in his hand he knew Cui Buqu was telling the truth. He tucked it into his lapels, then pulled Lu Ti toward the door, step by step.

Every member of the Lu family looked upon him as their mortal enemy as they followed tightly after him, but Su Xing paid them no attention. Though Cui Buqu had no martial arts to speak of, to Su Xing's mind, the man was somehow a more present threat than either Qiao Xian or Pei Jingzhe. It was the prick of his martial artist's intuition—inexplicable, but unfailingly accurate.

When Su Xing and Lu Ti were at a distance Su Xing thought sufficient for his escape, he spoke: "Qin Miaoyu can most often be found in three places in this city. The first two are Chunxiang House and Ronghe Building. The third is the small Qingzhuan house in the east of the city. Upon its doors hang banners with couplets that say, 'Green willows flourish beneath the light; the red walls glow, refreshed and bright.'"

Qiao Xian and Zhangsun had previously located Qin Miaoyu in the vicinity of Chunxiang House, so the moment they heard this, they knew Su Xing wasn't lying.

Su Xing took a deep breath, then leapt up onto the roof taking Lu Ti with him. "I've said all I promised, so I'll be leaving now." He smiled.

He wasn't particularly handsome, but the instant he was out of danger, he assumed a calm, steady aura. Seeing him like this, it made sense Lady Lu had fallen for him. It was her ill luck to have trusted the wrong person and lost her life.

"I have one more question," said Cui Buqu.

"Daoist Master Cui, now you're being greedy. I won't answer."

"Since your name isn't Su Xing, how should I address you?"

Su Xing was silent a spell. "Yin Zairong, as in 'a gentleman is made through his achievements, not his looks.'"

"Better it should be 'a gentleman is made through his *virtue*, not looks'!" Qiao Xian sneered. "You know, when she fought with us, she chose to risk escape rather than reveal your whereabouts!"

She wasn't referring to Lady Lu, but to Qin Miaoyu.

Su Xing was taken aback. The moment his focus slipped, a strong wind blew up from behind him. He made to dodge, but he was holding Lu Ti; there was no time. He had no choice but to shove Lu Ti away, pushing off him to veer to the side. But the person behind him seemed to anticipate his move; they swept to the side after him.

Su Xing was afraid Qiao Xian and the others would fall upon him at once. Unwilling to fight, he fled. To his surprise, the opponent's qinggong was superb—he shot past Su Xing to block his escape. A blast from his opponent's palm whipped toward him; Su Xing brought up his sword to block. Their eyes met, and Su Xing saw a terribly handsome face.

"Leaving in such a hurry? Perhaps you'll return my seal to me first," Feng Xiao said with a smile.

35

Su Xing had no interest in chatting with Feng Xiao and even less in testing his abilities. Right then his most important goal was to escape. Anything else could wait.

He'd lain low in the Lu family for many years, but his skills hadn't declined in the least. On the contrary, he was better now than when he'd left Goguryeo. Only death awaited him if he was caught; he ignored defense in favor of an all-out offense, every strike a killing blow as he beat Feng Xiao back.

Pei Jingzhe tossed his longsword to Feng Xiao, who caught it without looking. He thrust it forward to meet the whip sword Su Xing was slashing toward him and twisted. The blades vibrated with the internal energy of their wielders—Su Xing's slightly weaker. His wrist went numb as the whip sword shuddered and went flying, flung away by his opponent's blade.

Seeing things going south, he turned and gathered his qi to escape. His figure was like a soaring crane, bold and graceful. Even Qiao Xian exclaimed in surprise, "The foundations of his qinggong are solid; that doesn't look like the Goguryeon style."

"How do Goguryeons approach qinggong?" Pei Jingzhe asked.

Qiao Xian's face may as well have been covered in a layer of frost; she made no reply.

Pei Jingzhe's mouth twitched at the corner. He felt rather aggrieved. *I didn't poison your chief, and I didn't drag him all over the place either. I'm just a subordinate following orders. Give me a break!*

It was Cui Buqu who answered. "The Goguryeon and Fusang people are close, and their martial arts are similar. They emphasize stealth and cunning—hiding in the dark to seek a fatal strike, or defeating the enemy with lightning speed. They rarely employ this kind of light and agile style; among Goguryeons, such qinggong is usually practiced only by women."

"Did Qin Miaoyu teach it to him?" Pei Jingzhe guessed. "Yet he betrayed her too!"

Qiao Xian mouth twisted with cold disdain. It was rare for her to hold her tongue, but Pei Jingzhe didn't need her to speak to know her thoughts: all men in this world were callous creatures. He couldn't resist saying, "They were originally allies, but Qin Miaoyu turned her back on Su Xing and stole the jade for herself. Now Su Xing has betrayed her in turn. They're merely two dogs biting at each other."

"Perhaps Qin Miaoyu is no paragon of virtue," Qiao Xian said coldly, "but you have only to look at Lu Youniang to know what Su Xing is capable of. Compared to that, what's selling out Qin Miaoyu?"

Pei Jingzhe instinctively glanced toward the coffin and clammed up.

Within the space of that exchange, Su Xing's soaring figure had almost overleapt the bounds of Lu Manor. He was briefly surprised to find no one pursuing him—then his vision blurred, and agony tore through his shoulder. He collapsed to the ground. Even if he'd held onto his sword, brimming with power, it would have made no difference in his defeat.

The instant he hit the ground, a hand sealed his acupoints. Su Xing stared up at Feng Xiao, then closed his eyes in frustration. "Kill me, then! I only ask that it be quick!"

"The seal."

Pei Jingzhe understood. He came forward to search Su Xing's lapels for the seal he'd taken earlier, then presented it to Feng Xiao.

"Daoist Master Cui's words are my words," said Feng Xiao. "If the information you provided allows us to find Qin Miaoyu, the Jiejian Bureau will honor our promise and show you leniency."

Su Xing raised his head in disbelief. He'd never expected Feng Xiao would keep his word. From the other side, Lu Ti rushed at him, ignoring his own bleeding neck as he slapped Su Xing hard across the face. Su Xing was caught off guard. His head wrenched to the side, his cheek swelling instantly.

"Give me my daughter back!" Lu Ti said through gritted teeth, his expression ferocious. He would have choked Su Xing to death on the spot if Pei Jingzhe didn't reach out to pull him off. "Get out of my way!"

"See to Lady Lu's funeral first. The Jiejian Bureau will take care of this man." Without waiting for a reply, Pei Jingzhe struck Lu Ti on the back of the neck and knocked him unconscious. He gestured for the servants of the Lu family to take him inside.

Though the matter of Lady Lu was over, the case was not yet concluded.

"I've helped Deputy Chief Feng resolve things with the Lu family, and I've also helped you capture Su Xing. When will Deputy Chief Feng fulfill his promise to bring me Fo'er's head, I wonder?" Cui Buqu didn't bother being polite.

Feng Xiao slapped his forehead like he'd just remembered. "I forgot to tell you. On my way over here, I happened to see Fo'er in the distance heading toward the manor where you live. If I remember correctly, the envoy sent by Apa Khagan is also there, right?"

Qiao Xian's face paled. "Why didn't you say so earlier?!"

Eyes wide and innocent, Feng Xiao said, "You didn't ask me earlier. I was busy arresting Su Xing; I didn't have time to think. I only remembered just now. You should hurry, maybe you can still make it!"

Cui Buqu glanced at Qiao Xian, who sped off without another word.

"Is this how Deputy Chief Feng fulfills his promises?" Cui Buqu scoffed.

Feng Xiao smiled brightly, "I said I'd kill Fo'er, I didn't say when. Killing him now, killing him in the future—what difference does it make? Blame yourself for not being more specific. If you want to change the terms now, we'll have to renegotiate."

"State your conditions," said Cui Buqu.

"I want half the credit for the negotiations with Apa's envoy."

"Absolutely not," said Cui Buqu automatically.

"Then there's nothing to be done." Feng Xiao sighed regretfully. "You heard it too. Cui Buqu is the one you want. Don't kill the wrong person this time."

As the last words dropped from Feng Xiao's lips, a figure appeared on the rooftop above them. The newcomer jumped down, his saber slashing like the wind, straight for Cui Buqu.

Zhangsun Bodhi was long gone, and Qiao Xian had just left to pursue Fo'er. Suddenly there was no one to protect him. All he could hear was Feng Xiao saying coolly, "This person is a disciple of Fo'er, Songji. He's not a particularly skilled martial artist—but he's more than capable of killing you."

The saber was coming straight at him; in a moment, he'd lose his head. Pei Jingzhe's face paled in horror. He didn't have a heart of stone like Feng Xiao, yet there was no way he could dash over and rescue Cui Buqu in time. The only one who could save him was Feng Xiao.

In the face of death, Cui Buqu yelled, "I'll give you half the credit for the negotiations!"

"Wouldn't it have been better to agree earlier?" Feng Xiao said with a smile. He flew as fast as his words; in an instant, he was at Cui Buqu's side.

He waved his sleeve but made no other movement. Songji felt a powerful force surging toward him; he stumbled backward and fell. Pei Jingzhe ran up and seized him immediately.

Songji was Fo'er's youngest disciple. He'd become an apprentice late, and though he was the weakest of all of Fo'er's disciples, Fo'er loved him the most. When Fo'er came to the Central Plains to disrupt negotiations with Apa Khagan, he'd brought this youngest disciple with him. He'd intended Songji to gain some experience in the Central Plains but had initially permitted him only to track Apa Khagan's envoy, thinking to keep him out of danger. But Songji was young, and he yearned to perform great feats. Though his shifu had ordered him to keep back, when he'd heard Feng Xiao talking to Cui Buqu, he'd leapt out without thinking.

Who knew Feng Xiao would keep switching sides like this? One moment he stood coldly by, not caring a whit whether Cui Buqu lived or died; the next, he'd swept in to save him. Songji gnashed his teeth in frustration. But he'd already exposed himself and lost his opportunity to capture Cui Buqu—instead, he'd ended up captured himself.

Feng Xiao paid no heed to Songji. He laughed and said, "A gentleman's words are like swift horses. Ququ, you're the esteemed leader of the Zuoyue Bureau. You must not go back on your word."

The implication was clear: *Two can play at this game. You cheat me and I'll cheat you. We can drag each other down, and no one will come out the winner.*

"I'm no gentleman," Cui Buqu said, "but I will honor my promises. However, you must escort the buddha the entire journey west—if you help someone, you must finish what you start. Qiao Xian is no match for Fo'er, so you'll have to come back with me and kill him."

Feng Xiao smiled. "Actually, I lied. I didn't see Fo'er on the way here. If you want to find him, you should ask his disciple. His shifu will definitely come looking now that we've caught him."

Cui Buqu eyed him.

"You cheated me several times, so we'll call it even. Why don't we bury the hatchet and make peace?" said Feng Xiao.

Cui Buqu thought, *The fuck we're even*, but nodded agreeably. The two of them stared at each other, mouths curved in identical fake smiles.

Pei Jingzhe's lips twitched. *This really is too much!*

"We're done here," said Feng Xiao. "I'm going to find Qin Miaoyu first. Ququ, do you wish to come?"

"I will be negotiating with Apa Khagan's envoy tonight. If Deputy Chief Feng is interested, he is welcome to come and listen."

Feng Xiao was rather shocked to find Cui Buqu so cooperative. "I thought you'd try another scheme or two before letting me join," he said.

Cui Buqu sneered. "Do I look like that kind of indecisive, sloppy person?"

Feng Xiao cupped his hands and smiled. "Not at all. I was judging a gentleman's heart through a scoundrel's eyes."

The truth about Lu Youniang's death had been revealed. But for Lu Ti and his wife, it meant a Goguryeon had deceived them, living in their house for years under the name of their relative, and ultimately cost their precious daughter her life. They felt no more comfort now than they had when they'd believed Lu Youniang had drowned herself. When Madam Li came to, she wailed and cried, undone by regret. But Lu Youniang was already dead in her coffin. There was no way back.

When she walked in the underworld, would Lu Youniang rue that she'd misjudged that man so gravely?

The irreversible passage of time was the most agonizing thing in the world. A broken mirror could never be made whole; spilled water never recovered.

Feng Xiao and Cui Buqu didn't linger; they left the Lu family to their grief. When they reached the gates, they made to go their separate ways.

Cui Buqu suddenly paused in his step and turned to Feng Xiao. "I just remembered something. It's related to you, but I don't know if I should tell you."

Feng Xiao saw the affected concern etched on Cui Buqu's face and a sense of foreboding rose in his heart. "Then don't tell me."

"When I examined the corpse earlier, I put my hand in Lu Youniang's mouth. Some of the green bean pastry she'd eaten got on my hand, and I forgot to wash it after. I used that same hand to take your seal from Pei Jingzhe. I remember that you love cleanliness? I can't tell you how sorry I am."

Feng Xiao had no words.

Pei Jingzhe saw not a hint of guilt on Cui Buqu's face, but did observe that Feng Xiao's had turned rather green.

Cui Buqu wasn't foolish enough to wait around for Feng Xiao to come to his senses and take revenge. He disappeared in a flash, moving with tremendous speed and agility. It was night and day from his manner previously, frail and plagued with illness, coughing every second step.

Pei Jingzhe peered at Feng Xiao's face and said cautiously, "Sir, should we first go look for Qin Miaoyu, or...go back to bathe and change?"

"Find. Her." Feng Xiao squeezed those two words out between gritted teeth.

Pei Jingzhe was certain Qin Miaoyu would soon be finding herself in deep misfortune.

36

Q IN MIAOYU WAS GOGURYEON born and bred—and
that wasn't her original name.

In Goguryeo, everyone from the king to the aristoc-
racy was familiar with the culture of the Central Plains. Qin Miaoyu
had been adopted at a young age and taught various martial arts,
as well as the art of seducing men. At the age of twelve, she'd been
given a mission: travel to the Central Plains thousands of miles away,
disguise herself as a local, and bury herself until she received her
next task.

Since the Qin-Han dynasties, Goguryeo had been a vassal of the
powerful Central Plains. Some Goguryeons had even received hon-
orary official titles from several generations of emperors. However,
as Goguryeo gradually became stronger and the fires of war raged in
the Central Plains, the friction between the two nations increased.
Goguryeo was no longer content to remain a vassal.

It was under these circumstances that Qin Miaoyu and Su Xing
were sent to Liugong City as spies. Qin Miaoyu knew they were only
two of many Goguryeon spies lurking in the Central Plains. Perhaps
they'd go undiscovered their entire lives, or perhaps at some point
they'd die.

Though Liugong City was a small, remote settlement, it was linked
with various cities in the Western Regions such as Khotan and Qiemo

in the west. It was bordered by the Khaganate in the north, and its roads spilled into the interior regions of the Central Plains in the east. Its position was therefore both delicate and unique, and it was for this reason Goguryeo had chosen it rather than such flourishing locales as Luoyang or Yuhang in the heart of the Central Plains.

She'd spent her first four years in the Central Plains familiarizing herself with life here. The family she lived with had a matriarch with the surname Qin, who believed Qin Miaoyu's carefully crafted back-story and adored her like a blood niece. They also had a son of an age with Qin Miaoyu whom she referred to as a cousin. This son was a man of upright character who treated Miaoyu with the utmost care; the aunt had at one point thought to arrange a marriage between them. But Qin Miaoyu had refused time and again. She knew in her heart she'd never be afforded the chance to marry and have children like an ordinary woman.

One day, Yuchi Jinwu, who was at the time merely the nephew of the Khotanese king, arrived in Liugong City. Su Xing instructed Qin Miaoyu to seduce and marry Yuchi Jinwu and accompany him back to Khotan. He believed Yang Jian, then still the Duke of Sui, held immense influence and would inevitably seize power and become emperor in the future. If a new dynasty was established under this man, his dedication to progress would surely create friction with neighboring nations. Khotan was a small country in the Western Regions, but its location held strategic importance. It would very likely become a significant pawn in the game between great powers.

Qin Miaoyu had no way to refuse. She was alone in Liugong City, and both the level of her martial arts and her ranking among spies were well below Su Xing's. She followed his orders and created various opportunities to encounter Yuchi Jinwu, who was bewitched by her beauty and immediately offered to take her as his concubine.

But her aunt's family strongly opposed the proposal; they believed Yuchi Jinwu was a poor match for her. Her cousin drove him away from their door when he came to propose a marriage. But Qin Miaoyu insisted, and eventually, they had no choice but to believe she was vain and longed for shallow splendor on the arm of a rich man. They allowed her to be married.

She'd not returned to Liugong City since, and never again saw the benevolent Lady Qin and the family who'd treated her so well. After all, Yuchi Jinwu was the nephew of the king of Khotan, a prince and noble. Qin Miaoyu's life in Khotan was far finer than her life in Liugong City and held no shortage of luxuries and delicacies. But she still thought often of the Qin family, far away in Liugong City.

Even so, she knew she could not return. She never gave up her secret martial arts training, though her skills were still inferior—she would be considered a third-rate martial artist in the Central Plains at most. But this was a world where the strong were king, and this meager training was her only path to breaking free of her bindings.

Yuchi Jinwu was already wed to a legitimate wife in Khotan, along with several other lovely concubines. But Qin Miaoyu was both beautiful and talented, so he favored her above all. She lived like this for several years, up until he was appointed envoy by the king of Khotan and entrusted with escorting the tribute to the Central Plains. A few gentle words from Qin Miaoyu were all it took for him to agree to bring his beloved concubine along. He never imagined this trip would be the last he ever took.

When Su Xing had put a blade through Yuchi Jinwu's chest, splattering her face with her husband's blood, her eyes had widened, and she'd cried out softly. Su Xing had growled impatiently, "Shut up! Are you trying to attract more people?! Go finish off the two maids!"

He left Qin Miaoyu and went to take care of the Khotanese guards.

These were the Khotanese king's royal guards—they weren't just anyone. But in the Central Plains, where talent abounded, they were powerless against a stronger foe. Qin Miaoyu realized then that, despite her years of arduous training, she could only defeat a few comparatively mediocre members of the convoy. Were she to challenge Su Xing, she'd be lucky to last longer than ten moves.

In the instant that fact became clear to her, she discarded the last scrap of guilt she felt toward Yuchi Jinwu, and her hunger for the jade was born.

Because he loved and valued her greatly, Yuchi Jinwu had told her a secret: they hadn't brought one Jade of Heaven Lake from Khotan, but two.

For anyone who hadn't seen the true Jade of Heaven Lake, they would never suspect the second stone was a fake. This stone was also a real piece of beautiful jade discovered in a mountain not far from the true jade at around the same time, but it lacked the matchless radiance the true stone possessed. The Khotanese king wished to present both jades to the emperor of Sui to express his sincerity. Just before the assassination, Yuchi Jinwu had told Qin Miaoyu where each of the two stones was hidden.

Thus Qin Miaoyu knew something Su Xing didn't; she boldly gave him the fake stone. She hid the real one and returned to the city with Su Xing before secretly heading back to the scene of the murders. There, she took the real jade from its hiding place then snuck back into the city to conceal herself.

Qin Miaoyu knew the legend of the Jade of Heaven Lake—it could purify the body, shaping the tendons and cleansing the marrow. The temptation to enhance her martial arts was too great;

she couldn't help testing it. After several attempts, she discovered that if she exposed the Jade of Heaven Lake to the light of the full moon and channeled qi through her palm, she would receive a trickle of cleansing qi in response. Qin Miaoyu had discovered the jade's secret. She treated it like the most precious of treasures and practiced her internal cultivation day and night. When Qiao Xian and Zhangsun Bodhi followed the trail to her door and the assassin from the Thirteen Floors of Yunhai tried to take her life, Qin Miaoyu pretended to be harmless. She waited until Qiao Xian and her companion had defeated the assassin before slipping from their grasp and fleeing once more.

In truth, she'd also wanted to test her martial progress—and the results were astonishing. A few days prior she'd been a third-rate practitioner, yet now her internal cultivation had improved by leaps and bounds. The jade really was extraordinary. It was only a matter of time before she absorbed all the energy from within the stone and became a first-rate master.

But Qin Miaoyu was running out of time. Though she'd escaped from Qiao Xian and Zhangsun, she'd been seriously injured in the process. She had no choice but to go to ground in the city until she regained her strength. When Feng Xiao obtained the names of her three hiding places from Su Xing, Qin Miaoyu was in the middle of leaving the house through the back gate. The place was supposed to be top-secret, known only to Su Xing. She planned to take a risk and head to the city gates, disguised as a widow who wished to visit her parents. Then she would leave with a merchant convoy she'd contacted.

Qin Miaoyu had made up her mind: if this escape was successful, there was a boundless world waiting for her. No longer would she be a Goguryeon spy, nor anyone's thrall. She wanted to live proudly and openly, whether under the name Qin Miaoyu or another. She would live only for herself. With the jade in hand, even Su Xing couldn't order her around. Maybe she could even convince him to follow his own desires and leave too.

This grand plan fell to pieces the moment she spied a man standing beneath a tree not far from the back gates. He watched her, smiling.

He was extraordinarily beautiful.

Qin Miaoyu had seen all sorts, yet this was the first time she'd ever seen anyone so handsome. But the sight of him didn't stir up the butterflies of a young girl in love. This was an intuition only martial artists felt when confronting a strong foe—what washed over her was cold terror.

The Jade of Heaven Lake had not merely improved her cultivation, it had fine-tuned her sense of danger.

The handsome man smiled. "Qin-niangzi, your reputation precedes you. Today we finally meet, and you truly are as radiant as they say, not at all inferior to those famous beauties."

Qin Miaoyu calmed her fluttering heart and smiled. "May this one ask your esteemed name?"

"*Miaoyu*—clever speech. Your name is quite nice, but mine sounds better," the man said.

She had never met a man who talked to her in such a way. He was looking at her with appreciation, but it wasn't the appreciation of a great beauty. It was more like he was looking at a decently pretty flower.

"I'm called Feng Xiao," he said.

Qin Miaoyu's heart jolted, and not because she was sighing over the sound of his name. She knew this man.

"So it's the master of the Jiejian Bureau." Qin Miaoyu was incredibly sharp. Before Feng Xiao could say why he'd come, she straightened her robe and bowed. "I believe the gentleman has already met Su Xing. Was he the one who led you here?" she asked pleasantly. "I have the Jade of Heaven Lake, and I can reunite it with its rightful owner. In return, there is one thing I ask."

Feng Xiao stood with his hands clasped behind his back. "You're not qualified to discuss terms with me," he said leisurely.

Qin Miaoyu's smile was strained. "The gentleman misunderstands. Miaoyu's life is in your hands. How could I discuss terms? I merely wanted to inform you of this: that night, on the outskirts of the city, Yuchi Jinwu and the others were all killed by Su Xing. I only killed the two maids. If I hadn't done it, Su Xing would have. And if I hadn't taken the Jade of Heaven Lake, Su Xing would have sent it to Goguryeo long ago."

For the first time, Feng Xiao looked at her squarely. He studied her face. This woman was intelligent, he realized. She pleaded for neither her life nor her freedom. Instead, she stated what had happened that day, attempting to shift the blame and move him with reason. Presumably she'd already realized Feng Xiao couldn't be seduced and wouldn't let her off easily. She chose an unconventional gambit and attempted to blaze a new path.

"What does Goguryeo want with the stone?" Feng Xiao asked.

Qin Miaoyu didn't equivocate. Instantly she said, "I'm not clear on it myself, but Su Xing said the king suffers from a strange illness with no cure. Perhaps it is related."

Feng Xiao found her frankness deeply satisfying. Compared to Su Xing, this woman was indeed smarter and more canny. If not for her bad luck in being betrayed by her accomplice, she might have really managed to dissemble her way out of the city and become the fish that slipped into the great sea.

"Where's the stone?" asked Feng Xiao.

Qin Miaoyu untied the embroidered bag at her waist and took out a piece of jade, which she carefully handed to Feng Xiao.

The jade was the size of his palm, its body crystal-clear. At the center was a dash of blue-green, rippling slowly in the sunlight, as if alive. Before laying eyes on the real thing, Feng Xiao considered the jade he'd taken from Linlang Pavilion to be a rare and beautiful stone. But now he could immediately distinguish which was superior.

The object in front of him was the true Jade of Heaven Lake.

"Why is it so small?" he asked.

Qin Miaoyu glanced at him carefully. "I heard this object can enhance a person's martial arts, so I tried it." She could have attempted to hide it, but Feng Xiao would probably have guessed anyway. Her life was in his hands; it was better to be honest.

She didn't know that Feng Xiao was evaluating her intelligence. She saw how he made no move toward the jade and thought he was afraid she'd tampered with it somehow. Hastily, she said, "Feng-langjun, Miaoyu is completely at your mercy. I wouldn't dare try any tricks or schemes."

Feng Xiao's mouth twitched, but ultimately, he reached out and took the jade.

The instant it was in his hands, he felt a wave of bone-chilling cold. It was an indescribable feeling, like his entire body had been submerged in an icy river. Yet there was no discomfort. Instead, wisps of chill seeped through his limbs and bones and into his heart. His soul was bright and clear, as if touched by a divine hand.

But at that moment, Feng Xiao wasn't thinking how magical the jade was. He was thinking that, since he was going to hand it over anyway, anyone who could enjoy holding a stone that had been smeared with bean paste residue from a corpse's mouth was welcome to it. He was never going to touch it again, under pain of death.

37

QIAO XIAN RUSHED BACK to their residence. As soon as she arrived, she realized Fo'er hadn't traced them there at all—Feng Xiao had tricked her.

But Cui Buqu was still with Feng Xiao; at this thought, she turned to hurry back. She'd gone only a short way when, to her surprise, she ran into a perfectly composed Cui Buqu on his way home. Behind him was an eagle rider with a stranger slung over his saddle.

"This is Fo'er's disciple, captured by Feng Xiao. Lock him up somewhere—he'll be useful later when Fo'er arrives," Cui Buqu said.

He was talking about a living person like an object, but Qiao Xian nodded as if this was nothing out of the ordinary. She called someone to take Fo'er's disciple away.

Songji had braced himself to remain silent in the face of the most gruesome torture. But to his surprise, no one asked him a single thing as they prepared to drag him off. In a panic, he shouted in stilted Chinese, "Where are you taking me? My shifu will not stand for this!"

Cui Buqu had one foot raised to step inside when he suddenly stopped. He turned and stood in front of Songji. "Do you have some way to contact your shifu?"

Songji said nothing, his face a mask of defiance.

Cui Buqu threw a glance at Qiao Xian. "Tell him about the tortures he'll face at our Zuoyue Bureau."

"Yes sir," said Qiao Xian, face blank. "Moon through the Veil: we soak layers of paper in water and press them over your face, leaving you unable to breathe; eventually you suffocate. Or we may snap all the tendons in your arms and legs, toss you into the water prison naked, and allow hungry pythons to feast on your flesh. You'll watch your hands and feet as they're eaten, until the snakes have consumed everything and bite through your throat. This is called Hundred Birds Worship the Phoenix. There are also Blessings as One Wishes and Exquisite from Every Angle. Which do you like best? I'll explain them to you. Slowly."

Songji's face was so pale it was almost translucent, and he was trembling like a leaf. His Chinese was middling, but this he understood without issue. The most powerful thought in his mind just then was that the people of the Central Plains were terrifying—they even gave their grisly torture methods such beautiful names. He hadn't yet heard the explanations for Blessings as One Wishes and Exquisite from Every Angle, but he knew they must be still crueler and more horrific.

"What do you want?!" His voice cracked.

"Contact your shifu and plead for help," said Qiao Xian. "Get him to come here."

"You want to kill him," Songji said stiffly. "I won't do it."

"We won't kill him," said Cui Buqu. "But if you don't call him, we have other ways of letting him know you're here." He turned to Qiao Xian. "Hang him from the bamboo building."

There was a bamboo building next to the manor, its roof higher than those of the nearby structures. Standing on that building, one could see out over most of Liugong City. If they hung Songji up there, Fo'er would soon find out about it.

Qiao Xian watched them haul Songji away. Hesitantly, she began, "Fo'er is the Khaganate's number one expert..." She left the rest unsaid: that even if she joined hands with Zhangsun Bodhi, they might not defeat him.

Cui Buqu was unfazed. "No matter. Someone will come to help you."

"Feng Xiao?" asked Qiao Xian.

After a nod, Cui Buqu had a thought: "Where did you learn so many torture techniques?"

The Zuoyue Bureau was an agency that handled cases and investigations; it wasn't a prison of the Ministry of Justice, and it certainly wouldn't use techniques like "Blessings as One Wishes" or "Exquisite from Every Angle." Even the Ministry of Justice hadn't heard of such things.

Qiao Xian looked sheepish. "I just rattled off a load of nonsense. I only wanted to scare him."

Cui Buqu coughed twice, slightly relieved. "Excellent. Tailoring your words to the one you're addressing—this is something I would do too. I used to worry you were too rigid and would only be able to bully honest souls like Pei Jingzhe, while people like Feng Xiao would run circles around you."

Qiao Xian was speechless a moment. "Are you having pains in your chest again? This subordinate called for a doctor earlier. He's waiting in the front hall now; your lordship can go for an examination."

Cui Buqu's feet had been taking him to the front hall, but now he veered sharply away. Qiao Xian heard him mutter, "I just remembered. I touched the corpse with this hand, and I haven't washed it yet. I should go wash now."

Wordlessly, Qiao Xian stepped forward and grabbed Cui Buqu. She began dragging him toward the front hall without compunction.

"I'll have water and soap sent in. You were drugged with incense of helplessness. The residual poison was never expelled, and you spent a night exposed to the elements. You must let the doctor look at you!"

Qiao Xian usually obeyed Cui Buqu unconditionally. Only on the matter of his health did she become insistent. She'd seen Cui Buqu ill and bedridden too recently, coughing until he choked on his own blood. After the latest incident, everyone in the Zuoyue Bureau developed a tacit understanding: as long as they were there, Cui Buqu would never suffer that greatly again.

Cui Buqu wasn't a good-tempered man, but now, rather than scowling and castigating his subordinates as usual, he shut his mouth and let Qiao Xian draw him toward the front hall.

She couldn't help adding, "Last year...that incident. I don't want to see it happen again."

Cui Buqu was silent a moment. "It won't."

Last year, Cui Buqu had fallen seriously ill and almost died, scaring everyone in the Zuoyue Bureau out of their wits. Song Liangchen, one of the deputy chiefs, had strictly forbidden Cui Buqu from leaving his bed. He'd called in doctors to attend Cui Buqu in shifts, so that there was one at Cui Buqu's bedside night and day.

But Cui Buqu had been restless from birth. The instant he felt a little better he got up and began running hither and thither, yearning to leap from the capital to the ends of the earth. When the order for the negotiations with Apa Khagan's envoy came down, the expressions of everyone in the Zuoyue Bureau had been pitch-black—except Cui Buqu, who was in high spirits. He devised a vast and meticulous game of chess that lasted almost two months, and he didn't stop at pulling Feng Xiao onto the board; he placed himself there too.

Qiao Xian couldn't help but sigh at the thought, and her grip on Cui Buqu tightened. "If a doctor prescribes medicine, you must drink it."

The corner of Cui Buqu's mouth twitched. "I'm really fine."

"Then run a lap around that osmanthus tree right there. If you don't cough, you can skip the medicine."

Cui Buqu's face grew stormy. "Nonsense, who do you take my venerable self for? You can't order me around!"

They glared at each other, Qian Xiao refusing to back down. Finally, it was Cui Buqu who broke first. "Fine, I'll drink it!" He rolled his eyes.

Qiao Xian's lips curved in a small smile.

The maids here had all been hired as temporary help. Though their backgrounds were clean, they weren't members of the Zuoyue Bureau and therefore didn't know much about Cui Buqu's and Qiao Xian's relationship. They all thought Qiao Xian carried a torch for Cui Buqu—and that perhaps the sentiment was mutual. How could they know Cui Buqu's place in Qiao Xian's heart was far weightier than that?

To her, he was master and father, brother and friend.

Many years ago, before she was the woman she was now, she'd found herself in desperate circumstances. Her body had been covered in bruises, her left eye almost blind. She'd lain in the snow, her breath slowly fading, thinking it didn't matter if she never woke up. Whether she lived or died, nothing in this world would change. It was Cui Buqu who'd passed by and plucked her from the streets.

Qiao Xian knew she was merely a bit of side trouble he'd picked up. He had no particular interest in her—but if not for him, the woman she was today would never exist.

It wasn't until she'd been with Cui Buqu some time that she realized how fragile his body was. He was so delicate even a slight breeze could bring on a chill that would leave him bedridden for days. He fell seriously ill at the drop of a hat and looked like he might pass away any second. If they hadn't always managed to find a doctor in time, by now the grass on his tomb would surely have grown tall.

Yet it was this same sickly Cui Buqu who possessed an eidetic memory, who could strategize to perfection, who knew the stories of the jianghu like the back of his hand. He grasped all the world's affairs without needing to step out of the house.

She remembered something Cui Buqu had once said: *If you believe your existence is insignificant, no one else will take you seriously either. I'm different from you. I am who I am. Even if I fall ill, even if I'm on the brink of death, even if my limbs are crippled, no one can replace me, Cui Buqu.*

This kind of man—even if his life could be extinguished at any moment, he burned so brightly that no one could ignore him.

There was no doubt about it: the one in charge of the Zuoyue Bureau wasn't the strongest martial artist, Zhangsun Bodhi, nor the brilliant strategist Song Liangchen—and nor was it Qiao Xian. It was Cui Buqu. Zhangsun's martial arts could protect many people, but it was Cui Buqu who set everyone's hearts at ease.

There were many problems in the world that could be resolved with force, and there were also many that couldn't. But all these problems, when they fell into Cui Buqu's hands, would ultimately be resolved. It looked like Qiao Xian and the others were protecting Cui Buqu, but in truth it was Cui Buqu who protected them. As long as Cui Buqu was there, the Zuoyue Bureau was as stable as bedrock, and they were all free from worry. But though Cui Buqu had a heart of iron, there was one thing he hated more than anything else.

And that was drinking medicine.

No matter how much medicine one drank, even if they grew accustomed to its bitter and peculiar taste, they would never come to love it. To make matters worse, Cui Buqu could scarcely go a week without being made to drink several bowls of the stuff. Between holding his nose and drinking all that nauseatingly bitter medicine or letting Feng Xiao drug him with more incense of helplessness, he'd prefer the latter—at least then he could endure the suffering under his own willpower.

But Qiao Xian would never let him off that easily. So it was that, when Apa Khagan's envoy first laid eyes on the court ambassador she was supposed to negotiate with, she encountered a stormy, sullen face.

Since ancient times, whenever two countries met in negotiations, the envoys were almost always men. This was established convention.

In the Khaganate, the khagan's wife was known as the khatun. Though the khatun wielded some power in military and political affairs, the Khaganate wasn't a nation that held women in high regard. Thus, when the Zuoyue Bureau saw that Apa had sent a woman to negotiate, their first reaction was to doubt her identity.

The female envoy arrived with two guards and stayed within the manor for two days in seclusion. Her curiosity never drove her to come out for a look around, nor did she take the initiative to call upon Cui Buqu. She merely sat in her quarters and waited quietly for Cui Buqu's summons. Her patience alone was extraordinary.

The woman before them now wore a dark red dress, the styling obviously Göktürk, and even her hair accessories and braids had a foreign charm. Her face was slightly tanned, the corners of her eyes weathered by wind and sand, but she was nonetheless an exotic beauty. This beauty wasn't the kind appreciated by the people of the

Central Plains, who were used to fair and delicate skin, brows like distant mountains, and eyes like autumn pools. Instead, her beauty bespoke a powerful vitality that wouldn't bend to rain or wind.

Cui Buqu had just drunk a large bowl of bitter medicine and was in no mood to appreciate the unique allure of this female envoy. As soon as they were seated, he got straight to the point. "You are the envoy sent by Apa Khagan?"

It wasn't Cui Buqu's way to be overly welcoming, but in this case, his attitude gave her the mistaken impression that he looked down on her for being a woman.

"Correct. My Chinese name is Jinlian. May I ask Your Excellency's esteemed name?"

"Cui Buqu." Cui Buqu arched a brow. "You're named for the golden lotuses that grow on the grasslands?"

Jinlian looked surprised. "Correct. My Göktürk name comes from the golden lotus, so I'm called simply Jinlian in Chinese."

"Who are you to Apa Khagan? Why are you his representative? And how can I trust that what you say is the will of the khagan?"

Irked, Jinlian said, "I am Apa Khagan's khatun." She paused, then added, "The lesser khatun."

Cui Buqu had done his research on Apa Khagan, and he knew Apa Khagan had two khatuns. A lesser khatun held the same status a concubine might in the Central Plains. However, Apa's greater khatun was getting on in years and didn't handle such weighty matters. It was therefore the lesser khatun who most often supported him in affairs both major and minor. The fact that Jinlian had come personally demonstrated the importance of these negotiations to Apa Khagan.

Of course, for Jinlian to come herself, she must also possess courage and charisma no less than that of a man. It was small wonder she felt slighted when she saw this Central Plains dynasty had sent an envoy as feeble and sickly as Cui Buqu.

Noting her obvious displeasure, Qiao Xian said, "Our master here is the chief of the Zuoyue Bureau, with a rank equivalent to the Six Ministers. Even if you've never heard of the Zuoyue Bureau, you must have heard of Great Sui's Minister of Justice, who was formerly the Minister of Capital Affairs."

That year, the Ministry of Capital Affairs had been renamed the Ministry of Justice. Though this news had yet to reach the Khaganate, Jinlian had indeed heard of the Minister of Capital Affairs. Within the Department of State Affairs, the Six Ministers sat beneath the Left and Right Vice Directors. If Cui Buqu was equal to one of the Six Ministers, his official position was a high one.

Ruffled feathers somewhat soothed, she said, "It seems Cui-langjun is an accomplished man. It is I who was ignorant."

Cui Buqu inclined his head slightly. He didn't beat around the bush: "I trust Apa Khagan has an important message for us if the lesser khatun has come herself?"

Jinlian too seemed to dislike going around in circles or using obfuscating language. She answered promptly, "Yes. Ishbara is ambitious; he wishes to foment a war. I came for the sake of the peace between our two nations. How does your eminent emperor view this matter?"

Her words were lofty, but in truth, the rapid expansion of Ishbara's authority and influence had enraged the heavily encroached-upon Apa Khagan and forced him to this extremity. At Jinlian's urging, he'd realized the enemy of an enemy was a friend and sent her in search of an alliance with the Sui dynasty.

"Of course, His Majesty too wishes for long-term peace and stability at the border," Cui Buqu said. "However, Ishbara is determined to disturb Great Sui's peace; what can we do but counter force with force? If Apa Khagan is willing to work with us, a portion of Ishbara's territory may be allotted to him once the situation is resolved. You need only travel to Daxing City each year and offer quality horses as tribute."

Jinlian refused unequivocally. "We are not vassals of the Sui dynasty!"

"The lesser khatun doesn't wish to consider this further?" Cui Buqu smiled thinly.

Indignant, Jinlian snapped, "At first I thought you sincere. But it seems the people of the Central Plains will always try to take advantage of others! We would be the ones assisting you with Ishbara, so why should we submit to you?"

Cui Buqu was unruffled. "Our people have split our forces into several groups; two are even now heading to Bagha and Tardu Khagan respectively. As far as I know, they are both also at odds with Ishbara, so there's a good chance they'll agree to a proposal of mutual cooperation. If Bagha and Tardu agree and only Apa Khagan refuses, won't it be on your head?"

Jinlian's expression shifted.

Cui Buqu smiled. "Lesser Khatun, you are in the land of the Hans. If you complete this mission successfully, the chips in your hands will increase, and you will climb higher. But what if you fail? What awaits you may be the loss of Apa's Khagan's favor. In that case, will you still be able to realize your wishes?"

Jinlian looked at the man before her. She hadn't taken this man from the Central Plains, with his stark-white face and frail constitution—especially so compared to a Göktürk man—seriously. She'd felt disdain and dissatisfaction toward the emperor of the Central Plains for sending such an invalid to treat with her. But now his gaze was like an arrow, piercing the depths of her innermost mind. All her desires, concealed and unknown to others, had been bared to him in an instant.

Her back broke out in a cold sweat. "I don't know...what you're saying." She steadied herself with some effort.

"No matter." Cui Buqu looked at her with eyes full of pity. "It's just that after tonight, you may not have the chance to speak again."

"What do you mean?" Jinlian was instantly on guard. "You wish to kill me?" But why would Cui Buqu do such a thing?

Cui Buqu shook his head. "Not me; someone else."

Who?

As if in response to her unasked question, something whistled down from overhead. Jinlian rolled to the side without thinking. The next moment, the place where she'd knelt and the table in front of her were smashed to kindling.

The two Göktürk guards who'd accompanied her cried out, leaping forward to confront the intruder. But when Jinlian caught sight of the newly arrived enemy, her face drained of color.

Cui Buqu brought his sleeves together with perfect poise, as if he didn't realize the newcomer wanted to kill him along with Jinlian. He turned to her with great amusement and said, "Speak of the devil! The number one martial artist of the Khaganate, Fo'er. You must be familiar with him. Tonight our humble abode overflows with distinguished company. All we lack is a jar of good wine!"

38

FO'ER, UNDER ISHBARA'S ORDERS, had come to Liugong City with a single purpose: not to obtain the jade stone, but to disrupt negotiations between Great Sui and Apa Khagan.

Before Jinlian arrived in Liugong City, killing the Sui dynasty's envoy was the best way to accomplish this. But now Jinlian had appeared, and killing her would also bring negotiations to an abrupt end. Even if Apa Khagan somehow found another envoy with courage, smarts, and the willingness to risk life and limb traveling alone to the Central Plains, Jinlian's death would undoubtedly estrange the two sides, and their alliance would crumble before it began.

Thus, when Jinlian and Cui Buqu appeared in front of him at the same time, Fo'er didn't hesitate to disregard Cui Buqu and target Apa Khagan's lesser khatun.

Jinlian was a martial artist in her own right. She shot arrows on horseback and dueled on foot; in the Khaganate, she too was considered a heroine. Still, there was a clear gap in ability between her and the Göktürks' number one martial artist. She was driven into a corner within ten moves. Her two guards rushed in to save her; one was struck fatally in the chest, coughing up blood and dying on the spot, while the other's arm was broken, taking him out of the fight.

Qiao Xian and Zhangsun Bodhi had returned some time ago. Now they stood on either side of Cui Buqu, protecting him, but didn't move forward to rescue Jinlian.

Panicking, Jinlian shouted, "He's going to kill me! Do you plan to stand there and watch me die?!"

Slowly, Cui Buqu said, "Jinlian Khatun, Ishbara has forced your khagan to retreat time and again. If you perish, our Great Sui will still have allies in Bagha and Tardu Khagan. With or without you—it makes little difference. My position as an official will see neither promotion nor demotion on your account. Consider this carefully."

Jinlian was staring death in the face. She stood no chance against an elite martial artist like Fo'er. Still she fought onward, hanging onto her life by her fingernails. After fifteen moves, she could retreat no further. The force of a palm blast scraped past her shoulder and blossomed into agony, but Fo'er didn't stop. He truly intended to kill her.

Perhaps the Göktürks weren't as subtle as the people of the Central Plains in how they handled affairs, but their nobles engaged in no less backstabbing and infighting. Their bloodshed was no gentler than the power struggles seen elsewhere. Jinlian had married Apa Khagan in her teens and had climbed step by step to her current position. It had cost her unimaginable effort. How could she be willing to die so suddenly, in such a comical fashion?

"If Cui Buqu won't save you, I will."

A soft chuckle rang in Jinlian's ear. Seconds later, the overwhelming pressure before her eased. A figure stood in front of her, receiving the full brunt of Fo'er's all-out palm strike.

True qi burst outward from the two elite martial experts and shoved Jinlian several feet back.

Having walked the boundary between life and death seconds ago, Jinlian ignored the ripping pain in her upper back and felt only the drumming of her heart and the throbbing of her temples. She felt as if her feet were stepping on clouds, her entire body limp. At that moment, she was like anyone who'd barely escaped death. Her shocked gaze swept over her subordinates, one dead and one wounded, then fell upon the man who was fighting Fo'er.

Both moved as swiftly as wraiths; despite Jinlian's skills, she couldn't distinguish their strikes. She'd retreated a good distance, yet she could still feel their internal energy expanding toward her. She shifted farther away.

"Jinlian Khatun, how are your deliberations going?" Cui Buqu asked carelessly. "I seem to have heard Ishbara has several other extraordinary martial artists at his disposal. Besides Fo'er, there are two more powerful experts almost at the level of grandmaster. Should he dispatch a few more men, I fear you might not return to the Khaganate at all."

Jinlian gritted her teeth. She understood perfectly why Cui Buqu had stood by and refused to save her. This had been his goal.

But what could she do? This man's words had expertly targeted her weakness. She'd concealed her name and disguised her appearance to travel to the Central Plains, and her journey had been fraught with danger. She had managed to survive, but that didn't mean she'd be so fortunate on the return trip. Jinlian had believed that, once the alliance was established, Great Sui would dispatch soldiers to escort her back. But now they were at a stalemate, and if it couldn't be resolved, she'd have to return empty-handed and alone.

"The number of quality horses can be negotiated, and the nature of the alliance between the two sides has already been agreed.

The khagan will have no objections, and I can finalize the details on his behalf. However, I can't make the decision in regard to tribute. Here's what I suggest: Cui-langjun can travel with me to the khagan's encampment and meet with him personally. That will be far more effective than sending me back by myself."

Cui Buqu knew this was the limit of what Jinlian could offer, so he didn't push her further. He nodded. "Then I request that Jinlian Khatun please pen a handwritten letter and stamp it as proof of authenticity. I'll send it to the capital for His Majesty to review."

Quickly Jinlian said, "That won't be a problem. I already brought a letter from the khagan with me. I only need someone who can read Turkic."

"I can," said Cui Buqu. His brief, matter-of-fact answer made Jinlian look at him in a new light.

The negotiations were thus concluded, but the battle between Feng Xiao and Fo'er was far from over.

Fo'er's martial arts were slightly inferior to Feng Xiao's—but only slightly. While Fo'er might not be able to defeat him, he should certainly be able to escape without coming to harm. However, he'd come here tonight with two goals: an assassination and a rescue. Until he'd achieved both, he didn't intend to leave.

Fo'er's rise to prominence came at a time when the famed experts of the past had either become sect leaders or secluded themselves within the mountains and forests. They were difficult to trace and even more difficult to actually find. Since coming to the Central Plains, Fo'er had challenged masters one after another. His martial prowess was great, and the difficulty he'd had in finding worthy opponents led him to believe the reputation of Central Plains martial artists was overblown—until he met Feng Xiao.

Feng Xiao was a rare foe, the kind one might meet once or twice in a lifetime. His martial arts were swift and unpredictable, but his internal energy was steady and profound. His level of skill should have been impossible to achieve at his young age. Fo'er had suspected since their first encounter that Feng Xiao had learned under the tutelage of a great expert, or that Feng Xiao himself was a grandmaster who'd managed to reverse his aging. Fo'er had been beaten back at Huyang Forest, and now it seemed defeat was once again inevitable.

On top of that, while Feng Xiao alone was a daunting opponent, Zhangsun and Qiao Xian also lurked nearby. Though they merely watched for now, their presence sealed potential routes of attack and retreat, hemming him in from all sides until he was overwhelmed.

He caught a glimpse of Cui Buqu standing in the far corner, and a plan came to mind.

From within the dancing sparks, Fo'er's figure leapt toward the rafters. Though he was tall and broad-shouldered, the leap was like a white crane soaring into the air: light, nimble, and almost soundless. Feng Xiao pursued at once, but Fo'er had already burst out onto the roof. His aim wasn't to escape or even to rescue his disciple—instead, he raised his palm and struck down at the roof-tiles beneath his feet.

Oh hell, thought Feng Xiao. He only had time to shout "Run!"

With a roar, the entire roof collapsed. Broken tiles and bricks rained down, and the ten-foot pillars supporting the rafters swayed and fell under the shock waves of Fo'er's internal energy, burying the people inside.

In the blink of an eye, the place was flattened.

Those with some martial arts, like Jinlian, were better off. Though injured and caught off guard, she managed to avoid the worst of the collapse. But her surviving guard, who'd broken his arm, was not so lucky. He was crushed beneath the rubble, his fate unknown.

Feng Xiao's face was like a thundercloud. He finally discarded his carefree expression and turned to perform a rescue.

Pei Jingzhe had nearly been crushed by a pillar, and though he'd managed to dodge death, his cheek was patterned with scratches from flying debris, and his back burned with pain where it'd been struck. As he looked around, he remembered Cui Buqu, who knew no martial arts. His face paled. "Sir, Cui..."

Feng Xiao strode over and kicked at a pillar. Though he didn't appear to exert much force, the ten-foot pillar went flying and crashed down some distance away. Where it had been, a pale hand stuck out of the rubble.

Shocked, Pei Jingzhe ran over to help. When they managed to clear the debris, they found the hand didn't belong to Cui Buqu, but to Qiao Xian.

Qiao Xian and Zhangsun Bodhi had shielded Cui Buqu with their bodies, protecting him. All three were pulled from the wreckage; though his deputies had suffered some minor wounds, Cui Buqu himself seemed to be entirely unharmed.

"How did Deputy Chief Feng allow Fo'er to escape?" Cui Buqu asked with raised eyebrows.

Feng Xiao answered in his usual breezy way. "Of course it's because I saw you buried beneath the rubble. My heart burned with worry, and all I could think of was saving you. Ququ, it's really too unkind of you to complain. Here, feel my chest! My heart's still pounding away!"

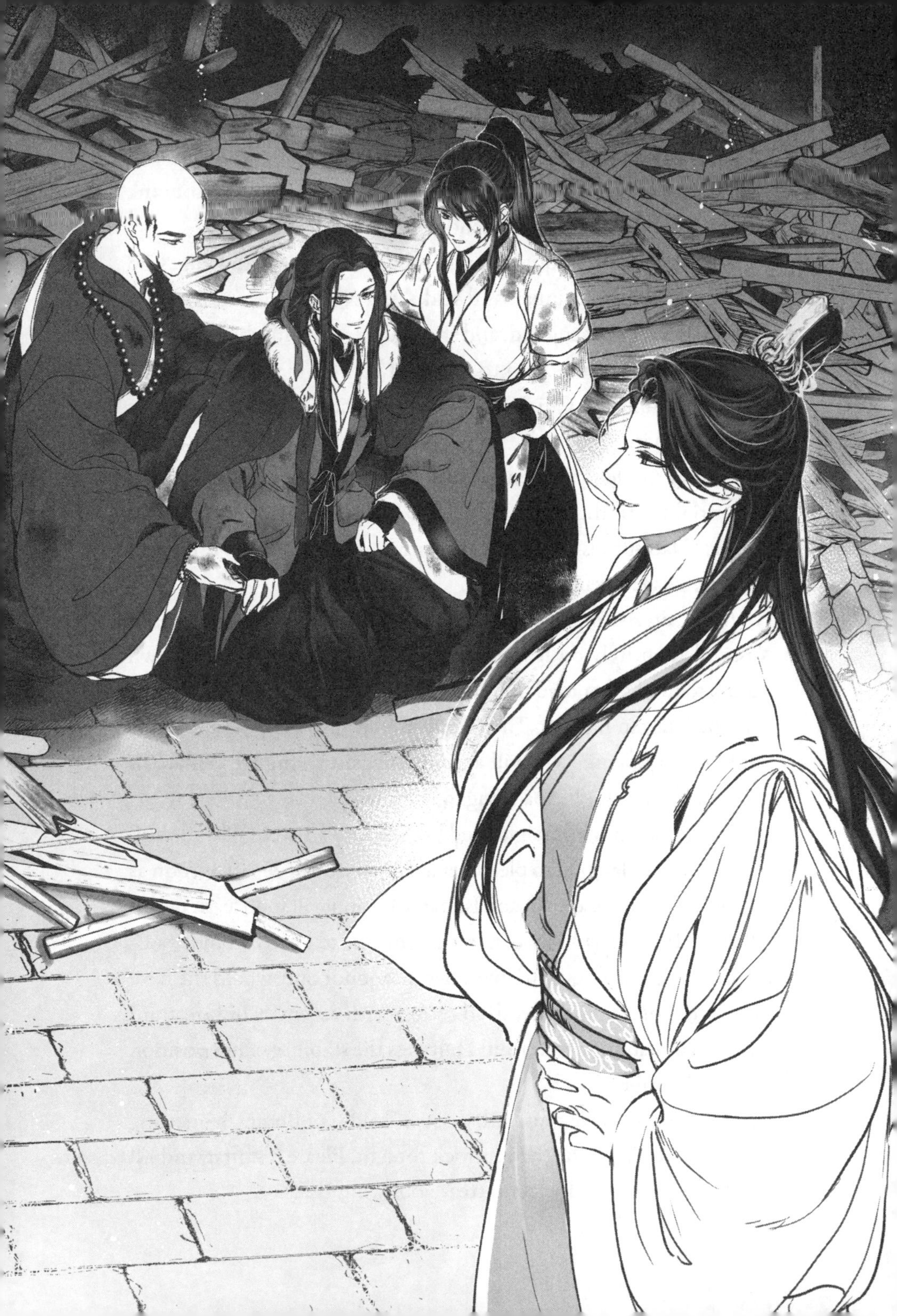

Pei Jingzhe thought, *Whose heart wouldn't pound? Are you a corpse?* But he was still Feng Xiao's subordinate, after all. He couldn't embarrass his superior, so he schooled himself to silence.

It was clear Cui Buqu was in no mood to debate with Feng Xiao either. He looked at Jinlian and said, "Apa Khagan's letter."

Jinlian's arm was injured, and she struggled to pull the document from her lapels. Qiao Xian took it and verified it wasn't poisoned before handing it to Cui Buqu, who shook the dust from his clothes and opened it.

A head suddenly leaned in close. Cui Buqu almost slapped the letter right into the interloper's face. "Hey, what language is this? Turkic? Daoist Master Cui is truly extraordinary. You can even read their language fluently!"

Ququ or *A-Cui* or *Daoist Master Cui*—the address he used depended entirely on his mood. Cui Buqu had long since grown numb to it. He skimmed the letter, making sure it really was penned by Apa Khagan himself. Then he stuffed it into Feng Xiao's hands and said to Jinlian, "We will accompany you to the Khaganate to personally meet with Apa Khagan."

Delighted, Jinlian straightened her spine to answer: "Wonderful! I must ask Cui-langjun to please set a date so we can depart as soon as possible. Fo'er has escaped, and Ishbara's faction will soon learn of this alliance. They won't hesitate to send someone to kill us on the road."

Bringing Cui Buqu back with her meant not only would she have protection on her journey, she'd return with an envoy of Great Sui. It was a contribution that would buttress the stability of her position within the tribe.

"There is much we must still discuss," said Cui Buqu. "It's getting late, and the khatun has had a shock tonight. Please rest first, and I'll send someone for a doctor to treat your wounds."

Jinlian nodded, finally allowing herself to slump with exhaustion. "Thank you very much, Cui-langjun. As for my two subordinates, I must ask Cui-langjun to arrange their burials."

She left with the aid of a maid's supporting shoulder.

Feng Xiao saw Cui Buqu about to turn away as well and grabbed his arm. Cui Buqu drew in a sharp breath. He'd just been crushed beneath a pillar; even with Zhangsun and Qiao Xian protecting him, he'd still sprained his wrist in the chaos. Now, as Feng Xiao tugged on him, his injury became apparent.

Qiao Xian glared and struck out immediately at Feng Xiao. He smoothly let go and stepped back saying, "Hold it. What did you mean by 'We will accompany you?' Who's *we*?"

The corners of Cui Buqu's lips turned up. "Me and you. That's the definition of 'we.'"

Feng Xiao was finally shocked into silence.

39

THE MOON AND STARS were above, wine and tea below. Feng Xiao and Cui Buqu sat facing each other. Outside the pavilion, a gentle breeze blew, and new grass sprouts peeked from the cold ground. If one ignored that the house had collapsed and Fo'er had taken his disciple and fled, it was a beautiful night.

Feng Xiao looked at Cui Buqu, who sat across the table from him.

He was in fact drinking neither tea nor wine; instead, he picked up a bowl of medicine. He hesitated. Then, with the expression of one bravely facing his death, he closed his eyes, tipped his head, and poured the medicine into his mouth. Anyone watching would have thought him committing suicide via poison. Cui Buqu had drunk many bitter medicines before, yet he believed the doctor who'd prescribed him this one might have a grudge against him. The sharp bitterness on his tongue made him shudder.

When he returned to his senses, he saw Feng Xiao watching him with great interest.

"How are things going with Qin Miaoyu?" Cui Buqu asked.

"We've retrieved the jade." Feng Xiao didn't add that the jade was only half its original size thanks to Qin Miaoyu absorbing its powers, nor that the pool of blue-green at the center had grown fainter. Those things had nothing to do with Cui Buqu. Searching for the jade had always been Feng Xiao's business, along with all the subsequent difficulties.

The case of the Khotanese envoy's murder was now considered closed. Though some unknowns remained, Su Xing and Qin Miaoyu had been captured and the jade retrieved. And, in line with their agreement, Feng Xiao was to acknowledge the Zuoyue Bureau's contribution in finding the jade and the murderer.

Cui Buqu was slightly surprised. "So Qin Miaoyu survived? I'm curious. What kind of secrets does she know that convinced you to let her live?"

"Am I naught but an indiscriminate killer in your eyes? Your words have shattered my heart! Even if I patch it, it will never be as it was!"

"Please speak in human tongue."

"A single woman traveled to the Central Plains as a Goguryeon spy and remained incognito for many years. That alone demonstrates her extraordinary fortitude."

Cui Buqu immediately took Feng Xiao's meaning.

The Khotanese king had no children, and Yuchi Jinwu had been his most valued nephew. If not for his death, he'd probably have inherited the throne one day. Considering Qin Miaoyu's abilities and Yuchi Jinwu's love for her, she may have very well risen to the rank of royal consort and become capable of effectively manipulating the royal court of Khotan.

The Goguryeons had placed such a pawn thousands of miles away. Of course their goal hadn't been merely to control the royal consort of a tiny nation far from their borders, but to use her to stir up the political situation in the Western Regions and thereby affect the Sui dynasty and the Khaganate. With the region's great powers at each other's throats, Goguryeo would be at an advantage. Whoever had hatched this plot must possess great foresight—though Goguryeo was a small nation, it clearly wasn't lacking for talent.

Unfortunately, the Goguryeon king's strange illness and the appearance of the Jade of Heaven Lake had made the Goguryeons impatient. They'd mobilized Qin Miaoyu and Su Xing much earlier than planned. If not for this, they might never have been discovered.

"Who sent Qin Miaoyu and Su Xing to the Central Plains?" mused Cui Buqu. "And whom else did they send?"

When the wise spoke to the wise, much breath was spared. Feng Xiao gave Cui Buqu an appreciative look. Though he had certainly caused the Jiejian Bureau a heap of trouble, it was rare to meet such a worthy rival. He had only one life, after all, and a peaceful and uneventful one would be far too dull.

Feng Xiao had previously surmised that, given Cui Buqu's abilities, many would want to recruit him even without martial arts. People like Cui Buqu had clear goals and the drive to achieve them. As long as he was offered a high enough position, Cui Buqu surely would have come. But fate laughs at the plans of men: Feng Xiao had ended up trying to recruit the chief of the Zuoyue Bureau.

Needless to say, Cui Buqu would never give up his position and lower himself to become the fourth deputy chief of the Jiejian Bureau. He might even hold a grudge for the way Feng Xiao tried to recruit someone out from under him.

There were so many grudges between them now that Feng Xiao found he didn't mind.

"The one who sent them is Go Un, the master of Go Nyeong. He's the brother of King Go Tang of Goguryeo and said to be the only martial arts grandmaster in the country."

Although Go Un didn't hold any official position, according to Feng Xiao's information, he exerted significant influence on

Go Tang's government. He'd also founded the Buyeo Sect, which played a role similar to the Jiejian Bureau. He was a spymaster acting in the interests of his own country, arranging infiltration into other nations and ferreting out secret intelligence.

There was no doubt about it. Su Xing and Qin Miaoyu were members of the Buyeo Sect.

"Qin Miaoyu holds a low position in Buyeo Sect. Go Un has always looked down on women; he relies on their sex appeal to perform low-level intelligence work. Only Su Xing had the power to contact the Buyeo Sect, but he doesn't know much either. All he could tell us was that the person who brought them to the Central Plains was called Yi-xiansheng."

A woman like Qin Miaoyu might be too timid and afraid to act out while young and inexperienced. But during the years she'd spent as Yuchi Jinwu's concubine, she'd had plenty of practice deflecting the schemes of his other wives and fighting to stabilize her own favor and position—all while collecting intelligence, contacting Su Xing, and seeking out advantages for Goguryeo. After all she'd learned, how could the Buyeo Sect possibly restrain her? It wasn't surprising she'd longed to throw off their yoke.

"Yi? As in *ease*?" Cui Buqu didn't care what plans Feng Xiao had for Qin Miaoyu. He was more interested in this "Yi-xiansheng."

Feng Xiao dipped his finger into the tea, then drew a single horizontal line on the table. "Yi as in *one*."

All came from one, and to one all would return. That *one*. One was the origin of all things, the starting point of all numbers, yet in its singularity, it could be infinitely great. Laozi[18] said, "Embrace the one, and set an example to all." In the beginning, the cosmos was one before splitting into heaven and earth, transforming into all things.

---

18   老子. A semi-legendary Chinese philosopher who authored the Daoist classic Tao Te Ching.

Anyone who'd use such a word as their codename was no ordinary person. This Yi-xiansheng wasn't just Su Xing's contact in the Central Plains. They likely held a high position in the Buyeo Sect. And whoever they were, they'd hidden themselves in the Central Plains for many years. If Qin Miaoyu had almost managed to become a Khotanese royal consort, Yi-xiansheng's false identity could not be a humble one.

The lesser hermit hides in the wilderness, while the greater hermit hides in the marketplace.

Things were getting interesting. They'd solved a case only to uncover another thread buried deep within. If they followed that thread, where would it lead them?

Cui Buqu trusted Feng Xiao had reached the same conclusions and was similarly intrigued. Perhaps he'd only told Cui Buqu this much in order to drag him into the snarl. But Cui Buqu had always been a restless person. The thornier the problem and the more difficulties he encountered, the more fascinated he became.

"I've told you so much," said Feng Xiao. "Shouldn't you return the favor?"

Cui Buqu smiled. "Of course. That's why I invited Deputy Chief Feng to come with me to the Khaganate to meet Apa Khagan."

Feng Xiao raised a slender brow. "So this is how you 'return a favor?' Aren't you just making trouble for me for the sake of it?"

"How could you think so?" said Cui Buqu. "I ask you, didn't you promise to bring me Fo'er's head?"

"I promised to kill Fo'er for you, but I didn't say when. Whether I kill him today or tomorrow, it still counts. I could even kill him a year from now. Right?"

Cui Buqu smiled without pleasure. "You heard what I told Jinlian tonight. Though she is the khatun of Apa, she has little power.

Her role was simply to travel here on Apa's behalf and deliver the letter he penned. If we wish to negotiate further, to try and grab more benefits for the Sui dynasty, I must personally make this trip to the Khaganate. Fo'er escaped you, so he'll definitely ambush Jinlian and me on the road. If we die, will you still get credit for cementing an alliance with Apa Khagan?"

"So you're saying I absolutely must go?"

"There's no such thing as a free lunch. If Deputy Chief Feng wants the accolades, he must make the trip."

Feng Xiao smiled. "You're not afraid I'll kill you on the return trip and take credit for all your work?"

Cui Buqu returned his gaze. "If that happens, I can only lament my fate. However, if I'm dead, then Deputy Chief Feng might find himself missing out on some interesting news."

"Such as?"

"Such as that I know who sent the two assassins from the Thirteen Floors of Yunhai. I also know that Yuxiu, the Prince of Jin's most trusted counselor, didn't come to Liugong City solely for the jade. He had other objectives. After all, though the Zuoyue Bureau doesn't have the manpower of the Jiejian Bureau, we still have our ways of obtaining information. How else could we survive?"

"Ququ…" Feng Xiao's tone was affectionate now. "I want to ask one more question. What makes you think I wouldn't want to go with you? Just seeing you every day improves my appetite!"

"So, Deputy Chief Feng has agreed," said Cui Buqu. "I thank you on behalf of Jinlian Khatun."

They stared at each other, their mouths curving into matching fake smiles. As for what curses they were swearing in their hearts, only they knew.

"Why call me Deputy Chief Feng? Haven't I already told you? Call me Feng-er. Or, if you're willing, Erlang. That would be even better."

Cui Buqu coughed twice and promptly disregarded Feng Xiao's nonsensical request. "We're going to the camp of Apa Khagan. To get there, we must pass through Qiemo and Kucha, which is a long, wind-blown journey. Make sure you get some rest."

With that he stood, drew up his cloak, and swept out the door with Qiao Xian close behind.

As their footfalls gradually faded into the distance, Feng Xiao smiled. He murmured, "Who wants me dead so badly? And they didn't even come themselves; they sent people from the Thirteen Floors of Yunhai. Perhaps they don't know martial arts and are jealous of my unparalleled magnificence. Alas—only the mediocre fail to draw envy, and I can't help being so handsome. What am I to do?"

On the other side of the door, Qiao Xian, who'd secretly turned back to eavesdrop, almost hocked up yesterday's meal. How could someone so shameless exist? She couldn't comprehend it.

Cui Buqu had sorely overestimated the state of his health. After the chaos of that night, he developed a low fever and lay insensible in bed for several days. It wasn't until the third that he showed signs of improvement. Even Jinlian, who'd suffered a serious injury that night, recovered more quickly. She couldn't help but worry he'd keel over before they set a single foot in the Khaganate.

"Worry not, Khatun." Cui Buqu was sitting on the bed wrapped in a blanket. He'd just drunk a bowl of medicine, and his expression was sullen. "I may be ill, and my body may be frail, but there's enough life in me yet to make it to the Khaganate. Qiao Xian will accompany us as well; she's skilled in medicine, so there's nothing to worry about."

He gestured for Qiao Xian to bring a scroll, which he slowly unrolled under the eyes of Jinlian and Feng Xiao.

"This is...a map?" Jinlian looked at the densely crammed annotations. The map looked familiar, though she couldn't tell precisely what it depicted.

"This is a map of the Western Khaganate, stretching from Qiemo in the south to the Sanmi Mountains in the north, and from Shule in the west to Gaochang in the east," Cui Buqu said. "It's not comprehensive, but even so, it's a more valuable gift for Apa Khagan than thousands of taels of gold or countless heads of livestock. The khatun's trip will not be vain."

Jinlian looked at him in disbelief. "You want to give me this map, then have me...offer borrowed flowers to Buddha? You want me to offer someone else's contributions in my name?"

She was a Göktürk, yet her Chinese was fluent enough to use an idiom like *offer borrowed flowers to Buddha*.

Cui Buqu's lips curved slightly. "I know the khatun strongly supports establishing a diplomatic alliance with our Great Sui. Otherwise, you wouldn't have risked your life and traveled here alone over thousands of miles. But surely there are scoundrels around Apa Khagan who will try to obstruct this goal. With this map in hand, will it not be that much easier for Khatun to achieve great things at Apa Khagan's side?"

Jinlian couldn't conceal her joy. She was a woman with intelligence and vision. She well knew that quality maps were closely guarded military secrets—such a treasure was far more precious than any gold, silver, or jewels.

Feng Xiao, watching coolly from the side, saw a deeper meaning in this interaction. Cui Buqu had offered the map to win over Jinlian, yet for any Göktürks with darker intentions, this map was also a warning: *Great Sui has grasped the terrain of the Western Khaganate. We can become your ally, or we can become your enemy.*

This move of carrot and stick, incentive and threat, was horribly clever. Feng Xiao couldn't help but sigh once more. Why couldn't such a talented man belong to the Jiejian Bureau instead?

THE STORY CONTINUES IN
Peerless
VOLUME 2

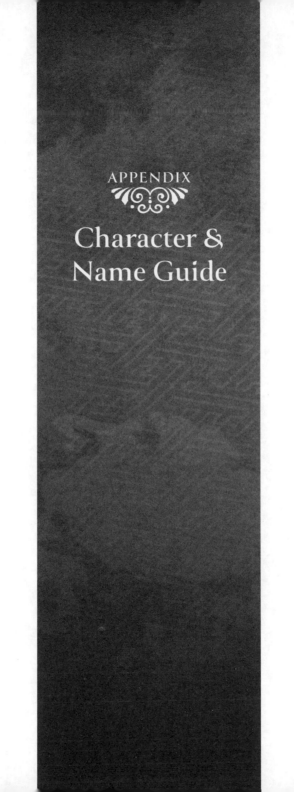

APPENDIX

Character & Name Guide

HISTORICAL PERIOD

Peerless is set in the first era of the Sui dynasty, Kaihuang. Emperor Wen of Sui (given name Yang Jian) established his dynasty in 581 AD after usurping the throne from the previous Zhou dynasty. Though Sui was a short-lived dynasty that eventually fell apart in the hands of his son, Emperor Yang, Emperor Wen is viewed as one of the most influential emperors of ancient China, both for his prosperous rule and for the reunification of the Central Plains after over two hundred years of war and turmoil.

CHARACTERS

FENG XIAO 凤霄 ("HIGH HEAVENS"): Deputy Chief of the Jiejian Bureau

CUI BUQU 崔不去 ("I WON'T GO"): Chief of the Zuoyue Bureau

JIEJIAN BUREAU

PEI JINGZHE 裴惊蛰: Feng Xiao's beleaguered assistant at the Jiejian Bureau.

ZUOYUE BUREAU

QIAO XIAN 乔仙: Deputy Chief of the Zuoyue Bureau

ZHANGSUN BODHI 长孙菩提: Deputy Chief of the Zuoyue Bureau

SUI IMPERIAL COURT

YANG JIAN 杨坚: Emperor Wen of Sui, the first emperor of the Sui dynasty. Also known by his Xianbei name Puliuru Jian.

DUGU QIELUO 独孤伽罗: Empress Wenxian

YUXIU 玉秀: A mysterious monk who shows up in search of the missing Jade of Heaven Lake.

LIUGONG CITY

COUNTY MAGISTRATE ZHAO 赵县令: The harried magistrate who governs Liugong City.

LU TI 卢缇: A businessman and the head of the Lu family, one of Liugong City's wealthiest clans. His manor ends up becoming the site of another case.

LU YOUNIANG 卢幽娘: Lu Ti's beloved only child. Engaged to Su Xing.

SU XING 苏醒: The nephew of Lu Ti, engaged to Lu Youniang.

KINGDOM OF KHOTAN

YUCHI JINWU 尉迟金乌: The deceased Khotanese envoy and prince, tasked with bringing the Jade of Heaven Lake to the emperor of Sui.

QIN MIAOYU 秦妙语: Yuchi Jinwu's beloved concubine, who mysteriously vanished with the Jade of Heaven Lake after the assassination of the envoy.

GÖKTÜRK KHAGANATE

FO'ER 佛耳: The foremost martial artist of the Göktürk Khaganate, who pledges loyalty to Ishbara Khagan, one of the most powerful khagans.

JINLIAN 金莲: Apa Khagan's lesser khatun who arrives in Liugong City as an envoy for negotiations.

GOGURYEO

GO NYEONG 高宁: A martial artist who shows up in search of the Jade of Heaven Lake.

NAMES, HONORIFICS, & TITLES

Diminutives, Nicknames, and Name Tags

A-: Friendly diminutive. Always a prefix. Usually for monosyllabic names, or one syllable out of a two-syllable name.

DA-: A character meaning "eldest." Can be used as a prefix.

-ER: Usually a character meaning "child." When added to a name as a suffix, it expresses affection. However, Feng Xiao's nickname, "Feng-er," uses a different character that means "second." Thus, in *Peerless*, "Feng-er" is an abbreviated way of saying "Deputy Bureau Chief Feng Xiao."

XIAO-: A character meaning "small" or "youngest." When added to a name as a prefix, it expresses affection.

Courtesy Addresses

GONGZI: A respectful address for young men, originally only for those from affluent households. Though appropriate in all formal occasions, it's often preferred when the addressee outranks the speaker.

LANG: A general term for "man." Can be used to politely address a man by pairing it with other characters that denote his place within a certain household. For example, "dalang," "erlang," and "sanlang" mean "eldest son," "second son," and "third son" respectively. "Langjun" is a polite address for any man, similar to "gentleman."

NIANG: A general term for "woman," which can be appended as a suffix. Follows the same pairing rules as "lang." "Niangzi" is a variant that can be used alone to address any woman, similar to "lady."

XIANSHENG: A polite address for men, originally only for those of great learning or those who had made significant contributions to society. Sometimes seen as an equivalent to "Mr." in English.

PRONUNCIATION GUIDE

Mandarin Chinese is the official state language of mainland China, and pinyin is the official system of romanization in which it is written. As Mandarin is a tonal language, pinyin uses diacritical marks (e.g., ā, á, ǎ, à) to indicate these tonal inflections. Most words use one of four tones, though some are a neutral tone. Furthermore, regional variance can change the way native Chinese speakers pronounce the same word. For those reasons and more, please consider the guide below a simplified introduction to pronunciation of select character names and sounds from the world of *Peerless*.

More resources are available at sevenseasdanmei.com

GENERAL CONSONANTS

Some Mandarin Chinese consonants sound very similar, such as z/c/s and zh/ch/sh. Audio samples will provide the best opportunity to learn the difference between them.

X: somewhere between the **sh** in **sh**eep and **s** in **s**ilk

Q: a very aspirated **ch** as in **ch**arm

C: **ts** as in pan**ts**

Z: **z** as in **z**oom

S: **s** as in **s**ilk

CH: **ch** as in **ch**arm

ZH: **dg** as in do**dg**e

SH: **sh** as in **sh**ave

G: hard **g** as in **g**raphic

GENERAL VOWELS

The pronunciation of a vowel may depend on its preceding conso-nant. For example, the "i" in "shi" is distinct from the "i" in "di." Vowel pronunciation may also change depending on where the vowel appears in a word, for example the "i" in "shi" versus the "i" in "ting." Finally, compound vowels are often—though not always—pronounced as conjoined but separate vowels. You'll find a few of the trickier compounds below.

IU: as in **yo**

IE: **ye** as in **ye**s

UO: **war** as in **war**m

CHARACTER NAMES

Fèng Xiāo

Fèng: as in **phone**

Xiāo: Sh as in **sh**eep, iao as in **yow**l

Cuī Búqù

Cuī: Ts as in pan**ts**, ui as in **way**

Bú: as in **boo**

Qù: Ch as in **ch**arm, u as in **oui**ja

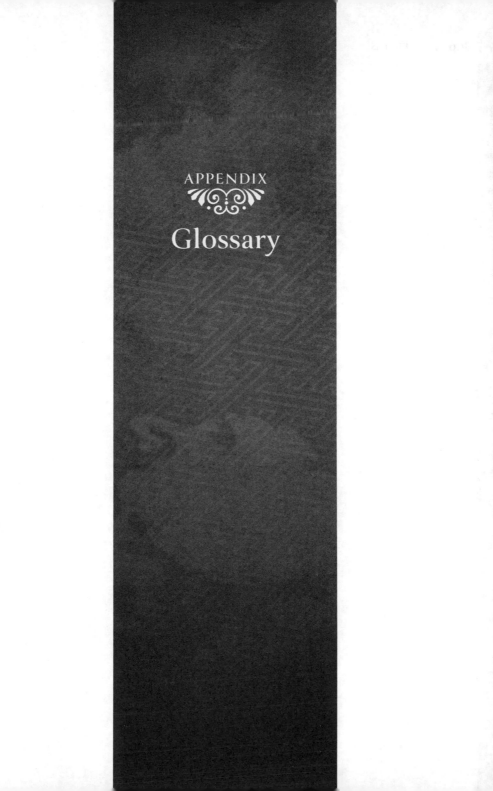

APPENDIX

Glossary

GLOSSARY

BUDDHISM: The central belief of Buddhism is that life is a cycle of suffering and rebirth, only to be escaped by reaching enlightenment (nirvana). Buddhists believe in karma, that a person's actions will influence their fortune in this life and future lives. The teachings of the Buddha are known as the Middle Way and emphasize a practice that is neither extreme asceticism nor extreme indulgence.

CONCUBINES: In ancient China, it was common practice for a wealthy man to take women as concubines in addition to his wife. They were expected to live with him and bear him children. Generally speaking, a greater number of concubines correlated to higher social status, hence a wealthy merchant might have two or three concubines, while an emperor might have tens or even a hundred.

COURTESY AND GIVEN NAMES: When men and women came of age in ancient China, they received a new name for others of the same generation to refer to them by, known as a **courtesy name**. Use of their original or **given name** was normally reserved only for respected elders and the person themselves—using it otherwise would be very rude and overfamiliar.

CUT-SLEEVE: A slang term for a gay man, which comes from a tale about Emperor Ai's love for, and relationship with, his male court official in the Han dynasty. The emperor was called to the morning assembly, but his lover was asleep on his robe. Rather than wake him, the emperor cut off his own sleeve.

DHARMA NAME: A name given to new disciples of Buddhism during their initiation ritual.

DAOISM: Daoism is the philosophy of the dao (道 / "the way"). Following the dao involves coming into harmony with the natural order of the universe, which makes someone a "true human," safe from external harm and able to affect the world without intentional action. Cultivation is a concept based on Daoist beliefs.

ERA NAME: A designation for the years when a given emperor was on the throne (or some part of those years). This title is determined by the emperor when they ascend the throne, and can often be used to refer to both the era and the emperor himself.

FACE: A person's face (脸 / lian or 面子 / mianzi) is an important concept in Chinese society. It is a metaphor for someone's reputation or dignity and can be extended into further descriptive metaphors. For example, "having face" refers to having a good reputation, and "losing face" refers to having one's reputation damaged.

INTERNAL CULTIVATION: Internal cultivation or neigong (内功) refers to the breathing, qi, and meditation practices a martial artist must undertake in order to properly harness and utilize their "outer cultivation" of combat techniques and footwork.

JIANGHU: A staple of wuxia, the jianghu (江湖 / "rivers and lakes") describes the greater underground society of martial artists and associates that spans the entire setting. Members of the jianghu self-govern and settle issues among themselves based on the tenets of strength and honor, though this may not stop them from exerting influence over conventional society too.

JOSS STICKS: Thin sticks of incense that are burned in ritual offerings at temples or during funeral rites.

PAIR CULTIVATION: Also translated as dual cultivation, shuangxiu (双修 / "cultivate as a pair") is a practice that uses sex between participants to improve cultivation prowess. Can also be used as a simple euphemism for sex.

PARASITIC CULTIVATION: Caibu (采补 / "harvest and supplement") is the practice of draining qi from a host to strengthen one's martial arts. As the bodies of men are believed to hold more yang qi while women hold more yin qi, the person in question will often "harvest" from the other sex to "supplement" themselves, which gives the practice its association with sexual cultivation.

QINGGONG: A real-life training discipline. In wuxia, the feats of qinggong (轻功 / "lightness technique") are highly exaggerated, allowing practitioners to glide through the air, run straight up walls and over water, jump through trees, or travel dozens of steps in an instant.

SIX MINISTRIES: The Six Ministries of the Department of State Affairs comprised the primary administrative structure of the Sui dynasty government, and included the Ministry of Works, Ministry of Justice, Ministry of Personnel, Ministry of Rites, Ministry of Revenue, and Ministry of War. The heads of these ministries had great authority and were appointed by and reported directly to the emperor.

SWORD GLARE: Jianguang (剑光 / "sword light"), an energy attack released from a sword's edge, often seen in wuxia and xianxia stories.

TRADITIONAL CHINESE MEDICINE: Traditional medical practices in China are commonly based around the idea that qi, or vital energy, circulates in the body through channels called meridians similarly to how blood flows through the circulatory system. Acupuncture points, or acupoints, are special nodes, most of which lie along the meridians. Stimulating them by massage, acupuncture, or other methods is believed to affect the flow of qi and can be used for healing—or in wuxia, to render someone unconscious.

Another central concept in traditional Chinese medicine is that disease arises from an imbalance of elements in the body caused by disharmony in internal functions. For example, an excess of internal heat can cause symptoms such as fever, thirst, insomnia, and redness of the face. Excess internal heat can be treated with the consumption of foods with cooling properties, such as lotus tea.

TRUE QI: True qi (真气) is a more precise term for "qi," one's lifeforce and the energy in all living things. True qi is refined in the lower dantian (丹田 / "elixir field") within the abdomen, which also holds the foundations of a person's martial arts, especially their internal cultivation.

In wuxia, a practitioner with superb internal cultivation can perform superhuman feats with their true qi. On top of what is covered under internal cultivation above, martial artists can channel true qi into swords to generate sword qi, imbue simple movements and objects with destructive energy, project their voices across great distances, heal lesser injuries, or enhance the five senses.

ZITHER: Also called a guqin, or qin, a zither is a stringed instrument, played by plucking with the fingers. It is fairly large and is meant to be laid flat on a surface or on one's lap while playing.

ABOUT THE AUTHOR
MENG XI SHI

Meng Xi Shi is a renowned web author whose works of fiction combine detailed research with witty writing, winning the hearts of readers around the world. Her works are published in China by Jingjiang Literature City. She goes by "Meng Xi Shi Ya" on Weibo.